WAR HAWK

WAR HAWK

A TUCKER WAYNE NOVEL

JAMES ROLLINS

and Grant Blackwood

First published in Great Britain in 2016
by Orion Books,
an imprint of The Orion Publishing Group Ltd
Carmelite House, 50 Victoria Embankment
London EC4Y 0DZ

An Hachette UK Company

1 3 5 7 9 10 8 6 4 2

A CIP catalogue record for this book is
available from the British Library.

ISBN (Trade Paperback) 978 1 4091 5448 8
ISBN (Ebook) 978 1 4091 5450 1

Printed in Great Britain by Clays Ltd, St Ives plc

www.orionbooks.co.uk

To all the four-legged warriors out there . . .
And those who serve alongside them.
Thank you for your dedication and service.

ACKNOWLEDGMENTS

To those many folks who have joined Grant and me on this journey with Tucker and his stalwart companion, Kane, I appreciate all your help, criticism, and encouragement. First, I must thank my critique group, which has been with me lo these many, many years: Sally Ann Barnes, Chris Crowe, Lee Garrett, Jane O'Riva, Denny Grayson, Leonard Little, Judy Prey, Caroline Williams, Christian Riley, Tod Todd, Chris Smith, and Amy Rogers. And as always, a special thanks to Steve Prey for the great maps . . . and to David Sylvian for always having my back! To everyone at HarperCollins who makes me shine: Michael Morrison, Liate Stehlik, Danielle Bartlett, Kaitlyn Kennedy, Josh Marwell, Lynn Grady, Richard Aquan, Tom Egner, Shawn Nicholls, and Ana Maria Allessi. Last, of course, a special acknowledgment to my editor for her talent (and infinite patience), Lyssa Keusch, and her colleague Rebecca Lucash; along with my agents, Russ Galen and Danny Baror (including his remarkable daughter Heather Baror). And as always, I must stress any and all errors of fact or detail in this book fall squarely on my own shoulders, of which hopefully there are not too many.

WAR HAWK

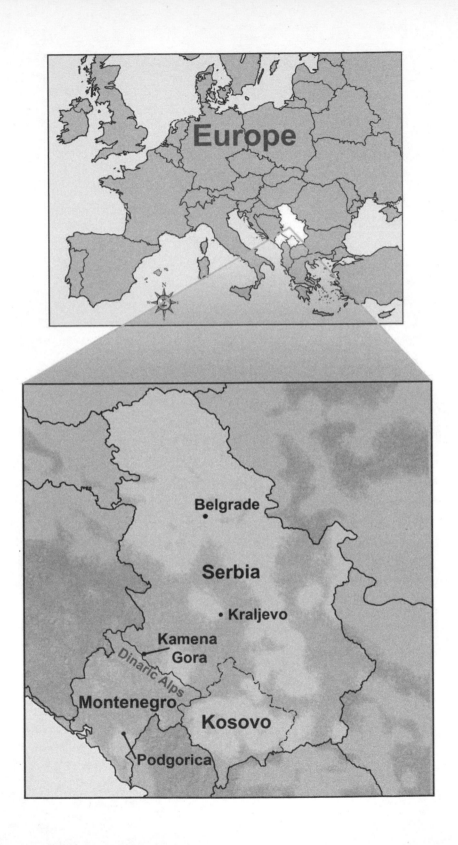

TRINIDAD & TOBAGO

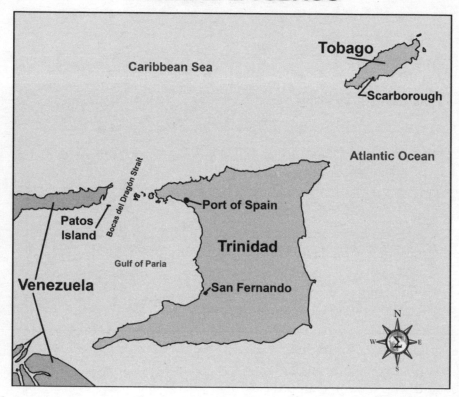

PROLOGUE

Few in the Abwehr's military intelligence knew his true name or even his intent here on British soil. The spy went by the code name *Geist*, the German word for *ghost*, and for him failure was not an option.

He lay on his stomach in a muddy ditch, with ice-encrusted cattails stabbing at his face. He ignored the midnight cold, the frigid gusts of breezes, the ache of his frozen joints. Instead, he concentrated on the view through the binoculars fixed to his face.

He and his assigned team lay alongside the banks of a small lake. A hundred yards off, on the opposite shore, a row of stately rural mansions sat dark, brightened here and there by the rare sliver of yellow light peeking through blackout curtains. Still, he spotted rolls of barbed wire mounted atop the garden walls of one particular estate.

Bletchley Park.

The place also went by a code name: Station X.

The seemingly nondescript country house masked an operation run by British intelligence, a joint effort by MI6 and the Government Code and Cypher School. In a series of wooden huts set up on those idyllic acres, the Allied forces had gathered the greatest mathematicians and cryptographers from around the globe, including one man, Alan Turing, who was decades ahead of his peers. Station X's goal was to break the German military's Enigma code, using tools built by the geniuses here. The group had already succeeded in building an electromechanical decrypting device called The Bombe, and rumors abounded about a new project already under way, to build Colossus, the world's first programmable electric computer.

But destroying such devices was not his goal this night.

Hidden upon those grounds was a prize beyond anything his superiors could imagine: a breakthrough that held the potential to change the very fate of the world.

And I will possess it—or die trying.

Geist felt his heart quicken.

To his left, his second in command, Lieutenant Hoffman, pulled the collar of his jacket tighter around his neck as an icy rain began to fall. He shifted, cursing his complaint. *"Gott verlassenen Land."*

Geist kept his binoculars in place as he scolded the head of the commandos. "Silence. If anyone hears you speaking German, we'll be stuck here for the rest of the war."

Geist knew a firm hand was needed with the eight-man team under his charge. The members had been handpicked by the Abwehr not only for their superb martial skills but for their grasp of English. Whatever the British might lack in military presence out here in the rural regions, they made up for by a vigilant citizenry.

"Truck!" Hoffman rasped.

Geist glanced over his shoulder to the road passing through the woods behind him. A lorry trundled along, its headlights muted by blackout slits.

"Hold your breath," Geist hissed.

He wasn't about to let their presence catch the attention of the passing driver. He and the others kept their faces pressed low until the sound of the truck's puttering engine faded away.

"Clear," Hoffman said.

Geist checked his watch and searched again with his binoculars.

What is taking them so long?

Everything depended on clockwork timing. He and his team had offloaded from a U-boat five days ago onto a lonely beach. Afterward, the group had split into teams of two or three and worked their way across the countryside, ready with papers identifying them as day laborers and farmhands. Once they reached the target area, they had regrouped at a nearby hunting shack, where a cache of weapons awaited them, left by sleeper agents who had prepped the way in advance for Geist's team.

Only one last detail remained.

A wink of light caught his attention from the grounds neighboring the Bletchley Park estate. It shuttered off once, then back on again—then finally darkness returned.

It was the signal he had been waiting for.

Geist rolled up to an elbow. "Time to move out."

Hoffman's team gathered their weapons: assault rifles and noise-suppressed pistols. The largest commando—a true bull of a man named Kraus—hauled up an MG42 heavy machine gun, capable of firing twelve hundred rounds per minute.

Geist studied the black-streaked faces around him. They had trained for three months within a life-sized mock-up of Bletchley Park. By now, they could all walk those grounds blindfolded. The only unknown variable was the level of on-site defense. The research campus was secured by both soldiers and guards in civilian clothes.

Geist went over the plan one last time. "Once inside the estate, torch your assigned buildings. Cause as much panic and confusion as possible. In that chaos, Hoffman and I will attempt to secure the package. If shooting starts, take down anything that moves. Is that understood?"

Each man nodded his head.

With everyone prepared—ready to die if need be—the group set off and followed the contour of the lake, sticking to the mist-shrouded forest. Geist led them past the neighboring estates. Most of these old homes were shuttered, awaiting the summer months. Soon servants and staff would be arriving to prepare the country homes for the leisure season, but that was still a couple of weeks away.

It was one of the many reasons this narrow window of opportunity had been chosen by Admiral Wilhelm Canaris, head of German military intelligence. And there was one other time-critical element.

"Access to the bunker should be just up ahead," Geist whispered back to Hoffman. "Ready the men."

The British government—aware that Adolf Hitler would soon launch an air war against this island nation—had begun constructing underground bunkers for its critical installations, including Bletchley Park. The bunker at Station X was only half completed, offering a brief break in the secure perimeter around the estate.

Geist intended to take advantage of that weakness this night.

He led his team toward a country house that neighbored Bletchley Park. It was a red-brick Tudor with yellow shutters. He approached the stacked-stone fence that surrounded the grounds and waved his team to flatten against it.

"Where are we going?" Hoffman whispered. "I thought we were going through some bunker."

"We are." Only Geist had been given this last piece of intelligence.

He crouched low and hurried toward the gate, which he found unlocked. The winking signal earlier had confirmed that all was in readiness here.

Geist pushed open the gate, slipped through, and led his team across the lawn to the home's glass-enclosed conservatory. He found another unlocked door there, hurried inside with his men, and crossed to the kitchen. The all-white cabinetry glowed in the moonlight streaming through the windows.

Wasting no time, he stepped to a door beside the pantry. He opened it and turned on his flashlight, revealing a set of stairs. At the bottom, he found a stone-floored cellar; the walls were white-painted brick, the exposed ceiling a maze of water pipes running through the floor joists. The cellar spanned the width of the house.

He led his team past stacks of boxes and furniture draped in dusty sheets to the cellar's eastern wall. As directed, he pulled away a rug to reveal a hole that had been recently dug through the floor. Another bit of handiwork from Canaris's sleeper agents.

Geist shone his flashlight down the hole, revealing water flowing below.

"What is it?" Hoffman asked.

"Old sewer pipe. It connects all the estates circling the lake."

"Including Bletchley Park," Hoffman realized with a nod.

"And its partially completed bunker," Geist confirmed. "It'll be a tight squeeze, but we'll only need to cross a hundred meters to reach the construction site of that underground bomb shelter and climb back up."

According to the latest intelligence, those new foundations of the bunker were mostly unguarded and should offer them immediate access into the very heart of the estate's grounds.

"The Brits won't know what hit them," Hoffman said with a mean grin.

Geist again led the way, slipping feetfirst through the hole and dropping with a splash into the ankle-deep dank water. He kept one hand on the moldy wall and headed along the old stone pipe. It was only a meter and a half wide, so he had to keep his back bowed, holding his breath against the stink.

After a handful of steps, he clicked off his flashlight and aimed for the distant glow of moonlight. He moved more slowly along the curving pipe, keeping his sloshing to a minimum, not wanting to alert any guards who might be canvassing the bunker's construction site. Hoffman's teammates followed his example.

At last, he reached that moonlit hole in the pipe's roof. A temporary grate covered the newly excavated access point to the old sewer. He fingered the chain and padlock that secured the grate in place.

Unexpected but not a problem.

Hoffman noted his attention and passed him a set of bolt cutters. With great care, Geist snapped through the lock's hasp and freed the chain. He shared a glance with the lieutenant, confirming everyone was ready—then pushed the grate open and pulled himself up through the hole.

He found himself crouched atop the raw concrete foundations of the future bunker. The skeletal structure of walls, conduits, and plumbing surrounded him. Scaffolding and ladders led up toward the open grounds of the estate above. He hurried to one side, ducking under a scaffold, out of direct view. One by one the remaining eight commandos joined him.

Geist took a moment to orient himself. He should be within forty meters of their target: Hut 8. It was one of several green-planked structures built on these grounds. Each had its own purpose, but his team's goal was the research section overseen by the mathematician and cryptanalyst Alan Turing.

He gestured for the men to huddle together.

"Remember, no shooting unless you're intercepted. Toss those incendiaries into Huts 4 and 6. Let the fire do the work for us. With any luck, the distraction will create enough confusion to cover our escape."

Hoffman pointed to two of his men. "Schwab, you take your team to Hut 4. Faber, you and your men have Hut 6. Kraus, you trail us. Be ready to use that machine gun of yours if there is any trouble."

The lieutenant's men nodded in agreement, then scaled the ladders and disappeared out of the open pit of the bunker. Geist followed on their heels with Hoffman and Kraus trailing him.

Staying low, he headed north until he reached Hut 8 and flattened against the wooden siding. The door should be around the next corner. He waited a breath, making sure no alarm had been raised.

He counted down in his head until finally shouts arose to the east and west. *"Fire, fire, fire!"*

Upon that signal, he slid around the corner and climbed a set of plank steps to reach the door into Hut 8. He turned the knob as the night grew brighter, flickering with fresh flames.

As more shouts rose, he pushed through the doorway and into a small room. The center was dominated by two trestle tables covered in stacks of punch cards. The whitewashed walls were plastered with propaganda posters warning about ever-present Nazi eyes and ears.

With his pistol raised, he and Hoffman rushed across and burst through the far doorway into the next room. Seated at a long table, two women sorted through more piles of punch cards. The woman to the right was already looking up. She spun in her chair, reaching for a red panic button on the wall.

Hoffmann shot her twice in the side. The suppressed gunfire was no louder than a couple of firm coughs.

Geist took out the second woman with a single round through her throat. She toppled backward, her face still frozen in an expression of surprise.

They must have been Wrens—members of the Women's Royal Naval Service—who were assisting in the work being conducted here.

Geist hurried to the first woman, searched her pockets, and came up with a thumb-sized brass key. On the second woman, he found a second key, this one iron.

With his prizes in hand, he hurried back to the main room.

From outside, there arose the *wonk-wonk-wonk* of an alarm klaxon.

So far our subterfuge seems to be—

The rattling blasts of a submachine gun cut off this last thought. More gunfire followed. Hoffman cursed.

"We've been discovered," the lieutenant warned.

Geist refused to give up. He crossed to a waist-high safe along one wall. As expected, it was secured by two keyed locks, top and bottom, and a combination dial in the center.

"Need to hurry, sir," Hoffmann rasped next to him. "Sounds like we got a lot of foot traffic outside."

Geist pointed to the door. "Kraus, clear a path for us back to the bunker."

The large soldier nodded, hefted up his heavy weapon, and vanished out the door. As Geist inserted his two keys, Kraus's MG42 opened up outside, roaring into the night.

Geist focused on the task at hand, turning one key, then the other, getting a satisfying *thunk-thunk* in return. He moved his hand to the combination lock. This was truly the test of the Abwehr's reach.

He spun the dial: nine . . . twenty-nine . . . four.

He took a breath, let it out, and depressed the lever.

The safe door swung open.

Thank God.

A quick search inside revealed only one item: a brown accordion folder wrapped in red rubber bands. He read the name stenciled on the outside.

THE ARES PROJECT

He knew Ares was the Greek god of war, which was appropriate, considering the contents. But that connotation only hinted at the true nature of the work found inside. The acronym—ARES— stood for something far more earth-shattering, something powerful enough to rewrite history. He grabbed the folder with trembling hands, knowing the terrifying wonders it held, and stuffed the prize into his jacket.

His second in command, Hoffman, stepped over to the hut's door, cracked it open, and yelled outside. "Kraus!"

"Komm!" Kraus answered in German, forsaking any need for further subterfuge. "Get out here before they regroup!"

Geist joined Hoffman at the door, pulled the pin on an incendiary grenade, and tossed it back into the center of the room. Both men

lunged outside as it exploded behind them, blowing out the windows
with gouts of flames.

To their left, a pair of British soldiers sprinted around the corner
of the hut. Kraus cut them down with his machine gun, but more
soldiers followed, taking cover and returning fire, forcing Geist's
team away from the excavated bunker—away from their only escape
route.

As they retreated deeper into the grounds, smoke billowed more
thickly, accompanied by the acrid stench of burning wood.

Another set of figures burst through the pall. Kraus came close
to carving them in half with his weapon, but at the last moment, he
halted, recognizing his fellow commandos. It was Schwab's team.

"What about Faber and the others?" Hoffman asked.

Schwab shook his head. "Saw them killed."

That left only the six of them.

Geist quickly improvised. "We'll make for the motor pool."

He led the way at a dead run. The team tossed incendiaries as
they went, adding to the confusion, strafing down alleyways, dropping anything that moved.

Finally they reached a row of small sheds. Fifty meters beyond,
the main gate came into view. It looked like a dozen soldiers crouched
behind concrete barriers, guns up, looking for targets. Spotlights
panned the area.

Before being seen, Geist directed his group into a neighboring
Quonset hut, where three canvas-sided lorries were parked.

"We need that gate cleared," Geist said, looking at Hoffman and
his men, knowing what he was asking of them. For any chance of
escape, many of them would likely die in the attempt.

The lieutenant stared him down. "We'll get it done."

Geist clapped Hoffman on the shoulder, thanking him.

The lieutenant set out with his remaining four men.

Geist crossed and climbed into one of the lorries, where he found
the keys in the ignition. He started the engine, warming it up, then
hopped back out again. He crossed to the remaining two trucks and
popped their hoods.

In the distance, Kraus's machine gun began a lethal chattering,
accompanied by the rattle of assault rifles and the overlapping *crump*
of exploding grenades.

Finally, a faint call reached him.

"*Klar, klar, klar!*" Hoffman shouted.

Geist hurried back to the idling lorry, climbed inside, and put the truck into gear—but not before tossing two grenades into each of the open engine compartments of the remaining lorries. As he rolled out and hit the accelerator, the grenades exploded behind him.

He raced to the main gate and braked hard. British soldiers lay dead; the spotlights shot out. Hoffman rolled the gate open, limping on a bloody leg. Supported by a teammate, Kraus hobbled his way into the back of the lorry. Hoffman joined him up front, climbing into the passenger seat and slamming the door angrily.

"Lost Schwab and Braatz." Hoffman waved ahead. "Go, go."

With no time to mourn, Geist gunned the engine and raced down the country road. He kept one eye on the side mirror, watching for any sign of pursuit. Taking a maze of turns, he tried to further confound their escape route. Finally, he steered the lorry down a narrow dirt tract lined by overgrown English oaks. At the end was a large barn, its roof half collapsed. To the left was a burned-out farmhouse.

Geist parked beneath some overhanging boughs and shut off the engine. "We should see to everyone's injuries," he said. "We've lost enough good men."

"Everybody out," Hoffman ordered, rapping a knuckle on the back of the compartment.

After they all climbed free, Geist surveyed the damage. "You'll all get the Knight's Cross for your bravery tonight. We should—"

A harsh shout cut him off, barked in German. "*Halt! Hände hoch!*"

A dozen men, bristling with weapons, emerged from the foliage and from behind the barn.

"Nobody move!" the voice called again, revealing a tall American with a Tommy gun in hand.

Geist recognized the impossibility of their team's situation and lifted his arms. Hoffman and his last two men followed his example, dropping their weapons and raising their hands.

It was over.

As the Americans frisked Hoffman and the others, a lone figure stepped from the darkened barn door and approached Geist. He pointed a .45-caliber pistol at Geist's chest.

"Tie him up," he ordered one of his men.

As his wrists were efficiently bound in rope, his captor spoke in a rich southern twang. "Colonel Ernie Duncan, 101st Airborne. You speak English?"

"Yes."

"Whom do I have the pleasure of addressing?"

"*Schweinhund*," Geist answered with a sneer.

"Son, I'm pretty sure that isn't your name. I'll assume that slur is intended for me. So then let's just call you Fritz. You and I are going to have a talk. Whether it's pleasant or ugly is up to you."

The American colonel called to one of his men. "Lieutenant Ross, put those other three men into the back of their truck and get them ready for transport. Say good-bye to your team, Fritz."

Geist turned to face his men and shouted, "*Für das Vaterland!*"

"*Das Vaterland!*" Hoffman and the others repeated in unison.

The American soldiers herded the commandos into the back of the lorry, while Colonel Duncan marched Geist over to the barn. Once inside, he closed the doors and waved to encompass the piles of hay and manure.

"Sorry for our meager accommodations, Fritz."

Geist turned to face him and broke into a smile. "Damned good to see you, too, Duncan."

"And you, my friend. How'd it go? Find what you were looking for?"

"It's in my jacket. For whatever it's worth, those Germans fight like the devil. Bletchley's burning. But they should be up and running again in a week."

"Good to know." Duncan used a razor blade to free his bound wrists. "How do you want to play this from here?"

"I've got a small Mauser hidden in a crotch holster." Geist stood up and rubbed his wrists, then unwound his scarf and folded it into a thick square. He reached into the front of his pants and withdrew the Mauser.

Geist glanced behind him. "Where's the back door?"

Duncan pointed. "By those old horse stalls. Nobody'll be back behind the barn to see you *escape*. But you'll have to make it look convincing, you know. Really smack me good. Remember, we Americans are tough."

"Duncan, I'm not keen on this idea."

"Necessities of war, buddy. You can buy me a case of scotch when we get back to the States."

Geist shook the colonel's hand.

Duncan dropped his .45 to the ground and smiled. "Oh look, you've disarmed me."

"We Germans are crafty that way."

Next Duncan ripped open the front of his fatigue blouse, popping buttons off onto the straw-covered floor. "And there's been a struggle."

"Okay, Duncan, enough. Turn your head. I'll rap you behind the ear. When you wake up, you'll have a knot the size of a golf ball and a raging headache, but you asked for it."

"Right." He clasped Geist by the forearm. "Watch yourself out there. It's a long way back to DC."

As Duncan turned his head away, a flicker of guilt passed through Geist. Still, he knew what needed to be done.

Geist pressed the wadded scarf to the Mauser's barrel and jammed it against Duncan's ear.

The colonel shifted slightly. "Hey, what are you—"

He pulled the trigger. With the sound of a sharp slap, the bullet tore through Duncan's skull, snapping his friend's head back as the body toppled forward to the ground.

Geist stared down. "So sorry, my friend. As you said before, *necessities of war*. If it makes you feel any better, you've just changed the world."

He pocketed the pistol, walked to the barn's back door, and disappeared into the misty night, becoming at last . . . a true ghost.

FIRST

GHOST HUNT

1

All this trouble from a single damned nail...

Tucker Wayne tossed the flat tire into the back of his rental. The Jeep Grand Cherokee sat parked on the shoulder of a lonely stretch of road in the forested mountains of southwest Montana. These millions of acres of pines, glacier-cut canyons, and rugged peaks formed the largest expanse of pristine wilderness in the Lower 48.

He stretched a kink out of his back and searched down the winding stretch of blacktop, bracketed on both sides by sloping hills and dense stands of lodgepole pines.

Just my luck. Here in the middle of nowhere, I pick up a nail.

It seemed impossible that this great beast of an SUV could be brought low by a simple sliver of iron shorter than his pinkie. It was a reminder of how modern technological progress could still be ground to a halt by a single bit of antiquated hardware like a roofing nail.

He slammed the rear cargo hatch and whistled sharply. His companion on this cross-country journey pulled his long furry nose out of a huckleberry bush at the edge of the forest and glanced back at Tucker. Eyes the color of dark caramel looked plainly disappointed that this roadside pit stop had come to an end.

"Sorry, buddy. But we've got a long way to go if we hope to reach Yellowstone."

Kane shook his heavy coat of black and tan fur, his thick tail flagging as he turned, readily accepting this reality. The two of them had been partners going back to his years with the U.S. Army Rangers, surviving multiple deployments across Afghanistan together. Upon leaving the service, Tucker took Kane with him—not exactly with the army's permission, but that matter had been settled in the recent past.

The two were now an inseparable team, on their own, seeking new roads, new paths. Together.

Tucker opened the front passenger door and Kane hopped inside, his lean muscular seventy pounds fitting snugly into the seat. He was a Belgian Malinois, a breed of compact shepherd commonly used by the military and law enforcement. Known for their fierce loyalty and sharp intelligence, the breed was also well respected for their nimbleness and raw power in a battlefield environment.

But there was no one like Kane.

Tucker closed the door but lingered long enough to scratch his partner through the open window. His fingers discovered old scars under the fur, reminding Tucker of his own wounds: some easy to see, others just as well hidden.

"Let's keep going," he whispered before the ghosts of his past caught up with him.

He climbed behind the wheel and soon had them flying through the hills of the Bitterroot National Forest. Kane kept his head stuck out the passenger side, his tongue lolling, his nose taking in every scent. Tucker grinned, finding the tension melting from his shoulders as it always did when he was moving.

For the moment, he was between jobs—and he intended to keep it that way for as long as possible. He only took the occasional security position when his finances required it. After his last job—when he had been hired by Sigma Force, a covert branch of the military's research-and-development department—his bank accounts continued to remain flush.

Taking advantage of the downtime, he and Kane had spent the last couple of days hiking the Lost Trail Pass, following in the footsteps of the Lewis and Clark expedition, and now they were moving on to Yellowstone National Park. He had timed this trip to the popular park to reach it in the late fall, to avoid the crush of the high season, preferring the company of Kane to anyone on two legs.

Around a bend in the dark road, a pool of fluorescent lights

revealed a roadside gas station. The sign at the entrance read FORT
EDWIN GAS AND GROCERY. He checked his fuel gauge.

Almost empty.

He flipped on his turn signal and swung into the small station.
His motel was three miles farther up the road. His plan had been to
take a fast shower, collect his bags, and continue straight toward Yellowstone, taking advantage of the empty roads at night.

Now he had a snag in those plans. He needed to replace the flat
tire as soon as possible. Hopefully someone at the gas station knew
the closest place to get that done in these remote hills.

He pulled next to one of the pumps and climbed out. Kane
hopped through the window on the other side. Together they headed
for the station.

Tucker pulled open the glass door, setting a brass bell to tinkling.
The shop was laid out in the usual fashion: rows of snacks and food
staples, backed up by a tall stand of coolers along the back wall. The
air smelled of floor wax and microwaved sandwiches.

"Good evening, good evening," a male voice greeted him, his
voice rising and falling in a familiar singsong manner.

Tucker immediately recognized the accent as Dari Persian. From
his years in the deserts of Afghanistan, he was familiar with the
various dialects of that desert country. Despite the friendliness of
the tone, Tucker's belly tightened in a knot of old dread. Men with
that very same accent had tried to kill him more times than he could
count. Worse still, they had succeeded in butchering Kane's littermate.

He flashed to the bounding joy of his lost partner, the unique
bond they had shared. It took all of his effort to force that memory
back into that knot of old pain, grief, and guilt.

"Good evening," the man behind the counter repeated, smiling,
oblivious to the tension along Tucker's spine. The proprietor's face
was nut brown, his teeth perfectly white. He was mostly bald, save
for a monk's fringe of gray hair. His eyes twinkled as though Tucker
was a friend he hadn't seen in years.

Having met hundreds of Afghan villagers in his time, Tucker
knew the man's demeanor was genuine. Still, he found it hard to step
inside.

The man's brow formed one concerned crinkle at his obvious

hesitation. "Welcome," he offered again, waving an arm to encourage him.

"Thanks," Tucker finally managed to reply. He kept one hand on Kane's flank. "Okay if I bring my dog in?"

"Yes, of course. All are welcome."

Tucker took a deep breath and crossed past the front shelves, neatly stocked with packets of beef jerky, Slim Jims, and corn chips. He stepped to the counter, noting he was the only one in the place.

"You have a beautiful dog," the man said. "Is he a shepherd?"

"A Belgian Malinois . . . a type of shepherd. Name's Kane."

"And I am Aasif Qazi, owner of this fine establishment."

The proprietor stretched a hand across the counter. Tucker took it, finding the man's grip firm, the palm slightly calloused from hard labor.

"You're from Kabul," Tucker said.

The man's eyebrows rose high. "How did you know?"

"Your accent. I spent some time in Afghanistan."

"Recently, I am guessing."

Not so recently, Tucker thought, but some days it felt like yesterday. "And you?" he asked.

"I came to the States as a boy. My parents wisely chose to emigrate when the Russians invaded back in the seventies. I met my wife in New York." He raised his voice. "Lila, come say hello."

From an office in the back, a petite, gray-haired Afghani woman peeked out and smiled. "Hello. Nice to meet you."

"So how did you both end up here?"

"You mean in the middle of nowhere?" Aasif's grin widened. "Lila and I got tired of the city. We wanted something that was the exact opposite."

"Looks like you succeeded." Tucker glanced around the empty shop and the dark forest beyond the windows.

"We love it here. And it's normally not this deserted. We're between seasons at the moment. The summer crowds have left, and the skiers have yet to arrive. But we still have our regulars."

Proving this, a diesel engine roared outside, and a white, rust-stained pickup truck pulled between the pumps, fishtailing slightly as it came to a stop.

Tucker turned back at Aasif. "Seems like business is picking—"

The man's eyes had narrowed, his jaw clenched. The army had handpicked Tucker as a dog handler because of his unusually high empathy scores. Such sensitivity allowed him to bond more readily and deeply with his partner—and to read people. Still, it took no skill at all to tell Aasif was scared.

Aasif waved to his wife. "Lila, go back in the office."

She obeyed, but not before casting a frightened glance toward her husband.

Tucker moved closer to the windows, trailed by Kane. He quickly assessed the situation, noting one odd detail: duct tape covered the truck's license plate.

Definitely trouble.

No one with good intentions blacked out his license plate.

Tucker took a deep breath. The air suddenly felt heavier, crackling with electricity. He knew it was only a figment of his own spiking adrenaline. Still, he knew a storm was brewing. Kane reacted to his mood, the hackles rising along the shepherd's back, accompanied by a low growl.

Two men in flannel shirts and baseball caps hopped out of the cab; a third jumped down from the truck's bed. The driver of the truck sported a dirty red goatee and wore a green baseball cap emblazoned with I'D RATHER BE DOIN' YOUR WIFE.

Great . . . not only are these yokels trouble, they have a terrible sense of humor.

Without turning, he asked, "Aasif, do you have security cameras?"

"They're broken. We haven't been able to fix them."

He sighed loudly. *Not good.*

The trio strutted toward the station entrance. Each man carried a wooden baseball bat.

"Call the sheriff. If you can trust him."

"He's a decent man."

"Then call him."

"Perhaps it is best if you do not—"

"Make the call, Aasif."

Tucker headed to the door with Kane and pushed outside before the others could enter. Given the odds, he would need room to maneuver.

Tucker stopped the trio at the curb. "Evening, fellas."

"Hey," replied Mr. Goatee, making a move to slip past him.

Tucker stepped to block him. "Store's closed."

"Bull," said one of the others and pointed his bat. "Look, Shane, I can see that raghead from here."

"Then you can also *see* he's on the phone," Tucker said. "He's calling the sheriff."

"That idiot?" Shane said. "We'll be long gone before he pulls his head outta his ass and gets here."

Tucker let his grin turn dark. "I wouldn't be so sure of that."

He silently signaled Kane, pointing an index finger down   then tightening a fist. The command clear: THREATEN.

Kane lowered his head, bared his teeth, and let out a menacing growl. Still, the shepherd remained at his side. Kane wouldn't move unless given another command or if this confrontation became physical.

Shane took a step back. "That mutt comes at me and I'll bash his brains in."

If this mutt comes at you, you'll never know what hit you.

Tucker raised his hands. "Listen, guys, I get it. It's Friday night, time to blow off some steam. All I'm asking is you find some other way of doing it. The people inside are just trying to make a living. Just like you and me."

Shane snorted. "Like us? Them towelheads ain't nothing like us. We're Americans."

"So are they."

"I lost buddies in Iraq—"

"We all have."

"What the hell do you know about it?" asked the third man.

"Enough to know the difference between these store owners and the kind of people you're talking about."

Tucker remembered his own reaction upon first entering the shop and felt a twinge of guilt.

Shane lifted his bat and aimed the end at Tucker's face. "Get outta our way or you'll regret siding with the enemy."

Tucker knew the talking part of this encounter was over.

Proving this, Shane jabbed Tucker in the chest with the bat.

So be it.

Tucker's left hand snapped out and grabbed the bat. He gave it a jerk, pulling Shane off balance toward him.

He whispered a command to his partner: "GRAB AND DROP."

Kane hears those words—and reacts. He recognizes the threat in his target: the rasp of menace in his breath, the fury that has turned his sweat bitter. Tense muscles explode as the order is given. Kane is already moving before the last word is spoken, anticipating the other's need, knowing what he must do.

He leaps upward, his jaws wide.

Teeth find flesh.

Blood swells over his tongue.

With satisfaction, Tucker watched Kane latch on to Shane's forearm. Upon landing on his paws, the shepherd twisted and threw the combatant to the ground. The bat clattered across the concrete.

Shane screamed, froth flecking his words. "Get him off, get him off!"

One of the man's friends charged forward, his bat swinging down toward Kane. Anticipating this, Tucker dove low and took the hit with his own body. Expertly blunting the blow by turning his back at an angle, he reached up and wrapped his forearm around the bat. He pinned it in place—then side kicked. His heel slammed into the man's kneecap, triggering a muffled pop.

The man hollered, released the bat, and staggered backward.

Tucker swung his captured weapon toward the third attacker. "It's over. Drop it."

The last man glared, but he let the bat fall—

—then reached into his jacket and lashed out with his arm again.

Tucker's mind barely had time to register the glint of a knife blade. He backpedaled, dodging the first slash. His heel struck the curb behind him, and he went down, crashing into a row of empty propane tanks and losing the bat.

Grinning cruelly, the man loomed over Tucker and brandished his knife. "Time to teach you a lesson about—"

Tucker reached over his shoulder and grabbed a loose propane tank as it rolled along the sidewalk behind him. He swung it low, cutting the man's legs out from under him. With a pained cry of surprise, the attacker crashed to the ground.

Tucker rolled to him, snatched the man's wrist, and bent it backward until a bone snapped. The knife fell free. Tucker retrieved the blade as the man curled into a ball, groaning and clutching his hand. His left ankle was also cocked sideways, plainly broken.

Lesson over.

He stood up and walked over to Shane, whose lips were compressed in fear and agony. Kane still held him pinned down, clamped on to the man's bloody arm, his teeth sunk to bone.

"Release," Tucker ordered.

The shepherd obeyed but stayed close, baring his bloody fangs at Shane. Tucker backed his partner up with the knife.

Sirens echoed through the forest, growing steadily louder.

Tucker felt his belly tighten. Though he'd acted in self-defense, he was in the middle of nowhere awaiting a sheriff who could arrest them if the whim struck him. Flashing lights appeared through the trees, and a cruiser swung fast into the parking lot and pulled to a stop twenty feet away.

Tucker raised his hands and tossed the knife aside.

He didn't want anyone making a mistake here.

"Sit," he told Kane. "Be happy."

The dog dropped to his haunches, wagging his tail, his head cocked to the side quizzically.

Aasif joined him outside and must have noticed his tension. "Sheriff Walton is a fair man, Tucker."

"If you say so."

In the end, Aasif proved a good judge of character. It helped that the sheriff knew the trio on the ground and held them in no high opinion. *These boys been raising hell for a year now,* the sheriff eventually explained. *So far, nobody's had the sand to press charges against them.*

Sheriff Walton took down their statements and noted the truck's blacked-out license plate with a sad shake of his head. "I believe that would be your third strike, Shane. And from what I hear, redheads are very popular at the state pen this year."

Shane lowered his head and groaned.

After another two cruisers arrived and the men were hauled away, Tucker faced the sheriff. "Do I need to stick around?"

"Do you want to?"

"Not especially."

"Didn't think so. I've got your details. I doubt you'll need to testify, but if you do—"

"I'll come back."

"Good." Walton passed him a card. Tucker expected it to have the local sheriff's department's contact information on it, but instead it was emblazoned with the image of a car with a smashed fender. "My brother owns a body-repair shop in Wisdom, next town down the highway. I'll make sure he gets that flat tire of yours fixed at cost."

Tucker took the card happily. "Thanks."

With matters settled, Tucker was soon back on the road with Kane. He held out the card toward the shepherd as he sped toward his motel. "See, Kane. Who says no good deed goes unpunished?"

Unfortunately, he spoke too soon. As he turned into his motel and parked before the door to his room, his headlight shone upon an impossible sight.

Sitting on the bench before his cabin was a woman—a ghost out of his past. Only this figment wasn't outfitted in desert khaki or in the blues of her dress uniform. Instead, she wore jeans and a light-blue blouse with an open wool cardigan.

Tucker's heart missed several beats. He sat behind the wheel, engine idling, struggling to understand how she could be here, how she had found him.

Her name was Jane Sabatello. It had been over six years since he'd last set eyes on her. He found his gaze sweeping over her every feature, each triggering distinct memories, blurring past and present: the softness of her full lips, the shine of moonlight that turned her blond hair silver, the joy in her eyes each morning.

Tucker had never married, but Jane was as close as he'd come.

And now here she was, waiting for him—and she wasn't alone.

A child sat at her side, a young boy tucked close to her hip.

For the briefest of moments, he wondered if the boy—

No, she would have told me.

He finally cut off the engine and stepped out of the vehicle. She stood up as she recognized him in turn.

"Jane?" he murmured.

She rushed to him and wrapped him in a hug, clinging to him for a long thirty seconds before pulling back. She searched his face, her eyes moist. Under the glare of the Cherokee's headlamps, he noted a dark bruise under one cheekbone, poorly obscured by a smear of cosmetic concealer.

Even less hidden was the panic and raw fear in her face.

She kept one hand firmly on his arm, her fingers tight with desperation. "Tucker, I need your help."

Before he could speak, she glanced to the boy.

"Someone's trying to kill us."

2

Tucker studied Jane's every movement as he held his motel door open. She passed by him, her back stiff, her fingers tightening on the boy's shoulder. Her gaze swept every corner of the room before stepping fully inside. Only after finding the place empty did she seem to relax, sagging, letting her exhaustion show. She guided her son inside and sat down on one of the twin beds with a small sigh.

The child—a blond-haired boy of three or four—climbed atop the bed and leaned against her side. Jane stroked his hair. His eyelids immediately began to droop.

Tucker took the opposite bed, sitting down, his knees almost touching Jane's. She shifted slightly farther away, a reflexive wary movement.

Perhaps catching herself, she placed a hand on her knee. "It's been a long drive," she offered.

Tucker knew it wasn't the drive that had shaken up the hard, competent woman he knew from six years ago. He gave her the leeway to open up with her story on her own and didn't press her.

Kane approached. He came with his nose held low, his tail wagging slowly, perhaps also sensing her tension.

A small smile creased Jane's lips. She patted the bed next to her. "Hey, handsome," she said softly. "I missed you."

At her words, Kane's tail swept more widely, plainly also recognizing Jane. The shepherd hopped smoothly onto the bed, gently enough so as not to disturb the drowsing boy on Jane's other side.

He lay down next to her and rested his snout on her thigh, his nose sniffing at the boy's tousled hair.

She rubbed one of Kane's ears, earning a contented *umph* from the shepherd.

Lucky dog.

Tucker watched as Jane turned and settled her son onto the bed, drawing a blanket over him. She was still strikingly beautiful. Her features were small, her eyes as blue as the deepest marine trench. He noted that she continued to keep herself wiry and athletic. In the army, she'd run marathons and practiced Kendo, excelling at both, earning her the nickname Zorro. Additionally, her tough physical conditioning had sculpted her silhouette into the most inviting curves.

With her son settled, Jane's gaze turned to him, sizing him up as well. He was a year older than her, his shaggy straw-colored hair several shades darker, his build just as athletic, but bulkier with muscle. He could tell she was searching through his many scars for the younger version of himself, the kid who would sweep her up in his arms and swing her around whenever they met, the one who could laugh easily, who didn't wake at night in sweat-soaked sheets.

They stared across the gulf of years between them.

Perhaps finding the depth of that gulf too much to face, she turned her attention back to Kane, to easier footing.

"Kane's gotten bigger, Tuck. How is that possible?"

Tucker let a small grin show. Jane was the only person in the world who called him Tuck.

"He pumps iron."

"Shush. He's as beautiful as ever." Her eyes found him again. "I heard about Abel."

Tucker felt a stab in his heart at the mention of Kane's littermate. His gaze flashed to the fall of knives, his nostrils suddenly filled with the smell of smoke, while his ears echoed with screams of his wounded teammates. His sight dimmed to a vision of a dark-furred form sprawled on red rock.

Abel...

A touch on his knee drew him back to his own body.

"I'm so sorry, Tuck," Jane said, her fingers squeezing. "I should have called. I should have stayed in closer touch."

"It's okay," he answered hoarsely. "Kane and I've been on the move a lot."

Jane straightened, her palm shifting to Kane's side. "I know how much you both loved him."

He swallowed hard.

"Well," she said, "at least most of the old gang is back together again. Wayne, Jane, and Kane."

An amused wistfulness softened her features. Back in Afghanistan, the rhyming confluence of their names had been a source of jokes among their unit.

Tucker paused a few moments to collect himself more fully, then nodded toward the sleeping boy. "So, Jane, tell me about this *newest* member of our gang."

She turned to the boy, her face softening with a love that glowed from her skin. "His name's Nathan. He'll be four in a couple months. To be honest, he's the other reason I never called. It's hard. I always thought you and I would . . . well, you know."

I know.

"Five years ago, I met a great guy—Mike. An insurance agent, if you can believe that."

"Why wouldn't I believe that?"

"You know what an adrenaline junkie I am. In the back of my mind, I always saw myself with someone risky. If not you, then a bull rider or a mountain climber or a cave diver. Then I met Mike. He was funny, sweet, handsome." She shook her head. Memories drew out a smile, while sadness welled in her eyes. "We fell in love, and I got pregnant."

"And where's Mike now?"

Jane looked to Nathan. "He died in a car accident three weeks after his son was born. He was so proud . . . so happy . . ."

Tucker hadn't been expecting that. He felt like he'd been punched in the stomach. "I'm so sorry, Jane."

She nodded, wiping at one eye. "After that, I pulled away from everyone. My son and my job became my entire life. At times, I thought about looking for you, but we'd been out of touch for so long already, and I didn't know what to say."

"I get it." He stared around the small motel room, ready to move on to a less uncomfortable subject. Jane had sought him out for a clear reason. "How did you find me here anyway?"

She shrugged. "Friends in shady places."

He lifted an eyebrow.

"Okay. I placed a credit card trace on you. If you truly want to stay lost, you'll have to work better at it."

She meant it as a joke, but he filed away her advice, reminding himself that he had become lax of late in covering his trail.

Getting careless.

Using her thumb and index finger, Jane tucked a stray lock of hair behind her right ear. Tucker remembered the mannerism; he loved it about her, though he'd never quite understood why. Just one of those things, he supposed. He found himself staring at her.

"What?" she asked, catching him looking.

"Nothing. Where're you living now?"

Jane hesitated. "I'd rather not say. It's not that I don't trust you. It's just the less you know, the better."

Tucker would have scoffed at this kind of cloak-and-dagger talk coming from anyone else. But this was Jane; she was as even-keeled as they came. Jane had been the best intelligence analyst in the 75th Rangers, attached to the Regimental Special Troops Battalion. In the past, she and Tucker had worked closely together coordinating missions, until she'd left the army seven months before him.

"Jane, you said you thought you were in danger. That someone was trying to kill you."

She took a deep breath. "I may just be paranoid. With my work, it comes with the territory. But with Nathan, I'm not taking any chances."

"Okay, then tell me what's going on."

"You remember Sandy Conlon."

Tucker had to think for a moment before he could place the name. It had been so long ago.

Jane slipped out a photo from a pocket and passed it over to him. He stared down at a younger picture of himself, grinning goofily, thrusting out his chest, his arm around Jane, who in turn had her arm around a shorter, slender woman with mousy brown hair, wearing black-rimmed eyeglasses. At their feet sat two proud young dogs, Kane and Abel.

A soft smile rose to his lips, remembering when this picture was taken. Sandy had been a civilian intelligence analyst attached to the 3rd Ranger Battalion out of Fort Benning, Georgia. She had been a frequent part of their gang. Thinking of her now, Tucker remembered her wry sense of humor, her bright laughter. This was another friendship he wished he'd never let slip.

"What about her?" he asked.

"She's gone missing. I hadn't heard from Sandy for about a month, so I called her mother three days ago. She lives outside Huntsville, up in the mountains. Backwater county. Banjoes, square dancing, moonshine, the works."

"Colorful. What did you learn from her?"

"Not a whole lot, but enough to make me worried."

"Go on."

Jane took a deep breath. "Sandy had taken a new position about a year and a half ago. Prior to that she was working as an analyst for the DIA."

Defense Intelligence Agency.

"In fact, it was Sandy who helped get me a job with the DIA. We worked alongside each other until she left."

"But you still work there."

She nodded.

Tucker knew better than to ask for more details. Jane's skill set had no doubt landed her work in a classified field.

Jane continued. "After Sandy left, we stayed in casual touch. E-mails a few times a week. Phone calls a couple times a month. That sort of thing. But for the past several weeks, I sensed something *off* about her. At first I thought she was just preoccupied, but when I pressed her about it, she kept saying everything was fine."

"And it wasn't."

"I could hear something in her voice, especially the last time we talked. She sounded scared."

From what Tucker remembered about Sandy, the woman wasn't one to scare easily. She had steel in her veins.

"Where was her new job?" he asked.

"Out at Redstone."

Tucker recognized the name. "Redstone Arsenal?"

She nodded.

Redstone was a U.S. Army post down in Huntsville, Alabama. It was home to a slew of military commands, mostly involved with the aerospace industry, including the Missile Defense Agency and NASA's Marshall Space Flight Center.

"And her job?"

"She never said. Maybe couldn't say. I assume she was hired as some kind of consultant out there. Involved with some highly classified project."

"And now she's gone?" he pressed. "And she left no word with anyone?"

"According to her mother, Sandy visited her three weeks ago, said she was going to be out of touch for a couple weeks and not to worry. But what struck me as strange was that Sandy also told her mother not to call the base or make any inquiries."

"Odd thing for her to say."

"I thought so, too." Jane let that sink in for a moment.

"If you had to guess," he asked, "what do you think happened?"

"Someone took her."

Tucker sat straighter, reacting to the certainty in her voice. "What makes you say that?"

"After speaking to Sandy's mom, I started making some discreet inquiries, checking on friends of friends. Both hers and mine. I hoped someone else knew something. Instead, I discovered two more of our mutual colleagues have fallen off the face of the earth. But far more disturbing, four others were dead."

"Dead?"

"All in the past month. One of a carbon monoxide leak in his house, another from a heart attack, and two others died in car accidents."

Too many for a coincidence.

"What's the common denominator among all of you?" he asked. "Did you work on something together? Were you all stationed somewhere?"

Jane looked into his eyes and said nothing, which was an answer in itself. Tucker knew her well enough to know she was holding something back, but he decided not to push it, remembering her earlier words: *the less you know, the better.*

"Why come to me?" Tucker asked.

She looked down at her hands. "At this point, I don't know whom to trust, but I trust you more than anyone else in the world. And you're . . . you're . . ." Her gaze shifted back to him. "Resourceful. And someone outside of all of this."

"Someone no one would suspect of helping you," he mumbled.

"And a new set of eyes. Don't think I've forgotten how good you are at looking past appearances to see the truth. I need that. I need *you*."

He stared at her, knowing there were depths to her last words that were too dangerous to plumb at the moment. If it had been anyone else, he would have slammed the door behind them and made sure he erased his trail from here. Instead, he leaned over and gripped her fingers, feeling the slight tremble in her hand.

"You've got me . . . and Kane."

She smiled up at him, stirring those depths. "Together again."

3

Pruitt Kellerman stood before the panoramic windows of his penthouse office. The view overlooked the expanse of Chesapeake Bay, but if he turned slightly, the view extended to the skyline of Washington, DC.

At this early hour, morning fog still shrouded the country's capital. It softened the city's marble-hard edges, erasing its monuments and domes. He imagined the mist eroding DC down to its shadowy heart, exposing the cancerous flow of ambitions that truly fueled the city, aspirations both petty and grand.

He smiled at his own reflection that overlay the distant capital, knowing he was the master of all he surveyed.

In a little over two decades, he had taken that city's dreams of power, its hopes and fears, and turned them into hard cash. Horizon Media Corp had become the dominant outlet for all those crying for attention, those weeping for redemption, those clawing for the top. His media empire controlled countless means of communication: television, radio, print, online. Over the years, he had learned how easy it was to control that flow of information. It was as simple as strangling some channels, while opening others more freely.

What few truly understood was that the old axiom *information is power* no longer held water. The true engine of power today was the *framing and delivery* of that information. In this era of sound bites and short attention spans, perception was everything, and Pruitt was a master at creating it, earning him the keys to that shining castle on the hill.

There wasn't a politician or a government servant beyond his reach. An election was coming up and already figures on both sides of the aisle were coming to him, hat in hand, recognizing who truly controlled their ambitions.

To maintain some distance, he had built the headquarters of Horizon Media on an island in Chesapeake Bay. Smith Island rested between Maryland and Virginia, and while it was mostly a national wildlife refuge, he had used his power to bend a recalcitrant zoning board to his will. He had picked one of the outer islands, the one closest to the coast, a sliver of eroding salt marsh that he expanded by dredging and filling, hiring a crew out of Hong Kong to fortify the foundations. He even had a private bridge built, along with employing a fleet of hydrofoils to ferry visitors back and forth.

A knock at the door drew his attention around. He checked his reflection, as he always did.

In his midfifties, he remained straight-backed and broad shouldered. He kept his head shaved, both to intimidate and as a matter of vanity, hiding a hairline that steadily receded. To further mask any signs of aging, he had begun to take injections of human growth hormone, a supposed fountain of youth. He also kept his body lean. Many had come to believe he was decades younger than his true age.

He straightened his silk tie.

Perception is everything.

The door opened behind him without his bidding. Such an action would have normally irked him, except only one person dared such an intrusion into his inner sanctum. He felt his stance relaxing as he turned, a smile coming to his lips.

"Laura," he said, greeting the young woman dressed in a prim navy business suit. "What are you doing here so early?"

She returned his smile just as warmly and waved to the hazy morning. "Like father, like daughter."

God, I hope not.

She crossed toward his desk, a folder tucked under one elbow. "I thought I should get a jump on the day."

He nodded with a long sigh and motioned to one of the chairs. His office was a masterpiece of Swedish modern architecture, with light wood furniture, brushed stainless accents, and minimal decoration. What dominated the room was the suite of giant ultrahigh-definition flat-screens that covered the wall behind a conference table. They silently displayed the channels he owned, showing talking-head anchors, while news stories scrolled along the bottom edges.

His daughter settled into the chair, brushing back a fall of auburn curls. Freckles dotted her cheeks. Few would consider her beautiful by today's unyielding standards, but over the years, Laura always managed to let her intelligence and charm win over a slew of suitors.

"Before today's news cycle kicks into full swing," she started, "I wanted to go over the message that legal has prepared in regards to this wiretapping business."

As director of communications, Laura managed the press, for both Horizon-owned outlets and independent alike. This latest case—this latest *nuisance*—concerned the accusation that Horizon Media had bugged the phones of the *Washington Post*.

"The *Post* has no proof," he groused, dropping heavily into his own leather chair. "Just word our response however you think best. I trust you. But stress the point that I had no prior knowledge of any such supposed activity. And if there's evidence to the contrary, we'll be happy to respond further."

"Done." Laura crossed an item off the list in the notebook on her lap. "So let's talk about the Athens trip on Friday. Somehow AP got wind of it."

"Of course they did."

Over the years, Pruitt had found it advantageous to allow a reporter to ferret out a nugget of information about Horizon now and again. It distracted attention from what he truly wanted to keep hidden.

Such was the case with this Athens trip.

"Just tell them the truth," he said.

She glanced up from her notebook, cocking an eyebrow with a small grin. "The truth? Since when are we in the business of disseminating the truth?"

He gave her a scolding look. "I thought I was the only cynic in the room."

"I learn from the master," she said, returning to her notes.

He sighed, wishing that weren't true. After Laura had graduated from Harvard Business, he had done everything possible to nudge

her away from working at Horizon. But in a world filled with vacu-
ous daughters of wealth who spent their days drinking Frappuccinos
and their evenings flashing their undergarments at paparazzi, he'd
gotten one who wanted to work hard for success and didn't have a
pretentious bone in her body. Still, since bringing her onboard five
years ago, he had done his best to insulate her from the darker side of
Horizon Media's enterprises, especially his plans for the next great
leap forward for the business.

She read from her notes. "In regards to the Athens trip, we're
saying that it's a part of Horizon's ongoing efforts to modernize and
consolidate the Greek telecom companies. We're also stressing that
both Horizon and the Greek government believe in a free-market
system, one of openness and transparency."

"That sounds perfect."

Pruitt was only too aware this statement would cause an uproar
among the antitrust zealots in this country and in the EU, but as it
stood, most of Greece's telecom industry was already headed toward
naked monopolization. Someone had to take the reins.

Might as well be Horizon.

"Anything else?" she asked.

"Yes, one more item on the agenda." He stood up, crossed around
the desk, and took her hand. "You're everything to me, you know
that, Laura, don't you?"

She smiled. "Of course. I love you, too."

"I'm worried that you don't take enough time for yourself.
Rumor has it you're here ninety hours a week."

"Dad, that's no different than a lot of people here."

"You're not *people*. You're my *daughter*."

"And I love my job. I can handle myself."

"Of course you can, but it's a father's prerogative to worry.
Besides, with your mother—"

"I know." Her mother had died of ovarian cancer when Laura
was fifteen. It had broken both their hearts, and in the mending,
the two of them had become even closer. She squeezed his fingers.
"You've done a great job, Dad. I'm a well-adjusted, average thirty-
something."

"You're anything but average, Laura."

She patted his hand in thanks, stood up, and smoothed her pencil skirt. "I should get going. I saw your bulldog waiting outside. He had that steely eyed stare that didn't look like good news."

That would be Raphael Lyon, the head of his personal security team.

Before she turned away, he wagged a finger at her. "Once this wiretapping nonsense is put to bed, you're to take a vacation. That's an order from your CEO."

Laura gave him a salute. "Yes, sir."

As she exited, Lyon entered in her place, striding stiffly forward into his office. The bulldog analogy was not unwarranted. The man was squat and heavily muscled. His hands were huge and armored with calluses. His face was permanently tanned from years in the desert. Every movement as he crossed to the desk screamed ex-military.

Rafael Lyon was formerly with the French Special Forces—Brigade des Forces Specials Terre. Six years ago, he had been facing capital war crimes charges for actions in Chad. At the time, Pruitt had found it advantageous to intervene on Rafael's behalf, mostly because Horizon-run newspapers had been implicated in riling up opposition forces in that country, stoking the fuels that ignited the country into a civil war. Still, when Pruitt spared Lyon from a long prison sentence, the man had become his most loyal asset, one who was not above getting his hands dirty, even bloody.

Pruitt knew better than to exchange small talk with the man. "So where do we stand with Garrison?"

Senator Melvin Garrison chaired the Committee on Energy and Natural Resources, which was currently studying a bill that would allow American defense manufacturers to use imported rare-earth elements in their products. Through a series of agents, Pruitt had been encouraging Garrison to ensure the bill never got out of committee.

Lyon shook his head. "He's not budging."

Pruitt smiled ruefully. "Is that so? Tell me about him."

"No vices or skeletons that I could find. Divorced, never remarried."

"Children?"

"A son and daughter. She's at Harvard premed. The boy is spending the summer backpacking across Europe. He's currently in . . ."

Lyon took a notebook from his pocket and flipped a few pages. "In Rome."

"Do you have anyone out there?"

Lyon thought for a moment, clearly knowing what was being asked of him. "I do." His gaze hardened on Pruitt. "How bad do you want him hurt?"

"No permanent damage, but enough that Garrison doesn't mistake the message. Let me know when it's done, and I'll call the good senator with my sympathies."

Lyon nodded.

"Good. Now where are we with the last of our wayward geniuses?"

"Snyder and his wife went off the road outside of Asheville. Faulty brake line. Not so original, but effective."

"And the last two?"

"We're closing in on one of them as we speak. The other—Sabatello—fell off the grid for the moment. We're working other leads. We'll find her."

Pruitt frowned. He had read the dossier on Jane Sabatello. "Given her background, that might be challenging."

"We'll find her," Lyon repeated. "She vanished with her son. Should make tracking her easier."

"Make sure you don't fail."

"For these last two, I assume you will want the same protocol as before?"

Pruitt nodded. "Their deaths must look accidental."

The truth must never get out.

4

Welcome to Rocket City...

Less than a day after parting ways with Jane in Montana, Tucker found himself on the opposite side of the country, cruising in a rental Ford Explorer through the wooded outskirts of Huntsville, Alabama. The place had earned its nickname, Rocket City, due to its proximity to the neighboring Redstone facility, home to both the military's missile program and NASA's space flight center.

Kane sat up front with him, his head out the window, taking in the scents of the surrounding Tennessee River valley. After being cooped up in a crate for the cross-country flight, his partner clearly appreciated the wind whipping through his fur, his nostrils drawing in the world.

Tucker reached over and patted the dog's flank.

Wish I could learn to live in the moment like you.

Instead, a nagging worry had formed a knot behind his eyes. He had hated to leave Jane behind at the motel, but she had insisted he go on ahead, wanting to get Nathan somewhere safe before rejoining him. Besides, Jane was too well known in this area. No one here knew his face. For now, he would have to take the lead alone.

Still, he had promised Jane that he would keep her abreast of his investigation. To that end, she had given him two telephone numbers that she called safe. *Leave a message on the first number—something anonymous about the birth of a baby or a family reunion or something,* she'd instructed him, *then wait ten minutes and call the second number.*

Though she had put on a brave face as he left for the airport, Tucker knew she was more frightened than he'd ever seen her.

Up ahead, a sign glowed alongside the interstate, half buried at the edge of a swampy woodland: FALLS VALLEY MOTEL.

"Almost home," he warned Kane.

He had chosen this place due to its remote location at the far western edge of Huntsville. Off to the left, the decaying remnants of an old concrete factory sat out in the swamps. Back in 1962, a levy had broken in a bend of the storm-swollen Tennessee River and flooded the shallow valley in which the factory sat. Rather than try to reclaim the already-abandoned factory, the state decided to make the best of a bad situation. Like the hulk of a sunken ship that becomes a reef, the factory had become the heart of a flourishing new ecosystem.

But it wasn't just the colorful seclusion of the motel that drew Tucker to rent a room here. Gate #7 of the Redstone Arsenal lay only two miles farther down the road. Whether this would make any tangible difference to his investigation, Tucker didn't know, but having the post within eyeshot would help him focus.

Reaching the motel, he pulled into the parking lot. The facility was made up of individual cabins spread through the neighboring forest. He checked in, asked for the most remote spot, and then drove to the far end of the lot to his room. Once inside, he found flowered wallpaper and an avocado bedspread straight from the 1970s, but everything was clean and smelled faintly of Lysol.

As he unpacked, Kane did a full inspection of the room. After seeming to find it passable, he plopped down on the queen bed, but not without a long, disappointed sigh.

"Yeah, not exactly the Ritz, is it?"

Tucker crossed and pulled open the drapes at the back of the cabin. The window looked east toward Redstone. Above the tree line, he could make out two hills—Weeden and Madkin Mountains—that rose from the forty thousand acres that made up the massive facility, over half of which were test grounds for missiles, rockets, and space vehicles. He had read that there were over two hundred miles of roads, and tens of thousands of square feet of buildings.

Redstone Arsenal was a city unto itself.

And somewhere in all that, Sandy Conlon had worked, perhaps on a project that had something to do with her disappearance.

But what?

There was only one way to find out. Though tired from all of the travel, Tucker was also jacked up by the prospect of the challenge ahead. And he suspected he wasn't the only one.

Kane watched him from atop the comforter, those dark eyes studying him as if anticipating what he would say next.

He smiled at his partner, which earned him a tail thump. "How about it, Kane. Ready to go to work?"

Kane bounded off the bed and headed to the door, his tail flagging high.

"I'll take that as a yes."

Before departing, he removed Kane's uniform from his duffel. The K9 Storm tactical vest was mottled to match the shepherd's black and tan fur. Not only was it waterproof, but it was also Kevlar reinforced. He checked the pinpoint night-vision camera folded next to his collar and its wireless transmitter. The equipment gave Tucker a two-way streaming visual and audio feed of the shepherd's surroundings. He could also communicate to Kane via a small custom-fitted earpiece.

He slipped the vest in place over Kane's shoulders and tightened the straps, feeling the dog's muscles trembling with suppressed excitement. After examining the vest for any rub points and testing the comm link, he did one final check. He cupped Kane's cheeks between his hands, staring deep into his partner's eyes.

"Ready, buddy?"

Kane pushed forward, touching his cold, wet nose to Tucker's.

"Who's the best dog?" he whispered.

A small lick to his chin answered him.

"That's right ... you are." Tucker straightened and turned toward the door. "Let's go explore."

9:19 P.M.

Night had fully fallen by the time Tucker's SUV passed through the gates of a small subdivision. His headlights swept over the bronze lettering at the stone entryway.

CHAPMAN VALLEY ESTATES

According to Jane, Sandy lived in this neighborhood. His rental's GPS led him through a maze of streets. The houses he passed appeared to be small mansions, none less than five thousand square feet, all on lots well over an acre. Each yard was neatly manicured, the homes set well back from the road. Through the open window, the evening smelled of lilac and freshly mowed grass.

Sandy, whatever you were doing, it must've paid well.

He slowed down as he neared his destination, then stopped when he was a hundred yards away. All of the driveways in the neighborhood were marked with identical rustic lamps, each bearing the street number. He noted the lamp at the foot of her driveway was dark.

A faint alarm bell went off in Tucker's head.

Maybe something, maybe nothing . . .

He sat for a moment, taking everything in. The warm air buzzed with mosquitoes and creaked with the calls of a thousand crickets. The road was otherwise quiet. No cars, no pedestrians, no barking dogs. Through a few neighboring windows, lights flickered from television sets or glowed from bedroom windows.

"Looks like everyone is settling in for the night," he whispered to Kane.

Except for us.

Tucker grabbed his shoulder pack and climbed out of the car with Kane. Together, they strode over toward her driveway, passing along Sandy's front yard as if just another local walking his dog.

Fifty yards from the street rose Sandy's home, a modern two-story French château with gabled windows and an attached three-car garage. There was even a tall stone fountain in a front courtyard.

Definitely paid well . . .

As he reached the driveway, he noted that all of the windows were dark. The fountain lay quiet and still.

With the street still empty, Tucker took ten quick strides down the driveway, then stepped off into a patch of oak trees. Kane kept to his heels as he dropped to one knee on a thick bed of damp leaves. He dug his night-vision monocle from a side pocket of his pack and panned it across the front of the house.

He counted four motion-triggered spotlights along the eaves, all evidence that Sandy likely had an alarm system.

But was it still operational?

Time to find out.

Twisting to the side, he powered up Kane's comm system, then donned his headset. He palmed the shepherd's cheek and pointed to the house.

"SCOUT," he whispered aloud, then circled a finger in the air. It was a command that Kane knew well: CIRCLE AND RETURN.

Kane took off toward the dark house, running low, already sweeping wide to make a full pass around the grounds. Tucker had worked alongside other military war dogs. He knew their capabilities, but Kane outshone them all, with a tested vocabulary of over a thousand words and the comprehension of a hundred hand signals. And while Kane's brain couldn't interpret full sentences, he could string together words and commands to complete a linked sequence of commands. But best of all, after working in tandem since Kane was a pup, the pair had grown to read each other beyond any spoken word or motioned signal.

They had come to trust each other implicitly.

Tucker watched proudly as Kane swept over the lawn, a dark arrow through the warm night. He also noted that none of the motion lights activated as the shepherd passed.

System must be off.

Suspicions jangled through him.

As Kane vanished around the corner of the garage, Tucker slipped his satellite phone into his hand. He thumbed on the feed from Kane's night-vision camera. A bobbling, washed-out image of tree trunks flashing past appeared on the screen.

When Kane reached the far side of the house, Tucker touched the microphone of his headset and sent a command to his partner's earpiece: "STOP."

Kane immediately obeyed, dropping down onto his belly. The shepherd kept his focus—and the camera's—on the rear of the modern château.

Tucker stared at the screen for several long breaths.

All seemed quiet.

"CONTINUE," he ordered.

. . . .

Kane pads through the damp grass, angling around bushes and flow-
ing through the deepest shadows. Ears stand tall, swiveling to every
noise: the whir of insects, a distant feline hiss, the rumble of a car on
a neighboring road. His nostrils flare with scents both familiar and
strange in this new place.

A squirrel darts from his passage, but he ignores the fire to give
chase.

He remains on the path given to him.

He circles around the house and back into the woods out front.
A faint breeze carries the tang of familiar sweat. He moves swiftly
toward it. His body craves the warmth behind that scent, the promise
buried there, of pack and home.

He finally reaches his partner's side.

Fingers find his scruff and welcome him with their touch, with
the dig of nails.

He leans closer, nudging the other's thigh with his nose.

Together again.

"Good boy," Tucker whispered in both greeting and reward,
acknowledging their partnership.

With Kane panting lightly at his side, Tucker sat back on his heels
and debated his next move. He had come here in the hopes of searching Sandy's residence. With the house dark and the outside motion
detectors off, it might be safe to proceed, but such a move was not
without risk. Still, it wasn't in his nature to lie back.

"On me," he finally ordered.

Keeping close to the trees, he headed toward the rear of the house.
During Kane's surveillance, he had spotted a back door into the
garage. He approached it cautiously, only to discover it was locked.
But the door's upper half was made of mullioned glass.

Using a small penlight, he searched through the window for
alarm wires and found none.

Good enough.

From his pocket, he withdrew a spring-loaded glass punch. He
folded a bandana over its steel head and pressed the tool against one

of the windowpanes and touched the button. With a muted crack, the glass shattered. He quickly tapped away the loose shards, then groped through until he found the dead bolt and flipped it.

He hurried inside, chalking up his first felony on this mission.

Breaking and entering.

He scanned the garage and found the usual contents: gardening and lawn equipment, a workbench, a few ladders hanging on the back wall.

But no car.

He crossed to the door leading into the house. He checked the knob. Locked. But he also knew Sandy's habits. He reached up and ran his fingers along the top of the molding.

Bingo.

He plucked the key, inserted it into the lock, and stepped through into the kitchen. After the humidity of the outside, the air conditioning felt refreshing, cooling the sweat on his skin. He held a hand up to one of the air vents. If Sandy had left the air conditioning running before she had disappeared, it seemed to imply she had intended to return here.

Worry iced through him.

He stood still and listened to the house, but all he heard were the telltale creaks of an empty house. He glanced down to Kane, who must have sensed his attention. The shepherd's ears were high, his muscles tense under his Kevlar vest. But his partner gave no indication that he detected anything out of the ordinary here.

Tucker touched his side. "Stay with me," he whispered as he began his search of the premises.

He made a quick survey of the house to get the layout. Sandy's taste in decor was southern cozy: deep-cushioned chairs, hand-scraped oak floor, maple cabinets. Yet, as homey as it all appeared, it all had a *staged* look. Nothing stood out of place. It felt unlived in, as if Sandy spent most of her time at work.

He looked for any evidence that someone had conducted a search before his arrival, but on his first pass, he found no sign of any trespassing beyond his own.

He ended up in an upstairs study dominated by a dark oak desk, which was flanked by tall bookshelves. He glanced through the titles, a mix of popular fiction and rows upon rows of books on computer languages, engineering, and programming.

Recognizing her interest, he stepped to her computer monitor. He followed a cord over the lip of the deck to a rectangular imprint on the carpet. It seemed the computer tower itself was missing. But did Sandy abscond with it or had someone taken it after she had vanished?

He searched the desk drawers, but found nothing unusual: bills, appliance warranties, letters, pay stubs, car payment vouchers, canceled checks, bank statements, and so on. They were all organized in labeled hanging file folders.

Hmm . . .

For someone so invested in computers, her recordkeeping was more old school. She seemed to prefer hard copies of everything.

A whine drew his attention to Kane. The shepherd stood by the lone window of the study. It offered a view overlooking the front lawn.

Tucker watched a black Chevy Suburban finish a turn into the driveway and glide toward the front door. Its headlights were off.

5

Tucker zoomed in on the license plate and memorized the number. This timely arrival couldn't be a coincidence. He didn't know who the newcomers were, but they weren't the police.

Must've triggered a hidden alarm.

Ducking away, he retraced his steps to the garage. Just as he reached it, the front door slammed shut inside the empty house. Tucker hurried to the back door of the garage, cracked it open, and searched the rear yard. *All clear.* He motioned for Kane to stick to his legs and slid out. Pressing to the brick wall, he sidestepped toward the front of the house. As he neared the corner, he heard something: the faint swish of a foot passing through the grass behind him.

Shielding Kane with his body, Tucker whispered to his partner, while reinforcing the command with a firm hand signal. "Cover right. Close hide."

The shepherd tensed, then bolted into the trees, vanishing immediately.

A harsh voice called out, "Stop right there!"

Tucker half turned, raising his arms, as a dark figure closed toward him. He whispered into his headset, "Circle rear. Quiet attack bravo." Then he yanked the headset down around his neck and called loudly in an affable southern voice. "Hey, there, buddy, I was just looking for Sandy. I'm Fred Jenkins. Neighbor across the street. Me and Libby take care of things for Sandy when she's out of town. Left me her key."

He held up the key, while noting the darker shadow of a gun

clutched in the man's right hand. Tucker kept a nervous smile on his face.

Nothing to see here, buddy . . . just a friendly neighbor . . .

"Hadn't seen Sandy for a while," Tucker continued. "Thought maybe she forgot to tell us that she was leaving for a spell. Then I saw that her lawn was turning yellow. What with all the heat of late, I wasn't sure her sprinklers were coming on, so I came back here to check the timer box." He pointed toward the back door to the garage. "But it looks like—"

"Keep your hands up," the man ordered as he stepped closer and lifted his arm higher, revealing his weapon: a semiautomatic pistol affixed with a barrel-shaped noise suppressor.

Not good.

"Sure, no problem," Tucker mumbled. "Didn't mean to—"

A twig snapped behind the gunman—an unusual misstep for Kane. The man began to turn as the shepherd sprinted out of the trees and leapt headlong at the gunman. He blindsided his target like an NFL linebacker. With an *umph*, the man went down hard, his head striking the edge of a stone planter bed. His finger, already on the trigger, jerked reflexively and fired off a round with a cough of the suppressor.

Tucker charged forward as the round buzzed past his ear. He kept moving, but the man had gone limp on the ground. Tucker slid on a knee in the grass next to the body as Kane retreated to the far side.

Tucker snatched the gun, a Beretta M9, and checked for the assailant's pulse, when a new voice barked harshly behind him.

"Freeze!"

Tucker grimaced.

Of course, there was more than one guy.

He hissed to Kane, who remained shadowed by Tucker. "CLOSE HIDE."

As Kane slunk around and ghosted across the lawn into the nearby bushes, Tucker yelled over his shoulder. "Okay, okay! No problem!"

"Don't turn around!"

Tucker had to act fast. Men with noise-suppressed weapons tended to shoot first and skip questions altogether. Probably the only reason Tucker hadn't been shot in the back already was due to the proximity of the man's partner.

Over his shoulder, Tucker said, "Your friend is hurt over here! We better get him—"

Without turning, he brought the Beretta up across his body and fired twice under his armpit. Even as the second round left the barrel, Tucker was spinning on his knees and dropping to his belly. He kept his pistol extended toward the gunman. Unsurprisingly, both of Tucker's shots had missed their target, but they had served their purpose. The assailant rolled himself around the corner of the house and vanished.

This guy's trained . . . seasoned . . .

Tucker sprinted to the front corner of the house, leading with his pistol, and peeked around. A bullet shattered into the stucco near his cheek. Tucker dropped to his belly, then peeked around the edge again. The man had reached his Suburban and taken refuge behind the open backseat door.

Why the backseat? Why isn't he—

The answer occurred as the man lifted a long gun into view. Tucker recognized the weapon: an M4 carbine, noise suppressed and equipped with holographic sights.

Before the gunman could get into position, Tucker squeezed off four quick shots into the Suburban's open door, shattering the window and pinging rounds loudly off the metal frame. His target backpedaled while returning fire in Tucker's direction, then disappeared around the Suburban's rear bumper.

Knowing the man intended to outflank him, Tucker didn't wait around. He gained his feet and retreated toward the neighboring tree line, firing as he went, careful not to empty his weapon. Ducking into the foliage, he broke contact and sprinted through the trees into a neighbor's yard. After fifty feet, he stopped behind a tree trunk and went still.

No gunfire. No footfalls in pursuit.

He waited a full minute.

From the direction of Sandy's home, an engine started, followed moments later by the hiss of tires on asphalt. His opponent's discipline must have kicked in. No matter who won, a firefight in a suburban neighborhood was a bad idea, so instead of hunting Tucker down, the man had likely collected his partner and fled.

Tucker let out the breath he'd been holding, then reseated his headset and whispered to Kane. "RETURN HOME."

10:24 P.M.

Ten minutes later—after making sure the Suburban had truly left—Tucker found himself back in Sandy's kitchen with Kane at his side. It was the last place in the house he had failed to search. As he checked every drawer and cabinet, Tucker felt the tension of each passing second building into a knot in his neck. The unknown assailant could return with reinforcements at any time . . . or the gunman could simply force Tucker away by alerting local law enforcement with an anonymous tip of a suspicious person at Sandy's address.

Either way, he had to move quickly, but so far he had found nothing.

Tucker leaned against the counter and pondered. His gaze settled on a key rack by the kitchen door that led into the garage. He had stepped right past it earlier.

Stupid . . .

He needed some sleep.

Crossing over, he found another example of Sandy's usual meticulous nature. Each key was carefully labeled: backdoor, patio, Mom's house. Standard household stuff. But the last hook—this one unlabeled—held a padlock key. On it was a yellow sticker with the number 256, and beneath it in smaller letters 4987.

Tucker recognized the type of key from his military days, when he shifted posts regularly.

"Self-storage," he murmured.

If he was right, the four-digit pass code would unlock the entry gate, and the unit itself was marked by a three-digit address.

But which storage place?

Huntsville was a military town, which meant there had to be at least a dozen within range of the Redstone complex.

Suspecting where he might find a clue, he returned to Sandy's study and reopened the file drawer that held Sandy's bill folder. He sifted through the bills but found nothing from a self-storage company. He moved on to her canceled checks; there were hundreds, going back to 2011. Tucker started there and worked forward. The earlier checks showed Sandy's address in Washington DC, before she moved back to Huntsville. Tucker flipped through the succeeding months and years, sifting through her life, until he came to Sandy's move to Alabama. Again he found what he expected: a payment to a moving company, followed by standard household expenses: telephone, water, cable.

Nothing significant.

What am I missing?

He closed his eyes and remembered Jane had mentioned that Sandy had become withdrawn about six months ago. Maybe that period deserved a closer look. Tucker flipped back through the checks to eight months prior, then moved forward more slowly, this time looking for anything that might coincide with Sandy's change in behavior.

At the five-month mark, Tucker found a lone check made out to Edith Lozier in the amount of $360. The memo line read *Loan repayment. Thanks, Edith!!!*

"Why would Sandy need a loan?" Tucker mumbled. He had seen Sandy's bank statements. She certainly didn't need to take out a loan, especially for such a small amount.

So why this check?

Tucker got out his satellite phone and did a local search for Edith Lozier. He got a hit in the neighboring town of Gurley, south of Huntsville. He plugged the address into the phone's Google Earth app. It appeared Edith Lozier lived off a highway in an industrial section of Gurley. Her home was within a fenced-off area containing a dozen Quonset-like buildings.

A storage facility.

The woman was most likely the business's live-in manager or owner.

Tucker smiled.

Gotcha.

11:48 P.M.

Shortly before midnight, Tucker slowed his SUV as it passed a sign that read GARNET SELF-STORAGE. The town of Gurley lay about twelve miles south of Huntsville, home to some eight hundred people, small enough for everyone to know everybody's business. Tucker had passed several other storage places on his thirty-minute drive here; one was practically around the corner from Sandy's home.

So why choose this place?

He glanced to the neighboring two-story building that matched the address of Edith Lozier. The windows were dark at this late hour. Who was this woman to Sandy? Clearly she was enough of a friend to accept a check written to her rather than to the business. He wondered what else Edith might know, but to go knocking on a stranger's door in the middle of the night might not warrant the warmest of welcomes.

Instead, Tucker patted Kane's flank as the shepherd rested his muzzle on the sill of the passenger window. "Let's first see what Sandy hid out here in the middle of nowhere."

Kane thumped his tail in agreement.

Tucker edged his vehicle up to the rolling gate of the facility and reached out to the pole-mounted keypad. He punched in the four-digit code found on Sandy's padlock key, and the gate clattered open. Tucker let out a long breath of relief and slowly idled his truck through the nest of Quonset huts, following signs to Unit 256.

"Home sweet home," Tucker mumbled as he braked before the numbered unit.

He and Kane hopped out. While taking a moment to stretch a few kinks loose, Tucker surreptitiously searched around. He spotted a security camera, sharing the same pole as a sodium light. Keeping his face out of direct view, he crossed to the unit's rolling door and tested the padlock. Sandy's key slid in smoothly, and a moment later, the padlock dropped into his palm. With the way open, he lifted the rolling door and aimed his flashlight inside.

For a moment, he simply stared at what lay before him, dumbfounded by the unit's contents.

"What the hell?"

Finally, Tucker stepped into the space and flicked on the overhead light. To keep his search private, he lowered the rolling door. As a precaution, he left Kane outside with a standing order.

GUARD.

Tucker was taking no chances of being ambushed again.

With his hands on his hips, Tucker slowly took in his surroundings, making a slow turn. A single card table and chair occupied the center of the room. Arranged before them in a semicircle was a set of six easel-mounted whiteboards, each scrawled with color-coded notes and flowcharts. To the left of the table, a pair of corkboards hung on the wall, pinned with hundreds of scribbled index cards. To the right of the chair, a dozen or more accordion folders sat on the concrete floor.

The intent here was plain.

Looks like Sandy had built herself a nerve center in here.

But to what end?

Tucker noted the conspicuous absence of a laptop. All of these notes and charts could have been easily created on a computer, especially given Sandy's previous job as an analyst. Instead, she had chosen to do all of this old school.

Just like her records at home.

But why?

Tucker snapped several pictures with his phone, then sank into the folding chair and stared at the boards. Sandy Conlon was a high-level mathematician and programmer. The formulas, codes, and keywords were beyond his grasp. Still, he noted a few bold or underlined words: *Turing, Odisha, Scan Rate, Expanded Spectrum, Clojure, Unstructured Data Collation . . .*

He shook his head.

Unless Sandy was conducting her own top-secret project, all this was most likely related to her work at Redstone. The fact that she was doing it *here*, and in this fashion, meant she didn't want anyone to know about it.

"Sandy, what were you up to?"

A low growl rose from outside.

Clenching a fist, he stood and looked back at the rolling door.

Someone was coming.

6

War is business . . . and business started early.

Pruitt Kellerman had left his public meetings in Athens before dawn and flown two hours north to the capital of Serbia. His private jet had landed in Belgrade as the sun crested the horizon. He had been driven in a bulletproof limo with blacked-out windows to Beli Dvor, the presidential palace located in the royal compound. He had given strict instructions to his advance team to keep this meeting private, to avoid even a whisper of press coverage. Even his daughter, Laura, was unaware of this side trip. To the world at large, the head of Horizon Media remained at his hotel in Athens, awaiting more meetings regarding Greece's telecom industry.

Unfortunately, the president of Serbia, Marko Davidovic, had chosen to ignore this memo. Upon arriving at the official residence, Pruitt found a lavish brunch awaiting him, attended by a slew of Davidovic's political cronies. The meal was in a grand hall, with black-and-white checkerboard marble floors, vaulted ceilings, and wrapped all around by grand staircases and balconies.

Pruitt endured the welcoming brunch with a smile fixed to his face and glad-handed whomever Davidovic put in front of him. He engaged the president's wife in polite talk regarding the midterm elections. In the end, it seemed those invited were the president's innermost circle, as Davidovic seemed equally keen to keep their upcoming joint endeavor a secret.

After an interminable time, Davidovic finally led Pruitt to a bookshelf-lined study and gestured to a leather captain's chair before a crackling fireplace, then took the opposite seat. The president was relatively young, in his late forties, with a boxy build and the broad shoulders of a farmer. His hair was still pitch-black, with a hint of silver at the temples.

A servant appeared and offered Pruitt a snifter of a dark liqueur.

"We call this Slivovitz," Davidovic explained as the servant left. "A native plum brandy." He lifted his glass. "*Ziveli!* To long life."

Pruitt raised his own glass, nodded at his host, and took a sip. The liqueur burned his throat, leaving a sweet aftertaste.

Not bad.

Pruitt sat straighter, ready to firm up their mutual plans. "You're a most gracious host," he started. "And your wife is lovely."

"My wife is a cow, but it is kind of you to say. She and I are comfortable with one another, and she has given me two strong boys. And the people love her, so who am I to complain? You never married, yes?"

Pruitt smiled inwardly. He knew Davidovic's chief of staff would have fully informed the president regarding the tragic death of Pruitt's wife. It was a question designed to unbalance his guest. Instead, Pruitt kept his face impassive.

"Widowed."

"Ah, yes, forgive me. And now I remember you have a beautiful daughter. Very smart, that one."

"Yes, she is," he answered with a touch of pride. Other emotions briefly flickered inside him: *shame* at deceiving Laura about all of this, but also *fear* that she might someday discover the truth.

"It is unfortunate she lost her mother so young."

Pruitt gave a bow of his head in acknowledgment, using the moment to settle himself. "It was long ago. But let us turn from the past to the future." He smiled blandly and cut abruptly to the heart of the matter. "I hear you have some reservations of late regarding our arrangements."

The president shifted in his seat, his dark eyes flicking to the flames of the fireplace.

That is how you unbalance an opponent . . . to let them think you know all their secrets.

"I am . . . reconsidering," Davidovic admitted.

Pruitt leaned back, cradling the snifter of brandy between his palms. "How so?"

"You stand to gain substantially from this agreement."

"Of course." Pruitt shrugged. "I'm a businessman."

"I understand, but—"

Pruitt cut him off. "You feel that *your* end can be improved."

Davidovic stared hard at him, dropping any pretense of graciousness. "I know it can be. You are asking me to provide facilities and transportation for your operational teams, along with all of the necessary immigration and customs interventions."

"As we agreed nine months ago," Pruitt said. "And in return for your cooperation, I will be handing you the first step to fulfilling a Serbian national aspiration—one close to your own heart."

Davidovic shifted again in his seat; his cheeks had darkened, and not from the flush of the brandy he downed now in one gulp. Pruitt's private intelligence network had supplied him with the hidden engine behind the Serbian president's ambition—a goal fueled by vindication and revenge.

During the border skirmishes between Serbian and Montenegrin forces back in the midnineties, Davidovic's home village of Crvsko had been attacked. A Montenegrin paramilitary group had razed the village, slaughtering his father and mother and his three sisters. Only his grandfather had survived and tried to defend Crvsko. Due to some brutal acts during the town's defense, the grandfather was later branded a war criminal by the Serbian president of the time, Slobodan Milošević. The grandfather had eventually died in prison.

This watershed event drove Davidovic into politics. He had positioned himself as a crusader for lasting peace in the Balkans—or so his platform declared. But Pruitt knew the truth and used that lever to sway the Serbian president to his side.

Pruitt continued, applying more force to that lever. "With my help, you'll realize your ambition—to finally set right what was wrong—while in turn earning the full support and praise of the world."

Judging by Davidovic's downcast eyes, he knew his words had struck home.

"And in return," Pruitt pressed on, "I'll receive the mining rights to a strip of land that no one wants." He shrugged and stood up. "If anyone should be *reconsidering* this deal, it should be me."

Pruitt turned and headed for the door.

Davidovic stopped him before he could take three steps. "Please, sit, Mr. Kellerman. I spoke out of turn. Let us forget this matter, attribute it to what you Americans call . . . cold feet."

Pruitt faced the president.

Davidovic waved to the abandoned chair. "Let us discuss the timeline."

Unmoving for a long ten seconds, Pruitt finally returned to his chair and sat down. He picked up his snifter, took a sip.

"My people will arrive in thirteen days."

9:03 A.M.

After finalizing plans, Pruitt was back in the limo with his head of security, Rafael Lyon, and headed to his private jet. He needed to return to Athens for a luncheon with Greece's main telecom company.

Pruitt sighed and loosened his tie, picturing Davidovic as the big man gave him a bear hug good-bye, the two of them the best of friends once again. "Are we certain that idiot isn't a war criminal himself? I've read about some incidents along the Serbian border."

"Rumors." Lyon shrugged. "Davidovic will behave himself until it is time. But we should—"

Lyon's cell phone trilled in his pocket, cutting him off.

Pruitt waved for him to answer it.

Lyon freed his phone and listened for several seconds. He asked a few curt questions, then disconnected. From the twin furrows between his brows, it was not good news.

"What is it?" Pruitt asked.

"That was Webster. There was someone at the Conlon woman's house in Huntsville."

It took Pruitt a full breath to disengage from his toe-to-toe confrontation with the Serbian president and remember who this woman was. Not that the two matters were unconnected.

"Who was the intruder?" he asked. "A burglar?"

Lyon shook his head. "Someone with training. He had a dog with him, too."

Pruitt frowned. "A dog?"

"A big beast, according to Webster. He believes the pair had military training. They sent Webster and his partner running with their tails between their legs. No pun intended."

Lyon's face was stone; he did not joke.

Pruitt sat back. Karl Webster came out of the military. He was no slouch, and over the years Pruitt had learned to trust the man's judgment. "What's his take on this guy?"

"Shots were exchanged, but Webster got the impression the intruder was purposefully avoiding hitting anyone. Which means this guy is careful, thoughtful, good under pressure."

Pruitt understood.

Dead bodies bring unwanted attention.

"Are there any leads on this mystery man?"

Lyon frowned. "Not yet."

"Could he have found anything at Conlon's home?"

"Nothing. It's been sanitized."

Let's hope so.

"Still, he wasn't there by accident," Pruitt said. "Someone must have sent him. And I could guess who that might be. Our last loose connection to Project 623."

Lyon nodded. "Jane Sabatello. It was my thought as well, but it gives me an idea."

Pruitt glanced harder at Lyon.

"We know her phone is a ghost," Lyon said. "All outgoing calls go through too many proxies to pin her down. But what about *incoming* calls? If she sent someone down to investigate Conlon, she'll be expecting updates from him."

Pruitt rubbed his chin, calculating in his head. This last matter was too important to leave to Webster alone, especially this close to their first true test. It was time to tie up these loose ends once and for all.

"I want you to go to Huntsville and work with Webster," Pruitt ordered. "With all the surveillance resources we have sitting idle at Redstone Arsenal, surely we can find this man. And when you do, make sure he and his dog disappear."

Lyon nodded. "Consider it done."

7

Someone was coming . . .

Trapped in Sandy's storage locker, Tucker needed Kane's eyes. He already had his satellite phone in hand after taking photographs of Sandy's makeshift nerve center. As Kane let out another low growl, Tucker tapped in the code to bring up the feed from his partner's video camera. He radioed Kane to go silent and keep out of sight.

"CLOSE HIDE."

An image—washed out into gray tones by the camera's night-vision mode—appeared on the screen. The view bobbled as the shepherd retreated to the rear bumper of the SUV. A figure appeared out from under the glare of a sodium lamp on a nearby pole—someone armed with a double-barreled shotgun. From the curves, it was plainly a young woman, her hair tied in a ponytail. She wore jeans, boots, and an untucked flannel shirt. She kept the shotgun firmly at her shoulder. From the way she carried it, she knew how to use it.

And she hadn't come alone.

A large beefy Doberman kept glued to her side, tensed and obviously trained.

"You in there!" she called out. "Come out! Slow now, you hear?"

Tucker could guess who this woman was. He pictured the security camera he had noted on the light pole earlier. He raised his voice and called back, "Edith? Edith Lozier?"

After a moment, the other answered, confirming his supposition. "Who are you?"

Tucker didn't want any misunderstanding with an armed civilian in the middle of the night. Apparently the caretaker of Garnett Self-Storage doubled as the security guard for the place. She must have seen him enter the storage facility and knew he didn't belong here, especially at this particular locker.

"I'm a friend of Sandy Conlon!" Tucker called back.

"Come out and show me some ID."

Tucker pocketed his phone, approached the rolling door, and slowly pulled it up. The woman backed two firm steps, keeping the shotgun at the ready in case he tried anything funny. She looked to be in her late twenties, with dark red hair and freckles across her cheeks. The Doberman kept its position, only lowering its head a few inches in an aggressive posture.

Once the door was up, Tucker lifted both hands, showing they were empty. From the corner of his eye, he noted Kane crouched in the shadow of the truck. He signaled Kane to remain hidden. He didn't want to startle the armed woman or her companion, not before he had a chance to explain himself.

"I have a dog, too," Tucker warned, figuring she had likely already spotted Kane on the security camera. "Come on out, big boy. Show the lady you're friendly."

Kane slunk out and joined Tucker. The shepherd's gaze remained fixed on the other canine. Edith eyed the shepherd, plainly noting Kane's gear. She still kept her weapon raised.

"Military dog?" she asked.

"Former. He did four tours in Afghanistan with me."

"So you're not from Redstone?"

He shook his head. "Just got into town. Looking for what happened to Sandy. She's been missing for a few weeks."

Suspicion still shone from the woman's narrowed eyes, from her ready stance. "How do I know you're telling the truth?"

"Sandy gave me a copy of her key," he explained. "Said to come out here if there was ever any trouble."

It was a lie, but from Sandy's caution in renting this place, he imagined Edith must have sensed Sandy was hiding something. To reinforce his claim, Tucker carefully reached into his shirt pocket and pulled out the photograph Jane had shown him back at the hotel in Montana. It showed the three of them in each other's arms. He had asked to keep it, figuring he might need to substantiate his relationship with Sandy at some point.

He passed it to Edith, who was careful to keep her weapon from his reach.

She glanced at the photograph, a frozen snapshot of a happier time.

"That was taken at Fort Benning," Tucker said. "We served together. All of us." He motioned to Kane.

Edith sighed, nodded, and passed him back the photo. She shifted the shotgun's barrel to her shoulder. "Sandy's gone missing?"

"For about a month. I came down here to find her." He glanced back to the storage locker. "I had hoped to find some clue here."

"A month ago, you say." Her gaze grew thoughtful. "That's about the last time I saw her myself. She came out here. Was in a big hurry. Usually she joins me and Bruce for a beer."

"Bruce is your husband?"

She patted the Doberman's flank. "Nope, somebody who'll never cheat on me."

Tucker smiled, fully understanding the love in her eyes, noting how the Doberman leaned against her side, returning the affection. "How well did you know Sandy?"

Her manner changed subtly, became guarded. Most people would have missed it, but Tucker's empathic skills went beyond his ability to relate to his canine partner. He could guess the source of Edith's hesitation. It likely centered on another of Sandy's secrets, one she only let a handful of people know about, especially due to the threat of this secret to her classified clearance ranking in the past.

"Don't ask, don't tell," he said with a shrug, letting Edith know he understood and further establishing his close ties to Sandy. "It's no longer an issue in the military."

"That may be true up north . . ." she mumbled sourly, but then shook her head. "I knew Sandy from a local gay bar. It's a close-knit community down here. When she needed a place to store some stuff, she approached me. Knew I could keep a secret."

He nodded. By now, Kane and Bruce had approached each other, sniffing and doing the usual dance of sizing each other up. "The last time you saw Sandy, did she give you any hint of where she might be going?"

"Said she was going to visit her mom."

That fits with the timeline.

"But I could tell she was scared," Edith said. "Told me she would be gone for a while."

"Did she ever tell you what she was doing out here with the locker?"

Edith gave a small shake of her head. "I didn't want to pry. She would often spend the night in there. I got the impression it had something to do with her work at Redstone, something that rubbed her the wrong way."

Hmm . . .

"And did she ever tell you what she was working on over there?" Tucker asked.

"Not Sandy. She knew how to keep her lips sealed and was loyal to a fault."

Tucker asked a few more questions, but it was obvious that Edith was as much in the dark as everyone else. Finally he asked a favor. "Whatever Sandy was working on in there looks important. In case anyone else comes sniffing around later, is there another locker we can move her stuff to temporarily?"

Edith nodded. "There's an empty space a few rows over."

Over the next half hour, Tucker got everything moved, said his good-byes to Edith and Bruce, and was back on the dark roads with Kane. As he rounded a tall hill, he could make out the glare of lights near the horizon, marking the massive complex of Redstone Arsenal. Whatever Sandy was working on, whatever *rubbed her the wrong way*, the answers lay out at that base. But he could not go traipsing in there himself.

Tucker admitted a hard truth to himself.

"I need help."

9:10 A.M.

Back at their motel room, Tucker slept for four hours, grabbed a breakfast of scrambled eggs and a stack of pancakes at a nearby diner, and then, armed with a jumbo cup of coffee, he settled before his laptop.

He had one immediate goal: find someone working at Redstone

who could serve as his eyes and ears on the military base. After his years in the service and multiple tours, he had accumulated a wide network of connections. It was one of the great aspects of the military: a bond of brotherhood that spanned years of time and swaths of the world. With military personnel regularly shifting posts and assignments, you eventually learned that you had a close friend—or at least a friend of a friend—on almost any base.

After hours of dragging up files and placing a few discreet calls to distant friends, he began to worry that this search was a lost cause. He came close to calling a secure, encrypted line, one that would connect him to Ruth Harper, his contact with Sigma, a covert force connected to the Defense Department's research and development agency. They owed him a favor or two. But he refrained from pulling out the big guns at this point, especially as he didn't know how intimately the military was involved with Sandy's disappearance.

Finally, as hunger pangs began to gnaw at his belly again, he found himself staring at a military ID on the laptop's screen, one with a familiar face smiling back at him. The man was a decade older than Tucker, with a blond crew cut, bushy eyebrows, and a ready smile.

"Hello, Frank. Good to see you again."

During Tucker's time in the Rangers, Frank Ballenger had been attached to his unit as a 98H, a communications locator/interceptor. Frank's role at the time had been to analyze intelligence and pinpoint an enemy, allowing people like Tucker to destroy them. While he and Frank hadn't been the most intimate of friends, they had gotten along well enough, mostly because Tucker had been curious about how the 98Hs did their job. Few shooters showed interest in the technical stuff—and to be honest, most of it went over his head. Eventually Tucker had to admit as much and summarized their relationship to Frank: *you line them up, and I'll knock them down.*

It would take Tucker another three years in the sandbox to realize how naive those words were. He found his right fist clenched on his knee and had to force his fingers to relax in order to call up Frank's phone number on Redstone's website. Frank was now a master sergeant, stationed at the base's Development and Engineering Center.

Hopefully he'll remember me.

He dialed Frank's number, expecting to go to voice mail, but instead a voice with a familiar Alabama twang answered. Tucker smiled, suddenly remembering now that Frank had grown up around these parts. No wonder he ended up at Redstone.

"Frank," Tucker said as an introduction, "I think I owe you a drink."

After a few minutes of small talk, Tucker soon realized that not only did Frank remember him, but Tucker must've made a significant impression on the older sergeant back in Afghanistan. The man also remembered Kane . . . and Abel.

"And Kane retired with you." Frank chuckled. "That's good to hear. You two were always tied at the hip."

Without offering any further explanation for the sudden call, Tucker coaxed Frank to meet at a local bar that evening. As he hung up the phone, he let out a long sigh. He glanced over to Kane, who lay on the bed. The shepherd had lifted his head when he heard his name mentioned during the call.

"Looks like we're going to meet another old friend."

Despite his satisfaction at reconnecting with Frank, Tucker could not dismiss the knot of anxiety at the back of his neck. After abruptly leaving the service, he had strived to leave the past in the past, to let sand cover all the blood and horror, but now he felt himself being drawn back.

Before a familiar cold sweat could build—which he knew would come if he didn't do something—he turned his attention to another mystery. He pulled up the photographs of Sandy's secret workstation and began plugging some of the words scrawled on her whiteboards into Google.

He didn't expect to find anything, but he needed to keep his head in the game. He searched one word after the other.

Odisha was a state in India.

Scan Rate could refer to any of a number of things.

Clojure was a computer programming language.

Turing might be a reference to a WWII-era cryptologist. Alan Turing was the man who broke the German Enigma code, an accomplishment that played an essential part in ending the war.

But what does he have to do with any of this?

Tucker continued down the list. All the remaining words seemed related to computer programming or high-level mathematics, except for one. He studied the photograph. Sandy had circled this phrase multiple times on the board: Link 16. A Google search revealed this could be a reference to a secure tactical data network, most often used to communicate with aircraft.

He stared at the emphatic circles drawn around that citation.

What was so important about that, Sandy?

3:45 P.M.

After hours of futile searching, Tucker finally admitted defeat. He leaned back and stretched the strain out of his spine.

I need to clear my head.

Kane shifted up from the bed, likely recognizing his partner's exhaustion and aggravation.

"How about some fresh air, buddy?" Tucker called over, earning a happy thump of a tail.

They left the motel and started driving. After stopping at a burger joint and splitting a cheeseburger and fries with Kane, Tucker drove aimlessly. He mostly wanted to get the lay of the land, to familiarize himself with Huntsville in case he ran into trouble.

The city was situated in the Tennessee River valley, surrounded on all sides by the Appalachian Mountains. The town itself was a jumble of antebellum mansions mixed with gabled Victorians and smaller saltbox homes lining shaded boulevards. Pedestrians and cars moved at a leisurely pace; no one seemed to be in a hurry.

Tucker relaxed, driving slower, even stopping to enjoy a few sights. At a big open park, he spent an hour tossing Kane's red rubber Kong toy; then another hour hiking along a shallow creek, where frogs hopped clear of their path and into the water. Kane bounded after them, splashing through the creek in a futile chase.

Finally, as the sun sank toward the horizon, stretching long shadows all around, Tucker called in a wet and happy Kane, and they returned to the SUV. Tucker drove a half mile north of the main gates to Redstone Arsenal and pulled into the parking lot of Q Station Bar & Billiards. He considered leaving Kane in the rental, but then thought the familiar presence of the shepherd might help Tucker gain Frank's cooperation. If anyone gave him trouble for bringing his dog into the bar, he had papers—courtesy of his friend Ruth with

Sigma—that listed Kane as a medical companion, allowing Tucker to take the dog almost anywhere.

As Tucker pushed through the double doors into the dimly lit interior, a few eyes glanced toward them, but no one said a word. The patrons then returned to their drinks or to the scatter of billiard balls on green felt. Tucker scanned the place as Lynyrd Skynyrd belted out "Free Bird" from a jukebox. To his left was a long bar, along with a row of booths pressed up against a low wall.

From the last booth, a hand waved.

Ah . . .

Tucker and Kane strode over.

Frank Ballenger greeted them with a warm smile, which turned somewhat crooked with amusement. "You and Kane . . . now that's a sight I haven't seen in a long time. You two make a fetching couple. Heard you two had to elope, even got yourselves into some trouble for it."

Tucker shrugged and shook the man's hand, doing his best to hide his discomfort. Frank must have made a few calls and had learned the circumstances surrounding Tucker's exit from the service, how he had absconded with Kane against orders. Eventually Sigma had helped clear up that sticky matter, as payment for services rendered. Still, as much as it bothered Tucker that Frank knew these details about his life, it was also a testament to the man's ability to gather intel.

Tucker slipped into the booth and waved Kane down. "Doesn't look like you changed much, Frank," he said, which was true. Though older than Tucker, the man looked wiry and solid. He clearly kept himself in shape.

"Thanks for saying so." Frank rubbed at his temples. "But I think these turned a bit silver since we left the trenches." He then reached down and slid a sweating bottle of cold beer toward Tucker. "Gotcha a Sam Adams. Hope that's all right."

"More than all right."

"It was really good to hear from you."

"Yeah, it's been awhile. Wasn't sure you would remember me."

"Hell yeah, I remember you. You were one of the only Rangers who ever paid any attention to what we communication geeks did. Plus you and your two dogs. I used to watch you working them when I had a break. It was impressive, like you all were reading each other's minds."

Tucker found his fingers tightening on the beer bottle, picturing Kane's littermate. Memories flashed like lightning, sharp and glaring, glinting with the flash of falling knives, booming with gunfire.

Frank must have realized something was wrong. "Hey, man, sorry. That was stupid of me to bring that up. I should know better."

Tucker breathed more deeply until he could finally unclench his fingers. "It's . . . it's all right."

It wasn't. Frank seemed to recognize this, and gave Tucker a few moments to collect himself.

After a couple of deep breaths, Tucker finally pressed on. "Master sergeant, huh? You've really moved up in the world."

Frank offered an understanding smile, moving to safer territory. "I'm a lifer. Who would a guessed? And stationed here in Huntsville, I get to see my family every weekend. But what about you?"

"Me? Nothing special. Odd jobs. Mostly security work, that kind of thing."

They shot the breeze for another half hour, exchanging memories, comparing notes, sharing gossip about mutual friends. Finally, Tucker moved closer to the matter at hand.

"Frank, how long have you been at Redstone?"

"Four years. It's nice. I'm now a cryptologic network warfare specialist." Frank read the confusion on his face and smiled. "I get that a lot. It's a new MOS, started in 2011. Covers mostly cyber warfare stuff."

Tucker gave a sad shake of his head. "The times are changing." He then cleared his throat. "Listen, Frank, I have a confession. I'm here for a reason."

"What? You mean beyond seeking out my delightful company?" Those bushy eyebrows rose higher, then settled back down. "Yeah, I figured. You all but dropped off the map after leaving the service and now you end up on my doorstep. It's okay, man. What's up?"

"I'm looking for a missing friend. She was stationed at Redstone."

"Missing?"

"For over a month. Her name is Sandy Conlon."

"Never heard of her, but that's no surprise. Redstone's a big place. Where'd she work?"

Tucker smiled sheepishly. "That's the thing—I have no idea. She never told anyone close to her. Never even mentioned the name of her command."

"Hmm . . . curiouser and curiouser. But if you're here speaking with me, you're thinking this has something to do with her post?"

"Just trying to cover all the bases."

Frank slowly nodded, the gears clearly turning in his head. "And let me guess . . . you haven't called the police or Redstone."

"I'd like to avoid that."

Those brows lifted again.

Tucker raised a palm. "I don't want to get you in any trouble, but I need to find her. She may not be the only one in danger."

Frank stared at him, studying him. A single finger tapped on the table. Tucker remembered this nervous tic of Frank's, marking when he was in deep thought, weighing the significance of some new intelligence.

Frank finally came to a conclusion and leaned back, a wry smile fluttering. "Let me do some poking around. If there's any trouble, it'll be like the old days. As you used to say: I'll line 'em up, and you'll knock 'em down."

Tucker lifted his beer and clinked it against Frank's bottle. "Deal."

6:08 P.M.

Karl Webster paced the length of the cavernous cement-block bunker, which housed the installation's engineering lab. With the sun already down and the technicians safely back in their cabins for the night, he had the place to himself. The bunker was cordoned off into several work spaces, each assigned to explore another facet of the project. But in the center, resting on the concrete floor and hidden under a large tarp, was the latest prototype.

He ran his fingertips along one of its shrouded wings, which spanned an efficient meter and a half. The techs called it a Shrike, named after a little bird—a stone-cold killer—that captured lizards and insects, even other birds, and impaled them on the thorns of an acacia tree to pick apart at their leisure.

He smiled at how apt that name was. Though he only oversaw

security for the project, he could not discount the flicker of pride at the accomplishment here. But now all his hard work was at risk.

All because of one man—and his damned dog.

He pictured the trespasser whom he had discovered skulking about Sandy Conlon's house, and the brief firefight that had followed. The man had subsequently escaped and vanished into the shadows.

Yet another problem to deal with . . .

A knock drew his attention to the bunker's main door.

And here came another.

The door opened and in stalked Rafael Lyon, head of security for Horizon Media. He pushed past one of Karl's men and entered with a dark glower on his scarred face, the fluorescent light shining off his shaved scalp. The man wore black tactical gear with a rifle over his shoulder. His flight had landed in Huntsville only forty minutes ago, but he clearly was not one to let any grass grow under his boots.

"What have you discovered about the bastard who got away?" Lyon asked brusquely, skipping any pleasantries.

Despite the man's thick French accent, Karl heard the accusation in his words. He also read the threat in the narrow pinch of those eyes. He knew this was no idle attempt at intimidation. Failure would not be tolerated.

Still, Karl clenched a fist, embarrassed and angry that Pruitt Kellerman had felt the need to dispatch his pet bulldog here. Karl had spent twenty years in military service, most of them in the sandboxes of Iraq and Afghanistan, first as a grunt, later in Special Forces. He didn't need any help.

"I already have a handle on the situation." Karl Webster kept his voice low and calm. "I'm only waiting on a call that should resolve this matter to everyone's satisfaction."

"And I'm here to ensure that happens."

The two men glared at each other, a storm building between them. Before it could break, Karl's phone chimed in his pocket. He pulled it out and answered it. He listened to the caller for several minutes, asked two questions, and got the answers he needed.

Lyon never took his gaze off him.

Karl smiled back coldly. "I know how to find our target." He glanced over to the tarp-shrouded Shrike. "And how to deal with him."

8

After a couple more drinks with Frank Ballenger at the bar, Tucker headed back to his motel. It had rained while he had been chatting with Frank, leaving the night air muggy and smelling of warm asphalt. Kane sat on the passenger seat, his muzzle resting on the doorframe of the open window.

Tucker sped west away from the traffic of the city, then turned south along the edge of the massive swamp that backed up to his motel. His headlights swept over cypress branches gauzed in Spanish moss. Unseen insects ticked against his windshield.

Alone on the road, he glanced out the side window and spotted the dark silhouette of the abandoned concrete factory in the middle of the swamp. He remembered the story of the levee break along the Tennessee River and tried to picture the subsequent flooding that had turned the industrial field into this vast plain of swamps and marshes. From the roadway, he could make out catwalks and conveyor belts that still connected the various buildings and silos, with metal buckets still dangling.

Suddenly the SUV's radio blared to life, startling him, making him swerve slightly on the lonely road "... *Evening, folks, you're listenin' to WTKI, Huntsville talk radio ...*"

Scowling, Tucker turned off the radio. As he did so, the engine sputtered, the dashboard lights flickered, and the vehicle began to slow.

Uh-oh ...

Kane's head pivoted toward him. The shepherd let out a whine of complaint.

"Hey, it's not me."

The radio came on again, then went silent. The windshield wipers began to flap.

What the hell...

Tucker steered the SUV onto the shoulder—and just in time. With a double cough, the engine died.

He sighed and patted Kane's flank. "Buddy, it's finally happened. We're being abducted by aliens."

Figuring the more likely cause was a loose battery connection, Tucker reached down and popped the hood latch. He climbed out with Kane and crossed to the front of the SUV. Under the glow of the service light, he studied the engine for a moment, then began checking wires and connections.

Everything seemed okay.

From the swamp, a muffled buzzing sound arose, faint at first, then slowly increasing in pitch.

Kane stalked over to a neighboring grass berm that overlooked the swamp.

Tucker joined him.

A loud *thunk* drew their attention back to the dead Explorer on the side of the road. Something had struck the SUV's quarter panel. Steam burst from the engine.

Recognizing that particular sound, Tucker ducked and drew Kane closer.

Someone was shooting at them.

Two more bullets slammed into the truck. The windshield shattered. With an explosive hiss, one of the rear tires burst. Now the rounds were coming faster, one every couple of seconds, all centered on the SUV.

Reacting quickly, Tucker signaled Kane to follow—then he turned, sat on his butt, and slid down the grassy embankment and into the swamp.

Kane obeys the command and leaps high.

As he flies, his nose takes in strange scents: mold and moss, rot and algae. He hears the creak of branches, the whine of bats, and the cries of distant birds—then he strikes the cold water and plunges deep, wiping all his senses clean. Water muffles his ears, blinds him, too.

As his heart pounds, his paws paddle for purchase, but find only more water. Then claws strafe along the bottom. He scrabbles, his paws sinking into mud—then his pads brush against something solid. Tree roots. He pushes off them until his nose breaks the surface, returning the world, first in scents, then in sounds.

He thrashes, his eyes searching, his ears tucked back in wariness and fear.

Something grabs his nape, then his collar.

He turns to instinctively snap, but his nose swells with the scent of familiar breath as he's drawn close.

"Easy, easy there, buddy . . . I gotcha."

Gripping Kane's nylon collar, Tucker scissor-kicked deeper into the swamp and sheltered behind the bole of a large cypress tree. He kept the trunk between him and the road. He took a moment to massage Kane's neck, to further reassure the dog.

"Good boy," he whispered.

Kane's coat was plastered with moss. Tucker fared little better, his face and arms coated in slime. He draped more moss over the dog's shoulders.

Good camouflage . . . and we might need it.

Tucker leaned against the trunk and spied toward the road and their abandoned Explorer. What the hell had just happened? No doubt they had been ambushed—but how? Had someone tampered with the vehicle while he was talking with Frank inside the bar? Though this seemed the most likely explanation, it didn't account for the timing.

And what about that buzzing?

As if summoned by this thought, the sound returned. Kane tensed, and his head swiveled to the right, then slowly tracked the target as it crossed back toward the embankment. It whispered over the dark treetops and came to sweep over the road. After another moment, the buzzing rose steeply upward, fading away and vanishing into the darkness.

Unbidden, one of Sandy's keywords popped into Tucker's head.

Link 16.

He swore under his breath as he now suspected the significance behind that reference. From his earlier Google search, he had learned Link 16 was a military tactical data exchange, mostly used to communicate with aircraft, including UAVs—unmanned aerial vehicles—or drones. Such vehicles were used more and more by all branches of the military, both for surveillance and for aerial attacks. They ranged in size from the massive Global Hawks to the smaller Ravens.

But what's hunting us?

He had no way of knowing, but it was clearly a hunter/killer version. He stared up past the black treetops. He knew drones could see not only in the dark but through clouds, dust, and smoke. Their vision was sharp enough to read a license plate from two miles up.

As he searched the patches of sky, Tucker's hairs stood on end. He and Kane had been hunted by helicopters in the past, most recently in Siberia, but this was much worse—like treading water at night with a shark circling beneath you.

Only this time the threat came from above.

With his eyes now adjusted to the darkness, he surveyed his surroundings. Even with the moonlight filtering through the canopy, he saw nothing but black water and jumbles of cypress trees. He knew, with a hunter in the sky, that returning to the road was not an option. Glancing over his shoulder, he pictured the drowned concrete factory far off into the swamp. It could offer better shelter.

But what then?

From his earlier canvass of the Huntsville area, he knew about a half mile past the factory were the grounds of a country club. It meant a lot of open water to cross, with an unknown number of enemies in the sky and maybe on foot.

Still, it was safer than the open road.

Tucker groped around until he found a clump of moss. He mashed it through his hair and draped strands over his shoulders like a dank shroud.

Kane studied his new look with his head cocked to one side.

Tucker leaned closer and whispered, "Boo."

The shepherd licked his face.

"Yeah, nothing scares you."

Tucker turned and headed away from the road. As he sidestroked into the deeper water, Kane paddled alongside him, the dog's snout just above the surface. Tucker chose a path that hugged root mounds and fallen trees. Still, after only thirty yards, he felt a sting at the edge of his right ear—and a few feet ahead of him something splashed into the water.

Goddamn it . . .

He grabbed Kane's collar, hugged the dog close, and whispered in his ear. "HOLD YOUR BREATH."

Tucker ducked with Kane beneath the surface. He kicked and dug with one arm, swimming hard toward a half-submerged log. He surfaced with Kane beneath it, keeping both of them pressed against the curve of bark. Somewhat sheltered from above, Tucker watched and listened.

So far, no more bullets came.

He strove to pick out any telltale buzzing. But as his breath heaved and his heart pounded in his ears, he couldn't be sure.

Closer at hand, an owl hooted three times. A moment later, the heavy flapping of wings passed overhead, followed by a feeble screech as the hunter found its dinner.

Let's hope that's the only successful hunter this night.

Tucker reached up, touched the edge of his ear. He winced at the tiny gouge in his flesh. But he had no reason to complain. Another inch to the left, and the round would have drilled through his skull.

Knowing they had to keep moving, Tucker floated the log slowly through the water. He tried his best to stay hidden from the drone, but eventually the log snagged into a tangle of roots, forcing them to continue on a labyrinthine path that kept them pressed against logs, tree trunks, and root mounds. Whenever they reached a stretch of open water, they continued underwater, only surfacing long enough to snatch a breath.

Then after what seemed like hours, Tucker's toes touched solid ground. After a few more steps, the mud underfoot turned to something even firmer. He reached down and scooped up a fistful of rough pebbles.

Gravel.

They had reached the edge of the factory complex. The jumble of buildings, silos, and moss-shrouded catwalks rose fifty yards away.

With the goal in sight, Tucker continued more slowly. As the embankment sloped upward, he soon found himself having to crawl in order to keep only his moss-covered head above the water's surface. Finally, he shimmied out of the shallows and up a gravel shore. With Kane pressed to his side, he chose a path through a stand of tall reeds to keep them hidden.

But it wasn't enough.

Without any warning, a burst of rounds shredded through the reeds and pelted into the gravel.

Tucker bunched his legs and shouted to Kane, pointing toward the ruins of the factory.

"RUN AND HIDE!"

Kane wants to ignore the order, to keep the pack together. But he trusts his partner and obeys.

He races low to the ground, his ears high, his tail straight back. He hears gunfire roaring in short spats. He knows guns, knows the damage they can cause. He swerves through bushes, around piles of old equipment, under the rusted hulk of a massive vehicle with flattened tires.

Rounds ping off metal and ricochet off gravel with bright sparks in the night.

By now, he has left the other far behind him. Kane's blood races with the urge to turn and return to his side, but he sticks to the path assigned him. He clears the vehicle's bulk and crosses the last distance toward a black doorway in the nearest building.

Behind him, gunfire erupts—but it no longer chases him.

With no choice but to obey his last order, Kane flies over the threshold and into the waiting darkness.

As soon as Kane had leapt from his side, Tucker had dodged away in the other direction. By splitting up, he had hoped to divide the drone's attention as its operator tried to decide which target to pursue.

It seemed to work initially. The gunfire had momentarily ceased as he and Kane took off. That lapse had allowed Kane to get a head start in his flight toward the factory. Still, gunfire rained down from above soon thereafter. First toward Kane's path—then the drone's deadly attention returned to Tucker.

But Tucker had used the distraction to reach a small thicket of trees. Rounds tore through the canopy and pelted into the ground. Tucker dodged past trunks as shards of tree bark peppered his face.

Don't look back . . .

With his heart pounding and his thighs burning, he focused on the goal ahead: a tall silo that speared into the night sky.

Slipping and sliding, Tucker dodged from tree to tree, hoping to present less of a target.

Crack!

A branch above Tucker's head snapped.

Crack!

Something tugged at his pant leg, but he ignored it and kept running and weaving. Moonlight brightened ahead, reflecting off water, warning that he had reached the end of the copse of trees.

He didn't slow.

He burst out of the tree line and dove low across what appeared to be a shallow lake, likely a former industrial pond for the factory. He slid beneath the surface as a scatter of rounds spat around him, but then the fusillade suddenly stopped.

Had the drone run out of ammunition?

With no way of knowing, he surfaced briefly, listening for any telltale buzzing, but he heard nothing. He pictured the drone banking away, readying to come back around again for another run. Confirming this conjecture, the nattering whine returned as he swam, growing louder by the second.

He searched for the enemy.

There!

Silhouetted against the moonlit sky, he spotted a fleeting, elongated shadow as it circled toward his position. It appeared to be a fixed-wing drone, but there was something off about it. The drone wasn't quite a shadow, more like a fuzzy, mottled shape that seemed to blend into the stars.

Some kind of stealth material, he realized.

Tucker swam faster, aiming for a dark, diagonal line that rose from the pond's far bank. It was an old rubber conveyor belt that climbed toward a door high up the neighboring silo. He had no better option, especially with the whine of the drone almost upon him again.

Tucker dove back underwater, praying the pond's reflective surface would hide him from the hunter in the sky. He kicked and paddled his way to the submerged end of the conveyor and ducked underneath it; only then did he risk coming up for air.

He glanced over his shoulder, studying the sloping belt and the metal buckets that dangled from beneath it. His plan had been to climb up to that silo door, keeping to the underside of the conveyor. The scheme had seemed far better from a distance.

But up close . . .

Above his head, the scaffolding dripped with Spanish moss. Wrist-sized vines snaked around the crossbeams and angle irons. What little steel Tucker could see was scabrous with rust. Even the rubber belt was worn thin with multiple holes.

He doubted the structure would hold his weight—and certainly not for long.

Any further reservations came to an abrupt halt as a fresh spatter of rounds tore into the conveyor, pinging off the scaffolding and ripping through the belt.

The drone must have spotted him after all.

Tucker lunged up, grabbed a crossbeam, and began to climb along the bottom of the conveyor belt, doing his best to use the large metal buckets as shields. If the drone didn't kill him, the ascent might. He lost his footing several times as pieces of the conveyor's support scaffolding gave way under his weight.

Still, he kept going.

Another round punched through the belt and sparked off a crossbeam beside Tucker's hand.

He cursed brightly—but then the barrage abruptly stopped.

The hunter must be circling around again.

He started counting in his head. When he reached thirty seconds, the buzz of the drone's engine returned. It seemed there was roughly half a minute from one pass to the next. Knowing this, he took shelter beneath one of the buckets as the drone swept over, raining rounds all around. The conveyor's scaffolding shook and shimmied. More sections came crashing down.

Tucker could swear that the entire structure had begun to list to one side.

Not good.

Then the world went silent as the drone banked away for the next pass.

Counting down in his head, Tucker moved quickly. He had only this one chance. He pulled himself around the scaffolding and onto the top side of the belt. He stood up, teetering on the decomposing rubber. The belt swayed under his weight—or maybe it was the scaffolding, as the structure groaned beneath him.

Either way, he had only one path open to him. He headed up the conveyor's slope—at first cautiously, then with more urgency as the distant buzzing rose in volume.

He ran the countdown in his head.

Another fifteen seconds . . . plenty of time, he promised himself. *Only another thirty yards to go.*

He glanced over his shoulder.

A mistake.

His left foot plunged through the rubber, and he belly slammed onto the belt. He jerked his leg, but his boot was stuck in a tangle of vines below.

No, no, no—

He yanked harder and managed to pull his foot out of the boot. With his limb free now, he rolled and pushed back to his feet. Whether from his struggling or from the simple ravages of time, the entire conveyor's structure began to give way, slowly toppling sideways.

Tucker sprinted.

The pitch of the drone increased, seeming to come from everywhere.

Out of time!

Six yards ahead, the end was in sight. The dark opening in the silo loomed, a black hole that led to who knows what? He didn't care. It was either death by bullet or death by falling.

A bullet punched through the belt behind him.

Three yards to go.

Tucker flung himself headlong as the scaffolding collapsed beneath him. He dove through the opening—and found nothing but open air on the other side.

With a gasp of defeat, he plummeted into the dark.

9

Tucker squeezed his eyes shut as he fell, certain a bone-shattering impact was coming. But instead, after plunging for a long, frightening breath, he struck a surface that caved under his impact, knocking the wind out of him. Gasping, he slid and tumbled down a steep slope, then struck the far side of the metal silo with a ringing bang.

He lay on his back, gulping air back into his lungs. His fingers dug into the surface beneath him. *Sand.* He rested his head back as more rivulets of grains sifted around his body. This must be a sand collection silo for the factory.

Overhead, a scatter of rounds pinged off the outside of the silo, echoing through the hollow space. But he knew he was safe for the moment—at least from the drone.

So far, he had seen no sign of any hunters on the ground. But he knew the military often used drones to flush out quarry, to chase them into the arms of ground troops. He had to assume that might be the case or that others might be circling down upon his position.

Gotta keep moving.

But first he had to find Kane—which could prove challenging. After leaving the meeting with Frank, Tucker hadn't bothered to equip the shepherd with his Kevlar jacket and communication gear. He mentally kicked himself for not doing so, but how could he have anticipated this aerial ambush on the road back to his motel?

Okay, so we do this old school.

By now, his eyes had adjusted to the darkness. In the faint moonlight coming through the conveyor opening, he spotted another door

opposite the one he had dived through a moment ago. The dark rect-
angle was about two yards up the wall on this side. He imagined it
led into the main factory building. As well as he could tell from his
brief and frantic survey of the grounds, there were four silos attached
to the central building, one at each corner, like turrets on a castle.

When he and Kane had split up, the shepherd had taken off for a
silo on the other side of the main building. Kane was likely still holed
up in there, following Tucker's last order: RUN AND HIDE.

Intending to reach his partner there, Tucker knee-walked through
the sand to the ladder that led up to the dark door. He wrapped his
hands on one of the rungs and gave it a tug, then another. Satisfied it was
solid enough, he mounted the ladder and climbed up to the doorway.

He poked his head through and discovered a catwalk extended
from the door and crossed high above the main collection floor of the
factory. Large sections of the roof had caved in, allowing moonlight to
better illuminate the cavernous space, which stretched a football field
wide and twice as long. Below, old equipment and a row of massive ore
carts—each the size of a train car—had rusted to the concrete floor.
Above, a labyrinth of steel beams was entwined in a jungle of vines.

Tucker frowned, trying to judge the viability of using the catwalk to cross to the other side of the main floor. He pictured the
conveyor's structure collapsing a moment ago as he leapt for his life.
If the catwalk didn't hold under his weight, it was a four-story drop
to the hard concrete floor.

To his left was a skeletal staircase that led down to the floor, but
the middle section had broken away. He might be able to leap the
gap, but once he landed on the lower section, would it hold him? He
had no way of knowing.

So which way?

As he hesitated, a familiar buzzing swept by overhead as the
drone continued hunting for its escaped quarry. Disturbed by its
passage—or by the drone's ultrasonic whine—several roosting bats
took flight from the vine-encrusted beams and shot out through the
collapsed sections of the roof.

Tucker eyed them, wishing he had wings, too.

He knew he could wait no longer. If the drone failed to flush
him out, ground forces would soon be closing in on this position,
if they weren't already here. He took out a small LED flashlight to

better study his two options: the collapsed stairs or the rickety vine-encrusted catwalk. Neither was a great choice.

Damned if I do, damned if I don't.

Tucker decided to take his chances with the catwalk. At least it was still intact, unlike the staircase. He proceeded cautiously, testing each step, his senses tuned for any warning. With the catwalk continuing to hold secure, he increased his pace.

Then a familiar humming grew in volume. The drone had returned, still timed, it seemed, to pass over the factory grounds every thirty seconds, intending to keep him pinned down.

Tucker paused on the catwalk until the drone left, fearful of being spotted through one of the holes in the roof. Once clear, he set off again. He was halfway across the main factory floor when he heard a series of rapid, overlapping pops ahead of him.

Oh, shi—

The catwalk broke from the scaffolding ahead. The section of grating underfoot fell at a steep angle, throwing him onto his back. His flashlight bounced out of his grip and rolled over the edge. His body followed, sliding down the grate. His fingers clawed, but he could find no purchase.

As his legs slipped over the edge, something brushed his face.

A vine.

He grasped it without thinking. The rest of the catwalk tore free beneath him. He fell with it, but he jerked to a stop, hanging by the vine, swallowing a scream. He heard the clattering crash below him but refused to look down.

With his heart hammering in his chest, he firmed his grip and looked up. The edge of the remaining catwalk was almost within arm's reach. If he climbed another foot, he should be able to—

A tearing sound was the only warning. The vine ripped free from its neighbor and Tucker dropped ten feet before again jolting to a stop.

With his eyes squeezed tight, he took three deep breaths.

Up was no longer an option.

He finally stared down. He was still three stories above the floor. Directly below him were the ruins of the broken catwalk, now a tangle of sharp steel. But ten feet to his left was the row of giant ore carts he had spotted earlier, still rusted to their tracks. The angle was wrong to tell if they held anything, but the closest one was under one of the large holes in the roof.

It'll have to do.

Tucker began swinging his body, first right, then left, dolphin-kicking his legs to build up momentum. Above him, the vine creaked, and debris rained down on his head.

"Come on, come on . . ."

He kept swinging, extending the arc each time, picking up speed. Then the vine popped and started to give way. Knowing he could wait no longer, he let go—and flew toward the nearest ore cart. He balled his limbs tight and dropped into the train-car-sized cart. He hit the inner wall on the far side and rebounded into three feet of rainwater that filled the bottom of the cart.

Despite the cushion of the pooled water, he hit the bottom hard enough to bruise his tailbone. He sputtered up, gasping out his relief. He stared at the hole in the roof, grateful for whatever past showers had filled this cart. Still, the water's surface was covered in a thick layer of scum: a mixture of algae, bird droppings, and bat guano. It clung to his clothing like a foul paste, reeking of rot and ammonia.

"Getting really tired of this place," he muttered.

A quick search revealed a row of toe- and handholds sculpted into the cart's inner surface, a ladder for workers to climb into and out of these massive carts. Tucker waded to it and started climbing.

Now to find Kane . . .

As his head cleared the top edge of the cart, he noted the flashlight he had dropped a moment ago. It glowed amid the wreckage of the catwalk—but that wasn't the only light source now.

Outside the factory, a beam of light swept along a wall of grime-encrusted windows. A figure stepped through one of the broken-out panes, moving cautiously into the factory, an assault rifle fixed to his cheek.

"The crash came from in here," the man said, leaning toward a radio affixed to his collar. "Lyon, hang back while I check it out."

Tucker ducked his head as the beam swept toward him. He quietly slipped back into the dank water. As he had feared, an armed detachment had been sent in on foot. He listened as the hunter crossed closer, likely drawn by Tucker's flashlight, intending to check the debris for his body.

"Got something," the gunman radioed. "They're here. Maintain watch outside. Shoot anything that moves."

"*Roger*," came the reply.

Tucker pictured Kane, hoping the shepherd stayed out of sight. But that thought gave him an idea.

Kane crouches in the shadow of a doorway. Ahead stretches a vast space. His senses extend into it. He smells dank water, along with the droppings from all manner of beast and bird. He had been drawn to this spot after hearing a thunderous crash. Before, he had been holed up in a neighboring space to this one, where he had been obeying his last order.

HIDE.

From this spot, he had watched his partner fall from above, heard him land with a loud splash, followed by a sharp gasp. Kane had wanted to run out, to bark, to demand to know if the other was okay, to re-form their pack once again.

But he obeys, stays hidden.

Now another man stalks the space, coming with light and with the scent of gun oil. Kane slinks lower, refusing to break command. His heart pounds, his chest heaves in quiet breaths, stirring dust motes and the spoor of mice.

Then a new noise piques his attention, drawing his ears straight and stiff.

A soft whistle, meant to sound like a bird.

But Kane knows the true source.

It is a new command.

He knows what he must do and rises up to obey this new order.

Kane lifts his muzzle and howls into the night.

Tucker hung by his fingertips from the top edge of the ore cart, his toes jammed into the ladder, his legs bunched under him. He had waited until he heard the armed hunter draw close to his hiding place before signaling Kane. The shepherd understood a vocabulary broaching a thousand words and the ability to comprehend hundreds of hand signals. But recently Tucker had begun training his partner with audible cues.

Like the soft call of a mourning dove.

It was the equivalent of the command SOUND OFF.

As Kane's howl echoed across the cavernous factory, seeming to come from everywhere at once, Tucker shoved with his legs, vaulted over the lip of the cart, and dropped toward the enemy below.

Caught off guard and startled by the dog, the gunman still reacted with surprising speed. Possibly alerted by the scuff of Tucker's boot, the hunter started to bring his weapon up, but Tucker fell heavily upon him anyway. He crashed atop the figure, grabbed the man's face, and slammed the back of his head into the concrete floor again and again. The body went immediately limp, out cold, maybe dead.

Tucker checked for a pulse.

Nope, just out cold.

Good . . . a dead body wasn't worth the trouble.

He whistled sharply, ordering Kane to his side, knowing he had to act fast. There was at least one other hunter out there. Tucker grabbed his opponent's weapon. It was a compact, noise-suppressed Heckler & Koch MP-5 SD with optical sights. It was a good weapon.

But an even better one arrived.

A dark shadow arrowed out of the darkness and came close to bowling him over.

He caught Kane up in a one-armed hug, gave him a kiss on his ruff. Any further greeting would have to wait. Still, Tucker could not discount how happy he was to have Kane at his side again. He felt whole now, more centered.

Over the man's radio came his partner's voice: *"Webster, you there?"*

Tucker heard a faint French accent. He quickly patted down the unconscious man until he found the radio handset. He tapped the transmit key twice. It was a radio-silent *roger* signal. In soldier parlance, it meant the sender wasn't free to speak.

Tucker got a double click in reply, confirming the other understood.

It also corroborated that these hunters had military training.

Tucker acted accordingly, knowing this Webster guy's partner wouldn't wait long for an update. He gestured for Kane to stick to his side. He crossed back to the tall ore cart, dropped to his knees, and crawled underneath it. With Kane next to him, he sheltered behind one of the metal wheels frozen in the old tracks.

Tucker lay flat and flicked the MP-5's selector to three-round bursts.

He didn't have long to wait for the French soldier to make an appearance. The only warning was a shift of shadows by the silo door where Kane had been hiding. The man outside must have been drawn in that direction by Kane's howl a moment ago. The soldier came in low, stalking forward with his assault rifle tracking left and right. A flash of moonlight revealed a heavily scarred face with a crooked nose.

This guy had seen his fair share of fights.

Tucker instinctively knew he could take no chances with this one. He adjusted his aim lower, laying a red dot on the man's chest. His finger tightened on the trigger. But as he fired, the man suddenly sidestepped left. Tucker had witnessed this kind of intuitive action before in combat—when a soldier gets that *something ain't right* feeling in the pit of the stomach. It can force one to duck, run, or take cover. It was a phenomenon that veteran soldiers never discounted and that few talked about lest they jinx themselves.

Whoever this Frenchman was, he had been shot at plenty of times.

Still, despite the target moving, Tucker's first two rounds struck home, hitting the man in the chest; the third went wide. Rocked by the bullets' impacts, the man stumbled backward through the silo door he had entered. For him to still be on his feet, he must be wearing body armor.

Silence followed.

Tucker stayed tense, expecting an immediate barrage of return fire. He searched the factory for other hunters, any backup for these two. No one showed themselves, and a moment later, he heard distant splashing from outside.

Was the French soldier fleeing—or going for help?

Through the optical sight of his MP-5, he spotted a rifle abandoned on the floor near the door. He remembered hearing a metallic thud when he had fired earlier. One of the rounds must have struck the other's weapon, likely damaging it and knocking it away.

No wonder the other took off.

Wounded and disarmed, the man must be retreating so he could live to fight another day. No ego, no fear, just the pragmatism of combat. Here was yet another indication Tucker was dealing with a professional.

But Tucker could not count on the soldier being gone for long. He could return with additional reinforcements at any time. Tucker had been lucky that this pair had underestimated him, placing too much trust on that deadly eye in the sky.

A low buzzing overhead told him that threat remained.

Tucker crawled out and searched the unconscious man. The gunman appeared to be in his late forties or early fifties, craggy faced, with auburn hair, graying at the temples. Tucker found two spare magazines, a portable radio, and a set of vehicle keys, but no identification of any kind. In a leg pocket, Tucker withdrew a paperback-sized device that he could not immediately identify. He found the power button and pushed it. A blue screen glowed to life, revealing a grid of touch-buttons.

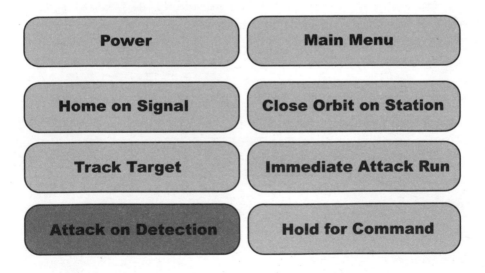

Tucker ran his fingers along the engraved four letters along the top of the portable unit: CUCS. From his years in Afghanistan, he knew those initials stood for Core UAV Control System. This was essentially the remote control unit for the drone that had been hunting them.

Tucker noted the one highlighted button.

Attack on Detection

Tucker frowned, fearing what this meant, remembering the actions of the drone, how it had seemed to hunt and fire at him all on its own. It must have some autopilot feature, capable of autonomously attacking once a target was acquired.

Tucker knew such robotic drones were currently in various stages of investigation by a slew of military contractors.

Looks like someone is well along that road.

Tucker examined the CUCS control module. It could be his ticket to escaping this swamp and the hunter in the sky, but he knew nothing about operating drones. With a shrug, he went for the most direct approach: blindly pushing buttons.

What could go wrong?

He tapped the button marked CLOSE ORBIT ON STATION. A light blue rectangular box appeared beneath the rows of buttons, along with a miniature keyboard. A flashing prompt appeared, asking for a password.

Enter Password

|

Hitting this obstacle, Tucker tried tapping the MAIN MENU button, but he got the same password prompt.

He sat back on his heels and muttered, "Well, that was too good to be true, wasn't it, Kane."

The shepherd wagged his tail.

Tucker rubbed his chin, puzzled by one detail. If this drone is set to fire at will, how did it know *not* to attack this Webster guy or his French partner? He stared down at the portable unit. The most obvious answer was that these CUCS were equipped with a targeting exclusion program, some signal that radioed the drone not to shoot whoever was holding the unit. Which begged the question: *did the device require a command to enable this shielding program?*

Tucker stared toward the swamp.

There was only one way to find out.

He gathered what he had taken from Webster, collected his abandoned flashlight, and clipped the MP-5 around his waist. He then headed in the opposite direction from the Frenchman. He reached a broken section of windows on this side and waited for the drone to make a pass and vanish again.

Thirty seconds.

He boosted Kane through the window, hopped out after the dog, then set off at a sprint for the swamp. He wanted to get under as much cover as possible when the drone returned, just in case he was wrong about the protective shield of this device.

Reaching the swamp, he splashed into the water and aimed for the densest section of cypress trees and tangles of root mounds. A glance at the stars showed him he was still headed on a path that should take him to the country club on the far side of the swamp.

"A half mile to go, buddy," Tucker promised Kane.

He was counting on the drone backing off once he reached a public space. Whoever was running this campaign certainly seemed to like to keep their secrets.

Tucker continued toward the refuge of trees, waiting for the return of the drone's engine buzz. As if on cue, the sound rose from the south. Tucker waved Kane toward a nearby root mound.

"HIDE."

Tucker followed the paddling shepherd but he hung back a yard, staying in plain view. He searched the sky and spotted a shifting section of stars, marking the stealth-camouflaged drone's passage.

Ready to leap if it targeted him, he clutched the CUCS in one hand, trying to get it to protect him by sheer willpower.

As he held his breath, the drone whisked overhead—and away. It continued its search pattern, oblivious of its former target. He let out a long sigh of relief. He knew the smartest plan from here would be to make a beeline for that country club. But he knew he had a small window to gather some intelligence about his opponents. So instead he veered at an angle and circled back until he reached a section of bullet-riddled trees.

Using a penknife, he pried one of the rounds free and examined it.

The bullet appeared to be a standard NATO sniper round—7.62 by 51mm—but it sure hadn't acted like any *standard* bullet. He examined the hole in the trunk, noting the angle of impact—then glanced up. The drone had always fired from *above* the canopy, but the round had entered the tree at a perfectly *horizontal* angle.

Suspicious, Tucker panned his flashlight over the water. After covering fifty feet, he spotted something floating in the water. It looked like a stick, but was too straight and too white for that.

He crossed over and retrieved it. The object—made of some kind of exotic polymer and roughly six inches long—was outfitted with tiny maneuvering fins and had a small bulge on the underside, which he imagined housed a guidance pod.

He glanced over to the tree.

Put *that* round with *this* cartridge, and he suspected what was shot from the drone.

"PGB," he whispered to the night.

A precision guided bullet.

He turned and stared toward the sky.

What the hell have we stumbled into?

11:48 P.M.

Two hours later, Tucker was back at his motel room and stood under the spray of a blisteringly hot shower, happy to flush the filth and grime of the day away—and to clear his head.

After crossing the last half mile of swamp, he and Kane had slogged out onto the grounds of the country club. He could only imagine the sight they made as they skirted the parking lot: some swamp rat and his muddy dog. Once safely at the club's valet station, he had called a taxi. From the way the late-night diners at the club's restaurant had eyed him through the window, he half expected a squad car to come collect them. But a yellow cab had arrived, and the valet was kind enough to sneak them a few towels from the golf locker room to use as makeshift seat cushions.

Their path back to the motel took them past where the SUV had been ambushed. But there was no sign of his Ford Explorer.

Apparently someone had it towed away, likely covering their tracks.

So much for my rental deposit.

Still, Tucker wasn't all that worried. As was his habit with rentals, he kept nothing inside that could trace back to him and had used one of three false driver's licenses and a matching credit card to rent the vehicle. The room was booked under another alias and a different card.

As an extra precaution, before reaching the motel, Tucker had the driver stop at a nearby construction site and acquired a length of two-by-four that was now jammed beneath the door's knob. Though there was no evidence that anyone had turned over his room, he would change motels tomorrow.

Still, questions nagged at him concerning this ambush.

How had this faceless enemy found him, how did he draw their attention, and how much did they know about why he was here?

The most obvious answer to these questions was one Tucker didn't want to believe. Only one person knew about his presence here and the reason behind it.

Frank Ballenger.

Tucker reached back and twisted the shower knob from hot to cold. The freezing water jolted him, steeling him for what was to come.

Tomorrow I'll settle that score.

10

The next morning, Tucker put his house in order. He cleared out of his motel, rented a new SUV—a silver Dodge Durango—under a false ID, and headed out to Athens, some twenty miles west of Huntsville. There, he checked into another motel, the Stone Hearth Inn. As Kane sniffed out every corner of the new room, Tucker called Frank Ballenger and arranged to meet for lunch a few miles from the Redstone Arsenal military base.

On his return to Huntsville, Tucker took a detour to the country club and retrieved the confiscated MP-5 rifle he had hidden in some hedges after exiting the swamp last night.

He was taking no chances with this meeting.

As an additional precaution, Tucker arrived at the restaurant an hour early. He canvassed the immediate area: searched the parking lot, noted all the exits and entrances to the establishment, and mapped out the surrounding streets. He then spied upon their meeting location from a Starbucks across the street.

The Cotton Row Restaurant stood on the southwest corner of the city's courthouse square, occupying a former cotton exchange building. It was a three-story brick structure with patio seating under taupe-colored awnings and a second-floor balcony lined by black iron railings.

Frank Ballenger arrived promptly at noon and sat at one of the outside tables shaded by an awning. Tucker kept watch for a full fifteen minutes, making sure the man hadn't been followed. Only then did he walk across the street with Kane.

Frank stood up, shook his hand, and smiled down at the shepherd. "I thought maybe you two were standing me up." He then frowned at Tucker's arms, which were crisscrossed with scratches and pointed to the small bandage on Tucker's ear, where a round had nicked him. "What in God's name happened to you?"

"Got lost in a swamp," Tucker replied stone-faced.

"What are you talking about? How?"

The man's shock seemed genuine. Tucker normally trusted his snap judgment of people's reactions, leaning on his innate talent to read people, but after last night, he remained wary.

"Frank, did you burn me?"

"What?"

Tucker sat down, drawing Frank with him. "After leaving the pub, I got ambushed near the swamp."

"Ambushed?" Frank leaned back, his eyes rounder. "And you think I . . . Tucker, I wouldn't do that. Not on my life."

Tucker stared into the man's eyes. The other's gaze didn't waver.

"First of all, I'd never betray a brother," Frank insisted. "Never. Second, even if I wanted to, who would I call? I don't know anybody like that."

"Could you have inadvertently alerted someone, said something out of hand?"

Frank thought for a moment, then slowly shook his head. "I can't see how. I didn't even make any calls about Sandy Conlon until this morning."

So he couldn't have accidentally tipped someone off.

None of this made any sense.

Frank leaned forward. "You gotta believe me."

Tucker sighed, reading nothing but a sincere genuineness. "I do believe you."

"Then we're good here?"

"We're good."

Frank let out a long breath, then settled back. "Tell me what happened."

Tucker recounted the electrical malfunction that had stopped his Ford Explorer on the empty road and the subsequent firefight that drove him into the swamps.

"Hmm," Frank murmured. "I'm guessing they must have used some sort of remote kill switch to incapacitate your vehicle. Nice."

"It wasn't *nice* from where I was sitting. But is such a thing doable?"

"Easy enough. It's just a matter of wirelessly hacking into a vehicle's CAN bus." Frank read Tucker's wrinkled brow. "Stands for controller area network. Everything on modern cars is digital nowadays, meaning they're hackable."

The waitress appeared and took their orders.

Once she left, Frank continued. "I now get why you suspected me. Occam's Razor: the simplest solution is usually right. But I know it wasn't me, so how did they get on to you?"

"And who are *they*?"

"Exactly. Who else knew you were down here?"

Tucker wasn't comfortable mentioning Jane, even to Frank, at least not yet. "Just the person who sent me," he offered lamely.

Frank seemed to understand his reticence. "And you trust this person."

Tucker nodded.

"Then they must be tracking you somehow. Maybe your phone."

"I doubt it. It's deeply encrypted." His satellite phone was a gift, courtesy of Ruth Harper at Sigma Force . . . in case she ever needed to reach him or vice versa.

"Let me see it." Frank held out his palm.

Tucker considered for a moment, then handed it over.

Frank proceeded to efficiently examine the phone: pushing a series of buttons, studying the screen, even opening the back panel and removing the SIM card. He spent a full minute poking around the innards with a plastic pick from a ridiculously complex Swiss Army knife—then he finally reassembled the phone and returned it with a low whistle of appreciation.

"I'm not even going to bother asking where you got it. It's damned sophisticated, but even this device could be tracked. Though I'll admit that it'd take some serious know-how."

"Even if you're right, it doesn't explain *how* I got on these hunters' radar in the first place. They'd have to know about me to think to track me."

"True. Which brings us full circle back to who else knew you were down here. Could this person who sent you to Huntsville have told someone else?"

Tucker couldn't imagine Jane doing that. Her level of paranoia when they met in Montana had been sky high. "I don't think so."

"Then what about *after* you got down here? Who besides me have you run into? Could someone have tagged you locally?"

Tucker pictured the two-man team that had waylaid him outside of Sandy's house. Had they somehow identified him after that encounter? And then there was Edith Lozier, the caretaker of the storage facility . . .

Maybe I haven't been as cautious as I thought I was.

"It's possible," Tucker admitted.

"Okay, then let's set aside that mystery for now. As a precaution, I suggest you keep your phone powered off with the battery pulled out. I might be able to rig some new components down the line that'll make it harder to track, but it'll take a few hours to get everything I need."

Tucker lifted an eyebrow. "You can do that?"

"It wasn't my good looks that got me promoted to a cryptologic network warfare specialist."

Tucker recognized the amused glint in Frank's eye from back in Afghanistan, when the man had tried to clarify the finer points of communication interception.

"As a soldier in this new era of cyber warfare," Frank explained, "I've had to hone a few new skills since back in my field days. Like hacking into systems. I'll gather up the components I need for your phone and see if I can batten down its hatches more securely. I can bring what I need to your motel tonight. Hopefully by then I'll have some more information about Sandy from the feelers I sent out this morning."

"Good."

Tucker realized one other task that might be best suited to Frank's new skill set. He pictured the remote-control device for the attack drone. As a precaution, he had powered the CUCS unit off and buried it a mile from his old motel. If anyone could glean any clues from that device, it would be Frank.

"Before you come to my motel," Tucker said, "there's something else you might want to take a look at."

"What is it?"

Tucker hadn't gone into great length about the unique nature of the drone that had hunted him through the swamps. He decided to get Frank's unbiased take on the operating system running the drone before filling in those details.

"I think I'll let you be surprised," Tucker said.

Frank cocked his head slightly. "Sounds to me like I'm getting an early Christmas present."

6:17 P.M.

As the sun set on another warm Alabama day, Tucker returned to the Stone Hearth Inn in Athens. He had spent the remainder of the afternoon with Kane out in the local parks, where the shepherd had demolished three tennis balls and trudged through five more streams. Maybe it would've been wiser to hole up out of sight, but he doubted the enemy would be bold enough to strike in broad daylight with witnesses all around.

Besides, Kane had needed to stretch his legs, to work through some of the tension from last night.

And so did I . . .

As pleasant as the day was, Tucker kept glancing to the sky, one ear always listening for a telltale buzz. He recognized such wariness was triggered in no small part from his own PTSD. Though he had suffered only a few scrapes, the attack at the swamp had affected him, stirring older wounds, those that had scarred over but never fully healed. After leaving Afghanistan, Tucker had been plagued by flashbacks, nightmares, and insomnia, leaving him emotionally numb. While he had gone through mandatory counseling with psychologists who specialized in treating vets, he had found greater peace out in the open, on the road, with Kane by his side.

Still, he knew those nightmares remained, just under his skin.

Maybe that was why he still kept accepting such high-risk jobs, to challenge that enemy within. One psychologist suggested he was perhaps suicidal, but Tucker knew deep down that wasn't the case. He wanted to live, and if he ever doubted it, he only had to look to the shepherd at his side. At his bedrock core, Tucker knew he would never recklessly endanger Kane in some veiled attempt at ending his life.

Instead, it was one counselor who offered Tucker his greatest insight, refining the diagnosis of PTSD to one born of *moral injury*, a wound where Tucker's fundamental understanding of right and wrong had been deeply violated by his experiences in Afghanistan. Tucker suspected his recent path through life was an ongoing attempt to find his center again, to make amends—not so much for what he did, but for what he had failed to do. It was what gave his life purpose, to tilt at the injustices of the world.

In the meantime, there was pizza—yet another reason to live.

On his drive back to Athens, Tucker had picked up two pepperoni pies and a six-pack of Sam Adams lager. He had barely placed them on his room's small dining table when there was a knock at the door.

As punctual as ever, Frank greeted him with a one-armed hug, carrying a small duffel in his other hand. He eyed the room as he entered and offered a halfhearted, "Great digs."

Tucker didn't miss the sarcasm in the man's voice. The place certainly wasn't the Ritz, but it was clean and cozy, with a decor that could be considered shabby-chic.

As they settled in, Frank helped himself to a slice of pizza and a beer, then plopped down on the bed next to a curled-up Kane, who gave Frank a single tail-wag hello. Tucker had already fed him a giant bowl of kibble.

"He looks happy," Frank said.

"He's now the king of Huntsville's parks and waterways."

"Damn, and here I forgot to bring him his crown." Frank zipped open his duffel. "But I did bring some other goodies. Pass me that phone of yours and let me see if I can't lock that baby up tight."

Tucker handed the satellite phone over.

Between bites of pizza, Frank opened the back panel and began fiddling with it: unscrewing this and rearranging that before finally inserting a new SIM card. "That ought to do it. At least, until we find out what tracking gear the opposition is working with."

"What do you mean *we*?"

Frank passed back the phone and smiled wryly. From his duffel, he pulled out the CUCS unit and placed it on the bedspread. He stared lovingly at it. "Such a beauty. Of course, even with your directions, I had a hell of a hard time finding where you buried this treasure. I've barely had time to do more than a cursory exam. Still, impressive sophistication . . ." Frank tore his gaze from the drone's remote control to face Tucker. "Looks like you're playing in my sandbox. You can't kick me out now."

"It could get ugly, Frank."

"Judging by your condition, it already has." Frank lifted his palms. "Listen, I'm more than happy to leave the rough stuff to you and Kane. I'll be a strictly behind-the-scenes guy."

Tucker sighed, weighing what to say. He knew Frank's expertise could prove valuable in this search, but Tucker preferred to operate alone. Unable to decide, he said, "Tell me what you learned about Sandy, then I'll consider your offer."

"Fair enough." Frank shrugged. "I know she comes from around these parts like me. Her only living relative is her mother, who lives up in the Appalachian high country, one of the poorest counties, where folks are notoriously wary of strangers."

Tucker remembered Jane mentioning that Sandy's mother was one of the last people to see the missing woman. He also remembered Edith Lozier, the caretaker of the storage facility, telling him that Sandy was headed to see her mother after making a hasty exit from her locker.

"It might be worth checking out," Frank said.

"Why's that?"

"The mountain people are a close-knit group, bound as equally by their traditions as by their suspicions. They know how to keep their secrets tight to their chest. If Sandy wanted to bury something away from prying eyes, that would be a good place to look."

Tucker slowly nodded. Frank was right. It might be worth a day trip. "What did you learn about Sandy's role closer at home, here at Redstone Arsenal?"

Frank frowned. "Not much. I learned she's not attached to any official military command. She's part of some quasi-private team—something called The Odisha Group."

Tucker sat straighter. He remembered seeing that name—

Odisha—circled on one of Sandy's whiteboards in her makeshift command center. Frank was on the right track. It seemed the man's skill set extended beyond motherboards and computer code.

"What was that group working on?" Tucker asked.

"Above my pay grade, I'm afraid. All I could discover without raising alarms is that the group is mostly made up of mathematicians and statisticians. They operate out of a newly constructed housing unit in a remote corner of Redstone. It's all segregated with access controlled by MPs. As far as I can tell, the group mostly lives there."

"You said they were *quasi*-private. What did you mean by that?"

"To operate at Redstone, they surely have the base commander's approval and support, but as I understand it, Odisha operates independently. They're run by a private company."

"Which one?"

Frank shrugged again. "That'll take some more digging. Perhaps if I knew more details . . ."

Tucker hesitated, then decided he was putting Frank more at risk by withholding information. "I think it's high time I gave you the rest of the story about Sandy's disappearance."

Frank leaned forward. "Do tell."

Tucker started with the intruders he ran into at Sandy's house and ended with his discovery of her storage locker. "Whoever chased us through the swamps may be the same pair that showed up at Sandy's place. At least I'm pretty sure one of the men was."

That guy named Webster . . .

Frank interrupted his story. "Back up, you said you got the license plate number off the men's Suburban at Conlon's house."

Tucker nodded.

"Good. Give that to me before I leave. If that vehicle ever passed through one of the gates at Redstone, there'll be a record of it. It might be a good place to start." Frank waved to him. "Go on. What else happened?"

Tucker continued with his story, filling in more details about the nature of the drone that had hunted him and Kane.

With a pizza slice halfway to his mouth, Frank blinked several times and blew out a breath. "Whoa," he murmured. "I've got like a few hundred questions."

Tucker smiled. "I thought you might."

"First, let me see that sniper round you dug out of the tree trunk and the guidance pod you found floating in the water."

Tucker walked over to his pack, retrieved the objects, and passed them over.

Frank remained silent for a full minute while he examined both. "Definitely the assembly for a PGB, a precision guided bullet. But this is beyond anything I've seen. I'll do my best to pick it apart later at my place." His gaze returned to Tucker. "As for the attack drone, how was the accuracy of its targeting systems?"

"Good, but not perfect. A lot of near misses. Why?"

"Did it seem to get better over time?"

Tucker thought back, then slowly nodded. "Now that you mention it. I thought maybe it was because I was slowing down, but you may be right."

"Hmm . . ."

"What?"

"From the level of engine muffling you described, along with stealth camouflaging, we're talking about a next-gen level of drone technology. If that's the case, one of the engineering facets currently under investigation—where the most money is being funneled at the moment—concerns building drones that can not only operate autonomously but *learn* on the fly."

Tucker felt a sinking in the pit of his stomach. "You think that's what we encountered out there? Some new prototype?"

"I do. But the question remains, how *autonomous* was that damned thing? Can it be given a whole mission profile and execute it?"

"As in, fire and forget?"

"Or even worse. With current tech, drones can already zero in and target various features of an enemy: visual identities, electronic emissions, travel routes, that sort of thing. But the next-gen drones will likely be programmed to make independent judgments upon what they find out there."

"Including shoot to kill."

Frank nodded. "Removing humans from the equation. To save the lives of boots on the ground, there has been growing pressure to give such robotic warriors greater autonomy and decision-making capability."

Tucker swallowed, trying to imagine that future war.

Or maybe I don't have to imagine it.

The buzzing of the drone's engines filled his head.

Frank continued. "Both military designers and independent programmers are racing toward that goal. It's a gold rush out there right now. Even Blackwater, the private military firm, added an unmanned division to its business model back in 2007, opening the door for robotic mercenaries, autonomous drones operating beyond the stricture of military command."

Frank must have noted Tucker growing paler, but the man apparently wasn't done. "One more thing. Whoever engineered that drone, you can bet it wasn't their only model. Drones come in all shapes and sizes, built for various purposes, designed to travel through the air, across the ground, or even underwater."

Tucker took these words of caution to heart.

Frank sat back and smiled. "So what do you think?"

"About what?" Tucker forced out.

"Do I have the position? Can I stay onboard with you and Kane? I told you I could be of use to you."

Tucker didn't hesitate. "You're hired."

Frank's grin broadened. "What do you want me to do first?"

"Look into the Suburban's license plate and see what you can find—but be careful."

Frank nodded. "What are you going to do?"

Tucker pictured Frank's description of where Sandy's mother lived. "I'm going to buy myself a banjo."

11

Maybe I should've bought that banjo after all . . .

As Tucker headed east into the mountains, the signs of traditional civilization began to fade. Once off Highway 35 and onto the back roads, the way quickly grew more potholed, the homes more scattered, diminishing into simple cabins. He filled up at a gas station with a rusted pump that looked like it dated from the fifties. As he passed along, children stopped playing in yards and stared at him, the girls in faded dresses, the boys in baggy shorts. Tucker waved to one man on a porch, who simply narrowed his eyes.

Tucker felt as though he had slipped backward into the depression era.

"Kane, I say we cross this place off for our next canoe trip."

The shepherd wagged his tail. Unsurprisingly, Kane remained fixated on the rural scenery, occasionally whining as he saw kids running and laughing, plainly disappointed he was missing out on all the fun.

Eventually the terrain steepened, and the slopes grew heavily wooded with oaks, the foliage already a riot of fall golds and reds.

Tucker slowed as he watched for the occasional road sign, following the directions Frank had given him. Sandy's mother—Beatrice Conlon—lived some thirty-five miles deeper into the mountains, outside a hamlet called Poplar Grove.

He passed farmhouse after farmhouse, all of them made of clapboard and seemingly held together by layers of peeling white paint. He came upon the occasional church, usually a small saltbox affair with a truncated steeple. After another forty minutes of driving, Tucker finally reached Poplar Grove. The town was little more than a four-way stop, with a hardware store, a diner, a grocer, and a gas station.

"What?" he mumbled as he braked at the intersection. "No Starbucks?"

He continued forward at a snail's pace until he spotted a faded sign for Davis Road and turned left. After another half mile, the road's blacktop ended, becoming a dirt-and-gravel tract. He followed to where it dead-ended.

Ahead, past a fencerow and a field of weeds, sat a trim yellow farmhouse with a wraparound porch. A mailbox at the edge of the drive read CONLON.

Tucker patted Kane's side. "Looks like we're home."

As he exited, Kane hopped out next to him, sniffing all around. Tucker shielded his eyes and studied the farmhouse. Aside from the chirping of crickets, it was perfectly quiet.

Frank had warned him this was shoot-first country when it came to trespassing.

Hopefully we'll at least get a warning shot.

Tucker cupped his hands around his mouth. "Anybody home?" he shouted.

There was no answer. He tried again, but still got no response.

He headed toward the driveway, which was little more than two ruts through the weeds. Before he could set foot past the fencerow, a female voice yelled at him, "Whatya want?"

Tucker stopped and motioned for Kane to stick beside him. A figure stepped out of the porch's deeper shadows.

"Ms. Conlon?" Tucker called out.

"Who's asking?"

"My name is Tucker. I tried calling but—"

"Get on outta here. I'm not buying what you're selling, mister." She began to fade back into the shadows.

"No, wait! I'm a friend of Jane Sabatello's. She asked me to come down to check on—"

The woman moved to the porch rail. "You lookin' for my Sandy?"

"Yes, ma'am."

"Find her yet?"

"No, ma'am."

"Then whatcha here for?"

"If I can learn a bit more about your daughter, it might help me find her."

After ten long seconds, she finally waved an arm. "Okay, then. Come on over."

So much for the warm welcome.

Tucker crossed up the driveway toward some side steps that led up to the porch. The closer he got, the more he appreciated the quaint farmhouse. Despite its age, it looked well maintained. The same couldn't be said for the yard. By the time he reached the porch, Kane's fur was covered in thistles and burrs.

"Name's Bea," the woman said and nodded to Kane. "There's a burr brush near the door. Get 'im cleaned up before he comes in."

She stepped through the screen door and let it clap shut behind her.

Tucker grabbed the brush and spent a few minutes dethistling both Kane's fur and his own pant legs. Once done, he pulled open the screen door and entered a small living room. The carpet was cream colored, perfectly clean, as was the furniture. A pair of Tiffany-style lamps sat on oak tables to either side of a couch. A wall-mounted television faced the seating area. There was also a prominent crucifix above the screen, and on the table, a rosewood framed photo of the beatific smiling face of Jesus Christ.

"Shut the door, will ya?" Bea called from the kitchen at the back of the house. "Got the AC going."

"Sure."

"You like lemonade?"

"Yes, ma'am. Thanks."

Bea joined him carrying both a bowl and a tray containing two glasses and a pitcher. The woman was in her midfifties, trim and tan, her graying blond hair tucked into a loose bun. She wore khaki pants, work boots, and a plaid long-sleeved shirt.

She placed a bowl of water before Kane. "Belgian shepherd?"

Tucker smiled. "Most people think he's a *German* shepherd. I think it's his accent."

His attempt at humor fell on deaf ears.

"I watch a lot of dog shows," she said. "Westminster and such. He's handsome. And smart, too, I'll bet."

Tucker's smile grew larger, prouder. "He is that."

She waved him to a recliner next to the sofa, then poured him a glass of lemonade. "Sorry about the unfriendliness out there. Kinda bred into us, I guess."

"No problem. I've learned over the years that a healthy suspicion of strangers is often warranted." He patted Kane's side as the shepherd settled next to him. "Give me a dog over a person any day of the week."

Bea offered a small smile as she sank down to the sofa, but he also noted the knot of worry between her eyes. "So you were a friend of Sandy's?" she asked.

"We knew each other at Fort Benning, but I haven't talked to her in years. It was Jane who called me. Thought I could help."

Bea nodded. "Jane's a good girl." That knot grew tighter as the woman's gaze returned to Tucker. "Do you think you can help find Sandy?"

"I'm going to try."

"I believe you, but I'm worried. She always calls. No more than a few days goes by without her phoning me. Plus she was acting oddly for the past couple months."

"How so?"

The woman rubbed her palms together, plainly worried. "She's been kinda drawn into herself, which ain't like her. Sandy's always been a pip. And the last time she was up here, about three weeks ago, she asked if anybody'd been up here asking about her."

"Had there been?"

"Not here. And if anyone had been in town, I woulda heard about it."

He leaned back, trying to get a complete picture of Sandy's life. "Do you know what she was doing at Redstone, what project she was working on?"

Bea shook her head. "Secret stuff, I'm sure. She never said, and I knew better than to ask. I assumed it was related to computers, math, and such. She was always a smart kid."

Tucker nodded. "Did she ever mention any names, any friends she worked with?"

"Only one. A gal named Nora Frakes. Sandy liked her. She even brought her to dinner here a few times. Nice gal. A little saucy, but nice all the same."

Tucker heard a flutter in the woman's voice, a flicker of unease in her eyes as she glanced toward a window. Nora Frakes was likely closer than a *friend* to Sandy, but Bea wasn't about to admit that to a relative stranger in her house.

Tucker decided to switch the subject to safer ground. "Tell me about Sandy. How did she get interested in math and computers?"

Bea's smile reappeared. "Like I said, she was a smart kid. But elementary school didn't spark her. Neither did middle school. But when she hit ninth grade she had a math teacher who took a shine to her. Next thing you know, she's doing algebra, calculus, trigonometry, computer science. It was like she just bloomed—honor roll, valedictorian, got a full scholarship to MIT from the air force, which she joined after she graduated."

"It sounds like she certainly found her niche."

"You could say that. If not for that math teacher, she'd probably be waitressing with a baby on her hip. Instead, she spent six years with the air force. When she got out, she did some stuff in Washington—I think with Jane."

Tucker nodded, remembering Jane telling him that the two women had worked alongside each other in DC.

"Then Sandy found this job at Redstone," Bea continued. "I think mainly to be close to me. It's been heaven having her around."

"And the last time you saw her was a little over three weeks ago."

"That's right."

Tucker read some vacillation in the woman, some hesitation or reluctance about that last visit.

She's not telling me something.

He remembered Frank's comment about these mountain folks keeping their secrets, about their innate distrust of outsiders. He needed to break through that wall.

While reaching into his pocket, Tucker quietly signaled Kane.

MAKE FRIENDS.

Kane rose and crossed over to the sofa and rested his chin beside Bea's left knee. She smiled down and gave him a scratch behind the ear, which set Kane's tail to swishing more vigorously, eventually involving his whole hindquarters. Tucker knew Kane wasn't play-acting. Tucker could read the shepherd's body language like a book.

The shepherd instinctively liked Bea, who from her fixation with dog shows clearly returned that affection.

She patted the couch cushion.

Kane jumped up and curled into a ball next to her.

"He's a delight," she murmured.

"And he has good sense about people." Tucker leaned forward and slipped over the photograph that Jane had given him. It showed the three of them arm in arm, grinning like fools. "So did Sandy."

Bea took the photo and ran a finger over her daughter's features. "She was so much younger here."

Tucker matched her sad smile. "We all were. Even my dog, Kane, there."

Bea squinted at the pair of war dogs squatted at their feet in the photo. "That's Kane?"

"When he was—"

Bea sat up straighter, staring at Tucker with wider eyes. "You're the soldier with the *two* dogs."

Tucker was taken aback by her reaction.

"I remember Sandy telling me about you, but I must've forgotten your name. Still, I remember Sandy's stories. About you, about Kane, and the other dog . . ."

"Abel," Tucker said, his voice cracking.

Kane lifted his head at the mention of his littermate's name. A small whine escaped him. Bea's hand dropped to reassure the dog.

"That's right. Kane and Abel." She glanced over to the crucifix above the television. "Like from the Bible."

He nodded, momentarily unable to talk.

She reached out and touched his knee. "I know what you lost. Sandy told me about that, too. I'm so sorry."

Tucker swallowed, struggling not to let those dark memories overwhelm him.

Have to stay on point here.

"Th . . . thank you," he mumbled, then cleared his throat. "Listen, Ms. Conlon—"

"Please just call me Bea."

He nodded. "Bea, if there was anything Sandy might have left here, something that might point to what happened to her or what she was working on, I need to know."

Bea didn't hesitate. She simply stood up and said, "Wait here."

She disappeared up a set of stairs and returned a minute later. She held out a USB flash drive. It was stainless steel and about the size of Tucker's thumb—larger than most he'd seen. There was no label or markings of any kind.

"Sandy said if anything ever happened to her that I was to give it to someone I trusted." She handed it to Tucker. "My daughter loved you all. I could tell whenever she talked about you."

Tucker accepted the drive, momentarily speechless.

Bea continued. "Sandy also said to warn whoever I gave this to that her coworkers could be in danger, too."

Her coworkers? That had to be the other members of The Odisha Group.

"Even with that big brain of hers, Sandy always had a bigger heart," Bea said. "She'd step in front of a train to rescue a puppy. Whatever got her into trouble, I don't think she ever wanted to put her friends at risk."

Was that why she had been so secretive?

Tucker squeezed the drive in his palm, sensing its importance. "Thank you."

"I hope it helps," she said. "But promise me one thing, Tucker."

"Name it."

"If somebody did something to my daughter, you'll set it right."

Tucker nodded. "Count on it."

2:02 P.M.

I'm going to get lost.

By midafternoon, Tucker and Kane had said their good-byes to Bea, but only after she insisted on making him a lunch of fried bologna sandwiches. They were now headed down the mountains—but not the same way they came up this morning. Tucker had asked Bea about the route by which Sandy usually headed back to Huntsville. As he suspected, the locals knew a more scenic shortcut out of the Appalachians.

He was now driving along Skyline Road, where the forests were notably thicker, mostly pines, so densely packed he could barely see a few feet past the tree line. He shifted the Dodge into a lower gear as the road crested a ridge and swept down the next hill in a series of steep switchbacks.

As he rounded a bend, a sharp-edged ravine appeared on his left. There was no guardrail or fence. Beyond the shoulder he caught glimpses of bright green water far below. He passed a red warning sign that read:

HIGHLY ALKALINE WATER
NO TRESPASSING BY ORDER OF
THE UNITED STATES ENVIRONMENTAL
PROTECTION AGENCY

Tucker slowed down, studying the lake below.

Must be a flooded quarry.

Tucker felt a deep unease as the road circled the toxic body of water. According to Bea, Sandy had left the farmhouse well after sunset. At that time, Skyline Road would've been pitch-dark. He pictured another dark and lonely road, another drowned industrial area. He and Kane had been waylaid where it would have been easy to hide their bodies.

Could the enemy have chosen a similar spot to ambush Sandy?

Fearing the worst, he slowed the Dodge and pulled over to a wider section of the shoulder. He exited with his backpack—and as an extra precaution, from under a blanket he pulled out the MP-5 assault rifle he had confiscated two nights ago and slung it over his shoulder. With Kane at his side, he began walking along the road-side closest to the quarry's edge. He eventually found a section of disturbed gravel on the shoulder. Beyond this patch, the weeds had been flattened in a telltale double stripe, headed toward the quarry.

Tire tracks.

Tucker followed them to the ravine's edge. He got out his bin-oculars and scanned the half-mile-wide quarry. Far to his right, past a cow gate bearing another red warning sign, a service road cut down along the cliff face and ended at a shoreline of boulders and dun-colored gravel.

Tucker spent a full five minutes panning the lake's surface. Then, thirty feet from shore, he spotted the barest outline of something.

He zoomed in. It took another thirty seconds to recognize what he was seeing.

The hemmed end of a seat belt.

It floated like a lone strand of kelp.

Tucker's belly turned to ice.

He lowered his binoculars and marched over to the service road. The gate was no obstacle. He hopped over it, while Kane ducked under it. Together, they headed down the road toward the shoreline. The crisp scent of pine was soon overpowered by a metallic scent, a mix of salt and oil, with an underlying bitter tang.

Tucker stepped to the lapping bank of the lake and studied the floating seat belt offshore. He followed its length into the green murk and made out the glint of silver below, the same color as Sandy's Ford Taurus.

"Maybe it's just her car," he said, holding out hope.

He didn't relish what he had to do next.

He turned to Kane and waved a finger in the air. "PATROL. FULL ALERT."

Tucker did not want any surprises. He dropped his bag and half hid his rifle under it. He then stripped naked. With his LED flashlight clamped between his teeth, he waded into the water until it reached his chest, then swam over to the hovering seat belt.

He girded himself for a breath.

Just do it.

He took a deep breath and did a pike dive into the colder depths. The alkaline water stung his eyes, a burning reminder to hurry. He reached the bumper with a single kick. He clicked on the flashlight and shone it along the bumper until he found the license plate.

It was a match for Sandy's.

No question now.

He kicked again and twisted around to the driver's-side door. A few feet farther along the sedan's side, the side panel was crushed inward. He ran his fingers over the damage and discovered a trio of crisp sharp-edged punctures through the steel.

Bullet holes.

Tucker pointed his flashlight through the open driver's-side window and searched the passenger compartment, both front and back.

Empty.

Out of air, Tucker rose to the surface. He treaded water, breathing deeply, blinking the sting from his eyes. So where was she? Had they kidnapped her and dumped the car to cover their tracks? Something told Tucker this wasn't the case.

There was only one place he hadn't searched.

Tucker glanced to shore, where Kane remained on watch. Tucker lifted a thumb's-up toward the dog. Kane barked once, his way of sounding the ALL CLEAR.

With apparently no danger setting off his dog's keener senses, Tucker dove down again. He kicked to the driver's door and eased his torso through the open window. He clawed around until he found the trunk release. He pushed the button, hoping the battery had enough juice to pop the trunk. Otherwise, he would have to climb all the way back up to the Dodge and fetch a tire iron.

Instead, a muffled clunk sounded behind him.

He shoved out and pulled himself over to the rear of the car. He paused at the bumper, set his jaw, then rounded the corner to the trunk.

Tucker stifled the rush of air from his mouth.

A body stirred inside the compartment. The face was pasty, the skin rippled and already sloughing off in places. The mouth was half open, and milky-white eyes gazed back at him. As he stared in horror, limp arms floated upward as though trying to reach to him for help.

It was Sandy Conlon.

Tucker hovered there, his mind blank before mentally shifting gears. He'd seen plenty of dead bodies. This was no different.

But it was . . . it goddamn was.

Despite the disfigurement of her face, Tucker could clearly see a bullet wound in her left temple. He also saw that her belly had been slashed open. It was most likely done postmortem, to puncture organs that would have filled with gas during the decomposition process. If the trunk had sprung open later, her body still wouldn't have floated to the surface, but rather it would have remained in place until the alkaline water had dissolved her flesh.

He cursed silently.

Those sons of bitches...

Tucker writhed back to the surface, fury burning the chill from his body.

If he hadn't stumbled upon the car, the trunk might have been Sandy Conlon's eternal tomb. Whoever had done this, they tossed people away like garbage. He remembered Jane telling him about the deaths and disappearances of her other colleagues. The same fate likely awaited Jane and her son, Nathan, if he didn't do something.

That's not going to happen.

He swam toward shore.

It ends here.

SECOND

ATTACK RUN

12

Chased by ghosts and fleeing from a faceless enemy, Tucker made good time reaching the rendezvous point. After clearing the Appalachian Mountains and leaving Sandy's body where it lay for now, Tucker had called Jane, telling her they needed to meet face-to-face.

She had suggested a highway diner in Kingsport, Tennessee, three hundred miles north of where Sandy was murdered. Tucker could guess why Jane had chosen Kingsport. The city lay halfway between Huntsville and Washington. Jane was most likely hiding with her son in DC, a place she knew well.

Today he hoped to find out precisely *why* she was hiding—and from *whom*.

It was time he got more answers.

Fueled by that desire, he reached Kingsport in under four hours and pulled into the parking lot of a fifties-themed diner off Highway 81. A bell jingled when he entered. It sounded gratingly loud— but at least it matched the decor. The booths were stitched in red vinyl fabric, the tables topped by black-and-white-checkered Formica with chrome trim. He gave the hostess his usual service-dog pitch to cover Kane's presence, then crossed to where Jane was seated in a rear booth.

This late in the evening, the diner was only half full. The clink of forks on plates and the soft babble of conversation filled the space.

Good.

He joined Jane. She had placed Nathan in a booster seat beside her. The kid was currently staring at his own reflection in a spoon.

Jane stood and embraced Tucker. "It's good to see you," she whispered in his ear, then she pulled back and studied his face. "You're hurt."

He shrugged. "Just part of the job description."

She fingered the abrasions along his jawline, then lightly grabbed his chin and turned his head. She frowned at the bandage on his ear. "If I asked, I don't suppose you're going to tell me the truth?"

"Actually, I would. Later, though."

"Hmm." Jane dropped to one knee and greeted Kane with equal affection. "You're supposed to be keeping him out of trouble."

"I'm doing my best."

She grinned. "I was talking to Kane."

She waved the shepherd into the booth. Kane settled between Tucker and Nathan.

The boy pointed. "Bog!"

"*Dog*, honey," Jane corrected softly.

"Bog, honey!"

Jane shook her head with exasperation. "Close enough."

Nathan shoved a finger toward Tucker. "Hi!"

"Hi, yourself."

Apparently it wasn't a good enough answer for the boy. Nathan returned his attention to Kane, wagging a hand in front of the dog's nose and getting his fingers licked. From the giggling, that was clearly much more entertaining.

As Tucker watched the boy and dog play, he found himself imagining what it would have been like if Nathan had been his son, Jane his wife, about that road not taken. He stifled that train of thought. Now was not the time to start second-guessing his choices—both those in the past and what was to come.

Tucker realized he had been staring too long and returned his attention to Jane. "Sorry."

"No apology necessary. I spend a lot of my day staring at him. It's one of the superpowers children possess."

The waitress arrived to take their order: a cheeseburger and fries for Tucker, a Cobb salad for Jane, and a fruit cup for Nathan. The waitress placed a coloring sheet before the boy, who set to work with a handful of crayons.

Kane sighed as he was abandoned for the boy's new project.

As they waited for their food, Jane leaned back and looked like she was bracing herself. "I could tell on the phone that you didn't have good news. So spill it."

Tucker glanced at Nathan, cocking an eyebrow

Jane understood. "It's okay. When he's coloring, he's oblivious."

Tucker cleared his throat and decided to be blunt. "Sandy's dead."

Jane stared a moment, frozen in place, then closed her eyes. Her lips tightened, trembling, and a couple of tears squeezed out her lids and ran down her face. She gave a shake of her head and dabbed at her eyes with a napkin. "Of course, that's what I was afraid of . . . but to hear it. I didn't want to give up hope."

Tucker hated to take that from her. "I'm sorry."

"Tell me what happened."

Tucker told her about his discovery at the quarry. He left nothing out.

"Do you think she went quickly?" Jane asked.

Tucker swallowed, remembering the bullet wound on her temple. "I hope so."

"Have you told her mother?"

"I . . . couldn't."

She reached over and patted his hand. "I'll do it tomorrow. Once I'm somewhere safe. I'll explain everything and ask her to keep quiet for now."

"Good." Tucker studied his hands. "But, Jane, it's time to lay all our cards on the table. I'm going to tell you everything I know, then you're going to do the same. Agreed?"

She nodded.

After glancing around to be sure none of their fellow diners were within earshot, Tucker started talking, recounting the firefight at Sandy's house, the discovery of her storage locker, his meeting with Frank Ballenger, and the ambush at the swamp.

"And you're sure it was a drone that attacked you?" she said.

"And probably Sandy, too."

Jane took a deep breath. "And we know Sandy wasn't the first to go missing or to die suddenly. The only connection is that we were all part of Project 623, a program under the auspices of the Defense Intelligence Agency."

"What were you working on?"

"Mathematics, computer programming, cryptology, statistics. No one was ever given the big picture, the endgame. We only had knowledge of the piece of the puzzle assigned to us. But, Tuck, I know we were operating in the black—*far* into the black. So much so that I'm not a hundred percent certain we were even working for the DIA."

"Where was this all happening?"

"In a nondescript building in Silver Spring, Maryland. They had heavy security and strictly controlled access, including conducting regular pat downs and searches. Even our computers' firewalls had firewalls."

"How long did Project 623 run?"

"We were disbanded eight months after we started."

"And at the end, you never learned the ultimate goal of this project?"

Jane shook her head.

"What about the name? Project 623. Does that mean anything?"

"It does. What do you know about Alan Turing?"

Tucker stirred. "I saw that name written on Sandy's whiteboard in her locker. He's that British mathematician who broke the German military code."

"The Enigma code. But that accomplishment barely scratches the surface of Alan Turing's true genius. His work laid the groundwork for the modern computer. Arguably, every piece of computing tech you see today exists because of him. At Bletchley Park, where he worked outside of London, he invented the first electromechanical machine, a rudimentary computer. It was used to break the Nazi code. With this knowledge, Allied forces were able to predict German troop movements, feed the Nazis false information, and reroute supply convoys around hidden U-boats. Breaking Enigma shortened the war and saved hundreds of thousands of lives."

Tucker nodded. He had read as much when he had performed a Google search on the few clues written on Sandy's boards. "And as I understand it, Turing was arrested by the Brits a few years later."

Jane nodded. "It was discovered he was gay, and he was convicted of gross indecency. He was given the choice of prison or chemical castration. He chose the latter. His security clearance was revoked, and he was ostracized. Two years later he killed himself."

"Unbelievable," Tucker muttered. "But what does that have to do with the name of the project—623?"

"Alan Turing was born on June 23."

Working from a hunch, Tucker mentioned something that Frank had dug up. "After Project 623 shut down, Sandy joined a new classified group at Redstone. It sounds a lot like that setup in Silver Spring. Closed campus, all locked up tight, etcetera. It's called The Odisha Group. Does that name mean anything?"

Jane began to shake her head—then stopped. "No wait." She pulled out an iPad and typed for a few minutes. "I was right. Turing's father worked for the Indian Civil Service. He was stationed in Odisha when Turing was born."

"So another program with a connection to Alan Turing." Tucker stared hard at Jane. "It seems too much of a coincidence. I think whoever closed down Project 623 reopened something similar over at Redstone."

"But why move it there?"

"More important, why start killing members of 623 so long after the first project shut down? And why did they spare Sandy until now?"

Jane thought for a long moment. "My guess," she said softly. "Sandy was the brightest of us by far. Maybe instead of starting from scratch after Project 623, they needed Sandy to keep the momentum going. She got the offer from Redstone only one month after 623 closed up shop. But if she was their rainmaker, why kill her?"

Tucker clenched a fist. "Whatever the answer, I'm going to keep going until I find it."

Jane reached across the table and gave his fist a squeeze. "I know you will."

"This all must tie to Alan Turing's work, but how?"

Jane shrugged. "Though everyone at 623 was kept in the dark about the project's end goal, it didn't stop us from speculating."

"Explain."

"There have always been rumors that Turing was working on a secret project, both during the war and after."

"What project?"

"First, you have to understand that at the outset of his career, Turing recognized the limits of computers. He hypothesized a supercomputing device, one that would blast through those barriers. He named it the Oracle and believed that building randomness into a computer was the key to creating it. He even proposed putting radium into one of his computers, hoping that its unpredictable radioactive decay would trigger that chaotic randomness he sought. Of course that was never done, and most believe that Turing never went any further in trying to create the Oracle."

"But you're thinking that might not be the case."

She just lifted her eyebrows.

"Why?" he asked.

She leaned closer. "One day, just a few weeks before Project 623 was shut down, we were all called into a room and shown a series of blown-up photographs. They were photos of equations and algorithms taken from what looked to be an old lab journal or notebook. They were rudimentary but groundbreaking."

"What were they related to?"

"An innovative way to analyze vast amounts of data, specifically what's called *big data*."

Tucker shook his head, confused.

Jane sighed. "On any given day, the Internet produces over three quintillion bytes of data. A quintillion is one followed by *eighteen* zeros."

"That's certainly *big*."

"And it's growing larger every year."

"What kind of data are you talking about?"

"You name it. Business trends, disease tracking, worldwide crime statistics, traffic conditions, meteorology. Collecting all that data is the easy part. The hard part is what to do with all the noise. How do you collate it, analyze it, share it, visualize it?"

"Has anyone ever tried?"

"They're doing it all the time. Take the Los Angeles Police Department. They started a pilot program using big data for what they called *proactive policing*. They achieved a twenty-six percent decrease in burglaries. But even their methods were crude, just scratching the surface of what could be possible. At Project 623, we were assigned to explore those handwritten algorithms to learn how to better extract information and exploit the results."

"To what end?"

"I think we were trying to create the ultimate electronic espionage system, a version of Turing's Oracle. Those equations we were shown were designed to penetrate *any* encoded data. No information would be safe, not in the private sector, not in any government. We're talking about a living, self-adjusting code breaker."

Tucker felt queasy. "It would be the beginning of a whole new kind of warfare. No bullets and bayonets. Just exploited data."

"Exactly. Nothing would be private any longer. Which is also why that advanced drone that hunted you has me worried."

"Why's that?"

"One of the biggest trends in big data is RSD—remote sensing devices. It's a euphemism for drones. While there's a staggering amount of data coming from the Internet, it's only a fraction of what's truly out there. There are also radio waves, microwaves, landline communications, and so on. The goal of RSD is to build something that can *actively* go out and gather data. Something small, unobtrusive, and smart."

Like a drone capable of learning.

"And you're thinking Sandy's group might have been working on something like that?" Tucker asked.

"Redstone is home to NASA's Marshall Space Flight Center and other commands involving high-altitude, long-range avionics. If an outfit wanted to experiment with the next generation of smart drones, that would be a good place to start."

"Do you really think Sandy would have participated in such a program?"

"I can't imagine she knew at first. Even back in Silver Spring, she grew nervous about the direction things were taking. We all did, really, but it was worse for her. Maybe that's why she set up that storage locker, so she could try to either stop or expose those involved."

And she was killed for it.

Jane reached over and grabbed his wrist. "Someone has to get into that place at Redstone. That's the only way we're going to learn anything more."

"I'm already working on that. But I'm going to need you to work on this." He reached into a pocket and slipped out the USB flash drive that Bea had given him. "Sandy hid this at her mother's house. I tried to open it, but it's deeply encrypted. She also warned her mother that her coworkers at Odisha could be in danger."

Jane looked ill. "You're thinking those assassins might start cleaning house like they did with the Project 623 team?"

"Maybe they've already begun."

Starting with Sandy.

Jane frowned at the drive, as if he had just placed a rattlesnake atop the table. Still, she covered it with her palm and drew it to her lap. "I'll see what I can do."

"And be careful," Tucker warned.

"Only if you do the same."

Then we're both screwed.

11:48 P.M. CDT
Huntsville, Alabama

As Tucker pulled into the parking lot of his motel, he found Frank Ballenger sitting on the wooden bench outside his door.

"You keep long hours," Frank said as he stood and greeted them. He gave Kane a pat on his chest, but even the shepherd was too tired to respond with more than a weak wag of his tail.

Tucker appreciated his dog's response. After driving to Kingsport and back, his butt and legs were asleep. "What's with the bags? Planning on moving in?"

Frank glanced down to the three black waterproof cases and shrugged. "I'm taking some vacation leave."

"Come again?"

"For a month. I've got the time."

"So instead of going to Hawaii, you're moving in with me and Kane?" Tucker stuck his key into the door's lock, pushed it open, and let Frank pass. "What's in the cases?"

"The tools of my trade. Hopefully everything a man needs to deal with killer drones."

"Frank, you said you were going to be my behind-the-scenes guy. This sounds more like frontline soldier stuff."

Frank shrugged. "I know we were never best friends, Tucker, but we were still brothers in green. Somebody on my post is trying to kill you guys. You came to me for help, so I'm going to help."

Tucker wasn't sure Frank truly understood what was at stake. Maybe it was high time he did. "Listen, Frank, I found Sandy Conlon."

"What?"

"They shot her, ripped open her belly, and stuffed her in the trunk of her car. That's who we're dealing with, Frank. If they catch us, we can expect the same or worse."

Tucker's words had the desired effect. Frank walked to the room's desk, pulled out the chair, and sat down. He stared silently at the wall for a while. Finally he looked at Tucker. "Okay, yeah, I'll admit that scares the bejesus out of me. But it doesn't change anything. I'm either in all the way or not at all."

Tucker sighed, not willing to bend on the matter.

"You're going to need my expertise," Frank pressed. "Especially when you hear what I learned while you were driving all over the country."

Tucker frowned. "What?"

Frank lifted one of his cases to his lap, undid the snaps, and opened it. He removed a familiar length of white polymer. It was the guidance pod Tucker had recovered from the swamp.

"I did some tinkering with this. The avionics on this are beyond micro, and the circuit boards are made out of some kind of rare-earth element. I don't know which one, yet. Something exotic for sure. And see these raised veins along the surface? They're acid ducts."

"Acid?"

"Meant to dissolve this cartridge after firing, to leave nothing salvageable. But it plainly malfunctioned, suggesting this is a prototype—like the drone itself—something still in the beta stage of testing."

Great . . . and I got to be a guinea pig.

"But they're close to perfecting this," Frank warned. "Very close."

Tucker took this in. "What about that license plate number I gave you, the one on the Suburban outside Sandy's house?"

Frank returned the sabot to the case. "You guessed right on that matter. The plate number belongs to one of eight Suburbans assigned to the same area where The Odisha Group is segregated. But here's the kicker. The vehicles are all registered to a single private defense contractor."

"Who?"

"Tangent Aerospace."

Finally, a name . . .

"They're based out of Las Cruces, New Mexico," Frank explained. "Unfortunately, I don't know much more. At least not yet. It's on my to-do list."

"Were you able to assign any names to that particular Suburban?"

"No. It's a fleet vehicle. Any Tangent worker could've used it. But I did get a list of all Tangent workers at Redstone."

"Let me see it."

Frank turned, pulled out a hard-copy printout from his case, and handed it over.

Tucker scanned it, looking for one name—and found it.

"*Webster . . .* Karl Webster," he read off the sheet. "Head of Tangent security."

"You know that guy?"

Tucker slowly nodded, picturing the sprawled body inside the abandoned factory.

Gotcha.

He handed the printout back to Frank. "Time to go to work."

"What're we going to do?"

"Go hunting. Find out what's really happening over at Redstone."

Frank stood up. "If we're going hunting, I'm going to need a gun."

"Are you still sure you want to go all in?"

Frank chewed his lip, plainly giving it full consideration, then said, "I'm all in."

Tucker clapped him on the shoulder. "Then welcome aboard. I hope you don't live to regret it."

"If it's okay with you, I'm just going to hope to continue *living.* Period."

Tucker nodded.

Now there's a smart man . . .

13

As midnight approached, Tucker lay sprawled on his stomach in the tall grass of a riverbank. Crickets sang all around him, while frogs chirruped from the Tennessee River behind him. Kane—already outfitted in his K9 Storm tactical gear—crouched at Tucker's hip.

Together, they waited, watched, and listened.

Fifty yards ahead, a perimeter fence stretched through the woods. It enclosed the remote corner of Redstone Arsenal that segregated The Odisha Group from the main military base. It was like a private gulag, tucked deep into a pine forest. Beyond the fence, a well-lit dirt road circled the small forest that hid the cabins of The Odisha Group. It was patrolled regularly by Tangent security teams in black Suburbans. As they passed, the drivers would pan a spotlight along the razor-wire-topped fencerow.

A burst suddenly came through the headset of Tucker's portable radio. *"Hey, Jimmy, you there?"*

It was Frank, laying extra thick on his Alabama drawl.

Tucker tried his best to imitate him, hoping the radio's static helped mask his feeble attempt. "You got me. What's the word?"

"Spotted some eye shine, so Buster's on the run. Any luck your way?"

Tucker gritted his teeth, not knowing who might be listening to their radio chatter. As a precaution, he and Frank had worked out a code, taking advantage of Frank's knowledge of raccoon hunting along the Tennessee River. It was a favorite pastime for local hunters, who had developed their own unique jargon for the sport.

Frank's radioed message meant that he had spotted another of the Suburbans making its way along the perimeter road. Frank was hidden farther to the south, dressed in camouflaged hunting gear like Tucker.

Tucker checked his watch.

The night patrols seemed to be running every fourteen minutes.

Tucker radioed back to Frank to close on his position. "If Buster loses the trail, let's try our luck farther down the bank."

"*Will do, Jimmy.*"

To establish their cover, he and Frank had left Huntsville at dawn yesterday and driven down to Lacey's Spring, a small town on the far side of the Tennessee River from the military post. They rented a hunting cabin near the river, where they'd spent the better part of the last forty-eight hours lounging in lawn chairs, fishing in the river, or drinking beer from Piggly Wiggly cozies.

Just a couple of good 'ol boys blowing off steam.

Tucker imagined their presence at the cabin did not go unnoticed by base personnel, so as a precaution, he kept Kane inside, out of sight, fearing the shepherd might be recognized. To mask his own features, he wore a slouch hat and mirrored sunglasses whenever he went out during the day.

Only after he felt confident that their presence here wasn't considered a threat did he set their mission in motion. Two hours ago, they had floated across the dark river on rubber rafts, choosing a spot out of the direct sight lines of the base. From there, they had split up to spy on the encampment.

With the patrol schedule now worked out, it was time to move forward.

Frank arrived ten minutes later. Together, they waited for the next Suburban to grind along the dirt road, flashing its spotlight along the fencerow. Once the vehicle moved on, Tucker led Frank and Kane through the woods to the fence. He searched to make sure the boundary wasn't electrified or alarmed.

As he did so, Frank breathed heavily behind him, glancing all around.

"Take it easy, Frank," Tucker whispered.

"I'm fine." His words came out like a croak.

Tucker glanced back. He had spent the past two days refreshing Frank's memory on the finer points of soldiering, but being told something wasn't the same as experiencing it firsthand.

"I'm okay," Frank assured him, and hiked his pack higher on his shoulder. "I got this."

Tucker removed a pair of wire cutters and started snipping a hole in the fence.

"Lights!" Frank hissed, grabbing his shoulder and knocking the wire cutters out of his grip.

Tucker followed Frank's pointed arm toward a glow rising from the south, coming up the road. To cover up their work, Tucker took out some camouflaged duct tape and resealed the few snips in the hurricane fencing. He then backed to the woods and waved everyone flat.

As the headlights drew closer, Tucker realized he had left the pair of wire cutters at the base of the fence. He couldn't risk them being spotted.

He rolled to Kane and pointed to the cutters. "RETRIEVE."

The dog immediately bolted from hiding and ran low through the grass. Kane snatched the wire cutters in his teeth, then smoothly circled back, flowing like a dark shadow. The shepherd dropped next to him just as the Suburban's tires hissed along the dirt road, drawing even with their hiding place.

The vehicle's spotlight swept across the fence, casting slivers of light through the grass around Tucker, Kane, and Frank.

"Not a muscle," Tucker whispered.

The Suburban passed them and kept going, its spotlight skimming ahead.

Tucker caught a glimpse of the vehicle's interior through the window. In the glow of the dashboard, he spotted only the driver. He waited until the Suburban rounded the next bend, its taillights fading into the trees.

Frank let out a long breath. "Did we trigger something by cutting the fence? I've read about these new tamper-resistant fiber-optic wires that the military is building into their fences."

"If that were true here, there would've been more than the one patrol closing in on us. No, the explanation is something much simpler. We assumed the patrols ran like clockwork, but the smarter play from a security standpoint is to vary the schedule every now and again. To catch any trespassers off guard."

"Like they almost did us."

"All the better to keep us on our toes."

"If you say so."

Tucker returned to working on the fence, snipping faster, opening a two-foot-square hole through the barrier. Once done, he signaled Kane to take point, sending the shepherd through first. Kane dashed across the border and vanished into the woods on the far side of the perimeter road.

Frank followed next, then Tucker, who hung back to replace the section of cut fence and resecure it with camouflage duct tape. As Tucker joined Frank at the forest's edge, Frank searched around.

"Where's Kane?"

Tucker pointed a few yards down the road. "Right there."

Kane lay flat in the grass; his mottled coat and similarly camouflaged tactical vest had rendered him a loglike lump on the ground.

Frank shook his head. "Kane's done this a few times, huh?"

"More than a few times."

"Makes me feel like a wet-behind-the-ears newbie." Frank stared into the dark forest. "How far to the compound, do you think?"

"A quarter mile. But we're not going that way."

"What do you mean?"

Tucker checked his watch, dropped his pack, and began preparing.

"Why walk when we can drive?"

11:58 P.M.

"I got lights in the distance," Frank said. "Heading this way."

Right on time.

Tucker was down on one knee next to Kane, double-checking all of the shepherd's gear, making sure the earpiece was situated correctly, then aligning the vest's collar-mounted night-vision camera. Kane already sensed it was time to go to work, staring at Tucker with eager brown eyes.

But first there was one final bit of preparation.

Tucker brought his face close to Kane's. "Who's my buddy?"

A warm tongue lapped his nose.

"That's right. You are." Tucker pointed into the depths of

the woods and gave a string of orders. "COVERT SCOUT. STOP AT STRUCTURE. STAY IN COVER. GO."

Kane twisted to the side and sailed away, his paws gliding silently over the pine needles as he vanished through the trees.

Frank sidled next to Tucker. "He understood all that?"

"And more."

Tucker had sent Kane in advance, ordering the shepherd to follow through the woods to the Odisha camp, to be Tucker's eyes and ears on the ground. In the meantime, he had his own duty.

He crossed back to the edge of the road as the headlights of the next patrol rounded the far curve and trundled toward them. Its spotlight swept along the fencerow, oblivious to the two men hidden in the woods nearby.

Tucker waited for it to pass, then rolled low and swung a thick branch against the rear quarter panel of the SUV. The dull bang reverberated up his arm as he fell behind the Suburban's bumper and crouched out of sight. The brake lights flared as the vehicle ground to a halt.

Spying under the vehicle, Tucker watched the driver's door pop open. A pair of booted feet dropped into the dirt, accompanied by a soft curse. The driver must have believed he struck something. There were deer throughout these woods.

As the man circled toward the rear, Tucker lifted his new weapon. A day earlier he had purchased the unique handgun. It was a Piexon JPX Jet Protector, engineered to fire wads of concentrated pepper spray. Tucker had been at the receiving end of this weapon in the past. The impact had felled him to his knees and left him incapacitated for twenty minutes.

Tucker waited until the guard reached the back wheel—then rolled out of hiding with his weapon raised. He laid the red dot of the handgun's aiming laser on the bridge of the startled man's nose and pulled the trigger. With no more than a sharp hiss, the charge shot from the barrel. A maroon splotch burst across the guard's eyes. The man dropped to his knees and started gasping.

Yeah, I feel for ya . . .

Tucker strode forward, raised the JPX, and cracked the butt into the man's head. His body slumped forward and went still.

Frank joined Tucker, his eyes huge. Together, they dragged the guard into the woods, where they quickly flexi-cuffed him around the trunk of a tree and gagged him. Tucker frisked the man, passing Frank a portable radio and a Beretta M9. He also found a wallet and checked the driver's license: Charles Walker.

Frank stared down at the man. "I think that's my first felony assault."

"Well, there's a first time for everything."

Tucker led him back to the idling Suburban. He retrieved the guard's cap, which had fallen off his head when they had dragged his body into the woods. He dusted it off and tucked it atop Frank's head.

"You're driving," Tucker said.

"Where to?"

"To pay our neighbors a visit."

Frank shoved the Beretta into his belt. "Sounds like the only hospitable thing to do."

12:12 A.M.

Seated in the passenger seat of the Suburban as Frank drove, Tucker studied the video feed from Kane's night-vision camera. Frank continued along the perimeter road, going slowly, aiming for the cutout that led toward the Odisha compound in the middle of the woods.

But before reaching the camp, Tucker wanted to know what he would find there.

On the screen of his phone, he watched as Kane skimmed through the forest. The trees quickly began to thin and a clearing appeared ahead, brightly lit with sodium lamps mounted on poles.

Kane slowed his pace and slunk lower to the ground.

Good boy.

The shepherd finally stopped, sliding under the low branches of a pine.

Tucker squinted at a set of six log cabins and a pair of cinder-block buildings. The grouping was split by a gravel road. In the middle was a turnaround with a white flagpole rising from the center. At this late hour, the cabin windows were dark. He spotted no movement.

Was anyone still there? Are we already too late?

That was a fear that had plagued Tucker over these past three days after speaking to Sandy's mother. The plan tonight had been to rescue the group and hightail it out of here. But what if the others were already dead, murdered like Sandy and the rest of Project 623?

There's only one way to find out.

"We're coming to the turnoff that leads to the camp," Frank warned. "What do you want me to do? Head in or circle around another time?"

Tucker had no idea what the usual routine was for changing patrol shifts. If they came in too early, it could raise a red flag.

He studied the feed from Kane. To the left of the cabins was a small gravel parking lot with a fleet of Suburbans parked there. "Frank, how many vehicles did you say Tangent had registered at Redstone?"

"Eight."

"There are six parked at the camp right now. Which means, beside us there's another Suburban out there somewhere." That made him uneasy, as did the remaining vehicle in the parking lot. "There's also a huge moving van sitting over there."

"Sounds like someone's planning on bugging out of here."

Tucker remembered Jane's story, how Project 623 had been shut down, only to resurrect under a new name, at a new location.

And the old team members were eliminated.

"We've got to go in," Tucker said. "We can't risk waiting."

Frank's fingers tightened on the wheel, the knuckles going white, but he nodded. "I agree. So what's the plan?"

"Grab the Odisha people, pile them in the back of the Suburban, and drive out the main gate."

Frank glanced to him, his face tight with disbelief. "You really think it's gonna be that easy."

Tucker shrugged. "A guy can always hope."

14

So far so good.

Tucker sat shotgun beside Frank as the Suburban approached the cluster of cabins. He kept low in his seat, trying to stay out of sight while keeping his JPX handgun ready in case he had to silently take someone out.

"Where now?" Frank asked, braking as they neared the gravel parking lot.

"We should get as close to the cabins as possible." Tucker pointed. "There's a turnaround in the middle. Stop in front of the second cabin on the right."

"Is that where Kane wants us to go?"

"Seems to be. And I've learned never to second-guess him."

While en route here, Tucker had ordered his four-legged partner to make a quick and furtive circle of the encampment, allowing Tucker to get a lay of the land. The four cabins to the left bore placards with winged logos on their doors.

Tangent Aerospace, the private defense contractor running this outfit. The placards likely marked the security detail's cabins. The last of that row had the words MESS HALL etched into the lintel.

On the opposite side of the turnaround squatted two massive cinder-block bunkers with a small airstrip behind them. A riot of antennas and communication dishes sprouted from their roofs. Glowing keypads secured all the entrances, which included a set of small hangar doors. Those buildings had to house The Odisha Group's work spaces. At this late hour, all the buildings' windows were dark. Apparently no one was burning the midnight oil.

All the better for us.

From Kane's canvass of the encampment, Tucker had noted signs hanging on the remaining two cabins' doors: MEN'S BUNKROOM and WOMEN'S BUNKROOM.

He was counting on the civilian personnel being housed there.

Frank edged the Suburban to a stop in front of the women's bunk. It was where Sandy likely lived while working here, and where Tucker had the best chance of finding Nora Frakes, the woman Sandy had brought home to meet her mother.

Frank's door was closest to the steps leading up to the cabin. As Frank exited, Tucker grabbed the MP-5 assault rifle and followed out on the driver's side, scrabbling low, and dropped to a knee next to the Suburban. He hoped any casual look this way would only reveal Frank's head, his face and features shaded under the guard's cap.

Holding his breath, Tucker braced for some alarm, some shout of challenge.

But the night remained quiet.

"Check the cabin window," Tucker ordered, plagued by a persistent worry.

Were any members of The Odisha Group still here?

As Frank climbed the three steps to the porch, Tucker tapped a button on his radio, sending out a signal for Kane to return. From the video feed, Tucker knew the shepherd was in the woods behind the cabins on this side. He trusted his four-legged partner had already caught his scent, likely even heard his words a moment ago.

On the cabin porch, Frank peeked through the nearest window. He then hurried back to Tucker and whispered, "Can't see much. They have blackout curtains. From around an edge, I spotted bunks but couldn't tell if anyone's in them."

A shift of shadows past Frank's shoulder coalesced into the familiar shape of Kane. The shepherd angled around the corner of the cabin and joined them in the shelter of the Suburban's bulk. Tucker scratched the dog's ruff, welcoming his friend back.

Kane remained stiff, still on guard, likely sensing Tucker's tension.

Tucker pointed under the porch steps and clenched a fist. "HIDE. SILENT GUARD."

Kane nudged Tucker's knee, as if acknowledging the command—then darted beneath the porch, becoming a shadow again.

"What now?" Frank asked.

"Let's see if anyone's home."

Tucker headed up the steps, letting Frank fall behind him. At the door, he tested the knob. Locked. With an aggravated sigh—*couldn't anything be easy?*—Tucker tapped lightly on the door, cringing at even this soft noise.

He held his breath, then heard someone curse inside, followed by the thump of feet landing on wood. Pine boards creaked as someone approached.

"Who is it?" a woman called out groggily.

Tucker thought quickly. "Bed check," he mumbled gruffly, trusting that security might periodically do a head count.

Another curse, then a dead bolt released.

As the door started to open, Tucker pushed inside, almost bowling the woman over. Frank came in at Tucker's heels. Tucker quickly closed the door behind him.

The woman—a thirty-something brunette wearing pajama bottoms and a red football jersey for the Alabama Crimson Tide—backed away, clutching a hand to her throat, eyeing them up and down.

"Who . . . who're you?"

"We're friends of Sandy Conlon."

To avoid setting the woman into full panic at two strangers in her dark cabin, Tucker found the light switch and flipped it on. Fluorescent ceiling lights flickered to life, revealing a pair of bunk beds to each side of the room, along with a couple of desks piled high with books and journals. At the rear, a short hallway likely led to bathrooms.

"Sandy?" the brunette asked, her face scrunching with confusion. "What're you talking about?"

A second occupant stirred from a lower bunk—the rest of the

beds were stripped and empty. A blanket was tossed back with irritation. "Diane, what the bloody hell is going on?"

The brunette backed until she was beside the other woman.
"Nora, these . . . these guys say they're friends of Sandy's."

This news drew a deep frown from the woman in the bed.

Nora . . . that had to be Nora Frakes.

Nora reached to a bedside table and pulled on a pair of eyeglasses,
fashionably bulky in a nerdy way. She was black, in her late twenties,
with her dark hair cut into a short crop. She had a slight British lilt
to her voice.

"Who are you?" she asked, rolling out of the bed to her bare feet,
wearing a set of thin pajamas.

"My name is Tucker Wayne. I served briefly with Sandy at Fort
Benning." He pointed a thumb at Frank. "This is Master Sergeant
Ballenger. He works at Redstone, at the main base."

Frank nodded his head. "Ladies."

Nora studied them, still on guard. "Why're you dressed in camouflage? What's going on?"

Knowing time was running short, Tucker needed to cut to the
heart of the matter. "Sandy's dead."

He watched emotions flicker across Nora's features. For a fraction of a second, a crooked smile flashed, as if she believed this was
all some joke, then a crinkle of concern formed between her brows,
ending with her eyes wide and fearful.

Diane was not so subtle, her voice sharpening with disdain.
"You're lying. She quit. Joined another outfit. Up in North Carolina."

"That's what your bosses want you to believe. But they shot
her in the head. Dumped her body in the trunk of her Ford Taurus.
You're all in danger."

Nora stepped forward, thrusting her chest out in challenge.
"Prove it."

"You know Bea Conlon."

"Sandy's mom?"

"I know you've been to her house a few times." Tucker pulled his
satellite phone from his pocket and extended it toward Nora. "Her
number's already keyed up. She's waiting by her phone."

Tucker had prepared for this moment yesterday, knowing he
would need to gain this group's trust quickly—and decided Nora

might be the best way to achieve that. Jane had already informed Sandy's mother of her daughter's death and readied Bea for this midnight call.

Tucker punched the number and held out his phone.

With a frown, Nora grabbed it and put it to her ear. She waited a breath as the secure line connected. "Bea? It's Nora."

As Nora listened, her breathing grew heavier, her shoulders slumping. When she finally spoke, it was a feeble whisper. "I . . . I'm so sorry, Bea." She glanced over to Tucker, her eyes glassy with tears. "And he can be trusted?"

After a moment, Nora closed her eyes and nodded. "We'll talk soon."

She turned slightly away and handed back the phone to Tucker. Her shoulders began to shake. Tucker stepped forward and scooped an arm around the young woman. She stiffened, but then leaned into him.

"Oh my God . . ." Nora whispered.

Diane remained still, her eyes on all of them at once. "He was telling the truth?"

"Sandy's dead, Di."

Diane backed away, as though trying to put distance between herself and this news. "What're we going to do?"

"We're all going to get out of here," Tucker said, and pointed to the door.

As if summoned by his gesture, there was a firm knock, followed by a curt voice. "Ladies, you okay in there?"

Everyone froze.

Tucker had kept his voice low, but that didn't mean he hadn't been heard.

Nora moved first, motioning them to the far side of the door. "Everything's fine, Karl!"

Tucker came close to tripping on his way over, remembering the printout of Tangent employees that Frank had supplied him.

That had to be Karl Webster out there . . . the head of Tangent security.

Tucker flattened against the wall next to the door. With his phone still in his hand, he pulled up Kane's camera feed. The angle of view was low, from under the porch, indicating the shepherd had remained in hiding, still keeping silent as ordered. Tucker didn't see anyone else positioned around the Suburban.

So most likely it was only Webster out there.

Closer at hand, the doorknob began to turn, but Nora was already there. She grabbed the handle and pulled the door partly open, shielding the view inside with her body.

"I saw your light was on," Webster said.

"Wasn't feeling good," Nora explained. "That chili tonight didn't exactly sit well, if you get my drift."

Webster chuckled—which made Tucker want to rip the door open and shoot the man in the head, remembering Sandy's watery pale face rising from the trunk of her sunken car.

"You need anything?" he asked. "Pepto or something?"

"I think the worst is over. I should be able to gut it out." She put a hand on her belly. "At least I hope so."

"Well, you shouldn't have to deal with Johnson's cooking much longer. We should be wrapping things up over the next week."

Tucker pictured the moving van parked in the lot.

"You'll all be back in your own beds before you know it," Webster said.

More likely they'd be dead.

A board creaked out on the porch. "Have you seen Chuck?" Webster asked. "That's his Suburban sitting in the turnaround. I thought maybe he was in here."

"Uh, no," Nora answered. "I did hear him pull up, and the door slam. Have you checked the kitchen? You know how he likes his midnight snacks." She clutched her belly again and groaned. "Or maybe you'll have better luck at the latrine . . . or out in the woods."

"You may be right. He did have a double helping of Johnson's chili."

"God help him."

Webster chuckled again and retreated. "Hope you feel better, Nora."

"Thanks."

She closed the door and leaned against it for a moment.

Tucker pressed an index finger to his lips. He checked Kane's feed and waited until Webster left. He nodded approvingly toward Nora. Her inventive subterfuge probably bought them a few extra

minutes, but that was about it, especially if the Suburban continued
to sit out there unattended.

"We need to haul ass out of here." Tucker stepped forward and
flipped off the light switch. "How many others of you are there?"

"Only Stan and Takashi," Nora said. "Over in the other bunkroom. There were another two men, but Karl said they both left for
home last week."

Nora looked truly sick, as if imagining those men suffering the
same fate as Sandy.

"Let's hope they made it." Tucker turned to Frank. "You need to
buy us more time."

"How?"

"You gotta play Chuck a little longer. Take that Suburban for
another loop around the camp and come back. Make it look like you
just came in for a pit stop and took off again." Tucker glanced at his
watch, remembering the schedule of the patrols. "That should buy us
fourteen minutes to get everyone together and moving."

Frank's eyes were wide in the dark.

"Are you up for this?"

Frank nodded and tugged his cap more firmly on his head. "Back
to work for Chuck."

Tucker clapped Frank on the shoulder, then stepped to the window and peeked out to make sure it was all clear. He didn't see any
sign of Webster, but there was a light in the mess hall cabin.

Tucker pointed to the door. "Go!"

Frank dashed out, hopped the steps, and slid behind the wheel.
The engine coughed and started. Tires spat gravel as the Suburban
sped away, circling the turnaround.

As the Suburban neared the mess hall cabin, a figure appeared
on the porch.

Webster.

Tucker cringed, but Frank flashed his high beams at the man, as
if signaling everything was fine. The bright light also momentarily
blinded Webster, who shielded his eyes against the glare. As the Suburban passed his position, Webster lifted an arm, acknowledging the
driver.

Frank continued on, making the turn onto the exit road and vanishing.

Tucker let out a long breath and turned back to the room.

"We need to get those other two men over here right now."

Nora glanced to Diane, who had retreated to her bunk. The two women exchanged a silent look.

Diane nodded and stood. "I'll get them."

The brunette turned her back on the door and marched toward the bathrooms.

Tucker cast a questioning look toward Nora, who unabashedly stripped out of her pajamas and into jeans and a black T-shirt.

"Fraternizing is frowned upon here," Nora explained, "but human nature won't be denied. Bonds form, especially when you're isolated like this. So we've taken to keeping our bunkrooms' back windows unlocked. It's only a couple steps between our two cabins. All the easier to manage that late-night booty call."

Tucker imagined Tangent knew about these dalliances and had learned to turn a blind eye to them. He hoped that blindness continued tonight.

As he waited, Tucker used the time to get some answers. "They're closing up shop here. Do you know where they're going? A timeline? Anything?"

"No, but I did hear Karl mention something called White City, but I'm guessing that's code of some sort. Either way, it'll take them awhile to move all of the drones and support equipment."

"You said *drones* . . . as in plural."

"They're all variants of a single smart design, engineered to learn on their own. We call them DEWDs: dedicated electronic warfare drones. Some of these UAVs are engineered for data collection and surveillance, others for jamming transmissions, and then there are the hunter/killers. Nasty work, those."

No kidding.

"The two men who left early were the ones who oversaw that particular project—but none of us would have had any success with our projects without Sandy."

"Why's that?"

"She was the one who made the breakthrough on the design for the central operating system, the brain for all the DEWDs. She was so damned smart. She called her breakthrough the Grand Unifying Theory of cryptology. Or GUT-C."

Tucker got the pun: *gutsy.* He pictured all that Sandy had done in secret. Not only was she smart, she was also damned gutsy herself.

Nora sank to her bed and donned a pair of red sneakers, trying to hide the pain of her loss.

"Do you have any idea about the plan for these next-generation drones?" Tucker asked.

Nora shook her head. "We only build them. It doesn't pay to be too curious around here."

"What about your work area at the bunkers? If we could collect proof—"

Nora frowned and stood. "Only Karl and his men have the access codes for the building's keypads. They keep us on a tight leash here. While we can pretty much come and go during our down time, they continue to track our cell phones, probably monitor our calls, too. But in our line of work, that's pretty much par for the course."

A scuff of heel on wood drew Tucker's attention to the back hall.

Diane led in two young men. One was short and blond, the other Asian. Each man carried a duffel and wore a wary expression.

"Stan and Takashi," Diane said. The woman still looked dazed, at the edge of panic.

"This is for real?" Takashi asked, his eyes narrow and suspicious.

Stan took Diane's hand. "Nora, you're sure about Sandy?"

Nora nodded to both questions, folding her arms across her chest.

Tucker waved them all toward the door. "Time to—"

A sharp cry erupted outside, followed by a heavy thump.

Kane sinks his teeth deeper into the ankle of his opponent. The taste of blood washes over his tongue. From under the porch, he tugs the booted leg farther through the open stairs, trapping the man.

A moment ago, he had watched the same man come up the steps and knock on the door. He had come casually the first time with no weapon in hand—this time, he came running low, a rifle pressed at his shoulder.

Kane caught the familiar tang of threat off the man's body, heard the pant of his breath.

All Kane's senses jangled with danger.

His last order still glowed behind his eyes.

HIDE. SILENT GUARD.

But the menace here outshone that command.

So he acted on his own and grabbed the man by the ankle when he tried to glide up the steps. He yanked him off his feet, sending his body crashing to the boards with a sharp cry.

A growl rises now unbidden, as blood washes through his senses, narrowing his sight. The other brings his rifle around and points it between the steps at Kane.

Kane only sinks his fangs in deeper, crushing to bone, refusing to let go.

The two lock gazes on each other.

Kane holds fast—knowing he could die, but trusting another more.

He hears the door open atop the porch, followed by a muffled pop.

A splotch of darkness strikes his opponent in the face. A bitter scent wafts back to Kane, burning his nose and eyes. The other writhes in agony, gasping and spitting.

He hears a new command from above. The words cut through his blood haze, calming his heart with their familiarity, soothing him.

RELEASE.

After getting Kane to let go, Tucker dashed down the steps with his JPX handgun in his fist. Webster—even blinded and in blistering pain from the wad of pepper spray—tried to raise his rifle and fire toward the porch.

Tucker jumped down and kicked the steel-shod tip of his boot into the man's temple—and his body went slack.

Out for the second time, you bastard . . .

Kane rushed from under the porch to his side. As Tucker crouched, he holstered his JPX and slung his MP-5 to his shoulder. He had to resist shooting Webster where he lay, but Tucker wasn't that cold-blooded. Besides, he couldn't risk making more noise, especially not knowing if anyone heard Webster's cry a moment ago.

Tucker listened and heard the telltale crunch of tires on gravel. Lights flared from the direction of the parking lot. Frank was on his way back here.

Webster must have grown suspicious, possibly tried to reach Chuck on the radio. When that failed, he must have figured something was wrong. But had he alerted any other—?

Gunfire erupted from the parking lot.

Crap.

Muzzle flashes flared from one of the cabins across the turnaround. Rounds pelted the porch and gravel around him, but the shots went wide, indicating the shooter feared hitting his boss on the ground.

Taking advantage of that caution, Tucker motioned to Kane, and they flew low up the steps and through the door. Nora slammed it behind them.

"Stay down!" Tucker warned as bullets shattered the windows to either side of the door, ripping through the blackout curtains. He pointed to the back hall. "Head that way!"

Tucker followed them, herding them away from the fusillade of bullets. He imagined the shooter was strafing the front of the cabin to keep his quarry pinned down.

Tucker pulled out his radio and called up Frank. "Forget the turnaround! Meet us behind the cabin!"

He got no response, but he imagined Frank was busy. Gunfire still echoed from the parking lot. He joined the others in the bathroom, which consisted of toilet stalls and a long washbasin along one wall and curtained shower cubicles on the other side. Directly ahead was a window, still open from earlier.

Crouched low, Takashi looked wild-eyed, wincing with the crack of each gunshot. Stan cradled Diane under him.

Nora joined Tucker, eyeing Kane. "What now?"

The answer came from outside with a squeal of brakes.

"Follow me," Tucker said. "Out the window. Don't think, just get into the backseat of the Suburban."

Tucker hurried to the window and spotted the waiting vehicle. The SUV's engine smoked, and the windows were spider-webbed with cracks and bullet holes. Frank had come in dark, with the headlights off.

Good.

Frank shouted from inside. "Come on! Hurry!"

Tucker lifted Kane and got the shepherd through the window,

then dropped next to the dog. He kept down on one knee with his rifle up, scanning right and left. He waved for the others to exit the cabin.

As they piled through, Tucker pointed to the SUV. "Move it!"

Nora charged forward first and yanked the backseat door open for the others, staying low. As she did so, a scatter of shots pelted the vehicle's rear bumper and shattered the door window above her head.

Goddamn it . . .

Tucker spun with his rifle raised and spotted a figure hugging the corner of the cabin. He waited for the gunman to pop back out and placed three rounds into his chest. Shouts rose from all around as Webster's men closed in on their position.

A cry rose closer at hand, coming from Diane. "Stan!"

Tucker looked over and watched the blond man fall from where he must have been sheltering his girlfriend. He toppled sideways, shot from behind, blood pouring from his shoulder.

Diane clawed at his jacket, trying to get him up. Then Takashi was there and manhandled his friend into the backseat with Diane's help. Nora climbed in after them.

Tucker slammed the door behind her and hollered to Frank. "Go! Circle around the outside of the cabins."

Frank looked wide-eyed at him. "What're you—?"

"Kane and I'll meet you on the other side. Look for us behind the mess hall."

Frank looked like he was going to argue, but Tucker smacked his palm on the door. "Go!"

Frank twisted back around, gunned the engine, and set off.

Tucker ran alongside the Suburban—but only to the rear of the next cabin, the men's bunkroom. He crouched there next to Kane as the SUV continued onward.

He lifted Kane's muzzle. If their group was to have any chance of escaping, he and Kane had to create as much confusion as possible. He stared into the dark brown eyes of his partner, hating to ask this of Kane, but knowing it was necessary.

Tucker pointed between the two bunk cabins. "HIDE AND SEEK. SHADOW ATTACK BRAVO."

The order would send the shepherd sprinting through the camp, attacking any targets briefly, and hightailing it away. The tactic was designed to spread panic—and few things did that better than seventy pounds of snarling muscle sliding through and haunting the shadows.

But it was also dangerous.

Tucker hesitated, but only for a moment. "Go."

Kane took off and swept around the corner.

Tucker rose, grabbed the sill of the open window, and pulled himself into the men's bathroom. He dashed low to the front of the cabin. He unlatched the door and eased it open a few inches, then dropped to his stomach, his assault rifle pointed out the door.

The grumble of the SUV passing along the back of the encampment to the left had drawn the attention of Webster's men.

A cadre of six guards came running down the center of the turnaround.

Tucker aimed his rifle and strafed into the group, dropping two men and sending the others scattering to either side. In the confusion, he shoved to his feet, shouldered open the door, and dashed out. He sprinted directly across for the mess hall.

Rounds spat at him, but the potshots went wide.

Off to his right, Kane let out a series of growling barks, accompanied by a man screaming. Two gunshots came from that same direction. Tucker's throat clamped with fear for his partner—but he kept going.

As gunfire rings out, Kane stalks the shadows, slipping through them with ease. His senses stretch through the darkness. His ears note every shout, every crunch of boot, every hurried breath. His nose picks up the wafting trail of damp sweat, the whisper of gun smoke. He follows those trails, coming upon his prey from behind.

His teeth rip tendons . . .

His bulk slams bodies facedown into mud . . .

His claws rake flesh . . .

Then he is gone, back into the shadows, where he howls his fury and threat until it echoes everywhere.

Then he moves on.

. . . .

Praying Kane was still okay, Tucker reached the mess hall, vaulted the steps, and crashed through the door. He raced past rows of trestle tables and aimed for the set of swinging doors that led into the kitchen, figuring there must be an exit back there. He entered the kitchen, leading with his weapon, and saw a door directly ahead.

Perfect.

He hurried toward it—only to have it open before him.

The growl of the Suburban's engine rose from outside, coming closer.

A guard backed into the kitchen, plainly intent on ambushing the Suburban as it drew even with the mess hall.

With the gunman's attention focused outside, Tucker picked up a cast-iron frying pan from the stove, stalked up behind the man, and walloped him across the back of the head. Bone crunched, and the guard collapsed with a grunt of surprise.

Tucker snatched the man's rifle and slung it over his shoulder.

The more firepower, the better.

Tucker opened the back door to the kitchen and searched left and right as the Suburban trundled toward his position. He freed his phone and radioed Kane. "Break and return to Jeep."

Of course, the Suburban wasn't a Jeep, but the command directed Kane back to the vehicle, which the dog's sharp ears surely heard and could easily track.

As Frank slowed the SUV, Tucker waved for him to keep going. Tucker paced alongside the vehicle. Two more men tried to ambush them, but Tucker chased them off with a fierce barrage of gunfire.

He kept watch for Kane, then spotted a flow of shadows in the alleyway between two of the cabins, coming his way. It was Kane. Before the shepherd could reach him, a figure rolled low into view on the far side, leveling a rifle at the dog.

Tucker yelled. "Break left!"

Ever obedient, Kane dodged as the guard's weapon flashed. The shepherd yelped. Tucker resisted the impulse to look that way. Instead, he focused on the gunman and fired two rounds. The man toppled sideways.

Tucker dropped to a knee. Kane rushed up to him and shoved hard against his side, panting heavily.

The Suburban's front door popped open behind them.

Nora called out, "Come on!"

Tucker hauled Kane up in his arms, twisted around, and barreled into the passenger seat. "Go!" he yelled to Frank, letting go of Kane only long enough to slam the door shut.

Tucker hugged Kane tight.

Be okay, buddy . . .

15

As Frank stamped the accelerator, sending the Suburban surging forward, Tucker ran his hands over Kane's body. When he reached the shepherd's right hindquarter, Kane winced. Tucker felt a patch of hot blood matting the thick fur, but it seemed to be only seeping, likely just a graze.

"It's all right, buddy."

A warm tongue licked his face with a slight inquiring whine.

"Yeah, I'm okay, too."

Tucker settled Kane into the footwell and scooted around. Kane hadn't been the only one shot. Diane was in the backseat, shaking with sobs, cradling Stan's head in her lap. Nora crouched over the man, pressing a wad of cloth to his upper chest. Takashi had climbed into the rear compartment to make room, but he loomed over the two women, his face a mask of concern.

"Nora, how is he?" Tucker asked.

She glanced up to him. "A lotta blood. He's out cold. I found what looks like an exit wound by his collarbone."

Tucker kept his face stoic. The guards had been firing hollow points, rounds capable of shredding everything in their path. Even with medical attention, Stan would not likely make it.

Nora must have suspected the same. "I can't find a pulse and—"

The back window shattered behind her. Bullets peppered into the rear of the Suburban.

"Get down!" Tucker shouted.

By now, Frank had cleared the last cabin. He made a sharp turn, crashing through the low branches of a pine, and reached the exit road that cut through the forest surrounding the camp. With the way clear, he sped faster toward the encircling perimeter road.

Tucker watched for any pursuit, but so far, the path behind them remained dark. But he knew that wouldn't last for long.

"We're almost to the perimeter road," Frank warned. "Do we go right or left?"

It was a good question. *Right* was the shortest path to the main gates that connected the segregated camp to the larger military base. *Left* would circle them first through the wilder sections of the woods before swinging back to those same gates.

So neither was a great option. At the moment, Tucker had no way of knowing if Tangent had alerted Redstone's military police. There could already be a shoot-to-kill order on their heads spreading throughout the base.

Frank glanced over to him, waiting for an answer.

Tucker twisted around in his seat. "Can everyone swim?"

Nora frowned at him. "Yes, but why?"

Tucker faced Frank again. "Turn right. Go to where we cut through the fence. We'll try to make it to our boat and cross the river."

"We'll be sitting ducks on the open water," Frank warned.

"That's why we all better be able to swim."

Frank looked none too happy with this decision. Still, when he reached the perimeter road, he turned right. He barely slowed, sending the back end of the SUV fishtailing in the loose dirt.

Behind them, Tucker spotted headlights through the trees, racing up the road they had just left. After the initial confusion of the firefight, Tangent was in pursuit.

"We got company on our tail," Tucker warned.

"I saw 'em." Frank shoved hard on the accelerator, picking up speed.

Tucker faced the backseat again and lifted up the MP-5 that he had grabbed from the guard from the mess hall. "Does anyone know how to use this?"

"Me, I guess." Takashi lifted a hand. "Sometimes the guards let me target practice with them."

Good.

Tucker passed the weapon across to the young man in back.

"Shoot through that hole in the back window if any of the others get close," Tucker instructed him. "But stay low."

Takashi nodded, looking sick, but he rolled with his weapon into position.

Turning back around, Tucker reached up and hit the switch for the sunroof. As it opened, he balanced on the passenger seat and rose up through the sunroof. He positioned his rifle on the top of the Suburban and used the gun's optical sight to spy on the road behind them. As soon as the first of Tangent's Suburbans sped into view, Tucker fired a trio of bursts into the windshield, stitching across the glass. The SUV veered wildly and crashed into the security fence, but a fleet of four other vehicles skirted the wreck and continued their chase.

Tucker lost sight of them as the perimeter road curved away, but the pursuing headlights continued to glow through the trees. He estimated it was only another quarter mile to where he and Frank had cut through the fence.

He called down to Frank. "When we get to the spot, brake hard, unload everyone, and get them through the fence and to the boat."

"And you—?"

"I'm going to continue in the Suburban before those bastards see you, try to draw them off, then Kane and I'll abandon the SUV and set off on foot." *Hopefully we can lose ourselves in the woods long enough to cut through the fence at a new spot.* "But don't wait. We'll swim across the river and find you on the other side."

"Tucker!"

Frank's shout wasn't in disagreement. The Suburban braked hard, throwing Tucker against the front edge of the sunroof. He hauled around as Frank skidded their vehicle through the dirt. Around the next bend, a Suburban sat sideways across the road, its headlamps doused.

Earlier, Tucker could only account for *seven* of Tangent's Suburbans. Here must be the missing *eighth*. Likely the driver had been out of the camp and had only returned recently through the main gate, just in time to set up this blockade.

From his vantage in the sunroof, Tucker caught a glimpse of a familiar scar-faced figure crouched on the far side, a rifle balanced on the hood of the SUV.

It was the Frenchman from the ambush at the swamp.

With no time to aim, Tucker fired wildly at the parked Suburban. The Frenchman shot at the same time. Rounds shattered glass and pinged off metal all around.

"Ram him!" Tucker yelled before Frank came to a full stop.

Frank obeyed and hit the accelerator again. The Suburban's engine howled, and the vehicle shot forward, casting up a rooster tail of dirt behind the vehicle. Tucker dropped back into his seat, cradling Kane.

The SUV struck the other with an explosive crunch of metal. Twin airbags deployed, slamming Tucker's body. Frank let out a strangled cry, echoed by the others in the back. The airbags deflated within a fraction of a second, filling the interior with a flurry of talcum powder.

Coughing and waving at the air, Tucker popped up and noted that Frank had succeeded in striking the rear quarter panel of the other SUV. The impact had knocked the vehicle askew, far enough for them to pass—if they hurried.

"Go, go, go . . ." Tucker urged.

Frank understood and ground them past the wrecked Suburban. As they cleared its bulk, a dark figure dashed away and into the trees to the left. The Frenchman shot at them as he retreated, but Tucker lifted his rifle's barrel past Frank's nose and returned fire through the driver's-side window, chasing the man deeper into the forest.

But the Frenchman wasn't the only threat any longer. While the man hadn't stopped them, he had delayed them long enough for the other Tangent forces to close the distance behind them.

Bullets thudded into the Suburban's back end.

Takashi opened fire from the rear compartment. The young man's barrage drove off the lead vehicle, sending it veering to the side, where it slowed and momentarily blocked the others behind it.

Takashi lifted his head up and looked back, wearing a proud grin.

Tucker yelled, "Get d—"

Takashi's forehead exploded outward as a single gunshot rang out. Beyond the man's falling body, Tucker spotted a dark figure standing at the edge of the forest, a sniper rifle at his shoulder.

The Frenchman.

Frank continued around the curve of the perimeter road, and the gunman vanished out of sight behind them.

1:24 A.M.

Gasping in pain, Karl Webster stood before a mirror in the cabin bathroom. Through his swollen eyelids, he could barely make out his reflection. He looked like a goddamned raccoon, only with a blistered, red mask. His sinuses still stung not only from the capsicum in the pepper spray but from the hit of ammonia salts his men had used to wake him after pulling him to safety during the firefight.

By the time he had woken, the assailants had fled aboard one of his own Suburbans. Then a minute ago, Rafael Lyon radioed that he had arrived at the encampment's main gates, apparently already fully abreast of the situation. He claimed he was going to set up a blockade on the perimeter road, boasting that he would deal with this group once and for all.

Karl heard the blame in the man's words.

Furious, he dunked his face into the washbasin for the third time. It was full of a mixture of dish detergent, water, and milk. He blinked his eyes and rubbed his skin, letting the cooling center him.

As he straightened, one of his men stepped into the room. "We're ready, sir."

He nodded and limped around on his bandaged ankle.

Lyon didn't know whom he was dealing with—*certainly not with these assailants and definitely not with me.*

Karl Webster had an ace up his sleeve, a backup in case Lyon failed.

"Get those birds up in the air," he ordered his teammate. "It's time to end this."

1:26 A.M.

Twisted around in his seat, Tucker watched behind their SUV. He focused on the back road, doing his best to avoid staring at Takashi's crumpled body in the rear compartment. Tucker's breathing wheezed through his clenched teeth as he pictured that French assassin. Fury threatened to narrow his vision into a pinprick.

Then a warm tongue licked his wrist. At his knee, Kane must have sensed his anguish and distress, offering his support. In turn,

Tucker's fingers found the dog's scruff and dug deep, reassuring the shepherd.

They were all shell-shocked.

In the backseat, Diane sobbed, huddled into a ball. Nora lay over Stan's body. From the glassy-eyed stare of the blond man, he must have already bled out. Frank glanced over at Tucker. His pained expression was easy to read, full of guilt, desperate for what to do next.

The lights of the pursuing vehicles were gaining on them. His early plan to dump off the others and lead the enemy away was no longer an option. Instead, he pointed ahead and to the right, to where the forest beyond the security fence had thinned out.

"Make a hard right. Don't brake if you don't have to."

Frank nodded, understanding.

They needed to reach the river as soon as possible.

Frank eked out more speed, then yanked on the wheel. The Suburban bumped off the road and rammed into the fence. Their vehicle's three-ton bulk burst through chain link. Once clear, Frank juked the SUV left and right, doing his best to avoid trees, sideswiping a few trunks. Branches slapped and scraped their flanks.

Tucker left the navigating to Frank. He craned around and stared up at the road. Headlights reached the break in the fence and stopped back there.

Why aren't they coming after us?

Worried, Tucker turned around as the Suburban's nose bucked over the uneven terrain. He spotted moonlight glinting off water up ahead.

"Don't slow," Tucker warned. "Take us straight into the river."

"Bank's high. We're gonna catch some air."

He nodded and turned to Nora and Diane, their eyes shining fearfully back at him.

"The river's not too wide here. Maybe a hundred yards."

"Oh, God," groaned Diane.

"It'll be okay. Once we get to the other side, we'll be safe."

It was a lie, but a necessary one.

Hope helped you survive.

Diane balled a fist in Stan's shirt. Nora reached over and forced her to let go. "He's gone, Di. We'll have to leave his body. Stan wouldn't want you to die because of him."

She pulled Diane to her side, her eyes on Tucker, silently asking what to do.

"When we go in," Tucker instructed, "the interior will fill up quickly. Go out the windows. Try to stay together, but don't fight the current. Just get to the far bank and wait. If we get separated, we'll find you."

"I see something," Frank said, drawing all their attentions forward. The river loomed only thirty yards away. "Above the water to the left."

It took Tucker half a breath to spot a dark object hovering close to the shore.

"It's a Wasp," Nora said, her voice strangled. "A surveillance drone."

"Does it come with any firepower?" Tucker asked

"No." She scanned through the open sunroof. "It's meant to paint a target, then a Shrike is summoned to take it out."

Tucker pictured the fixed-wing drone that had hunted them through the swamps.

So that's what you call it.

"We may be okay for the moment," Nora continued. "Shrikes take longer to get airborne. Wasps are easier, meant to be sent in advance at a moment's notice. But if it paints us and tracks us . . ."

A Shrike will be on our asses before long.

Tucker now understood why the Tangent guards had hung back. With the river under watch, they could take their time sending men on foot, intending to catch their targets in this snare.

"What do we do?" Frank asked, starting to hit the brakes.

Tucker pointed forward. "Stick to the plan. Don't slow down."

As Frank pushed them faster, Tucker grabbed his rifle and popped back through the sunroof. Careful of low-hanging branches, he raised his assault rifle and wrapped the shoulder harness around his forearm to steady his aim.

Frank shouted up at him. "Hang on!"

The Suburban blasted out of the tree line, bounced over a bank of river rocks, and shot high over the water. Once clear of the forest,

Tucker fired at the drone as it hovered in the air, held aloft by four propellers. He strafed without stopping, emptying the entire magazine, knowing he would have only this one chance.

A handful of rounds struck true. The Wasp bobbled in the air—then tilted sideways and crashed into the river.

Now our turn . . .

The Suburban—front-heavy with the engine—nosed down. Tucker dropped back into the cabin, sheltering Kane under him. The vehicle struck hard. Water sprayed over the windshield and began flooding through the front windows.

Tucker shouted above the torrent, "Everybody out!"

Frank boosted to his knees on his seat and rolled through the driver's-side window. Tucker made sure Nora and Diane got out safely, then lifted Kane, pushing the shepherd through the flooding window on his side.

By the time Kane was clear, the water had risen to Tucker's nose. Past the windshield, the headlight beams glowed green in the swirling sediment. He took a deep breath and pushed off to follow the others—but then jerked to a stop.

His left foot was tangled on the seat belt. He yanked his leg. Nothing happened. A rush of panic filled his chest. The Suburban, now fully flooded, sank rapidly into the depths, plunging nose-first toward the bottom. The body of Takashi floated over and bumped against him, as if urging Tucker not to abandon him.

Tucker fought harder, twisting his foot and rotating his ankle. Finally, his leg came free. He kicked out the window and toward the watery moonlight. Seconds later, he broke into the night air.

Kane dog-paddled over to him, which plainly took effort. Already the current had hold of them. He looked downstream. There was nothing but swirling water under the glow of the moon. He spun around, looking, looking—

Twenty feet to his right he spotted a flailing arm. Frank's head surfaced next, sputtering and coughing.

Tucker called, "You okay?"

"Think so! Where're the girls?"

"Here!" Nora's voice called out of the darkness.

Tucker spotted her waving. The current had carried her farther, at least fifty yards downstream.

"I have Diane! She's hurt!"

Frank started swimming in that direction, but Tucker called him off. "I'm closer. Head for the far bank." He pushed Kane to follow the man, adding a firm command. "Swim to shore."

As the pair set off, Tucker kicked and paddled downstream. The current helped him reach Nora quickly. She had Diane under one arm, holding the woman's head above water. Blood dribbled from a scalp wound. The brunette looked dazed, but awake, more in shock than anything.

Tucker took Diane from her, and they headed together to shore. Nora's gaze kept sweeping the night sky. Tucker followed her example, knowing what she feared.

Had Tangent sent out more than one Wasp? Was a Shrike already in the air?

Tucker swam faster.

As he neared the bank, he spotted Frank and Kane running down the sandy shore toward their position. Frank helped haul Diane out of the water. The woman's limbs were weak and wobbly. Tucker saw a long gash in her jeans, flowing with fresh blood. She must have cut herself on a jagged piece of the wrecked Suburban during her escape.

"We need to get out of sight," Tucker said and urged everyone into the woods.

He knew this night's hunt wasn't over.

16

Once deep within the woods on the far side of the river from the military base, Tucker called them all to a halt. It was time to regroup versus running blind.

He helped Diane down to a log and briefly inspected the handkerchief he had hastily tied around her upper thigh. Blood seeped through the cloth. They needed to get her medical attention, and the closest town was the little hamlet of Lacey's Spring. Tangent would surely have eyes on that place.

Following Tucker's example, Kane sniffed at Diane's leg wound, then settled to his wet haunches with a huff, as if sensing their plight.

Though the night was warm, Nora shivered, soaked to the skin.

Frank pulled a fatherly arm around her and pulled her closer.

Nora leaned into him, but her eyes never left the skies. "They won't give up, you know," she muttered. "They're just regrouping. Probably lost us in the water."

Together they scanned the breaks in the canopy overhead. Tucker's ears remained tuned for any telltale buzz of a drone's engine. As encumbered as they were, with only the trees for cover, a Shrike would make short work of them.

But first it needs to find us.

So far he had spotted no other Wasps in the air, but Nora was right. He knew more of the surveillance drones would soon be sweeping through the woods, followed behind by a Shrike. Nora said The Odisha Group had built a dozen Wasps and a pair of Shrikes. They also had something called a Warhawk, a larger wedge-shaped drone outfitted with a 20 mm cannon loaded with depleted uranium rounds.

So there was no telling what might be sent after them.

"We need to get back to our cabin," Frank said. "Get to my cases."

"Why?" Tucker asked.

He knew Frank had spent the downtime inside the rental cabin working on equipment nestled in the cushioned interiors of his cases, which included the CUCS module for the Shrike hunting them in the swamp. They had left the remote control at the cabin, powered off, guessing whatever protective frequency it broadcasted was likely recalibrated after Tangent had found it missing. If they tried to use it now, it would likely only serve to announce their position.

"It's risky," Tucker warned. "It won't take them long to put two and two together and come searching that cabin."

"Then we'll have to move fast," Frank said. "I can grab what I need and we can pile into the Durango and get the hell out of Dodge."

"They'll have the roads watched."

"But maybe I can blind those eyes."

Nora turned to him. "How?"

"I analyzed the signaling technology inside one of your CUCS units and found it's a closed two-way system. The remote control not only communicates to the drone but *receives* feedback."

Nora nodded. "It's a looped system, so we can monitor the prototype's functionality from the ground."

"I built something that can track that signal, so we'll know if a drone is nearby broadcasting its unique signature."

"Is that possible?" Tucker asked.

Nora turned to Frank and peppered him with technical questions that were above Tucker's head. She finally turned back to him. "It's possible."

Frank nodded. "And I think I might be able to tweak the device into broadcasting a jamming frequency up to the drone."

In other words, blinding it.

"But I haven't had a chance to make those changes to it," Frank warned. "Or test it, of course."

"I can help him," Nora said. Her eyes were glassy in the dark, her mind already working on this puzzle.

"We'll have to be quick," Tucker warned.

He got Diane back on her legs, but he had to practically carry her now, her breath wheezing fearfully in his ear. She was close to passing out.

Luckily, the cabin was only a quarter mile away, and they reached it in good time, motivated and with a plan. Still, Tucker had them hold back, hidden in the woods behind the cabin. The place appeared dark, but he had Kane circle the log structure to make sure no one was around. Only then did he and Frank risk climbing into the place through a rear window.

As Tucker grabbed a first-aid kit, Frank secured his two hard-shell cases and tossed them through the window. They then both bailed out and retreated into the woods. The Dodge Durango was parked fifty yards away on the shoulder of a forest access road.

Before approaching the vehicle, Frank dropped to a knee at the edge of the forest and opened one of his cases. He pulled out the CUCS device recovered from the swamp and removed a metallic, spiral-shaped antenna, which he passed to Tucker. "Hold it up as high as you can."

Tucker did as instructed, while Frank grabbed a dangling wire from the antenna and plugged it into his device. He also hooked a small laptop to it, which he balanced on his knee.

Nora bent over his shoulder, watching him while he worked. As the CUCS unit powered up, a tiny screen bloomed with what appeared to be a frequency map. Frank fiddled with dials, getting the occasional suggestion from Nora.

"There!" Nora said, pointing at the screen. "See that ping in the M-band. That's from a Wasp hunting us."

Tucker searched the skies, holding aloft the antenna like some mystical sword against that invisible threat. "Has it found us?"

Nora shook her head. "If it spots a target, you'll see another spike in the X-band. That's the signal for a Shrike or Warhawk to begin an attack run. From there, those killer drones will continue the hunt until they eliminate their target or are called off. You'll know that by a strobing pulse in the S-band."

Definitely don't want that.

Tucker continued to crane his neck. "Can you trace the Wasp's signal? Find out where it's at?"

"Turn in a slow circle," Frank ordered as he opened the laptop.

Tucker obeyed, trying not to get tangled in the antenna wire, until Frank and Nora simultaneously ordered him to stop.

Nora bent closer to the laptop screen, her face illuminated by the glow from it. "See there? That pinpoint is the drone's FLIR—its forward-looking infrared radar. Because of power limitations, the range isn't particularly good."

"How good?" Tucker asked.

"Max of five hundred yards. It's probably sweeping along the river's edge, trying to acquire us. But it looks like it's being directed to come straight at us."

Probably tasked with surveilling the cabin.

"We've got maybe ninety seconds," Nora said. She snatched the keyboard from Frank's knee and began typing rapidly on it.

"What're you doing?" Frank asked.

"Trying something. You just get the CUCS ready to broadcast."

Tucker stared in the direction of the river. "Can you jam it before it gets here?"

"Better." She smiled, typing even more swiftly while staring down at the screen in Frank's hand. "I know the tracking software the Wasp employs. I wrote every line of that code. I think I can hack it on the fly and take control."

Tucker frowned down at her. "And do what with it?"

"You name it." She continued typing. "We can use it to call down a Shrike and rain hellfire upon those Tangent bastards and smoke them all."

Tucker liked the sound of Nora's plan, but he stared over at Diane, who sat slumped against a tree, her head hanging. Kane sat beside her, leaning against her, as though keeping watch on a wounded comrade. Tucker felt a swell of affection for the shepherd, knowing his big heart, that boundless well of compassion inside the dog.

He suddenly felt very tired, knowing he'd lost half of Nora's team. But it was replaced just as quickly by that steely determination ingrained in all Rangers.

"As tempting as that is," Tucker said, "we need to look down the road. To level the battlefield for the next fight."

Which I know will come.

He knew this was far from over, and they would need to gather every asset available.

"What did you have in mind?" asked Nora.

"Let's grab it." He faced Nora and Frank's stunned expressions. "Do you think you two could commandeer that Wasp and recruit it to our cause?"

Frank shifted on his knees. "We can sure as hell try. We got nothing to lose."

Nora nodded.

"Then do it."

The two set to work. Unfortunately, hacking into the Wasp proved to be more difficult than Nora had anticipated. With it closing in, her fingers flew over the keyboard. Frank offered suggestions, which were met with expletives or nods of agreement.

"It's almost on us," Frank warned.

Tucker searched through the canopy. At this point, there was no way they could outrun the drone, not in the SUV, certainly not on foot.

"It won't let me in," Nora moaned.

Frank put a hand on her trembling shoulder. "You can do this," he said, his voice firm and calm. "Just focus. Put everything out of your mind."

She took in a deep, shuddering breath and bent closer to the screen as code flew across it.

Frank suddenly pointed. "Stop! What about that?" He read a line of code aloud. "*Transmit autonomous run upon acquisition . . .*"

"Maybe," Nora said. "I don't—"

A low whine echoed through the forest, silencing her.

They were out of time.

"Screw it," Frank said and reached over and punched the return key.

They all held their breath—then the wall of code broke into two blinking lines:

CANCEL ALL TRANSMISSIONS
TRANSFER CONTROL TO CUCS 12958

"CUCS 12958?" Tucker asked. "Is that us?"

Frank grinned triumphantly. "Damned straight."

Nora returned to typing. "Lemme see what I can do from here."

Moments later, Nora brought the Wasp over their heads and into a holding pattern above the access road. The drone was X shaped, a yard wide, and painted a matte black. It hovered six feet off the ground, humming with the soft whine of its four propellers, one at the tip of each crossbar.

"I'm sending a signal to the Tangent ground monitoring station," Nora explained. "Telling them that the Wasp has incurred a propulsion malfunction. Making it look like it plummeted into the river."

So it'll be considered lost.

Smart.

Tucker watched as she expertly lowered the Wasp to the road, making a soundless landing. They all stared toward the idling drone.

"What now?" Frank asked.

Tucker stalked toward it. "We make those bastards pay."

7:17 A.M.

By the time the sun was up, everything looked brighter—if not better. Tucker was headed east along Highway 20, having just cleared Tuscaloosa. He had stopped to refuel their SUV at a large truck stop and let Kane take a bathroom break. He left Frank to fill up the Durango, while he got an update from Jane on his satellite phone.

"She may lose her leg," Jane said, reporting on Diane's condition. "But at least, for now, her—"

An eighteen-wheeler sitting beside the diesel pumps started its engine, drowning her words out. He stepped farther away, pressing his phone to his ear. "Say again."

"I said, at least her cover seems to be holding."

He sighed.

So good news and bad news.

Hours ago after leaving Lacey's Spring, Tucker had made contact with Jane. He had everyone—and the acquired Wasp—loaded into the Durango. The original plan had been to take the evacuated members of The Odisha Group to Atlanta, where Jane had mobilized a team she trusted to take them off the grid. But with Diane in grave condition, they had shifted operations to Birmingham. Jane constructed a cover story for Diane, which included a fake Virginia license and the tale of an abusive boyfriend to help explain her injury.

"When will the doctors know more?" he asked.

"Within the next twenty-four hours. If they don't get the sepsis under control, they're going to take her leg."

"How's she holding up?"

"According to my guy out there—who's posing as her concerned brother—she's scared, but she knows to keep playing along." Jane's voice grew softer with concern. "How about you? How're you doing?"

"As well as can be expected."

He glanced over as Frank hooked the gas nozzle to the pump. In the backseat, Nora crouched over a laptop. He and Frank had tried to get the woman to stay behind in Birmingham, but she had refused. She warned them that they still needed her help, especially if they wanted to put the Wasp to use. Unfortunately, Frank couldn't disagree with her.

Still, Tucker suspected Nora was driven less by a need to be useful than a desire to exact revenge upon those who had killed her friends, especially Sandy. As he drove through the night, he saw her tears as she looked out at the passing scenery, unable to sleep. With the adrenaline worn off, the weight of her loss must have finally struck her. He understood this reaction all too well. In the heat of a firefight, as friends were lost or wounded all around you, you kept moving. It was only later, in the dark of night, that you could measure those losses and try to make sense, to mourn, to find a way to live with your grief and guilt.

"Where are you headed now?" Jane asked, drawing his attention back.

"Las Cruces, New Mexico."

It was their only lead, one that came again courtesy of Nora. She had told them that Tangent was closing up shop at Redstone, moving operations to advance the next stage of this operation.

But what was it? What required such secrecy that it left a swath of dead bodies in its wake?

"We know Tangent Aerospace is headquartered out of Las Cruces," Tucker explained. "That alone makes it worth checking out, but Nora also mentioned a name she had overheard regarding the new operation. A place called White City. I think it might be code for the army's White Sands Missile Range."

"Just outside Las Cruces," Jane mumbled. "Makes sense."

"Hopefully we'll find out more once we're there."

"Just watch your back."

"If I don't, I know someone who will." He glanced down at Kane, who noted his attention and wagged his tail. Kane had a bandage taped over the bullet graze across his hindquarter, but the dog looked ready to go.

After saying his good-byes, Tucker hung up and walked back to the Durango with Kane. Frank was washing the windshield with a little too much diligence, overly focused on such a simple task.

"What's wrong?" Tucker asked.

Frank glanced over at him, giving him an incredulous look. "What's wrong? You have to ask?"

"I do. You've barely spoken since we left Birmingham."

Frank stepped over, tossed the squeegee into a blue detergent bucket, and sighed heavily. He combed his fingers through his hair and lowered his voice after a glance at Nora. "We were supposed to be rescuing those kids, but we got half of them killed."

Tucker had been expecting this conversation. "And they'd all be dead if we did nothing," he countered. "At least Nora and Diane have a chance now."

"But if we'd been more careful, thought things through more . . ."

Tucker recognized this familiar lament, having heard it all too often, both from other soldiers and from his own lips. "Frank, combat sucks. Terrible stuff happens. Even the best soldiers make mistakes, and sometimes they get people killed. You can let it cripple you, or you can learn from it and move on."

Frank looked down at his toes. "I . . . don't know if I can do that."

Tucker decided it was time for some tough love. "Then this is where we need to part company."

Frank jerked his head up. "What?"

"You heard me. If you can't pull it together, you're a liability. More likely to make a mistake. You could get us all killed."

"I wouldn't—"

"Not intentionally, but your head is in a bad place. I need you completely *here*—or gone altogether. I'm going to take Kane for a walk. You've got ten minutes to decide."

He left Frank and took Kane over to a grassy area. He hated to be so stern with the man, but sometimes it was better to rip off a bandage and let a wound air out. Kane used the time to sniff out a few precise spots and lift his leg. After the allotted time, Tucker led the dog back.

He found Frank already in the front passenger seat. He opened the back door so Kane could jump in next to Nora.

"We all set?" he asked.

Nora mumbled some acknowledgment, Kane wagged his tail, and Frank stared for a long breath and nodded.

Tucker climbed behind the wheel. "Then let's hit the road."

10:22 A.M. EDT
Smith Island, Maryland

"So you lost them?" Pruitt Kellerman repeated.

He stood at his desk, his back to the view of Chesapeake Bay and the Washington skyline. He leaned with his fists on the desk's polished surface and brought his face closer to his computer monitor's built-in camera.

On the screen, the faces of Karl Webster and Rafael Lyon stared back at him. Neither man answered. Behind their shoulders, he could make out Tangent's ground monitoring station, consisting of banks of computer workstations, all lit by dim halogen lighting.

"Have I got that right?" Pruitt asked.

Webster answered, his eyelids swollen and pinched. "Sir, they're all most likely dead."

"It's the *most likely* part that worries me."

"The vehicle they tried to escape in is sitting at the bottom of the Tennessee River. We didn't find anyone inside, but the current is fierce. Any bodies could be halfway to Kentucky by now."

Lyon cut in. "We're monitoring police scanners in the cities along the river for reports of drowning victims."

"What else have you learned?"

Webster answered. "We now know they were staying at a cabin

across the river. The manager remembered the dog. We've got descriptions of both men, but no credit cards. They paid in cash."

By now Lyon's brow had folded into deep angry ridges. He was not a soldier who tolerated mistakes, especially his own. "We did pick up two incoming calls to Sabatello's phone."

Webster shifted uncomfortably in his seat at the mention of Jane Sabatello; a flicker of guilt flashed across the man's features, likely from being reminded of another of his failures, of how he had let the woman slip through his net and escape.

"We know the caller is using a satellite phone," Lyon continued. "A nonstandard model with enhancements."

"Enhancements?"

"Encryption, proxies, that sort of thing. Definitely reeks of black ops."

"Do you think this guy is someone from our own government?" Pruitt asked. "Or an outside player?"

"Too soon to say. Another call or two and we should be able to get an ID."

Pruitt straightened, stretching a kink out of his back, refusing to let this setback unnerve him. "Assuming one or more of the Odisha people escaped, what damage could they do?"

"None," Webster said a bit too quickly. "No individual had the complete picture of the project, I'm sure of it."

"What about stage two? Were any of them aware of *where* you were moving operations this week?"

Webster slowly shook his head. "I don't see how. My men were under strict orders not to talk."

Pruitt frowned.

Hardly an ironclad guarantee.

He knew from personal experience that there were always leaks.

"Do we delay for now?" Webster asked. "Wait to make certain we're clean before proceeding?"

Pruitt tucked his chin, calculating odds and evaluating risks. If he jumped at every shadow, he would not be where he was today. One did not rise high by ducking low. One had to be bold.

"No," he decided, "we stick to our timetable."

Lyon's lips tightened into a thin grin of satisfaction. "Yes, sir."

When it came to bloodshed, the man was always eager.

"However," Pruitt cautioned, "when you both get to White City, put up some extra coverage."

While I might be bold, I'm not stupid.

"If that man and his dog escaped and end up at our door, let's make sure they're properly welcomed."

THIRD

WHITE CITY

17

Tucker entered the hotel room to find Frank and Nora bent over their spoils from the raid on Redstone. The Wasp rested on the carpet. The drone's inner workings were exposed, with equipment and tools strewn all around it.

"We've named him Rex," Frank announced with a grin.

"Rex?"

Frank motioned to Kane, who followed at Tucker's heels, sniffing at the two bags of Chinese takeout in his hands. "You have Kane. We have Rex."

Nora simply rolled her eyes and leaned over the open braincase of the drone with a tiny screwdriver in hand. "It wasn't a unanimous decision."

Tucker crossed and placed the food on a small dining table next to a kitchenette.

Late last night, they had reached Las Cruces after changing rental cars twice while en route across the country. Once here, he picked a hotel on the outskirts of the city. It was a golf course resort made up of casita-style rooms about a half mile from Mesilla Valley Bosque State Park. Their two-bedroom unit had polished cement floors, a small kiva fireplace, and best of all, a deep soaking tub in the bathroom. He came close to sleeping away the entire night in the damned thing.

At the crack of dawn, after a short breakfast of huevos rancheros and oatmeal, Frank and Nora had set about examining the Wasp in more depth. Tucker had watched them remove the top canopy and get to work, but as their language grew technical, full of jargon that could not possibly be English, he took Kane out for a tour through the neighboring state park. Its three hundred acres bordered the Rio Grande. With the park mostly empty, they spent the morning exploring trails through scrublands, meadows, and riverside woods.

But now it was time to get back to work.

"Besides naming it, what else have you learned?"

"Rex is beyond awesome," Frank said, sounding like a kid on Christmas morning. "Everything is self-contained inside its skull. Battery, guidance system, radar, even a ten-terabyte solid-state hard drive."

He pointed to the skull, the drone's spherical central housing. It was twice the size of a basketball, supported by a trio of spider-leglike landing struts. The drone had two wings that crossed at its midline, forming a large X, with four teardrop-shaped protrusions at the ends that housed rotatable, variably pitched propellers. The whole thing weighed a scant twenty pounds.

Frank waved a hand over its small bulk. "The exterior is made of carbon fiber."

"One that's micro-honeycombed to trap light," Nora added. "A type of stealth coating."

Frank nodded. "It's a beast."

"But can you tame it?" Tucker asked.

Frank grinned. "Between my own moderate genius and Nora's knowledge, I'm sure of it."

Good.

Tucker began unloading the boxes of Chinese food and opening them. "What about the Wasp's original purpose? Are there any clues about what we might be facing ahead?"

Nora sat back on her heels and nodded. "I believe it's the next-gen soldier for a new type of warfare."

"What warfare is that?"

"The rise of *information* warfare."

Tucker frowned. "What are you talking about? Like hacking?"

"It's a lot more sinister and far more dangerous than that. It's a combination of brute-force electronic warfare, cyber attacks, and psychological operations."

Frank nodded. "You need to listen to Nora."

"Go on," Tucker urged. "Explain."

"Everything nowadays is connected, intertwined, overlapped," Nora began. "It's a wobbly digital house of cards. It wouldn't take much to topple it, to create chaos. And this is not unknown to the powers that be. Nations, including the U.S., are investing billions to establish military commands for this new type of warfare, to learn how to topple a foreign country's house of cards, while beefing up one's own."

Frank nodded. "Unfortunately, both Russia and China are already ahead of us."

"I don't understand. What exactly do these attacks look like?"

"Like I said," Nora continued, "it's basically three pronged. *Electronic warfare* is intended to mess with transmissions, like jamming weapons guidance systems or interfering with air traffic control. *Cyber attacks* involve not only stealing data but disrupting a nation's entire infrastructure—its power plants, water and gas utilities, railway systems, and on and on. The last, *psychological operations*, or psy-ops, is the most fucked up. Its goal is to degrade a populace's morale by spreading misinformation through both social media and news outlets, intending to inspire fear and spread panic."

Frank sighed. "It's this very threat that my role at Redstone—as a cryptologic network warfare specialist—was established to combat. It's becoming a whole new battlefield out there."

Tucker eyed the Wasp with more worry. "And this is its soldier?"

Nora nodded. "Equipped with Sandy's decryption algorithm, one capable of decoding anything and everything and learning from it, Rex is more than merely a surveillance drone. It can secretly eavesdrop and record any airwave transmission. Even its landing struts are data collectors. Land this baby on any broadband, DSL cable, or phone line, and it'll suck data like a vampire."

"What about offensive capabilities?"

"Nothing in the traditional sense," Frank said. "But Rex comes equipped with directed-burst transmitters. Get him close enough— say, a half mile—and he can scramble any circuits, including some hardened military stuff."

"So let me get this straight," Tucker said. "This flying electronic warrior can collect data and intelligence on an enemy and leave behind a path of destruction in its wake."

Both Frank and Nora nodded.

"Then how do *we* put it to use?"

Frank glanced to Nora, his expression turning sly. "We may have a big surprise for Tangent."

2:22 P.M.

From across the street, Tucker studied the headquarters of Tangent Aerospace. It rose forty stories, forming a towering glass wedge which loomed over Las Cruces. Its surface blazed in the afternoon sunlight.

Tucker sat on a roadside bench heavily shadowed by mesquite trees. He wore a ball cap and dark sunglasses to hide his features as he studied the main gates of Tangent's forty-acre campus. Past the high wrought-iron fence, the corporation's grounds had been landscaped with meandering creeks, English gardens, and gurgling fountains, an oasis of green set amid the desert landscaping of the city's business district.

He watched a handful of Tangent personnel eating a late lunch, seated under umbrellas on a wide garden patio. Some chatted and laughed; others were bent with their heads together in deep conversation. He wondered if any of them knew of all the bloodshed these past days. Fury stoked inside him at their nonchalant attitude. Whether culpable or not, they were cogs in this machine.

Still, he forced that anger back down, knowing it was born partly of his PTSD. Following a battle, his paranoia always ran high. He ended up looking for enemies everywhere. Even now, a fist had formed on his knee, and he had to relax one finger at a time to get it to unclench. He knew this feeling would pass, but one bit of therapy always helped.

He reached his hand down and ran his fingers through the ruff of Kane's fur. The shepherd sat on his haunches beside the bench, watching birds flit through the mesquite branches overhead. For Kane, the ordeal at Redstone was in the past. The dog lived in the here and now, enjoying the shade, the birds, and Tucker's company. He always found Kane's attitude reassuring. For his four-legged partner, what might happen tomorrow or the next day simply didn't exist.

Tucker kept his hand on his dog's side, absorbing that sense of peace. After another ten minutes, his breathing grew less strained, and his blood pressure lowered. Finally, Tucker stood up, ready to return to the resort where he had left Frank and Nora doing some final work on the Wasp drone.

His assignment this afternoon had been to canvass Tangent Aerospace's headquarters. He took note of the number of guards, the security procedures at the gate, and the position of cameras. More important, he had taken a few discreet photographs of the forest of antennas on top of Tangent Tower.

Someone was certainly transmitting and receiving lots of data.

His task finished, Tucker headed away with Kane at his side and returned to his new rental, a Honda Pilot. Once back at the room, Tucker shared what he learned with Frank and Nora and showed them the photos.

"No way we're sneaking in there," Tucker concluded as Frank examined the pictures of Tangent's gates.

Nora swiped back over to the picture of the nest of antennas atop the tower. "There might be another way. As far as I can tell, it looks like they've got almost every kind of transceiver up there, from ELF—extremely low frequency—to microwave."

"And everything in between," Frank added. He smiled at Nora. "Think Rex is ready for a little reconnaissance?"

Nora glanced to the reassembled Wasp drone. "Only one way to find out."

Frank turned to Tucker. "While you were gone, we accessed and made active the electronic warfare suite buried inside Rex's operating systems. The drone should now be able to do what it was engineered for."

"To suck data covertly," Tucker said.

Nora nodded. "Once in the air and within five hundred yards of the tower, Rex should be able to start a dialogue with those antennas and hack into Tangent Tower without anyone growing the wiser."

"Still, we'll have to tread lightly," Frank warned. "Remember Rex is a prototype. There are sure to be bugs that haven't been worked out yet."

"For that matter, we should also only launch Rex at night," Nora added. "The drone is equipped with all manner of cloaking and jamming equipment, but it could still be spotted by the naked eye."

Tucker considered the timetable. "Then we do this tonight. We have to assume Webster and his convoy are en route with everything from Redstone, if they're not already here. Whatever the next stage of this operation is, we need to find out *where* it's scheduled to take place."

Nora frowned. "I thought you believed Karl was heading over to the White Sands Missile Range?"

"I still believe that," Tucker said. "But White Sands is spread over three thousand square miles. We need to know exactly *where* on that base Webster's operations are located."

Frank dropped to one knee next to the drone. "Then we'd better—"

A knock on the door made everyone freeze.

Tucker motioned the others down, then slipped out the JPX handgun holstered at his shoulder. He angled to the door, keeping out of direct line of fire if anyone should shoot through it. He moved to a neighboring window and peeked through the curtain.

A quick glance revealed a familiar slim shape of a woman, her blond hair tied back into a ponytail, her face half hidden by a sunhat.

After making sure she was alone, Tucker crossed over and opened the door.

The newcomer smiled. "Hey, handsome."

But her eyes were on Kane as the shepherd came forward to greet her, wriggling his hind end and sweeping his tail happily. When the woman's gaze rose and found Tucker's face, she found a less welcoming greeting.

"What the hell are you doing here, Jane?"

18

Tucker drew Jane inside and marched her off to the suite's bedroom. He ignored the questioning looks from Frank and Nora. Kane pushed into the room before he could shut the door, plainly insisting on being a part of this reunion.

"You shouldn't be here," Tucker started, feeling his face heat up. "You know that. You're putting yourself at risk . . . not to mention us."

"Oh calm down. Who do you think I am? I took all the necessary precautions."

"Which included not calling me and telling me you were coming?"

"Correct. That was one of the *precautions*. If I reached out to you via my phone, we'd be compromised."

Tucker realized she was right. The plan had always been for him to call her, not the other way around.

"Besides," she said, "if I had called, you'd have tried to talk me out of coming. Or worse, packed up and moved."

True.

"What about your son?" Tucker asked, picturing Nathan's innocent face.

"I've got him safely stashed away for now. Nobody'll find him. And at this point in the game, it's probably better that I'm not at his side."

Even truer.

"And to answer your question, *what the hell am I doing here?*" Jane added. "I'm joining your damn team."

"What if it gets you killed? What about Nathan then?"

"Tuck, they won't stop coming after me until this is over, and I'm tired of being hunted by these bastards. Remember, I was army, like you. We don't wait for a fight to come to us, right? We take it to them."

Tucker read Jane's expression, one he had seen all too often in the past: her jaw set, her gaze focused, and an obstinate glint shining in those eyes.

There's no talking her out of this.

Tucker sighed. "Fine . . . for now."

She shrugged. "Good enough."

She stepped forward and wrapped Tucker in a hug, pressing her face into his chest. Without thinking, he squeezed her back. It felt good. Familiar.

After too short a time, she pulled back and stared up into his eyes. There was so much that remained unspoken between them, but neither had the words to bridge the gulf of years that separated them.

He felt a sudden urge to lean down and kiss her.

Before he could act, she shifted farther back, turning away slightly. "Maybe you'd better bring me up to speed."

He nodded, disappointed . . . but also relieved.

"First of all, let me introduce you to Kane's new buddy." Tucker led her back to the other room and pointed to the drone. "Jane, meet Rex."

He then introduced both Frank and Nora.

Nora gave her a hug. "Sandy talked a lot about you, Jane. I'm sorry we're meeting under these circumstances."

As the two women shared a few stories about Sandy—some of which were accompanied by tears, others with soft laughter—Frank tugged Tucker aside and lowered his voice. "Is this smart? It's bad enough Nora is putting herself in harm's way . . ."

Tucker recognized the worried look in the man's eyes. Frank was likely picturing what had happened to the rest of Nora's team. Tucker stared at the two women, connected by a ghost. The two shared a grim sisterhood. Both were the lone survivors of their respective units—Project 623 and The Odisha Group.

Tucker knew Frank's fear.

Will we get them both killed?

Tucker finally answered Frank's question. "It might not be smart, but it is necessary. And for now, that'll have to do."

His answer seemed to offer Frank little solace.

Welcome to the club.

Jane finally waved the two men closer and nodded to Nora. "She's the other reason I risked coming out here."

"Why's that?" Tucker asked.

Jane reached into the pocket of her light jacket and removed a fat thumb drive, one Tucker recognized immediately. It was the drive that Sandy's mother had given Tucker.

"You were able to decrypt it?" Tucker asked.

"With help. But what was found on it was beyond my scope." She turned to Nora. "Plus there's something you should see."

At Jane's insistence, Frank lifted his laptop from the floor next to the drone and placed it on the room's desk. Jane inserted the drive into the computer's USB port. In short order, a window full of file folders opened.

The first was labeled NORA.

Jane stepped back. "Nora, I think this entire drive was meant for your eyes. Sandy left this for *you*."

Nora shifted front and center and stood there for a long breath—then reached with a trembling hand and opened the folder with her name on it. It held one item: a large video file. Nora glanced to Tucker, her eyes shining with fear.

Like her, he could guess what that file held. He shifted the desk chair behind Nora. She sank into it, took another deep breath, then opened the video.

A small window bloomed, revealing the smiling face of a ghost.

It was Sandy Conlon, seated in what appeared to be her storage locker. She looked nervous, edgy, while she double-checked that everything was recording properly.

At the sight of her, Tucker felt his own legs giving out as he struggled to reconcile this image with the decaying ruin rising from the trunk of the sunken Ford Taurus. As Sandy began to speak, memories from their past at Fort Benning flooded through him. Here again was that familiar southern drawl, the crooked smile, the nervous habit of pushing her black eyeglasses higher on the bridge of her nose.

Jane joined him, slipping an arm around his waist. "It's okay . . ." she whispered.

It wasn't.

As they all watched and listened, the ghost of Sandy told her story.

"Nora, if you're seeing this, I'm sorry. Maybe I should have let you know what I was doing, but I couldn't put you at risk . . . not you." Sandy's voice cracked, and emotions washed over her face: love for sure, but mostly fear and shame. She tried to soften it with a small laugh that broke Tucker's heart. "I blame my mother. Paranoia and secrets are as much a part of the mountains where I grew up as coal fires and moonshine."

Nora sat with her back straight and stiff. Tucker wanted to console the woman, but he sensed if he touched her she would crumble.

"Karl showed me some more of those journal pages," Sandy continued. "More like those that I had seen back in Silver Spring. At Project 623. He even admitted they were the work of Alan Turing, just like I had thought. I even spotted a date on what appeared to be the last entry: April 24, 1940. He showed me those pages after I had made the breakthrough in developing GUT-C."

Sandy was referring to the Grand Unifying Theory of Cryptography, the set of algorithms and code that were the core to all of Tangent's smart drones.

Jane glanced to Tucker to see if he understood what Sandy was talking about, but he waved and mumbled, "Later."

"As you know," Sandy said, "there were still problems with GUT-C. Holes even I couldn't fill. Karl hoped the new pages might help me finish the work to its completion. Which it did—but I did that coding in secret, away from Tangent's eyes."

She waved to encompass her storage locker. "Actually it wasn't that hard. Alan Turing had done all the heavy lifting. He could've completed it himself, given enough time and resources. In the end, the key was *chaos*, just as Turing hypothesized for his mythic Oracle . . . which you'll see in the code I wrote and left for you, Nora."

Tucker noted the rows of other files included on the flash drive.

This must be why Jane had come. It would take someone intimately involved in all of Sandy's work to fully understand it.

Sandy continued. "Turing called his new set of algorithms ARES, likely a play off the name of the Greek god of war. But the acronym actually stands for Artificial Reasoning Engine Structure, a rudimentary blueprint for the first AI computer. I think even he knew that the creation of such an operating system could only lead to bloodshed and ruin. And now considering our work with the drones, it looks like he was proven right. I feared what horrors might be wrought if my rudimentary systems were perfected, so I completed the work in secret. I could not let Tangent get hold of it."

"And look what it cost you," Nora mumbled, wiping at one eye.

But Sandy wasn't done. "While working with Turing's algorithms, I also sought to discover *where* those pages originally came from. As long as they exist, others could do what I did."

Sandy sighed and gave a small shake of her head. "Unfortunately I could never get to the bottom of that rabbit hole, but I did discover some things. More rumors than concrete facts, but intriguing nonetheless. Like the date of that last entry, April 24, 1940. I did some research into the history of Bletchley Park, where Turing worked during that time. According to what I learned, there was a mysterious fire two days after the last entry, which almost destroyed the place. But digging deeper, I encountered hints and speculations that it was actually sabotage . . . or maybe even a German attack on British soil. Either way, it made me wonder if the journal fell into someone else's hands. Maybe even made it back to the U.S."

No doubt about that now, Tucker added silently.

"If so, *who* could possibly have it?" Sandy stressed. "I know both Project 623 and The Odisha Group were funded through government sources, but they were also privately run, suggesting one hand might be behind both operations, an unknown puppet master who is seeking to use those old journals to resurrect Turing's project for their own personal gain. But I was never able to discover *who* that might be. It was like chasing a ghost."

Tucker turned to Jane. "I think I know someone who might be able to help us with that, someone who can quietly pull some strings in Washington and discover *who* was truly behind your project and the one at Redstone."

Jane scrunched her nose. "Who are you—?"

Sandy interrupted her. "As you'll see, Nora, I succeeded in perfecting Turing's system. I did so for two reasons. First, to see if it was possible, but also as a fail-safe. Since I couldn't discover who's behind all of this, I wanted to discover a way to stop it in case anyone else followed in my footsteps. I figured I'd have to build it in order to know how to tear it down."

"Smart," Nora said, as if speaking to the ghost on the screen.

"With the code finished, I was able to create a mirror image of the same algorithms. It's a way to tear down any functioning version of my systems, even the GUT-C code that I developed already for Tangent. It will basically lobotomize any AI created through my designs."

Tucker noted a file that was named LOBOTOMY. It must contain the countercode to her operating systems.

Sandy leaned closer to the camera. "Nora, you must stop them at any cost. Alan Turing was abused and destroyed because of the truth of who he was. Don't let them do the same with his final work." Sandy finally sat back, stared at her hands, then back at the screen. "Nora, I love you. I never said it before, but I should have. I hope it's not too late."

A sad smile glowed on the screen as the video ended, freezing there forever.

Nora reached up and touched the screen, tracing Sandy's chin with a fingertip. Finally her hand fell away. Nora hung her head for a long breath.

When she finally spoke, it was soft and forlorn. "She was so bloody smart . . . and so beautiful . . ."

Jane went to her and pulled her close. "Nora, I'm so sorry."

Nora's shoulders shook as she quietly sobbed.

10:12 P.M.

Standing in the parking lot of the resort's golf course, Tucker shivered as he waited in the dark. After night had fallen, the desert temperatures had plummeted from the low eighties to just shy of forty degrees. He stood guard with Kane at the rear of their SUV. An hour ago, he and Frank had carried Rex out to the open grass of the course and launched the drone for its covert assault on the antenna array atop Tangent Tower.

He could hear Nora and Frank talking inside the Honda Pilot, the two of them helping guide Rex for this sortie. Jane was also with them, offering whatever technical advice she could.

He patted Kane's side. "Looks like it's just the two of us on guard duty."

Kane wagged his tail.

"Yeah, it's just the way I like it, too."

After another half hour, the back hatch opened, and Jane poked her head out. "You should see this."

Tucker leaned down to Kane and waved an arm. "CLOSE PATROL."

He did not want any surprises tonight.

The shepherd took off, gliding through the darkness and vanishing.

Only then did Tucker turn his attention to the darkened interior of the Pilot. As an extra precaution, Tucker had removed the bulb from the SUV's overhead lamp. The only light source came from the tiny screen of the jury-rigged CUCS control unit and the laptop attached to it. The view on the computer screen looked down upon the lit-up wedge of Tangent Tower. The feed came from Rex's camera.

"Should you be flying that close to the building?" Tucker asked.

Frank dismissed his concern. "We're at the drone's max elevation and in full stealth mode. Kane's not the only one that knows how to keep out of sight."

Nora added, "We need to be this close in order for Rex to hack into Tangent's systems without being detected."

"And how's that going?"

Frank grinned proudly. "Beautifully."

Nora was less enthusiastic. "We've only partially penetrated the data firewall. We don't dare push any deeper. Like Sandy mentioned, her central operating system still has some bugs and weaknesses in it. So we're pulling what we can slowly."

"A gigabyte a second isn't *slow*." Frank sounded wounded, as if Nora had insulted his best friend.

And maybe she had.

Nora waved a hand. "If Rex had Sandy's latest algorithms, there'd be no limits to what that drone could do."

With her mind on the task at hand, Nora's mood had much improved. Earlier, she had spent the evening in her room. Through the door, Tucker heard Sandy's faint voice as Nora reviewed the video several more times on the laptop. Tucker doubted the repeated viewings had anything to do with gathering more intelligence. Still, when Nora had finally stepped out, she looked more collected, her staunchness fueled by a fiery anger in her eyes.

Frank refused to let anyone trash talk his pet project. "Rex is not only gathering data at those speeds but processing what he's culling. It shouldn't be much longer until he finds something useful."

Jane nodded. "It's damned impressive. All Frank and Nora had to do was give Rex some search parameters, and the drone took it from there. The drone isn't just dryly compiling information. It's looking for anomalies, mapping trends, and doing some rudimentary analysis."

Frank explained. "I asked Rex to sniff out any communication between the tower and White Sands. Rex should be able—"

Nora interrupted Frank, drawing his attention back to the screen. Their chatter quickly dissolved into technical details beyond his pay grade.

Jane smiled at Tucker, lifting an eyebrow. She was clearly amused by the camaraderie of the pair and silently reminded him: *Remember when we were like them?*

He did.

Frank rolled to the side slightly. "I think we got something. Come see."

A map glowed in a corner of the screen. It showed the territory of White Sands with a cluster of blue dots near the northern end of the base.

"Rex managed to detect a series of communications over the last week, all directed to a specific set of GPS coordinates."

"What's more," Nora added, "there's been an uptick in that communication over the past twenty-four hours."

"Something's happening out there," Frank said.

Tucker could guess the source of that commotion.

Webster's convoy must have arrived from Redstone.

Tucker straightened. "Looks like someone should go out and see what all the fuss is about."

"So what's the plan?" Frank asked. "Another hunting expedition?"

"Don't think that'll work a second time."

"Well, whatever your plan is, let's not hang out there for too long." Frank pointed to the markers on the map. "That section of White Sands is home to the Trinity Site—as in the first detonation of an atomic bomb."

"What's your concern?"

"My *concern* is that at some point I'd like to have children. If we hang around that place too long, I'm afraid I'll start glowing, and my little swimmers will die."

Jane spoke up, a mischievous glint in her eyes. "I don't think you need to worry about that, Frank. We won't be blindly wandering the desert."

Tucker turned to her. She had spent a good part of the evening using his phone in private. She must have been prepping for what was to come. He didn't like her expression at the moment, having seen it all too often.

"Jane, when you get that look, I get worried."

She smiled. "You should be."

19

The next day, Tucker drove through the blazing desert. A straight strip of two-lane blacktop stretched through a dry desert of rock and scrub brush. Overhead, the sky shone a startling blue, unblemished save for a few cotton-ball clouds.

He headed west along Highway 360, which hugged the northern border of the White Sands Missile Range. The surrounding rugged territory and the mountains in the distance shared a history with Billy the Kid, Butch Cassidy's Wild Bunch, and the notorious Apaches, Cochise and Geronimo.

Struck by the breathtaking desolation of the area, Tucker found the vast expanse daunting. If the coordinates Rex had found were correct, their group would need to venture dozens of miles into restricted, heavily guarded territory.

But at the moment, his passengers were oblivious of such worries.

During the three-hour drive, Jane had fallen asleep in the backseat, with Kane tucked in a ball close to her belly. She was plainly exhausted, but he knew much of her fatigue was due to the heavy weight on her shoulders. Despite her brave words upon arriving on his doorstep, she was scared—not for her own sake, but for her son's. Last night, he had caught her looking at photos of Nathan on her phone, swiping slowly through them when she thought no one was looking, her eyes full of pain and love.

It was good she had these hours to rest—which was true for all of them.

Seated next to Tucker, Frank drowsed with his chin on his chest.

Though Frank did lift his head in time to see a green sign for the tiny town of Bingham flash past—population nine. Tucker slowed, noting a small general store and a little farther on a large sign for a rock shop.

Their destination was another twenty miles ahead along the highway.

It would soon be time to get everyone moving.

They had left Nora back in Las Cruces, where she was studying Sandy's code, seeing if they could use any of it to their benefit. This morning, Tucker had spoken with her after a Starbucks run. It looked like the woman hadn't slept all night. She seemed determined to finish what Sandy had started, no matter where it might lead. Past her exhaustion, Tucker also saw the haunted look in her eyes. He sensed her need to talk and had sat with her.

"You have to understand," Nora had eventually shared, waving at the screen of code in front of her, "this was Sandy's passion. She always felt a deep bond with Alan Turing, an affinity that transcended hero worship. Maybe because she felt a kinship with the man—not only for their common love of math and codes but because they shared a lifetime of prejudice, persecution, and secrets."

Tucker had understood.

For Sandy, it couldn't have been easy growing up gay in Appalachia.

"She seemed almost protective of Turing's memory." Nora offered a small sad smile. "I used to tease her, telling her the only reason she liked me was because I was both gay and British, like her hero."

From the way Nora spoke about Sandy, he knew their relationship went much deeper than that. So he let her talk, knowing it helped her reconcile her loss. Eventually she had returned to her work, looking more determined and less compulsive.

Jane stirred in the backseat, stretching an arm and stifling a yawn. "How much longer until we reach the Sirocco trailer?"

"Fifteen to twenty minutes."

She sat up, looking surprised. The movement woke Kane, who huffed at having his nap disturbed. She checked her watch. "Then we need to get ready."

The plan from here was dicey at best. White Sands had been in operation for some seventy years, home to decades of top-secret military projects. Base security was tight. Whether Jane's plan would be enough to get them to Rex's coordinates without being caught, only time would tell.

Jane pulled up her iPad, which tracked their progress. "There should be a turnoff on your left in another five miles. But we should pull over before that, get our eyes on our target first."

Tucker had already planned on doing that. Once close enough, he slowed and guided their SUV onto the shoulder of the road. "Better stay inside," he warned the others.

He climbed out into the heat, popped the hood, and spent a few minutes pretending to check the engine. He reached and undid the radiator cap, letting steam escape. Then he wiped his sweating brow and climbed back inside, leaving the hood propped open, as if waiting for the overheated engine to cool.

Once he was behind the wheel, Jane handed him a set of binoculars. "Follow the dirt road ahead back some hundred yards or so off the highway."

Peering through the binoculars, he did as instructed and found a white construction trailer sitting out there, fronted by unpainted wooden steps. A sign over the door read:

SIROCCO POWER
EL PASO, TEXAS

Frank had his own set of binoculars and must have noted the same sign. "Those guys are a long way from home."

Tucker panned around, finding nothing but open desert. He saw no evidence of the neighboring military base: no tall fence, no ominous warning signs. All he spotted was a rutted tract heading out into that rugged landscape. He knew fifteen miles due south was the Trinity Site, where Robert Oppenheimer and his Manhattan Project team detonated an eighteen-kiloton atomic bomb, forming a crater of radioactive light green glass ten feet deep and a thousand feet wide.

Tucker felt a shiver on the back of his neck.

This is where World War II ended and the Cold War began.

He returned his attention to the trailer and spotted a dusty, late-model white Ford Expedition parked alongside it, emblazoned with the Sirocco Power logo on its doors: a red-and-yellow mountain peak beneath a single blue lightning bolt.

"What do you think?" Jane asked.

"It'll have to do," he conceded.

She clapped him on the shoulder. "Now there's the can-do attitude I know and love."

Using Tucker's secure sat phone, Jane had spent all day yesterday discreetly searching for a chink in the armor of White Sands security, looking for the best way onto the base. Through her multiple contacts, she eventually found it.

Sirocco Power was contracted by the state of New Mexico to build eight hundred miles of power lines for wind and solar energy. A bone of contention with the Department of Defense was that fifty miles of those lines would run through a northern corner of White Sands. Still, with both the state government and the federal Bureau of Land Management backing the project, the Pentagon eventually folded, but not before gaining some concessions, which included the tight monitoring of any Sirocco employees at the work site.

At this early stage of the project, those employees only numbered two: a pair of engineers who were conducting land surveys in this remote corner. According to Jane, they rotated those engineers fairly regularly—which, considering how isolated it was out here, only made sense.

"Car's coming," Frank warned.

To the west, a gray Jeep with a yellow light on top headed their way.

Definitely military.

Uh-oh.

The vehicle must have come from the Stallion Gate ten miles farther up the road, marking the northernmost entrance to White Sands. Suspecting this was a routine patrol, Tucker got back out and returned to examining the engine compartment. He retightened the radiator cap as the vehicle drew abreast of the SUV.

As the Jeep slowed, Tucker raised an arm, giving them a thumbs-up. With the sun glinting off the vehicle's windows, he could see nothing of the interior, but he felt a pair of eyes watching him.

Keep moving, he silently urged.

Without a word, the Jeep's engine growled deeper, and the vehicle continued down the road and soon disappeared around a bend. He suspected they'd run his license plate number. He hoped the false ID used to rent the vehicle continued to hold water.

Not wanting to push his luck, Tucker spent a few more minutes tinkering with the engine before shutting the hood and rejoining the others. He wheeled the SUV around and backtracked to the nearby town of Carrizozo, where the team had dinner and mapped out their plan.

As the sun finally sank away, Tucker faced the group across the ruins of their meal. "Ready?" he asked.

It would be now or never.

He got nods all around. Kane, seated at his feet under the table, wagged his tail.

For better or worse, at least it's unanimous.

8:09 P.M.

Ninety minutes later, Tucker slowed the Honda Pilot as he neared the dirt road that led to the trailer belonging to Sirocco Power. He doused his headlights, made the turn, and coasted to a stop. A hundred yards down the darkened road, yellow rectangles of light marked the trailer's position, a lonely outpost here in the desert.

He and Frank got out, while Jane took the wheel with Kane in the passenger seat. The two of them donned ski masks and took off low through the scrub brush, while Jane turned on the headlights and continued slowly down the bumpy road toward the trailer.

As she did so, Tucker angled wide with Frank, circling toward the far side of the trailer from the approaching Honda Pilot. The plan was simple: to blitz the two engineers before they were any the wiser.

As Jane pulled up to the trailer's steps and rolled down her window, the door opened and a tall man took a step out.

Jane called over to him. "I'm sorry to bother you. I saw your lights on. I think I'm lost."

As Tucker approached the trailer from the shadows, he recognized the sweet charm in her voice, imagining her sheepish smile as she played her role.

"Where you trying to get?" the man asked, tugging a company

cap more firmly on his head as he headed over to her. He carried a beer bottle in his hand.

A glance through the nearest window showed another man lounging on a sofa inside the trailer, dressed in blue jeans and a T-shirt, watching a football game on a big LCD television.

Sorry to interrupt game night, boys.

On Tucker's signal, Frank ran out of the dark and blindsided the man, hitting him from behind and crashing his target headlong into the side of the SUV. At the same time, Tucker dashed through the door in a single bound. The fellow on the sofa only had time to swing his legs to the floor when Tucker pointed his JPX handgun at his face.

"You really don't want me to fire."

Outside, Kane growled as Jane let the shepherd loose.

"And you definitely don't want me to call my dog in here."

In a matter of five minutes, they had both men secured inside with flexi-cuffs around their wrists and ankles.

After gagging and blindfolding the pair, Tucker pulled off his ski mask. "Okay, listen up," he growled thickly. "We don't want no trouble, and we don't wanna hurt nobody. Where's your money, your stuff?"

The goal was to make this look like a robbery.

Frank frisked both men and came up with their wallets. He took the cash. "What about these credit cards?" he asked, thickening his southern accent.

"They track plastic, dummy," Tucker warned. "Leave 'em. Grab those cell phones on the table, though. And those walkie-talkies. Let's see what else they got."

Frank searched the double-wide trailer, discovering a locker with blue coveralls with the Sirocco Power logo on their pockets. Identification badges were pinned to the uniforms. He tossed them to Jane, who set to work, altering the badges using an X-ACTO knife and small photos of herself and Tucker.

To further support the robbery story, Frank began tossing the place.

Tucker used this time to study the survey maps tacked to the wall, noting the company's work sites dotting this corner of the mili-

tary base. He ripped down one of the charts, folded it, and pocketed it.

"Found some keys," Frank announced loudly.

"Take 'em!" Tucker said. "Probably belong to that SUV out back.
Maybe Spider can strip it for us."

Jane gave Tucker a thumbs-up, waving the two badges to get her
handiwork to dry.

"Okay, we're outta here." Tucker nudged one of the engineers
with his foot. "Just to show we ain't all bad, I'll call someone tomorrow. Get 'em to come cut you all loose."

With matters concluded, they all bailed out of the trailer. Tucker
turned off the lights as he exited. He felt a flicker of guilt at leaving
the men like this, but he had no choice. Too many lives were at stake.

Once outside, Jane hid their SUV behind the trailer, out of direct
view of the road. They'd retrieve the vehicle if they could. If not, he
was out another deposit.

So be it.

They quickly transferred all their gear, including Rex, to the
power company's Expedition, then set off back to the highway.
Tucker turned west and headed for the Stallion Gate.

"Holy crap, we pulled that off," Frank said from the backseat.

In the rearview mirror, Tucker saw the man's hair was matted
with sweat, his face flushed. "Looks like you got a second career to
fall back on if this army gig doesn't work out."

Jane smiled back at Frank. "You did good. Very convincing."

Far ahead, the lights of the base gates appeared, glowing in the
darkness.

Tucker's hands tightened on the wheel.

Now comes the hard part.

20

"Here we go," Tucker warned.

He turned left off Highway 380 and onto a smaller road that aimed toward the heart of the White Sands Missile Range. A sign on the shoulder read:

STALLION GATE
4 MILES

Jane swung around in the passenger seat to face Frank and Kane. "Time for you two boys to go into hiding."

In the rearview mirror, Frank looked worried—and rightly so. Still, the man crammed himself into the footwell behind Tucker's seat and pulled a blanket over his head. Kane followed his example and curled behind Jane's seat. She leaned back and tossed another blanket over the dog—then piled on a pair of sleeping bags, a small folded tent, a camp stove, sacks of groceries, all topped by a couple of backpacks.

"How're you all doing?" Jane asked once she was done.

Frank groaned from under his hiding place. "We're gonna get caught."

"If you keep fidgeting like that," Jane warned, "we definitely will."

Tucker glanced back and saw that Kane had already gone deathly still under his share of the pile, plainly understanding the intent here.

"Good boy, buddy," Tucker encouraged him, and reinforced the plan with a firm order. "STAY HIDDEN."

Tucker continued toward the lights that marked the Stallion Gate. To either side of the road spread a dark landscape of rolling sand, low hillocks, and spindly bushes, all etched in silver by the moonlight. To the east and west rose two mountain ranges, forming the rim of the basin where White Sands was nestled. It was a lonely stretch of desert that offered no hint of the advanced military base hidden here.

"I read in a brochure," Jane mumbled as she settled back into her seat, "that this road could be backed up for miles during the day with tourists coming to visit the Trinity bomb site."

"Well, that's one advantage of a midnight raid," Tucker commented. "No traffic."

After another few minutes, they approached the Stallion Gate. Given the secure nature of the facility, the entrance was underwhelming. A small guard shack sat on the shoulder of the road. A prominent stop sign stood next to it, illuminated by a tall streetlight. All that blocked the road was a pair of orange cones.

As Tucker pulled to a stop, he noted a small camera positioned under an eave of the shack, pointed toward their vehicle. A man in a gray uniform and baseball cap stepped out of the shack. He carried a clipboard in one hand and lifted his other arm in a lazy greeting, clearly recognizing the Sirocco Power's SUV. He stepped over as Tucker rolled his window down.

"Evening, guys," the guard started—then stiffened at the discovery of strangers inside the vehicle.

"Not just guys this time," Tucker corrected with a grin, pointing a thumb at Jane. They both wore the work uniforms confiscated from the power company's trailer. "This is Pam. I'm Pete. We're new to the team down here."

Jane waved and gave him a beaming smile.

Before the guard could look too closely, Tucker thrust out the altered ID badges. The guard briefly scrutinized them, then checked his clipboard. His brow furrowed, plainly failing to find them on the current list of Sirocco Power employees on site.

Anticipating this, Tucker sighed loudly. "Chris and Adam

rotated out yesterday." He had gotten the names of the two Sirocco engineers from their wallets. "Looks like Pam and I get to be in the frying pan now. At least for the next six weeks. Heard it's gonna be a scorcher tomorrow."

The guard nodded and returned their badges. "And freezing tonight."

Jane poked Tucker in the side. "Aren't you glad I told you to pack the heavier sleeping bags?"

"Still, I don't think we need this much camping gear for the one night." Tucker turned to the guard and rolled his eyes. "If my wife had her way, we'd have hauled the whole damned double-wide trailer with us."

Tucker had spotted the wedding band on the guard's finger and figured a little commiserating between husbands might help smooth things over. A small smile of understanding briefly appeared before the man went stoic.

Tucker cleared his throat. "Our plan is to camp at the project site farthest from the gate and work our way back here. Try to beat the worst of the heat tomorrow."

"Plus see the stars," Jane added wistfully. "I heard they're really beautiful at night."

The guard nodded. "Okay, but I'll need to inspect your vehicle. Can you roll down your back window and pop the rear hatch?"

Tucker nodded and hit the proper buttons. As the rear hatch opened on its own, the guard stepped over and shone a flashlight through the passenger window into the backseat, splashing the beam over the piled gear. Tucker held his breath, praying for Frank and Kane to remain perfectly still. Finally, the guard continued around to the open rear hatch. The flashlight settled on the object resting back there.

It was Rex.

Tucker hadn't bothered trying to hide it, counting on the presence of the drone to draw attention away from their two hidden stowaways.

"What's this?" the guard asked.

Jane twisted around to face the man, again flashing her smile. "That's mine. It's equipped with ground-penetrating radar. I use it to perform sweeps of the terrain. It's why Pete and I were called in. Its generator sends out spherical waves designed to diffuse basalt and give me—"

The guard lifted a hand, interrupting what would have been an even longer explanation if need be. "Got it."

Tucker reinforced their credentials with more technical talk. "The guys over at the Bureau of Land Management are worried the local gypsum karst deposits might mess with transmission ratio fall-off. We have to make them happy. You know bureaucrats."

This earned a small chuckle. "Tell me about it." The guard reached up and pulled the hatch closed. He came back around and leaned by the window. "Okay, you're good to go."

"Thanks," Tucker said, happy it had all gone smoothly.

Unfortunately, the guard wasn't done. "Once back in the shack, I'll activate your GPS unit." He pointed to the glove compartment. "Remember to stay within the twenty-five-mile perimeter allowed for Sirocco. If you stray outside of that area, you'll find yourselves in a mess of trouble."

Tucker nodded as if he intended to comply.

"And watch out for snakes," the guard added.

Jane slipped her hand into Tucker's, her voice turning coy. "In that case, maybe we better share *one* sleeping bag tonight."

The guard grinned. "Sounds like you have one smart woman there."

You don't know the half of it.

He waved to the guard and headed down the road into the dark desert. Jane kept hold of his hand for longer than the ruse required, but he didn't object. He could not discount how it felt to play her husband, appreciating her warm touch, the glimmer in her eyes, the tilt of her smile. All reminders of what might have been.

Frank finally interrupted, his voice muffled by the pile of gear. "What the hell was that stuff about a GPS unit?"

Tucker heard the fumbling sound of Frank climbing out of hiding. Kane did the same. But Tucker focused on Jane as she reached down and opened the glove compartment. A blinking amber light glowed from its depths, revealing a GPS unit, stamped with the Department of Defense logo on its front.

Tucker called back to Frank. "Think you can disable it?"

Frank leaned his head next to Jane's shoulder as he inspected it. "Maybe, but I don't think we should risk it. I wager it's been tamper-proofed."

Jane already had the map Tucker had ripped from the trailer wall and studied it. "That means we have a twenty-five-mile electronic leash attached to us. If we go any farther, men in black helicopters will come hunting us."

Tucker turned to Frank. "How far out were those communication markers that Rex picked up from eavesdropping on Tangent Tower?"

"At least *thirty* miles."

Jane looked to Tucker for a solution.

He had only one. "That means we'll have to ditch the Expedition and go the rest of the way on foot."

Frank didn't look happy with this option. "If we get caught in the open desert, we'll be sitting ducks."

Jane offered a solution. "Then let's not get caught."

9:01 P.M.

Karl Webster ignored the bustle of the makeshift command center behind him. He and his crew occupied a set of old concrete bunkers about two miles east of the test site. They had arrived less than forty-eight hours ago and were operating on an accelerated timetable to perform this test run tonight. Pruitt Kellerman had been firm on this schedule, especially after the raid at Redstone.

Beyond the concrete bunker, engineers and ground crew serviced rows of drones parked on the surrounding tarmac, readying the group for the midnight assault.

Nothing must go wrong.

Inside the bunker, technicians were seated at various terminals along the walls, busy with last-minute finessing of the drones' monitoring and communication equipment.

Karl, as head of Tangent security, had his own station. He had already cleared operations with the brass at White Sands. A total communication blackout of this immediate area had been initialized. While waiting for the approaching zero hour, Karl had been doing a final review of the various checkpoints surrounding this area. Earlier in the day, this off-limits region had been evacuated of any military personnel, but he was taking no chances.

And it was lucky he was so thorough.

On his monitor was video feed from the Stallion Gate thirty miles to the north. The footage was from an hour ago and showed a power company truck idling at that gate. Karl was well aware of the company's ongoing survey in that remote corner of the base and would normally have dismissed the vehicle's presence. The DoD contract limited the power company's vehicles to a patch of sand well beyond this restricted area.

But his paranoia was running high this night.

So he had studied the video feed more closely. There were two passengers, but their faces were obscured by the reflection of the streetlamp off the windshield. Then the guard on duty had shone his flashlight into the back of the SUV. Karl had caught a glimpse of the employees' faces. He didn't recognize the driver, but the other—a woman—turned to say something to the guard. Karl felt a cold chill travel through his bones. He knew that woman, that smile, all too well.

It was Jane Sabatello, the only one to escape his purge of Project 623.

He leaned closer to the image frozen on the screen as questions ran through his mind. *What are you doing here, Janie, especially now? How did you find out about this operation? Why did you foolishly come out of hiding?*

He balled a fist. While he might not have any answers, he knew she was the one who had sent that commando and his dog to investigate the disappearance of Sandy Conlon.

Karl squinted—his eyes still sore and puffy from the pepper-spray attack—and studied the shadowy image of the driver.

Was this that same man?

A barked order drew his attention back around. Karl punched the keyboard and closed the video feed as Kellerman's pit bull came stalking over to him after berating one of the techs for getting in his way. Rafael Lyon was dressed in commando gear with a prominent sidearm holstered at his waist. He carried a helmet under one arm.

"I just got off the phone with your boss," Lyon said with thick disdain, careful not to mention Kellerman by name in front of the others. "Are we still on schedule?"

Karl nodded. "All hell will break loose at midnight . . . as planned."

Lyon's left eye pinched very slightly. His gaze flickered toward Karl's monitor and back again. It seemed Karl was not the only one whose paranoia was running high.

"And no hiccups with security?" Lyon asked.

"None at all." Karl kept his face fixed. "And if anything changes, I'll deal with it personally."

9:19 P.M.

"This is as far as we can go," Tucker announced.

He brought the Expedition to a stop and shut off the engine. He opened his door, allowing in a frigid breeze, perfumed by some night-blooming desert flower. The temperature had dropped precipitously since they'd first climbed into the stolen vehicle.

The change brought back memories of Afghanistan.

Boil during the day, freeze at night—and get shot at the entire time.

"Let's get Rex in the air," Tucker ordered Frank as he climbed out.

They all offloaded. Kane stretched his legs and sniffed around the immediate area, lifting his leg a few times before he was satisfied enough to return to Tucker's side.

Frank hauled the Wasp drone out of the rear compartment and set about doing an internal systems check, testing Rex's thrusters and guidance fins. The plan was to use Rex to scout ahead of them, to search the coordinates that the drone had acquired by hacking into Tangent's communications.

"Is the bird ready to fly?" Jane asked.

Frank wiped his palms on his jeans. "Seems so. But I wish Nora were here. She knows far more about this tech than I do."

Tucker put a hand on the man's shoulder. "You'll do fine." Tucker looked up at the cloudless night sky, where the bright sickle of the moon hung amid stars as crisp as ice. "You certainly can't crash Rex into anything out here."

"We'll see about that."

Frank waved them all back, and a moment later Rex's engine

hummed louder and the craft rose fifteen feet off the ground and hovered. With its matte-black exterior, the drone was already nearly invisible in the dark.

"All set?" Frank asked, staring down at the glowing screen of the control unit.

Tucker didn't bother answering, knowing his friend was talking to Rex.

Frank ran a fingertip across the pressure-sensitive interface, and the drone shot forward with barely a whisper of its motors. Jane and Tucker joined Frank, flanking him on both sides. Together, they watched the feed from Rex as the drone began its aerial patrol. Most of the screen was devoted to a bird's-eye view through Rex's camera, while a row of blue-tinted rectangles flowed with readouts for altitude, speed, compass, battery level, and other flight data.

Frank sent Rex skimming south, slowly bringing the drone up to its top speed of sixty miles an hour. He kept Rex flying low, hugging the terrain as much as possible. Low hills and scrub brush—lit up brightly by the camera's night-vision capability—swept below the drone's path.

"You're doing great," Tucker said.

"It ain't me." Frank lifted his hand away from the drone's controls. "I just entered the coordinates. Rex is flying on his own under a feature called *contour matching*. And I would swear he's getting better at it, beginning to anticipate wind shear and changes in the terrain."

Like he's learning.

Tucker watched the drone make its own altitude adjustments, climbing and dipping over the wrinkled landscape of the desert. While it was amazing, it was also a touch frightening.

After another thirty seconds, Rex popped over one last hill and abruptly began to slow.

"He's approaching the target," Frank explained and returned his attention to the controls. "I'm activating Rex's electronic warfare suite. Just in case of trouble."

Rex continued to close in on the coordinates, skimming low.

"He's a hundred yards out," Frank said.

"See anything?" Jane asked.

"Looks like some buildings coming up," Frank said. "But so far

Rex isn't picking up any transmissions or movement. What do you want me to do?"

"Take Rex in another fifty yards," Tucker ordered. "But let's get a higher view."

Frank followed his instructions, sending Rex sailing upward as the drone approached the coordinates. A cluster of buildings—more than two dozen—became visible, ranging from bungalow homes to a stretch of storefronts that looked straight out of a Norman Rockwell painting, all centered around a town square.

"Can you zoom in?" Tucker asked.

"Hang on."

A moment later, the view narrowed and spanned one of the rows of homes. Curls of white paint flecked the exteriors, but most of the walls looked sandblasted down to cracked, gray wood.

"You sure these are the coordinates?" Jane asked.

"Yeah, but—" Frank flinched. "Wait. Rex just picked up some electromagnetic radiation. It's faint, but there's definitely some electricity flowing down there. Though it seems to be pooled in patches throughout the town."

"Any idea what it might be?"

"Not a clue. I'll get Rex circling. See what else he can find."

As the view swept wider, Tucker spied with the others. Something appeared on the far side of the little town, something that certainly didn't belong there.

"Is that what I think it is?" Jane asked.

Tucker nudged Frank. "Bring us closer, but be careful."

The anomaly sat outside the town's perimeter, parked in the sand. As Rex swept for a closer pass, there was no doubt.

"It's an army tank," Frank said.

"But not *our* army," Jane murmured.

Tucker recognized the foreign design, too. "It's a Soviet-era tank. A T-55, I think."

"And judging from its condition, it hasn't been there for long," Jane added. "Look. You can see tread marks in the sand where it was driven up here. With all the blowing wind, it shouldn't be that fresh."

Tucker estimated it must have been parked out there today.

And that wasn't all that had been left.

Beyond the tank was spread an array of Soviet-era military hardware: infantry vehicles, artillery pieces, along with trucks of various sizes. They all appeared in immaculate condition, untouched by the harsh sand and sun.

"What now?" Frank asked.

"I think Rex has done all he can," Tucker answered. "It's time we go look for ourselves."

Frank sighed and mumbled under his breath, "I was afraid you'd say that."

21

After ninety minutes of hiking over the rolling terrain, Tucker's group neared the derelict town. It lay over the next hill in a shallow bowl of a valley.

Two keen-eyed scouts kept watch on their surroundings: Rex in the air and Kane on the ground. Outfitted in his K9 Storm tactical gear, the shepherd ranged the desert under a tight MEDIUM ROAM SCOUT order, while the drone hovered a hundred feet above, offering a bird's-eye view of the surrounding terrain.

So far no one appeared to have noted their trespass, and periodic sweeps by Rex still showed no activity at the town ahead: no transmissions, no heat signatures, no movement. Even the Soviet tank remained dark and quiet.

As the group reached the last hill, Tucker waved for Jane and Frank to hang back. He signaled Kane with a soft whistle. The shepherd bled out of the shadows and glided up to his side. Together, they climbed to the crest of the hill and dropped to their bellies. A panoramic view revealed a wide sandy depression ahead, sheltering the cluster of wooden structures at its center.

Tucker got out his night-vision monocle and studied the town, making sure all remained quiet. After waiting another ten minutes, he motioned the others to come up. As they joined him, a coyote howled in the distance, the lonely note echoing across the dark desert.

Frank sprawled into the sand next to him. "Forget White City . . . should have named this place Spooky City."

"Amen to that," Jane replied, crouching next to Kane. "But let's hope this is the right place."

Only one way to find out.

"Stay low and follow me." Tucker lifted up. "As a precaution, we'll enter the town on the opposite side from where that tank is parked."

Frank stared up toward the night sky as he stood. "I'll set Rex to hovering a thousand feet overhead, to watch our backs in case of trouble."

And Kane will guard our fronts.

Tucker pointed to the edge of town and let the shepherd loose. "Scout ahead low."

Kane raced down the far side of the hill, sweeping around boulders and under bushes. Tucker lost sight of his partner in two breaths, but he monitored the shepherd's progress on his phone's screen. As Tucker and the others approached the town, Kane had already reached its outskirts and padded between buildings and across dark porches. Tucker kept an eye on the shepherd's progress. Kane gave no alerts, and the dog's relaxed gait suggested no immediate threats.

Trusting Kane's instincts, Tucker began to have his doubts.

Maybe we're at the wrong spot.

Still, he couldn't shake the knot of apprehension in his belly as his group reached the town itself. As if cued by a Hollywood director, a large tumbleweed bounced across their path and disappeared between a pair of buildings.

"If the ghost of Wyatt Earp shows up," Frank whispered nervously, "I'm outta here."

Continuing cautiously through the outlying homes—a few still framed by gap-toothed, weathered picket fences—they reached the sandy square in the town's center. The dilapidated facades of the surrounding structures appeared to be various faux businesses: a bakery, a clothing shop, even a general store. The last was fronted by a rickety porch with a bleached wooden sign dangling from the eaves. Faded letters read:

**ALICE'S PLACE
TEA PARTY SUPPLIES SOLD HERE**

"Looks like someone had a sense of humor," Jane commented.

With his nose to the control unit, Frank scoffed, "This sure ain't no Wonderland."

Maybe, but we've definitely fallen down a rabbit hole.

Tucker turned to Frank. "Where's the nearest of those electrical signals that Rex detected earlier?"

Frank tapped at his control unit with his nose bent to the screen. After a moment, he straightened and pointed across the square to the general store. "If we want any answers to this mystery, it looks like we're going to have to go ask Alice."

Tucker nodded. "Let Kane and me check the place out first. You two hold here."

He signaled the shepherd over to his side and headed across the square, counting on the robotic eye in the sky or Kane's keen senses to alert him of danger. Once at the storefront, Tucker climbed the steps to the porch. The boards creaked under his weight, setting his nerves on edge. He fell momentarily back to Afghanistan, remembering a small village outside of Fallujah where Taliban forces had ambushed his unit. Again, muzzle fire flashed behind his eyes. Blinded by the memory, he failed to stop his boot from cracking through a rotted board. He teetered sideways, but Kane was there, pressing against his leg, supporting him as always.

He regained his balance, patted the dog's flank, and crossed to the dusty window. A peek inside revealed the place was a shell, nothing more than an empty room with a low ceiling of open rafters and a plank floor. But out of the darkness on the far side, a pair of green lights glowed, like two venomous eyes shining from the shadows.

He eased over to the door, opened it slowly, and slipped inside with Kane.

He circled a finger in the air and pointed across the planks. Search.

The shepherd set off along the edges of the room, sniffing through some old scaffolding, a pile of unused boards. Tucker pulled out his penlight and flashed it along the floor. Scuffled footprints in the dust led to the pair of shining lights. They glowed from a matte-black steel box, about the size of a standard tool chest. A spiral antenna poked from its lid.

Tucker approached it cautiously, fearful it might be some sort of monitoring device, and didn't want to inadvertently alert whoever might be listening. Once closer, he noted a smaller string of blue and red LEDs blinking next to the antenna. The unit appeared to be completely enclosed with a keypad on the side facing him. A power cord connected the box to a pair of car batteries on the floor.

Kane whined from a far corner of the room. Tucker cringed, realizing he had not ordered Kane to remain silent. He glanced over and saw the dog sniffing and circling a patch of the floor. Tucker recognized the unusual timbre of Kane's warning. He had heard it all too often in Afghanistan and knew what it meant.

Fearful that the noise might be picked up, Tucker studied the lights on the box, but nothing had changed, suggesting the monitoring device—if that was what it was—was not tuned to pick up sound.

So what the hell is it for?

Wanting answers, Tucker walked back to the door and waved for Frank and Jane to join him.

As the others crossed the square, Kane repeated his warning, scratching at the floorboards. Tucker clenched a fist, ordering Kane to be silent.

I got your message, buddy. Let's deal with one mystery at a time.

Jane and Frank climbed up to the porch and entered the general store.

Tucker pointed to the box. "What do you make of that?" he whispered.

Frank shrugged and crossed for a closer look, drawing Jane and Tucker behind him. Without touching anything, Frank gave the unit a full inspection, cocking his head one way, then the other.

"Well?" Jane finally asked.

Frank frowned at the pair of car batteries. "That's definitely the source of the electromagnetic radiation that Rex picked up. And considering he detected other pools of similar radiation throughout this town, I wager we'd find a slew of these boxes planted all over."

"But what are they for?" Tucker asked. "And what are they doing here?"

Frank stood up, holding a palm to his aching back, and glanced around the space. His gaze clearly extended beyond these four walls. "We're only eleven miles from the Trinity bomb site. If I had to guess from the age and wear of the buildings, this mock-up of a town was built during the first atomic tests. The Trinity scientists couldn't agree on what would happen when they blew up their bomb. Some thought it might even set the atmosphere on fire."

Tucker shook his head, surprised they risked setting the damned thing off.

Talk about leaping without looking.

Frank continued. "They built towns like this all around the bomb site, not knowing how far the blast wave might reach."

"Clearly it didn't reach this far," Jane commented.

Frank nodded. "Back then, the scientists planted monitoring instruments throughout the various towns, to test both the strength of the blast and its radiation effects." He looked down at the black steel box. "Something tells me someone else is using this town in a similar fashion."

Tangent.

Tucker felt an icy finger trace along his spine.

Did we all just hike to ground zero of a new Manhattan Project?

From the worried looks on Frank and Jane's faces, they feared the same thing.

Tucker pointed to the door. "Let's get the hell out of here."

Frank nodded, but Jane moved over to the store's back window and raised a small set of binoculars.

"Jane, what're you doing?"

She waved Tucker over. "You can see the tank and the rest of the Russian equipment from here, parked outside the edge of town. I can make out the faint green glow from under the tank's treads."

"Another of the monitoring devices."

"Before we leave, maybe we should take a closer look." She lowered the binoculars. "Why has Tangent brought in all of this Soviet-era military equipment?"

It was a good question, but right now Tucker sensed time was running out, and he had learned to trust his gut.

"While this stuff is old," Jane pressed, "it's not obsolete. Lots of armies from former Soviet-bloc countries still use such tanks and equipment. What if this is a test run—not only against civilian targets like this town but against military ones?"

Tucker bit his lower lip. Jane was right. All of this smacked of a dry run. But what was the endgame here? Who did Tangent have in its crosshairs?

"If we had a closer look," Jane continued, "gathered all the makes and models, then maybe we could figure out the true objective of all of this. Find out what country—"

Frank cut her off. "Too late for that."

Tucker looked at Frank, who was studying the screen of his control unit, which flowed with video feed from Rex.

"We got company coming," Frank explained. "Black SUV, about a half mile out and moving fast. From the dust trail, it looks like it came from a set of old military bunkers a couple miles away."

It has to be Tangent.

"They'll be here in under a minute," Frank said.

Tucker stated the obvious. "Then it looks like we're not going anywhere."

11:33 P.M.

Karl Webster sat in the passenger seat as the Suburban rattled and bounced across the desert. In the distance, he could make out the dark silhouette of the weathered town, which he had codenamed White City.

He checked his watch and growled to the driver. "Faster, damn it. We're less than thirty minutes out from launch. I'm not going to let this glitch set us behind schedule."

"Yes, sir."

The Suburban shot faster, chewing through the terrain.

Karl turned to the backseat, where a pair of technicians huddled, dressed in gray coveralls, looking none too happy to be headed into the line of fire. "You know which units to check. I want us in and out of there in under fifteen. Got that?"

Both men nodded.

Karl swung around, hoping his ruse held out long enough for him to search the town. He didn't know if Jane Sabatello and her nameless companion with the dog had somehow reached White City, but he intended to make sure they weren't on-site to witness what was about to happen.

Worried, he clutched the assault rifle resting across his knees.

Back at the command center, he had faked a problem with one of the monitoring devices, creating an excuse to come out here. Rafael Lyon had squinted suspiciously when Karl had insisted on personally accompanying the repair techs. Karl had stated that he wanted one final boots-on-the-ground look at the site before midnight. Before Lyon could question him more intently, Pruitt Kellerman had called, wanting an update.

As that French bastard took the call, Karl had used that moment to break free of Kellerman's watchdog.

Still, this stunt would only buy him a narrow window of time.

He stared ahead as the SUV's headlights finally reached the outer edge of the town. The Suburban swept past the array of Soviet military hardware and parked next to the treads of the massive tank, an armored beast weighing forty tons.

The techs piled out while the driver stayed with the vehicle.

Karl took his rifle and followed the two men in coveralls into the town. He limped on his bandaged ankle, where that damned dog had savaged his leg. He used the pain to center himself, to keep focused on his objective . . . even if it meant going behind Lyon's back. Karl had started this mess and intended to clean it up once and for all. But first he had a mystery to solve.

He pictured the two figures in the Expedition photographed at the Stallion Gate, especially one of their faces.

Where are you, Janie?

11:34 P.M.

Tucker lowered his night-vision monocle and turned away from the rear window of the general store. He had waited until the incoming Suburban had braked to a hard stop, stirring up a cloud of sand and dust. He had wanted to know how many had arrived and counted four men: two technicians carrying toolboxes, a driver standing by the open door, and another.

Karl Webster, head of Tangent security.

What was he doing out here?

Tucker frowned at the monitoring device as he rushed away from the window.

Did we inadvertently trigger some alert, drawing these others here?

He suddenly worried that his choice of hiding places might not have been the wisest—not that they had any better options.

Thank God for Kane's sharp nose.

Tucker joined the others next to the open trapdoor in the floor. Earlier, Kane's particular whine had alerted him to this spot. He had not heard that unique note of warning from Kane for several years, not since Afghanistan. Beyond Kane's duties as a military war dog, the shepherd had been trained by a search-and-rescue team to hunt for bodies. *Cadaver sniffing*, it had been called, and it was one of Kane's grimmest tasks. His partner performed such duties with clear reluctance, expressed by the mournful note to that whine.

Alerted by Kane, Tucker had drawn Frank and Jane to the section of planks. If a body was buried under the floorboards, then perhaps there was a way for them to hide below, too. It took only seconds to discover the trapdoor, which led down to a series of tunnels beneath the town, connecting the various buildings. Old defunct power cables ran along the bottom, suggesting the tunnels were used to wire up the old equipment that Trinity scientists had used to monitor the town decades ago.

Once he reached the trapdoor, Tucker hopped through the opening and dropped to a low crouch with Jane and Frank. He pulled the door shut over them all. The pitch-black tunnel was only three feet high and about as wide.

"Let's move out," he said.

Tucker took the lead, crawling on hands and knees. Jane followed with Frank behind her. Tucker intended to use the tunnels to reach the far side of the town, where hopefully they could find an exit and slip away. To achieve that goal, he had sent Kane scouting ahead, while Frank monitored the enemy above through Rex's eyes.

As he led the others, Tucker checked the feed on his phone from his four-legged partner. The night-vision mode of Kane's camera showed a bobbling image as the shepherd traversed the maze. A small blinking dot of Kane's GPS tag marked the dog's path, slowly building a map of this subterranean system for them.

He watched Kane stop beside a crumpled figure that blocked the tunnel.

Must be the source of the odor.

The shepherd nosed the remains, as if trying to revive the corpse.

By Tucker's estimate, the body lay in the tunnels on the far side of the town square. The scent must have drafted through the tunnels to reach Kane's nose at the trapdoor in the general store.

He radioed to Kane's earpiece. "CONTINUE SCOUT."

Obeying the order, the shepherd backed away and found a side tunnel that led away in another direction. Tucker followed after his partner, tracing the glowing bread crumbs on the slowly extending map.

When they reached the turn that led away from the dead body, Tucker had them all hold. "I'm going to check the remains. Maybe they could give us some clue to what's going on here."

Jane came with him, while Frank stayed put, his face awash from the glow of his CUCS unit's screen.

Leading with a penlight, Tucker found the corpse ten feet down the side tunnel. The upper body was half curled on itself, the lower legs trapped under an old cave-in. The remains appeared mummified, with the skin and muscle dried to bone. From the short, brittle-looking hair, Tucker guessed it was a male. The cargo shorts and red shirt suggested it was likely someone young. A caving helmet lay in the dirt.

"I don't think we're going to get any answers here," Jane said. "The body must've been down here for at least a decade."

He nodded and searched the shorts, finding a wallet, a penknife, and a few crumpled dollars. He studied a faded Arizona driver's license, showing the smiling face of a collegiate-looking kid.

His name was Kyle Wallace.

"What was he doing down here?" Jane asked behind him.

Tucker found the answer in a laminated card tucked in the wallet. A logo showed what looked like a haunted house, with the initials APEC stamped atop it. Written along the bottom were the words ABANDONED PLACES EXPLORER CLUB. He shook his head. He had heard of such urban explorers who scavenged and searched lost and abandoned places.

"What do you think?" Jane asked.

Tucker sighed. "Wrong time, wrong place."

It was a soldier's motto. From his tours in Afghanistan, he knew how fickle fate could be: the misstep that exploded a hidden IED under your feet, the chance turn of the head that ended with a bullet through your skull, a sudden wind shear that crashed your helicopter into a mountainside, and on and on.

Jane reached forward and touched his arm, as if sensing the defeat washing through him. Her warm fingers slid down to his wrist and tugged gently. "Let's keep going."

He nodded, but not before pocketing the wallet. He intended to let Kyle's parents know the fate of their son. They deserved to know, especially as the kid's death had inadvertently offered them a possible way to escape this trap.

Tucker intended to make sure that death was not wasted.

He and Jane rejoined Frank and set off again, continuing to follow Kane's lead. As they crossed under another structure, faint voices rose from up ahead. Tucker doused his light and had Frank switch off the glowing screen of his CUCS unit.

Tucker motioned for the others to stop and crept closer to eavesdrop.

A man with a nasally voice echoed from above. "Looks fine to me. Green lights across the board."

A shift of weight creaked the plank floor. "Are you sure this is the one that was glitching?"

"Unit 417B. That's what Webster said was the problem."

"Maybe he got it wrong."

"Well, I don't want to be the one to tell him that. Let's just reboot this damned thing and get our asses out of here. It's less than fifteen minutes until this party starts. And I don't intend to be here when that happens."

"True dat," the other acknowledged with a harsh laugh.

Tucker mentally calculated and guessed the timetable was set for midnight. As he listened to their muffled movement, he willed them to work faster.

After three or four long minutes, the one with the nasal twang announced, "Fuck it. That oughta do it. Let's find Webster and haul ass out of here."

The tread of boots across the floorboards sounded explosively loud.

Tucker waited until he was sure they were gone and called softly to the others. "All clear."

He got them all moving again.

"What did you hear?" Jane asked.

Tucker used his penlight to check his watch. "I heard that we don't want to be here at midnight."

Jane winced. "How much time do—?"

"Nine minutes."

Frank offered even more bad news. "Rex is picking up two bogies in the air to the east. Another four are rising from those bunkers we spotted earlier."

"Drones?" Jane asked.

"Big ones." Frank stared toward the low roof. "Nothin' I've ever seen before."

Tucker remembered Nora mentioning another class of drone, something called a Warhawk. No matter what was coming, Tucker could guess the mission objective.

To level this place to the ground.

He also knew one other fact.

No way we're getting clear of here in time.

22

With his penlight clutched between his teeth, Tucker crawled as fast as he could through the tunnels. Frank and Jane wheezed and gasped behind him, struggling to match his pace. In one hand, he clutched his phone, following the electronic trail left by Kane as the shepherd sought an underground path to the far side of the town. In the upper corner of the screen, he watched the seconds on the digital clock winding toward midnight.

Less than a minute to go . . .

"Frank?" he called back, not needing to explain what he wanted.

Frank scrabbled along with his CUCS unit in one hand. "The first two drones are almost on top of us. Rex has tapped into their systems. The drones' weapons are hot, and an attack pattern is being actively calculated."

So Tangent was right on schedule.

He swore under his breath, knowing he would never reach Kane in time. They all needed to find the best cover. Overhead, the roof was a series of planks as the tunnel burrowed under the floor of another of the structures. Not good. These buildings were surely the targets, and once the bombardment started, the floorboards would offer no protection. He hurried to clear the structure, to reach the section of the tunnel that ran *between* the buildings, hoping being underground would offer them the best shelter to weather the coming storm.

"Faster!" he urged the others.

Tucker got them clear of the building behind them and continued deeper.

Frank yelled, "They're dropping cluster bom—"

Whump!

The earth lurched under Tucker's knees. He dropped flat to his belly as the concussion rippled through his body. A wash of dust swept up from behind and rolled over them. Coughing, he pushed up and continued deeper into the tunnel. The ground shuddered again with a chest-pounding thump. Tucker got slammed sideways into the wall.

More explosions echoed, coming faster and faster.

He glanced back and saw Frank sheltering Jane, the two huddled close to the floor. With his eyesight swimming, his ears ringing, he pulled his phone close to his nose, checking on the status of their last teammate.

The feed from Kane's night-vision camera showed the shepherd racing down a dust-choked tunnel, panicked, zigging and zagging. Then a burst of brilliance exploded, burning away the image on the camera's light-sensitive receptors.

Tucker's heart clenched into a tight knot.

The image returned a moment later, showing a cascade of dirt falling over the camera lens like a shroud—then only darkness.

Kane . . .

Kane breathes dust as the tunnel collapses around him. He flees blindly as the wall of dirt chases him, trying to swallow him up.

All his senses have been overwhelmed. The fiery flash had turned his vision into a red glare. The explosion had set his ears to ringing, followed by a dull deafness now. Sand and smoke clog his nose, stripping him of the trails of night breezes and mice spoor that had led him through the darkness earlier.

His world now is only panted breath and the burn of muscles.

Then a heavy weight strikes his hindquarter, crushing his legs down, sprawling him forward onto his chest. More of the roof falls over him, riding over his body. He claws with his front paws, gouging nails into the dirt. He drags his body forward, an inch, then another, trying to break free.

But he is too slow, too exhausted.

More dirt buries his hips, his back, his chest.

Still, he struggles, gasping his fear.

A wave of sand and dirt rolls over his shoulders. He howls through the darkness. Then more of the world closes over his neck and head, burying him to silence. A heave of his chest only finds dirt. He writhes, but only traps himself further.

He howls again—but only inside, casting out one last plea for help.

Tucker reached the trapdoor in the next structure and stood up, his forearms braced on the trembling dirt walls. He had left Jane and Frank in the insulated section of the tunnel between the last two buildings. From the digital map built by Kane's GPS, he pinpointed his partner's last position, but the building above had been struck by one of the drone's cluster bombs, shattering half its structure and demolishing the tunnel on the far side.

The only way to reach Kane now was across the open battlefield.

But the detonations were coming faster, every few seconds, sometimes above his head, sometimes far enough away that he heard only the muffled detonation through the dirt ceiling.

He stared up.

As bad as it was down in here, aboveground would be worse. The structures of White City would offer no protection against the bombardment.

Still, he didn't hesitate.

He reached up, placed his palms against the hatch, and pushed. Debris rained down on him. He closed his eyes and kept shoving, straining. With a crack, the trapdoor popped free. He pushed it aside, grabbed the edges with both hands, and vaulted himself out onto the floorboards.

Crouched low, he looked around. He had emerged into one of the bungalow homes—or what was left of it. One corner of the roof had caved in, and the back half of the structure was nothing more than splintered studs. Through the gaping hole in the wall, he saw a line of basketball-sized craters.

As he watched, fire and dirt erupted from the neighboring home, shattering wood high into the air. The bass note of the explosion pounded his ears.

He ignored the danger and checked his phone to orient himself.

Kane's last position was beneath a bungalow two doors away on his left.

Tucker turned in that direction and rushed to the front doorway. He creaked it open enough to check the night skies. He heard the buzz of drone engines, but they sounded like they were coming from every direction.

He flashed back to the hunt through the Alabama swamp, which pushed his heart into his throat. He squeezed his eyes shut, fighting against a numbing panic.

Put it away . . . stay on point.

As he opened his eyes, a black-winged shape swept down the street before him, unnervingly quiet. Even this close, its stealthy passage rippled the air, making it appear to be a ghostly mirage. Tucker felt his skin prickle with goose bumps, knowing what glided silently past him.

A Warhawk.

As he watched, it banked away to the right. A moment later, a series of explosions blasted in that direction, leveling more of the town. A hailstorm of shrapnel rained down over the bungalow.

Tucker shook away the palpable terror at the sight of that war machine.

Now or never.

He burst out the door, leaped the porch steps, and hit the ground running. He sprinted across the street, vaulted over the picket fence of the next house, and veered to the backyard. He didn't slow, aiming for the rear of the next bungalow. The place was in even worse shape than the one he had abandoned. It was just a section of roof balanced on a couple of walls.

He hurdled the shattered remains of its porch and skirted through a blast-damaged section of wall. Once inside, he searched the floorboards.

Where the hell is the trapdoor?

The others had been in the structures' corners. He checked the nearest one and found nothing. But in the second corner, he found the hatch—but it was half pinned under a collapsed section of wall. He stomped on the remaining exposed boards, shattering the slats under his boot heel. He then knelt down and clawed the pieces away, ripping his palms and fingertips to bloody shreds.

Come on . . . come on . . .

Once he had enough cleared, he jumped feetfirst into the shaft, then bent forward and crawled into the darkness. He clicked on his penlight and danced its beam across the walls and ceiling. In a white-knuckled grip, he kept one eye on his phone's screen, working his way to the last glowing bread crumb left by Kane.

He followed the tunnel to where it ended.

A wall of dirt and splintered wood filled the passage.

He reached it and started digging, yanking pieces of broken rafters. He pictured the skeletal remains of the young explorer, terrified that Kane would suffer the same fate.

As bombs continued to rain down upon the town above, he clawed and fought, tears blurring his vision.

Don't leave me, buddy . . .

Then his fingertip brushed over something furry.

A paw.

He scrabbled faster, clearing away more and more of the obstruction. Dirt fell over his own shoulders as he labored. He finally reached Kane's face. The dog's eyes were half open, caked with dirt. No breath moved the dust in the air.

I'm too late.

As more tears wet Tucker's cheeks and choked him with grief, he still tore at the dirt. His fingers caught the edge of Kane's vest and curled into the Kevlar-reinforced straps. Bracing his legs, using both arms, he dragged Kane's body out of the debris. Tucker fell onto his back and pulled the limp form over his chest, hugging his friend.

I can't . . .

Tucker didn't know what he was refusing, but he squirmed farther back and rolled Kane alongside him. He brushed dirt from his friend's nose and clutched his muzzle and heaved air through those cold nostrils, feeling Kane's chest rise and fall. With Tucker's fingers ripped and numb, he had no way of checking for a pulse, no room in the cramped tunnel for cardiac compressions.

More concussions echoed down from above, raining dirt over their forms, but Tucker didn't care. He simply held on to his friend, side by side, forcing breath into Kane.

He took in another chest full of air—only to be met by a faint whine from Kane, almost like a complaint.

"Buddy," Tucker whispered in his ear.

Kane stirred, his eyes blinking away the caked grime, paws weakly batting at Tucker's chest. Tucker rubbed his partner all over, digging fingers deep into the dog's ruff, his lips whispering reassurance, more sound than words.

Then finally a warm tongue licked the inside of his wrist.

Eyes stared back at Tucker, reflecting the meager light.

"Who's my good boy?" Tucker asked.

Kane leaned forward and touched his nose to Tucker's.

"That's right, you are."

12:22 A.M.

Hauling Kane in a fireman's carry, Tucker retraced his steps back to the first bungalow. After emerging from the tunnels, he had waited for a few breaths, noting that the squadron of wedge-shaped Warhawks had seemed to turn their deadly attention toward the cluster of Soviet equipment parked on the other side of town.

As explosions echoed from over there, casting up swirling plumes of fiery smoke, Tucker hurried across the blasted ruins of the town to rejoin the others. He didn't know how long this lull would last.

Once at the bungalow, he called down for Frank and Jane to join him. As he waited, he lowered Kane to his paws and examined the shepherd's body more thoroughly. There appeared to be no broken bones, and Kane's thick fur and reinforced vest had protected the dog from all but a few scrapes and cuts. As if irritated by the exam, Kane shook his coat. Still, the shepherd kept close to Tucker's leg, plainly needing the reassurance of his close company.

Tucker felt the same way and rested a palm on Kane's flank.

Frank and Jane climbed through the trapdoor. They were covered head to toe in dirt and dust. Once free, Jane hurried forward and hugged Tucker.

"Thank God . . ." she whispered in his ear.

He returned the affection and would have happily stayed in her arms, but they were not out of danger. He broke free of their embrace, letting Jane greet Kane, and turned his attention to Frank.

"Any success?" Tucker asked him.

"I think so, but I'd be happier if Nora were here to double-check my homework. She knows far more about these drones than I do."

"I'm sure you did fine."

Before leaving to find Kane, Tucker had tasked Frank to try to use Rex as a Trojan Horse in order to sneak code into the squadron of drones. Back in Alabama, the CUCS unit had shielded Tucker and Kane from the Shrike's targeting sights. He had hoped they could use Rex to achieve the same result, to create a blank spot in the drones' surveillance net, a hole through which they might escape.

Even with that protection, getting out of here would be risky.

As if reading Tucker's mind, Frank offered a thin smile. "I was also able to figure something else out."

"What?"

"Rex hacked into and got hold of one of the Warhawks' targeting cues."

"And that means what?"

Frank lifted his CUCS unit. "Come see."

Tucker joined him. The small screen showed a smoky aerial view of the battlefield below. Frank changed the camera angle and summoned a close-up of the nest of bunkers in the neighboring desert.

"While we hightail it out of here," Frank said, "we might want to keep those Tangent guys busy."

Tucker glanced over at Frank. "What're you thinking?"

"I'm guessing this is a shakedown cruise of the drones, testing if they're battle ready." Frank grinned at him. "But as you well know, when it comes to fighting, something always goes wrong. I think I can divert one of those Warhawks to target the bunkers, make it look like a malfunction. If nothing else, it'll give those guys something else to do rather than look our way."

Tucker matched his grin, picturing Karl Webster's face. "Do it."

12:25 A.M.

"The drone's not responding," the technician said, a panicked edge rising in his voice. "It's ignoring all shutdown orders."

In the command bunker, Karl Webster watched over the technician's shoulder. The screen flowed with code, while a smaller window displayed the video feed of a Warhawk sweeping back to its home base.

"What the hell is it doing?" Rafael Lyon asked, flanking the tech on the other side.

Karl leaned closer. "Maybe its self-diagnostics discovered a malfunction, and it's headed back for repairs. If I recall, that's a part of the design protocol for the drones."

The tech shook his head. "It should still respond to our transmissions—and it's coming in with weapons hot."

Karl noted the red glow on the schematic in the upper right corner of the screen, highlighting the Warhawk's cannon array and its twin nests of cluster bombs in its two holds. As he struggled to understand, he glanced over to another screen showing the fiery destruction of White City and the ongoing bombardment of the Soviet equipment parked on its outskirts.

While he had failed to discover any evidence of Jane Sabatello and her male companion out there, if the pair had been foolish enough to hole up in one of the buildings, both were long dead. If not, he already had their Expedition targeted for surveillance.

"Sir!" the tech gasped.

Karl turned back to the screen. The incoming Warhawk had almost reached the bunkers—but a blue glow had appeared on the drone's schematic, lighting up its nose cone.

He knew what that meant.

"It just activated its onboard EW systems," the tech said.

Electronic warfare.

Karl swung around and yelled to the others in the bunker. "Shut down all systems! All communications! Now!"

Before anyone could respond, the lights flared brightly within the concrete bunker. Computer screens flickered, the images dissolving into washes of pixels. Then the lights went out, sinking the place into darkness. A scatter of LEDs and dials glowed from the various monitoring banks, until they died away, too.

"What the hell happened?" Lyon asked. Iron-hard fingers grasped Karl's elbow, demanding the question be answered.

Karl broke free of that grip. He didn't have time to explain the Warhawk's comprehensive suite of EW features: from electromagnetic pulses capable of frying military-grade equipment to jamming technology that could permanently blind systems.

They had only seconds to go.

"Everyone down!" he hollered, knowing what was coming next. "Get under cov—"

The thunderous detonation jolted the ground under Karl's feet, throwing him headlong away from the bunker's entrance. His eardrums popped, and pressure pounded the air from his chest. He didn't remember hitting the floor, only lying there with blood pouring from both nostrils.

He finally rolled to his side and stared toward the front half of the bunker, aglow with smoldering fires. Through a cloud of oily smoke, he spotted the tip of a black wing sticking out of the rubble. He imagined the Warhawk's final kamikaze dive upon its target, igniting its deadly cargo in one mighty blast, enough to crush half of the command bunker to ruin.

He sat up and discovered Rafael Lyon glowering back at him, a deep gash across the French soldier's scalp, painting half his face in blood.

Karl didn't look away.

Despite the miscue in targeting the bunker—something they could diagnose later—the remaining test of the Warhawk squadron's capabilities had been an unqualified success. Kellerman should be happy enough with the results to continue with phase three.

Or at least, that's the way I'll spin it.

12:32 A.M.

From a high hill a mile away, Tucker studied the smoldering ruins of the town through a set of binoculars. Beyond the outskirts, piles of slag metal glowed against the dark sand, marking all that remained of the Soviet tank and equipment.

He was suddenly struck by the surrealism of it all: how decades of old military hardware could be obliterated by twenty-first-century drones equipped with an AI system created by a British mathematician from World War II.

He lowered his binoculars with a shake of his head, struggling to understand.

He rolled over to where Frank and Jane were huddled over the CUCS unit, monitoring events through Rex's eyes. Not only had Frank managed to keep them digitally cloaked from those hawks in the sky, but he had sent one of those raptors down upon the bunker complex.

A small curl of smoke still marked where the drone had crashed itself and its payload on the enemy's compound.

Tucker rolled to his feet, knowing they had to get moving, to get clear of the area before Tangent collected itself after the unexpected assault.

Kane heaved to his legs with a rare huff of complaint.

Tucker patted the dog's side gently. "You said it, buddy."

He joined the others and got them all moving again.

Jane strode alongside him. "Frank had Rex pull as much data as he could from the drone he commandeered, but he'll need Nora's help to decipher even half of it."

He nodded, too tired to consider all the ramifications.

During the hike back to the Expedition, he found Jane's hand in his own. He didn't know who took whose hand or when, but he didn't care. They continued in silence across the desert, happy to be alive.

At least, for now.

23

The next day, Tucker found himself drowsing on a motel bed. An air conditioner hummed nearby, doing its best to hold back the Texas heat. Kane was sprawled beside him, with Jane curled on the dog's far side.

Lucky dog . . .

Then again, they were all lucky.

As he lay there, he listened to the tapping of Frank's laptop keyboard and the low murmur of Nora's voice. After leaving White Sands, the group had returned to the trailer belonging to Sirocco Power and collected their Honda Pilot. Afterward, Tucker had driven the stolen Expedition and dumped it in the middle of the desert after thoroughly wiping it down. From there, the group had hurried back to the resort outside of Las Cruces and collected Nora in the middle of the night. She had still been awake, her eyes puffy and red from working on the code that Sandy Conlon had left on her thumb drive. Tucker skipped any celebratory reunion and got everyone, including Rex, packed up and moving again.

He drove the rest of the night to reach Lubbock, Texas, just before dawn.

On the drive here, Frank and Nora had sat in the backseat with their heads bent together. Frank pored through and shared all the data that Rex had collected, while Nora explained what she had learned about Sandy's code. He doubted the two had slept at all, even after arriving at the motel. While refueling the SUV, Nora had grabbed a six-pack of Rockstar energy drinks from the gas station's convenience store, while Frank stuck to coffee.

"What a beautiful piece of work," Frank said. "I think I'm in love."

Tucker forced open his eyes and rolled his head sideways. Frank sat cross-legged on the neighboring bed with his laptop perched atop his calves. Nora lay on her belly next to him, with her own computer near her nose.

Tucker grumbled, "You cruising porn sites again, Frank?"

The man looked flabbergasted, glancing from Nora back to Tucker. "I didn't . . . what are you—?"

Nora spared him any further embarrassment. "He's talking about Sandy's code for perfecting the AI operating system. It is beautiful."

Frank collected himself, nodding a bit too much. "That's right. The work she did is simply amazing. I barely understand half of it, but with Nora's help, I can appreciate the sheer magnitude of what she accomplished on her own."

Nora rolled around and sat up. "That's Sandy. When she sets her mind on a task, there's no stopping her."

Except to put a bullet through her skull, he thought sourly, but he kept that to himself.

"What's so amazing about it?" Tucker asked.

Frank rubbed his eyes. "It's how she extrapolated Alan Turing's algorithms and theories and found a practical way of implementing them."

Nora smiled, which seemed to erase the exhaustion from her face—or maybe it was her memory of Sandy. "Turing postulated that the crux to building his Oracle—a thinking computer capable of deciphering anything and learning from it—was to build chaos into its systems. He believed chaos or randomness was the key to creative intelligence."

Tucker remembered Jane mentioning how Turing had wanted to put radioactive radium into a computer, hoping its unpredictable radioactive decay would instill randomness into his machines.

Jane stirred, drawn by the conversation. She propped herself up and shoved a couple of pillows behind her back. "What did Sandy figure out?"

"You should really see the code to fully appreciate it," Nora said.

"But at its simplest, Sandy found a way to incorporate *irrational* numbers into the design of the neural nets used to operate the drones."

"If that's the *simplest*," Tucker said, "I'd hate to see what you call *complicated*."

Nora frowned, plainly trying to figure out a way to dumb it down for him.

Frank helped her. "You know computer code is all *zeros* and *ones*. Basically *current on* and *current off*. Sandy found a way to incorporate a whole range of numbers between fully on and fully off."

"Just like there's an infinite set of fractional numbers between zero and one," Nora added. "She figured out if you wire up a neural net in such a way that tiny changes in input trigger bigger changes in outputs, then a feedback loop will—"

Tucker lifted a hand, suppressing a groan. "Okay, I believe you, but how does that help us?"

Nora glanced at Frank.

The man gave a small shake of his head. "You tell him."

"What?" Tucker pressed.

Nora cringed. "To test Sandy's code, I inputted it into Rex."

Tucker glanced to the drone on the floor. Cables ran from its central core to Nora's computer. He tried to imagine what equipping Sandy's new AI with a set of wings might do.

Tucker's voice came out sharper than he intended. "What the hell, Nora? Why did you—?"

"Because I asked her to," Frank said, clearly protective of Nora. "Rex collected too much raw data last night. He got loads of information directly from the drones, but he also sucked up massive amounts of intelligence from those Tangent bunkers before that Warhawk took them out. *Way* too much for me to analyze. It would take me months to even scratch the surface."

Jane put a hand on Tucker's arm, seeming to be a step ahead of him. "They want to use Rex—an improved Rex—to sift through all that raw data and make some educated guess about Tangent's next move."

Frank nodded.

"It's actually pretty brilliant," Jane said, which drew a bashful smile out of Frank. She slid off the bed and joined the other two. "Let me see that code."

Knowing he was outclassed by this discussion, Tucker grabbed

Kane's leash. His partner was immediately up on his paws, showing no hesitation or sign of being nearly suffocated to death hours ago.

"Looks like it's just us," Tucker said.

He headed out into the midday heat. This part of Texas was suffering through a scorching Indian summer. He had grabbed a ball cap before leaving and tugged the bill farther over his eyes. As usual, his gaze swept the parking lot of the Motel 6. With no one about, he didn't bother hooking Kane's leash and headed off with the dog to a neighboring park.

He spent an hour tossing a red rubber Kong ball for Kane, both entertaining the shepherd and reestablishing a bond that went deeper than handler and dog. He also assessed the shepherd's physical health after last night. It took someone who knew Kane intimately to note how the shepherd began to favor his left hind leg—not with a limp, but by being a step slower if Tucker tossed the ball in that direction. Kane pivoted off that leg with less strength, more caution.

Tucker bent down on a knee, opening his arms as Kane returned a final time. He let off a small whistle between his teeth. Kane's ears perked straight up upon hearing this and ran at Tucker. The shepherd dropped the ball, abandoning his favorite toy, and ran full tilt into Tucker, knocking him onto his back. They rolled in the cool grass under the shaded branches of an elm tree, whose leaves had begun to turn a golden yellow.

They play-wrestled for a few minutes, with Kane pretending to bite at his wrists or licking ferociously at his face. Finally, Tucker lay on his back, with Kane sprawled at his side, pinning down Tucker's right arm. Tucker stared through the branches, while Kane panted happily. He could feel all the aches and bruises of the past several days—but also a deep well of contentment . . . especially with his best friend at his side.

He closed his eyes and came close to falling asleep when a shadow passed over him. His body tensed, instantly going alert. But Kane still lay on his arm, his tail wagging.

It wasn't a threat.

He craned back and saw Jane standing there, smiling down at them both.

"Got room for a third?" she asked.

He flopped his left arm across the grass, and Jane dropped down beside him. She snuggled close with her head resting on his shoulder. He could smell the perfume of her honeysuckle-scented shampoo.

"How are Frank and Nora—?"

Jane sighed, sounding disappointed, but not apparently because the others weren't getting anywhere. "I tried to keep up with them, but they moved beyond even my comprehension like twenty minutes ago. I only stayed longer to save face, then found an excuse to leave before they figured me out."

Tucker smiled. "I know what you mean. I felt like a dinosaur in there, a dusty relic from another era. All this talk of a new battlefield—an information war fought with digital code and smart drones—I might as well be a knight facing an armored tank."

She turned her head and smiled at him. "You'll always be my knight."

"Okay, that might be the corniest thing you've ever said."

She laughed. "Maybe . . . but it's true."

Despite his discounting of her words, he recognized she was being genuine. Likewise, he couldn't discount the warmth swelling through him. It was those damned eyes, aglow in the shade, so easy to get lost in. Memories of happier times played through him, rising easily out of the past, perhaps made even easier because he could never fully escape his haunted past. The two were entwined, part of the same fog of war.

Still, their lives had eventually pulled them apart. She'd had a family, a son, a whole existence beyond their shared history. He tried to picture her pregnant, raising a child alone, dealing with the grief of losing her husband. Even now, a familiar fear shone from her eyes, for Nathan.

"Listen, Jane, as your knight in shining armor, I think maybe we need to revisit your involvement here. After that close call at White Sands—"

"No," she said firmly. She propped up to an elbow and looked down at him. "You're not the only one who knows how to read people. You think sending me running back to Nathan will help protect him."

"If you get killed—"

"Then I get killed, and he lives." She dropped onto her back, still nestled against him. "Once I'm out of the way, Tangent will have no need to pursue Nathan. He'll be safe. And besides, it's no life to be always running, always looking over your shoulder. If there's a way to end this, then for Nathan's sake, I'll do anything and everything to give him that chance."

He heard the fierceness behind her words. At heart, she was still a soldier. She refused to sit on the sidelines when it came to protecting her son. Still, he sensed the hesitancy, the doubt, even the guilt. He read it in the seismic tremble in her body. She wanted to be back at Nathan's side.

"Tell me about him," Tucker whispered.

She stared sidelong at him. "What do you mean?"

He shrugged. "Like why did you pick the name Nathan?"

She frowned, as if trying to guess if he was teasing her.

"What's his favorite cereal?" he pressed her gently. "Is there a bedtime story he likes?"

She started slowly. "Nathan . . . he's named after my husband's grandfather, who died of cancer a year before Nate was born. As to breakfast, that boy is a Lucky Charms addict, but he only wants it with warm milk, which I find disgusting. Still, I love stirring his milk on the stove each morning, reminds me of warming his bottle when he was a baby."

Tucker heard the wistful smile in her words as she continued to share Nathan with him, building their lives together in bits and pieces.

"But he can sometimes be a handful, especially lately . . . he's getting to be that age, trying to find his independence, which both makes me proud and breaks my heart a little."

After a time, her words faded into a thoughtful silence. They continued to lie there. Finally, she whispered, "Thank you."

"For what?"

"For reminding me why I'm here."

Her arm drifted across his chest and hugged him, drawing him tighter to her. He rolled up and stared down at her. Her eyes shone with a renewed determination, but also an ember of something warmer, of what might have been . . . and maybe what could still be.

"Tuck . . ." she whispered, slipping fingers through his hair.

He leaned down and kissed her, needing to feel the heat of her lips, to ground him in the here and now, knowing she needed the same. She kissed him back without hesitation. As their breathing grew heavier, passions rising, she pulled back slightly, enough to speak, her lips still brushing his.

"Tucker, I still need to tell you about—"

"Guys!" a voice called from the motel.

Tucker fell to his back, pondering ways to kill Frank.

Jane twisted to face the man as he came running up. He was plainly oblivious to the poor timing of his interruption. "What is it?" she asked.

Frank was breathless. "Nora . . . she found something!"

3:33 P.M.

Back in the motel room, Tucker huddled with Jane and the others around Nora's laptop. "I don't understand," he said. "What am I looking at?"

Frank explained, "Buried inside the brains of the Warhawks, Rex discovered an identical subroutine program, one shared by all the drones. It was sort of like . . . well . . ."

Nora filled in the blank. "Sort of like a *pending* file, for lack of a better term. It was deeply encrypted, but the newly improved Rex had no trouble ripping it open. The file contained a bunch of directives, basically a to-do list for the drones. Most of those seemed connected to operations at White Sands, but deeper in that file, we found a list of directives that made no sense, all dated three days from now."

She pointed to the screen and the list that glowed there.

> 1868
> TSTT
> Opus Networx
> WOWnet
> Interserv
> Carib-Link
> Cablenett
> 110859 / 0604956
> 103543 / 0612014
> IATA: TAB, ICAO: TTCP
> IATA: POS, ICAO: TTPP

Nora scrolled further, revealing the list went on and on for several pages.

Tucker turned to her. "Okay, what does all of this mean?"

She returned to the beginning and identified what was listed on the screen. "These are a country's calling codes. Here are its Internet service providers, airport coordinates, and Internet protocol addresses." She pointed to a set of numbers. "These are emergency, military, and air traffic frequencies for the same country. And look here, this last section lists a bunch of local radio stations."

"What is all of this for?" he asked.

Frank answered, "It's everything someone would need to know to launch a cyber attack upon a country, to literally shut it down lock, stock, and barrel."

Tucker remembered that in this new era of information wars cyber attacks were a critical component.

"And here's the kicker." Frank put his finger on a line of data that read CARIB-LINK. "All this data is tied to a specific little dot in the Caribbean."

"Where?"

"The island of Trinidad."

Jane frowned. "Trinidad? You're talking palm trees, coconuts, calypso music. That Trinidad?"

Nora nodded. "One in the same."

"So you're thinking Tangent is going to orchestrate some sort of attack out there?" Tucker asked.

"Or maybe another test." Frank looked to Nora, who nodded. "We think White Sands was a test of only *one* feature of Tangent's new weapons systems."

Tucker pictured the burning city, the slag of metal glowing outside of town.

Frank continued. "We believe something *different* is going to be tested in Trinidad."

Jane raised a question in Tucker's own mind. "What about all that Soviet military hardware we saw at White Sands? That island can't have more than a few thousand military personnel and virtually no offensive munitions beyond light arms."

Nora nodded. "I checked online. Trinidad buys its weapons

from Sweden and the U.K. Definitely not Russia, let alone an arsenal from the Soviet era."

"So what are you thinking?" Tucker asked.

Nora faced him. "I think Tangent is about to test the next phase of its weapons system, something tied to attacking the digital infrastructure of that island country. It's scheduled for three days from now."

Jane bit her lower lip, getting that determined look in her eyes. "We need to get out there before that happens."

Tucker knew she was right, but first it would require taking another risk, one he had been avoiding until now.

All eyes turned to him, looking for guidance.

"Before we pack our sunscreen," Tucker told them, "we're going to need help."

FOURTH

SMOKE AND MIRRORS

24

Tucker sat with his forehead pressed against the aircraft window as the pilot banked the private jet—a Citation Mustang—across an expanse of indigo water. The green mound of Trinidad slid into view below as they began their descent toward the island's airport.

"I could get used to traveling like this," Frank commented from across the leather-appointed cabin.

Seated behind him, Nora murmured her agreement, a crystal tumbler of Coke in her hand.

Even Jane was impressed. "Tuck, you've certainly made friends in high places."

You have no idea.

Before leaving Texas, he had finally broken down and placed an encrypted call to Ruth Harper, his contact at Sigma command in DC. Until then, he had avoided approaching the covert group due to Sigma's direct involvement with DARPA, the Defense Department's research-and-development agency. Since Tangent Aerospace's work centered on advanced drone technology, he feared DARPA might be equally involved, especially considering the military's cooperation in all of this, at both Redstone Arsenal and White Sands.

While on his home turf in the States, Tucker had preferred to go it alone, but now that the trail led beyond U.S. borders, he knew he needed additional support. When he finally called Ruth, she had not seemed overly surprised to hear from him—which made him wonder if Sigma didn't have a way of tracking him all along. Either way, she had listened to his story, promised to make some discreet inquiries at her end, and arranged their new passports, along with concocting a cover story for their group's trip to Trinidad.

She had offered to ship out a Sigma field operative to join them, but he had refused. The less commotion they made in Trinidad the better. But more important, he didn't want anyone at his side whom he did not fully trust. Besides, the group's goal on this island should be a simple one. After sundown, they planned on sending Rex aloft over Port of Spain, the capital of Trinidad. They were going to use the newly improved drone to perform the task for which it had been built: to collect and gather intelligence. If Tangent was planning something tomorrow, Tucker intended to find out what it was and hopefully stop them.

Tucker had also been prepared to request one other favor from Ruth. Over the past two days of traveling, he had noted the occasional haunted look in Jane's eyes, a haze of worry, fear, and guilt. He knew her son was foremost in her thoughts. Tucker had suggested having Sigma gather up Nathan and get the boy somewhere safe, but Jane had soundly rebuffed him. She trusted those who were watching her son, and she didn't know these unknown "friends" of Tucker's. In the end, he hadn't pressed the matter, recognizing a mirror of his own paranoia in her eyes.

So they were on their own for now.

As the jet began its final descent toward the airport, Kane responded to the change of pressure by lifting his head from where he lay curled at the bulkhead and growled softly, plainly irritated. The shepherd was not a fan of small planes and tolerated such hops as necessary.

Tucker rubbed under Kane's muzzle. "It's okay, buddy. We'll be back on the ground soon."

Kane harrumphed and settled back down.

Frank continued monitoring their flight from across the cabin. "A lot of jungle down there." He glanced toward Tucker, the implication easy to read on his face.

While the island was only the size of Rhode Island, vast areas were sparsely populated and remote. It would be easy for Tangent to hide a drone fleet down there.

Nora spoke up. "Was that Tobago I saw when we circled around?"

"I think so," Tucker answered.

Trinidad was part of a republic that included the island of Tobago to the northeast. Dozens of smaller isles—some inhabited, others deserted—also shared the surrounding seas. The location and climate made this tiny island republic an important area for tourism, but due to large reserves of oil and gas, its main industry was petrochemical. This vast natural resource made this nation the third wealthiest in the Americas, after the United States and Canada.

Is that one of the reasons Tangent had targeted this place?

He had no idea. Any answers waited for them below.

After another minute, the Citation's tires touched down at the Piarco International Airport outside of Port of Spain. Tucker held his breath as they passed through customs, but Ruth's papers held up to scrutiny. Even the plastic crate that housed Rex was only given a cursory glance, the outside emblazoned with NOAA emblems. Ruth's cover story had the group posing as climate scientists associated with the National Oceanographic and Atmospheric Administration. If there were any deeper inquires, Frank and Nora had been scripted with enough technobabble about the weather to further support their cover.

In short order, the group cleared the airport and hailed a taxi. The day was already hot, the humid air smelling heavily of salt. Low-hanging puffy clouds filled the skies. The forecast was for afternoon showers, but the night would be clear, the perfect flying weather for Rex.

As they loaded into a yellow taxi van, Tucker studied an anomaly: several British FV432 armored personnel carriers were parked along the airport's perimeter fence.

Jane noted his attention and whispered to him. "Did you see all the Trinidadian soldiers patrolling the airfield's tarmac?"

He nodded. The soldiers all had assault rifles slung at the ready across their chests.

"Something's definitely up," he muttered.

"Maybe tonight Rex can find out what that's all about."

Tucker had a more immediate source for that information. After they all piled into the back of the van, he leaned toward the driver. "What's going on with all the military in the area? Is there something wrong?"

The young black man spoke with a Jamaican accent. "No trouble, mon. Nothing you need worry about. It's paradise here."

Still, Tucker caught the man's eyes in the rearview mirror.

Guy's nervous, plainly putting on a happy face for the tourists.

Tucker pressed the cabbie. "Listen, we got work on the other side of the island. I'm this team's security. If there's anything I should know about . . ." He reached forward and held out a folded hundred-dollar bill. "I'd appreciate the heads-up."

The bill vanished, and the driver squinted at Tucker in the rearview mirror before finally confiding to him. "We got an election comin' up in a couple days. Lots of tension, mon. No one likes President D'Abreo." Even the name drew a scowl from the cabbie. "His government . . . be corrupt as they come. Some say there could be rioting if he be reelected. So maybe you keep an extra eye on your peoples."

Tucker nodded to the man. "Thanks for the warning."

"But like I said, mostly just talk." The man offered a wide grin of reassurance. "Troubles come and go in Trinidad like the rains. You be fine."

Tucker hoped he was right.

As he sat back, Jane leaned closer. "Sounds like a powder keg is brewing."

One that wouldn't take much of a match to ignite.

Tucker sat back for the remainder of the ride. They passed two more APCs on their way to the city. The cab even had to go through an armed checkpoint before entering the capital.

Nora shifted forward from the van's third row. "Guy's right about the tension here." She lifted up the iPad she had been working on. "The government has been trying to downplay it, to keep it out of the media."

"Don't want to scare away the tourists," Frank guessed.

Nora nodded. "The main competitor for the current administration is a grassroots political party. Something called the TPP, the Trinidadian People's Party. They've been threatening violence if the upcoming presidential election doesn't go their way. They claim the current administration is crooked, including his entire cabinet ministry. The TPP is talking revolution."

Tucker eyed yet another armored carrier parked alongside the road. "Looks like D'Abreo is taking that threat seriously."

Frank's face had gone a touch paler. "We need to get Rex in the air. Find out what's really brewing here."

As they continued into the city, Tucker took stock of his surroundings. They had left behind the palm-lined highways and lush hills for a sprawling metropolis. Port of Spain spread for eighteen miles along the coast of the Gulf of Paria and was home to more than a hundred thousand people.

Tucker couldn't help but wonder what Tangent had in store for them.

What is the enemy's interest in this tiny Caribbean republic?

The taxi finally swept off the main drag and up a lilac-strewn driveway. They circled a central fountain and stopped before the lobby of the Hyatt Regency. A pair of valet attendants in starched white shirts hurried forward, opening doors and ushering them out with warm greetings. The only hiccup in their well-researched routine was when seventy pounds of Belgian shepherd hopped out of the backseat.

One of the attendants stumbled back, but the older of the two held his ground, firming his faltering smile. "Oh my . . . what a beautiful dog."

Without missing a beat, the man waved for the bellhops to come collect their luggage, then led them all into a marble-floored lobby. Faint calypso music played in the background. To the left, floor-to-ceiling windows looked across palm trees, white sand beaches, and the flat blue waters of the Caribbean.

Walking alongside him, Jane took Tucker's hand. "You take me to the nicest places."

"Let's hope it stays *nice*."

Within a few minutes, they were checked into a two-bedroom penthouse suite on the twentieth floor with a wraparound balcony that offered generous views of both the city and the gulf.

"Wow," Frank murmured, exploring the carpeted space. "This sure beats Motel 6."

More focused on the task at hand, Nora rolled the case holding the Wasp drone over to the main living area. She looked anxious to check on Rex after the long flight, to make sure there wasn't any damage. Her intensity drew Frank away from the view.

As she unbuckled the drone's case, Kane began his own duty, which involved thoroughly sniffing every corner of the room.

Jane had to sidestep the industrious dog to reach the bar. Someone had fully stocked it for them, leaving behind a gift basket of fruits and cheeses. Jane read the note aloud. *"Play nice . . . and don't forget the sunscreen. R. H."*

Tucker shook his head. Ruth Harper was certainly thorough.

Jane tossed the card aside and stepped behind the bar. "Anyone else want a drink?"

Tucker was tempted to follow her example, but he wanted to make sure one other detail had been properly arranged for them by their diligent benefactor. He moved to the closet. Inside, he found the hotel minisafe was already locked. He dialed in the code that Ruth had given him, got the green light, and opened the small door.

Three pistols lay inside: all SIG Sauer P225s. There were also matching shoulder holsters, extra magazines, and four boxes of 9 mm ammunition.

From behind the bar, Jane watched him remove the weapons. "Okay, those friends of yours . . . they're getting to be a little scary."

But they certainly have their uses.

He carried everything over to the sofa, inspected the pistols, and began loading the magazines. Steps away, Nora and Frank had Rex already hooked to a laptop, preparing the drone for tonight's sojourn.

Jane returned with two gin and tonics and settled onto the sofa next to him.

"Those both for you?" he asked.

She passed him one. "I think you're gonna need this."

She swirled her glass, tinkling the ice, and took a sip, as if gathering the courage to speak—but then the phone rang, echoing from various locations around the suite.

Tucker crinkled his brow and reached to the handset on the end table. He expected it to be a courtesy call from reception, making sure the accommodations met their expectations.

"Sir, this is Santiago from the front desk," a crisp voice responded as he answered. "We have a gentleman here who is inquiring if he could speak to you, but he didn't know your name—only showed me a picture of you."

A picture?

"So I thought it prudent that I confirm with you first before connecting the call."

Tucker felt warning bells going off in his head.

Did someone follow us from the airport?

Before responding, he palmed the receiver and spoke to Jane. "Get everything packed up again and ready to move." He returned to the receptionist on the phone. "Thank you, Santiago. You can put the gentleman through, but I'd appreciate if you didn't share our room number until I know who this is."

"Of course, sir. I'll put him on one of our lobby phones. Just a moment."

Tucker listened to a shuffle, a click, then a voice answered with a prominent French accent. "It's high time we had a chat, *mon ami*, don't you think?"

Tucker immediately recognized that harsh accent, picturing the scarred face of the soldier who had accompanied Karl Webster to the swamp.

Before Tucker could respond, the caller continued. "Let's say fifteen minutes in the lobby lounge. Just you and me."

The man hung up.

Jane stared wide-eyed at Tucker as he lowered the handset. "Who was that?"

"Trouble."

25

As the elevator doors opened, Tucker tugged at the edges of his cardigan sweater. He kept his hands away from the SIG Sauer holstered at his armpit. He had left Jane and Frank equally armed up at the suite, stationing Kane with them as extra security. He didn't expect the French soldier would be so bold as to attack him amid the midday bustle of the hotel lobby, but he wasn't going to this meeting unarmed.

Tucker exited the elevator and scanned the lobby, trying to spot anyone who looked his way. The caller had said he had come alone, but Tucker wouldn't put it past the man to bring backup. Tucker especially kept an eye out for the bulky form of Karl Webster.

Failing to identify anyone suspicious, Tucker followed a placard to the lobby lounge. It was an intimate space of red-cushioned chairs positioned around small coffee tables. A number of hotel patrons occupied various tables, but on the far side near the windows, a lone hand raised into the air.

Tucker's heart quickened at the familiar sight of his nemesis. The French soldier had shed his commando gear for loose linen trousers and a black silk shirt. If the man was armed, he hid it well. Still, Tucker approached cautiously. The man appeared to be in his midthirties, squat and heavily muscled, with a sun-weathered face and a shaven head.

As Tucker joined him, the man stood up and held out a calloused hand. "Good morning."

Tucker refrained from taking that hand, picturing Takashi's head exploding from a sniper round. Here was the young man's killer.

Seemingly not offended, the soldier lowered his arm and took his seat. "Thank you for taking this meeting."

Again Tucker noted how the man had not yet referred to him by name. He imagined part of the purpose of this sit-down was to unnerve him. Using Tucker's name would have had that effect.

Means the guy doesn't know who I am . . . at least not yet.

Tucker sank down to his own chair. "And who am I taking this meeting with?"

"Name's Rafael. Let's leave it at that."

Tucker had no way of knowing if this was the truth, but he didn't question it. He had ways of double-checking this information later. For now, he wanted to find out what this meeting was all about.

"You're a good tail," Tucker said. "I never spotted you at the airport."

Rafael shrugged at the compliment. "You did not make it easy to find you." The man reached to a pocket and pulled out a photograph, which he slid across the table. "And neither did Ms. Sabatello."

Tucker held back a flinch at the mention of Jane's name. Instead, he studied the photo. It showed his profile and Jane's face behind the windshield of the stolen Expedition. It must have been taken when they had stopped at the Stallion Gate at White Sands.

Rafael explained, "The day after our operations at White Sands we learned of a robbery report by a pair of Sirocco Power employees, which included the theft of their company SUV, a vehicle which miraculously turned up at White Sands bearing a pair of new Sirocco surveyors. You are resourceful, *mon ami.*"

But apparently not resourceful enough.

Tucker inwardly winced. He clearly hadn't covered his tracks as thoroughly as he had hoped back in New Mexico. Still, he kept his voice nonchalant. "I'm surprised it took you a full day to realize that your security at White Sands had been breached. It seems like we caught Karl Webster sleeping at his post."

Rafael's lips tightened before responding. Clearly Tucker had touched a nerve. "It is unfortunate—a lapse that will be dealt with once Webster shows his face again."

Interesting.

The head of Tangent security must have fled, knowing his days were numbered. Webster's failures had been mounting: first Jane had escaped his purge of Project 623, then Tucker had raided his encampment at Redstone, and finally Tucker and Jane had slipped through the cordon he had placed around White Sands.

No wonder Webster vanished.

Rafael collected the photo from the table. "I had no way of knowing what you two might have learned concerning our operations here in Trinidad, and unlike Karl Webster, I am not one to leave loose ends. So as a precaution, I placed the airport under surveillance, to watch for anyone matching your descriptions."

"Smart. So you found us. What next?"

"I've simply come with a proposal, a way to put this matter to rest."

"If it's along the lines of *leave the island or we'll kill you*, let's skip ahead."

Rafael smiled. In contrast to his tan face, his white teeth shone. "I know you don't frighten easily. Besides, why use violence when reason might work?"

"Then lucky for you, I'm a very *reasonable* man."

Rafael clearly recognized the sarcasm but chose to ignore it. "We have no quarrel with you. Yes, you've caused a lot of problems for Tangent, but my employer is willing to put it in the past."

"That's very generous of him, but just who is your employer?"

Rafael raised an eyebrow.

Tucker shrugged. "Worth a try."

From the man's choice of words, it sounded as if Rafael's employer was someone *outside* of Tangent, maybe the person behind all of this.

"Like I was saying," Rafael continued, "he is willing to put this in the past *if* you'll back off and return to your own lives."

"That's a lot to ask. Aside from getting to remain breathing and aboveground, what's in it for us?"

"Name a figure and I'll present it to my employer."

"Five million dollars."

Rafael didn't miss a beat. "I'm sure that can be arranged."

"And with that, you'd let us all go?"

"My employer is a man of his word."

Though Rafael betrayed nothing, Tucker knew this was a lie. He also learned one other thing from this exchange. The man had not mentioned anything about the drone that Tucker's group had stolen, indicating the enemy must still believe Rex was somewhere buried in the mud of the Tennessee River. Rafael had also given no indication that he knew about Sandy's research or about the thumb drive that Tucker had obtained from the dead woman's mother.

If these bastards knew about the tech in our possession, it would have been part of these negotiations.

"So do we have a deal?" Rafael asked and held out his hand again.

This time, Tucker took it. "We do."

It was a lie, but Tucker suspected Rafael knew as much. The soldier was no fool. This entire exchange was nothing more than a fishing expedition by the enemy, one meant to acquire information about Tucker and the others, while intimidating them at the same time.

And it seemed that fishing expedition wasn't quite finished.

"You never did tell me *your* name," Rafael said, his iron fingers still clamped on Tucker's hand.

Tucker squeezed harder. "I'll be going down to Starbucks tomorrow morning. You can always have me followed and see what name the barista writes on my cup."

Rafael chuckled and let his hand go. "You know, I like you."

"So it would be a shame if you had to kill me."

"Indeed."

"But it wouldn't stop you."

"Not for a second. And you?"

"Not for a *half* second." Tucker grinned. "And for your boss, even less than that."

Rafael accepted that threat with grace. "Then it's good we're all friends now."

"The very best of friends."

Rafael gave a slight bow of his head and departed. Tucker waited until the man left the hotel before returning to the elevator. Once inside, he kept his hands away from the hidden pistol, but his fingers adjusted the tiny camera lens hidden next to the middle button of his cardigan. He had stripped the surveillance gear from Kane's tactical vest and donned it before taking this meeting.

Rafael hadn't been the only one fishing.

Let's see if Ruth and her resources at Sigma can help identify this guy.

1:23 P.M.

An hour later, Jane continued her nervous pacing of the penthouse. A curious Kane sat on the sofa, his head tracking her path as if watching a tennis match. She moved like a caged lioness, all energy with no way to expend it.

After returning from his talk with Rafael, Tucker had kept them all locked down in their suite. He had pulled the balcony curtains closed after inspecting the sight lines to their rooms. While there were no buildings taller than the Hyatt nearby from which a sniper could take a shot at them, Tangent clearly had drones that could buzz past the building at any time.

Tucker also did not trust the Hyatt's privacy policy. A rich enough bribe to the right bellhop could reveal their room number. Tucker knew only one thing for certain about their accommodations.

We're trapped here.

Nora stirred from where she hunched over a computer, stretching a kink from her neck. She and Frank had been working on Rex, checking and double-checking everything, waiting for sunset. The pair—along with Jane's help—had also been trying to get the lay of the land.

Nora motioned for Tucker and Jane to join her. "Frank and I have been doing a little spitballing," she said. "Whatever Tangent is up to here, it has to be tied to that list of codes we pulled from White Sands. That list encompasses the entire digital infrastructure for these islands."

Tucker remembered the pages of country calling codes, radio stations, Internet protocols, and air traffic control frequencies—both civilian and military. He remembered Frank mentioning it was all anyone would need to wage a cyber attack and shut this tiny nation down.

Nora continued. "We began wondering what Tangent could gain by launching a cyber strike. There must be a significant payoff, something that would be worth trying to start a war between the current government and those TPP revolutionaries the cabbie described."

"What did you find?" Tucker asked.

She handed him an iPad. On the screen was a *Wall Street Journal* story dated four months earlier. "Read this."

Tucker scanned the piece. "This is all about the discovery of a new oil field," he mumbled, and looked up.

Frank nodded. "A deepwater deposit just off the northeastern tip of the island, someplace called Salybia Bay. Geologically speaking, it's a mother lode. The government is still debating how to proceed. Right now, it's a football that's still in the air."

"A very valuable football," Nora added.

Tucker tried to follow the thread of their premise. "You're thinking that Tangent—or whoever is truly behind all of this—is planning to destabilize the country, to turn Trinidad on its head, all in order to go after that oil field."

Jane started pacing again. Her eyes took on that familiar faraway look whenever she was concentrating hard. "Whoever backs the winner in this political conflict could be handed a fortune in paybacks afterward. They could auction off infrastructure contracts, direct kickbacks to the right parties, plus maybe collect a piece of the downstream oil output."

Tucker's stomach churned queasily. "What you're talking about is orchestrating a coup. That's classic spook stuff, the kind of operations the CIA ran in Guatemala and Chile."

Jane faced him. "Only instead of a government intelligence service pulling this off, it's a private company."

Tucker swallowed.

How can we even think of stopping this?

A phone rang sharply—but it wasn't the hotel line this time. Tucker crossed to his satellite phone sitting on the bar and answered it.

"Ruth, tell me you have something?" he said.

"Do I ever let you down, honey?" Ruth's southern drawl was always laid on extra thick whenever she was joking with him.

"What did you find out?"

"First, that the gentleman you met earlier is no gentleman." Ruth's voice sharpened, going serious. "His name is Rafael Lyon, and he's bad business. Former French Special Forces, outfitted with the BFST—Brigade des Forces Spéciales Terre."

Tucker closed his eyes. Back in Afghanistan, he had witnessed BFST's prowess firsthand. They fielded some of the finest shooters and toughest soldiers out there.

"Six years ago, Lyon ran into some trouble in Chad," Ruth continued. "Killed some villagers and got himself brought up on war-crime charges—that is, until those charges suddenly evaporated. After that, Lyon dropped off the map. Even his financials are run through a series of tax havens and Swiss accounts. He's definitely shady. I'll need more than an hour to discover who he truly is and who he works for."

"Are you thinking he's a mercenary for hire?"

"Maybe, but I don't believe a megacorporation like Tangent Aerospace would have hired a former war criminal, exonerated or not. Instead, I think you were right that there must be another player in all of this, an unknown puppet master who employs Lyon for his dirty work." Ruth sighed, plainly exasperated. "Anyway, that's all I could dig up over the past hour, but I have additional feelers out and hopefully I'll know more soon."

Tucker gave a small shake of his head.

"Except for one other bit of intel," Ruth added. Tucker could picture her wry smile. "Lyon used a credit card under his name three days ago to hire a car. I was able to contact the rental agency and get the VIN, which allowed me to access its GPS."

"You know where his car is?"

"Parked at West Bay Boats. He rented a runabout twenty minutes ago. I called the company office and was able to sweet-talk my way into finding out what he listed as his destination."

"Which was what?"

"Patos Island. It's a little blip about nine miles from Trinidad's westernmost tip. It lies just across the country's maritime border with Venezuela."

"How little of a blip are we talking about?"

"It's an islet that's a mile long and a quarter mile wide. All jungle, not a single human resident."

Which would offer someone plenty of privacy and cover to hide a drone fleet.

"Of course, he might have falsified that form," Ruth warned. "That might not have been his real destination."

That was certainly true, but there was only one way to find out.

He said his good-byes to Ruth, while getting assurances from her that she would still look into Rafael Lyon's true allegiances.

He then faced Kane. "Hey, buddy, you feel like playing pirate?"

2:34 P.M. EDT
Smith Island, Maryland

Seated behind his office desk, Pruitt Kellerman clutched the phone harder to his ear. On the other end of the connection, the noise of an outboard engine ate up the caller's words.

He checked his watch. He was due to meet with his daughter, Laura, to discuss a contractual dispute that arose following the telecommunications conference in Athens—then Rafael Lyon had called with an update from Trinidad. Pruitt wanted this latest matter dealt with as expeditiously as possible before Laura grew suspicious of all these urgent calls from Horizon's head of security. His daughter was no fool, and before long questions would arise, questions he would have a hard time satisfactorily answering without involving her— which must not happen.

"Say again," Pruitt yelled, irritated and angry. "You met this mystery man. Who is he?"

"Don't know," Lyon answered. "He's definitely an American citizen. Former Special Forces, if I had to wager. But he gave nothing away in our discussion. I couldn't even get a rise out of him when I mentioned Jane Sabatello."

"But you said he had a price. Five million."

Lyon snorted. "He has no intention of honoring that bargain. There's been too much blood spilled. Likewise, he knew we would never stick to our end of the deal."

"Then we put the screws to him. Every man has vulnerabilities . . . someone close to him, someone we can reach. We find that, and we've got him."

"But first we have to know *who* he is," Lyon reminded Pruitt. "His group is traveling under fake passports. Good ones. Papers like that take either lots of money or powerful connections to forge."

Pruitt swung his chair to look out across Chesapeake Bay toward the silhouette of DC. If Lyon was correct, this could be a troublesome development. Pruitt had made plenty of enemies, in both the political and private sector.

So who's pulling this guy's strings?

Lyon interrupted this thought. "Sir, it'll be hard to pin this man down. Let me handle him in my own way."

Pruitt quashed the urge to reprimand Lyon. Just as one doesn't tell a doctor how to remove an appendix, he was reluctant to tell a man with Lyon's experience how to deal with such matters.

At least not yet.

"Very well," Pruitt said. "What's your plan?"

Lyon shouted to be heard as the outboard motor whined louder in the background. "I left a trail of bread crumbs for our target to follow. If he's as good as I think he is, he'll pick up that trail, and I'll be waiting for him."

"Just get it done. I won't tolerate any more mistakes, not after all the security lapses by that incompetent bastard Webster."

"Don't worry," Lyon said. "By nightfall, it will be over—for all of them."

26

"How's it going?" Tucker asked Frank.

The man stalked around the drone sitting atop the coffee table, doing a final inspection. "Rex is not picking up any scents," Frank said. "We should be good to go."

Frank looked to Nora, who was seated at her laptop with wires trailing from the computer to the drone. She gave a nod of agreement.

It was a couple of hours after sunset and full night had fallen over the capital city. They had activated Rex's suite of sensors and had been monitoring for any telltale electronic signatures of Tangent's drones in the area. Apparently all remained quiet.

"I still don't like us splitting up," Frank said.

"It'll be hard enough for Kane and me to sneak out of the hotel on our own. With all of you in tow, it would be all but impossible to slip past whoever must be watching this place."

Frank did not look convinced. "But if we use Rex—"

"Rex has plenty on his plate tonight as it is. I need you and Nora to get this bird in the air and out into the night. While I investigate this island, you all tap into the digital infrastructure of the city and try to find out what the enemy is planning. Rex may be all that stands between Tangent and the destruction of this city. For all I know, this trip to Patos Island could be a wild goose chase."

And if not, it would be too dangerous to bring the others.

Tucker pressed the matter. "With Rex in the sky, having your back, you'll all be safer laying low here. If worse comes to worst, I'm leaving you and Jane with the other two SIGs."

Jane stood nearby, donning her shoulder holster.

Nora unhooked the leads running to the drone. "Tucker is right. We need Rex here, and I might need your help, Frank. Especially with that side project you and I were working on."

Tucker frowned. "What side project?"

Frank matched his expression. "You have your secret mission. We have ours."

Nora shook her head at their antics. "It's actually too technical to explain in a short time."

Jane smiled. "Tuck, I think she just called you stupid."

Probably right.

Tucker didn't feel like pressing the matter. "Fine. Let's get Rex in the air."

They all backed away as Frank used the CUCS unit to start Rex's motor and set the four propellers to spinning. A low buzz filled the space, tickling the small hairs on the back of Tucker's neck. The drone rose smoothly off the coffee table and hovered in the middle of the room.

It was an eerie sight to see this war machine hanging in the air, barely moving. Tucker knew that beneath that matte-black exterior was the true heart of the next generation of warfare. The prickling over his skin grew, as if he could feel the eyes of the drone upon him, this future electronic warrior staring down at its outdated and obsolete counterpart of flesh and blood.

Jane and Nora hurried to the balcony doors, pulled the curtains, and opened the sliding doors. Frank guided the drone forward and out to the balcony. Once Rex sailed beyond the railing, the women closed the doors and resecured the curtains. Nora joined Frank as he continued to monitor Rex's ascent above the city.

Tucker dropped to a knee next to Kane. He scuffled the dog's ears with both hands. "Ready to do some hunting, big boy?"

Kane's tail swished more vigorously, carving his excitement through the air.

He gave the shepherd a one-armed hug, then rose and grabbed his backpack, which held all of Kane's tactical gear. He already had his SIG Sauer holstered with spare magazines weighing down his pockets.

He checked his watch. "You know what to do?" he asked Frank.

The man waved at him dismissively, his eyes still on Rex's flight. "Go already!"

He headed to the door with Kane. Earlier, they had used Rex's electronic warfare suite to hack into the Hyatt's computers and extract the schematics for the hotel property and tap into the security cameras.

"Am I clear?" he called to Nora who sat at her laptop.

"Hall's empty," she confirmed for him. "The rest of the way down looks good, too."

He nodded to her, opened the door, and dashed outside. He led Kane to the stairs. They hurried down the steps, descending the twenty floors to the lobby, but Tucker continued to the subbasement level, where access was restricted. An electronic keypad secured the door to this lower level, but Rex had obtained the key for him.

Tucker tapped in the code and the door unlocked. He hurried through and into a cavernous garage space. Black limos with the Hyatt logo on their doors were parked along one wall. There was also an airport shuttle. He paused at the door to make sure the private garage remained empty. Failing to spot anyone, Tucker rushed to a locked and alarmed cabinet beside the first limo. He dialed in the proper code courtesy of Rex and got the green light. He opened the cabinet and searched the keys until he found the one for the shuttle.

He nabbed it, closed the cabinet, and rushed with Kane to the small bus.

Once close enough, he used the fob to electronically fold open the side door and waved Kane inside. He began to follow when the hotel door to the garage opened behind him.

Crap.

He lunged into the shuttle and hit the fob button to close the bus's doors. He stayed low, hoping he hadn't been spotted. But the shuttle's interior lights remained lit, apparently on a delayed timer. In the dark garage, the bus was lit up like a Christmas tree.

He heard a rush of steps coming his way.

He freed his pistol, his mind flashing through various scenarios. If it was one of Lyon's men, Tucker planned on dealing with him quickly. If it was simply hotel security, that would be a trickier matter. He thought of ways of subduing the man before any alarm could be raised, but even if Tucker was successful, the delay could upset the timetable. Everything from here depended on perfect timing.

A fist rapped on the door. "Is there room for one more?"

Despite all his planning, he had failed to anticipate this scenario. He stood up and hit the release for the door with the flat of his hand.

Jane smiled at him and climbed into the shuttle. "You didn't really think I'd let you and Kane leave without me?" She pushed past him and dropped into the driver's seat. She held out her palm. "Keys, please."

"Janie—?"

"The others have Rex to guard them, and Frank is armed and trained for combat. I'm not about to stay up there twiddling my thumbs while you and Kane put yourselves in harm's way."

She glanced back at him, her eyes stone cold. This was clearly not up for discussion. He knew a large part of her anxiety about waiting in the hotel likely centered on a certain towheaded little boy. She needed to keep moving. He sagged, accepting the inevitable, though not liking it. Kane, on the other hand, seemed more than happy to have the trio reunited. The shepherd nosed her and wagged his tail merrily.

"I'm obviously outvoted," he said.

Jane tapped her wrist with a finger. "And we're on a bit of a time crunch."

Tucker sighed and slapped the keys into her hand. "Try not to hit anything."

She scowled at him, started the engine, and got the bus turned around and slowly headed up the ramp toward the exit. She took her time. As she drew near the closed security door at the top, an electronic key on the dashboard flickered and the gate began to rise.

"Hunch down," Tucker warned her, while he crouched next to Kane. He checked his watch. "We have another twenty seconds."

She nodded, hunkering lower.

They watched the garage door continue to open.

"Five seconds."

Earlier, Tucker had anticipated that Lyon would not leave this exit to the hotel unwatched. And while the cover of a hotel shuttle bus might escape casual scrutiny, Tucker wanted extra insurance.

He watched the last second click away.

"Go," he said.

As Jane goosed the engine and got the shuttle rolling toward the open door, their unseen partner on this mission performed right on schedule. The scatter of garage lights blinked off as the electricity to the hotel was cut off. Outside, streetlamps flickered and went dark.

Good boy, Rex.

The drone, using its bundle of electronic warfare tools, had tapped into the city's power grid and blacked out this corner of Port of Spain. The island was plagued by periodic outages, so what was one more? The power would be restored in another minute, which offered Tucker and Jane the additional blanket of darkness to help cover their escape.

Unfortunately, cutting the power had one unanticipated effect.

The garage door started to lower ahead of them, likely an emergency precaution against looters. Jane noted the same and gunned the engine, jolting the shuttle forward. Tucker grabbed the back of the driver's seat to keep his position.

The bus shot under the dropping door.

They were not going to—

Tucker winced as metal grated on metal. Jane did not slow. Hunched over the wheel, she forced the bus forward, ignoring the grinding complaint of the descending door. They finally dragged free and made it to the street. Jane turned them sharply and got them moving even faster through the darkened section of the city.

Tucker straightened, glancing to the roof. "What did I tell you about not hitting anything?"

She waved him off. "Quit being a backseat driver."

9:03 P.M.

Tucker eased back the throttle of the old powerboat and glided to a stop. Swells lapped at the wooden hull, causing the craft to rock on the darkened surface of the water. High above, the sickle of the moon shone brightly in a cloudless sky. The engine puttered softly, as a balmy night breeze swept across the bow, bringing with it the salty scent of the Caribbean Sea.

Tucker checked the GPS map on his sat phone. "We should be about there." He gazed ahead but saw nothing but the black waters etched in traceries of silvery moonlight.

Kane hopped from the neighboring passenger seat and crossed to the rear bench. He lifted his nose to the breeze, sniffing deeply. The shepherd was once again decked out in his K9 Storm vest and tactical equipment. The weight of his gear always set Kane to full alert. The dog knew it was time to get to work.

Jane settled into the seat vacated by Kane. She picked at a curl of paint along the rail next to her and cast up an eyebrow toward Tucker. "Did you have to rent the worst boat they had?"

He shrugged.

The twenty-two-foot runabout was at least fifty years old, its wooden hull splotched by mismatched layers of varnish and fiberglass tape. Its vinyl seats and plastic dashboard looked held together by nothing more than duct tape and bailing wire. The Plexiglas windscreen even had a bullet hole directly in front of the driver's seat.

They had rented the boat from a small village northwest of Port of Spain. The proprietor of the tiny marina, a short man named Petrie, had shrugged when Tucker had questioned the boat's state. "Meh," he said. "Take, no take. Okay by me."

Since there was little other choice at that hour, Tucker chose to *take*.

Jane dug out a pair of the binoculars from her backpack, rose from her seat, and aimed the glasses into the darkness. "Well, it got us here," she said after a moment.

Keeping their speed at a moderate pace, it had taken them a half hour to cross the thirteen miles of open sea that separated Trinidad from this tiny island off the Venezuelan coast. These waters were called the Bocas del Dragón—or the Dragon's Mouth. Like the bullet hole in the windscreen, the name was not the most positive of omens.

Jane passed Tucker the binoculars. He searched the sea and spotted a dark smudge, a tiny speck of land, about a half mile off the bow. A churning white line marked where the surf met the shore, which appeared to be an unbroken line of ten-foot cliffs.

"It doesn't look like much," Jane said.

"It might be small, but it's got room enough to hide a small fleet of drones."

Jane huffed out a breath, plainly agreeing with him. "If Tangent was looking for a place from which to launch a coup, Patos Island would be a perfect choice. This empty spit of land lies just outside Trinidad's territorial waters but within a few minutes' flight of Port of Spain."

Tucker pulled out a set of sea charts from his pack, courtesy of the marina's proprietor. "According to the map, a set of coves breaks up these cliffs near the western tip of the island. I'm guessing somewhere around there is where Tangent would have set up its base of operations. We'll have to go in dark and hope—"

Kane let out a warning growl behind him. Tucker turned and looked toward his partner, who was still half up on the rear bench. The dog's body had gone taut. Kane's head panned from left to right, as though trying to pin down something. Suddenly his gaze snapped directly astern.

Tucker saw nothing but flat, black ocean. Farther in the distance, the lights of Port of Spain glowed.

"What's wrong with Kane?" Jane asked as another growl rolled from the dog's throat.

Tucker grabbed his sat phone and tapped to bring up the feed from Kane's camera. Through night-vision mode, the seas appeared far brighter, almost luminescent. On the screen, an object emerged from the deeper gloom, a spherical shape gliding ten feet above the surface of the water.

Tucker's heart filled his throat, recognizing that silhouette from the Alabama swamps. "It's a Shrike. Incoming."

27

"Get down!" Tucker yelled.

Jane dropped flat to the boat's floorboards, while Kane hopped off the rear bench and tucked himself against the backseat's riser. Tucker ducked lower and slammed the throttle forward. The aging engine growled, and the boat surged forward.

"Hold on to something!" he shouted.

He spun the wheel hard to port, then back to starboard, slaloming across the water, trying to confound the drone's targeting. But he knew that once the Shrike locked on to the boat, its rounds would shred the runabout—and them.

The only hope lay in getting them into the nearest cove.

He resisted the impulse to look over his shoulder.

Drive, drive, drive . . .

As Tucker kept up his serpentine maneuver, the island grew rapidly in size ahead of him. To his right, he spotted a break in the white line of surf.

One of the coves.

It was still two hundred yards away.

They'd never make it.

"Jane, grab our packs! We're bailing out."

Their boat was too large a target, but in the dark water, they'd be harder to spot.

Before he could order them to abandon ship, a geyser of water shot up a few feet off the boat's starboard bow. Spray washed over his face. Tucker imagined the drone was bracketing them, fine tuning for its next shot, which if he was right, should strike off the port side—so he spun the wheel hard to *starboard*.

As the runabout lunged into the turn, another plume erupted beyond the port gunwale. He then straightened the boat's course and aimed for the cove.

"Ready, Jane?" he called.

"As I'll ever be."

As Tucker abandoned the driver's seat, the runabout jolted. He got slammed forward, banging his forehead against the steering wheel. He blinked hard. His vision swirled. Glancing over his shoulder, he saw a jagged series of holes strafed across the floorboards near the stern. Water gushed through the openings.

"Over the side! Go!"

Jane got to her knees, threw her torso over the gunwale, then disappeared beyond the edge. Tucker reached sideways, grasped Kane's vest collar, and heaved the dog into his lap. He then stood up and rolled over the boat's other rail.

Dark seas enveloped them. Tucker got bowled through the water, holding hard to Kane. Once his momentum bled away, he kicked to the surface and broke into the air. Tucker released Kane from his embrace, but he kept ahold of the shepherd's collar.

Twenty feet ahead, the runabout sped into the cove. The Shrike fired down at it, chasing after it. The drone then silently shot upward at a steep angle, barrel-rolling to set up for another attack run.

"Jane?" he called out.

"Here, right here."

He spotted her and swam over. By the time he reached her, the runabout had disappeared from view around a sandbar in the cove. A loud splintering crash echoed to them as the boat ran aground.

Still, the Shrike dove out of the night skies and continued to fire in that direction, apparently not yet satisfied with the level of destruction.

But how long until it turns its attention this way?

Tucker pushed that thought out of his head and concentrated on swimming toward a sandbar fifty yards to his left. The others matched his pace. With every stroke, Tucker expected the Shrike to come skimming across the water, its cannons blazing in the dark.

But the distraction of the boat's flight and crash bought them the two minutes necessary to reach the sandbar's shallows. Tucker stood up and helped Jane to her feet. They trudged through the knee-deep water. Twenty feet to the right rose a wall of palm trees and brush.

Tucker pointed Kane in that direction. "COVER."

The waterlogged dog sprinted toward the trees, with Tucker and Jane chasing behind. The trio ducked into the undergrowth. Once a safe distance into the jungle, Tucker ordered them to drop flat. He rolled to Kane and gestured for the dog to crawl back to the edge of the tree line. He wanted to use the dog's night-vision camera to spy on the cove.

As his four-legged partner moved into position, he turned to Jane, who panted beside him. With his eyes adjusted to the dark, he noted a trickle of blood running from her scalp across her right cheek. Until now, the seawater had been keeping her face washed clean.

"You're hurt," he said.

She fingered the wound. "Burns like a mother. Clipped my head on the edge of the boat after bailing out."

She was lucky she hadn't run afoul of the boat's propeller.

Concerned, he risked pulling out his penlight. Shielding the brightness, he checked her wound, then her pupils. One seemed less responsive.

He doused the light. "Are you feeling nauseous?"

"Can't say I'm feeling great," she said, trying to pass off her words as a joke.

"You might have a slight concussion."

"Better that," she mumbled, "than floating facedown in the Caribbean Sea."

Let's hope it doesn't still come to that.

He huddled over his satellite phone and pulled up Kane's feed. Jane shifted closer to see. Shoulder to shoulder, they watched Kane sink low in the underbrush at the edge of the beach. The camera's view showed the curve of the palm-lined beach. Twenty feet from the waterline lay the remains of the runabout. The violent grounding had all but shredded the craft. A debris-strewn rut in the sand marked the runabout's path, ending at the capsized bow section.

Jane mumbled, "You're not gonna get your deposit back on that boat."

At least her humor was still intact.

"What now?" she asked.

Tucker waited a full minute, but he saw no further sign of the Shrike. His ears strained for its telltale buzz, but all he heard was the gentle slap of waves on sand.

Jane noted the same. "Has the Shrike left?"

"It could be off searching the neighboring waters." But another more disturbing possibility rose to mind. "Or maybe it's completed its mission."

Jane glanced to him, wrinkling her brow.

He explained. "Its primary purpose was likely to kill us, but failing that, maybe it had been instructed to drive us to ground here on the island and strand us."

He remembered how the Shrike had continued to fire into the wreckage of the beached boat, making sure the craft was completely disabled.

"If you're right," Jane said, "then Lyon's men must be close by, preparing a welcoming committee for us."

"Which means we need to move. While they might not know which cove we'd be stranded at, you can be sure they're closing in here now."

A low growl sounded in his earpiece. Kane's sharper senses must have detected something. Tucker could guess what that meant.

"We're about to have company," he warned Jane, then subvocalized into his throat mike, ordering Kane back to their side.

He helped Jane stand, but once on her feet, she weaved unsteadily. He had to grab her arm to keep her from falling.

"Oh, God . . ." she said, then jackknifed in half and vomited into the shrubs. She stayed bent over for several breaths, wiped her lips, and straightened. "Sorry."

"At least you missed my boots," he said, but he couldn't keep his words light.

Concern ached through him. She definitely had a concussion. With no way of telling how bad it was, he knew she shouldn't be moved, but they couldn't stay here. He scooped an arm around her waist and supported her. She didn't refuse his help, which alone told him how sick she was feeling.

In the distance, a new sound intruded—faint at first, then louder.

It was the thumping of helicopter rotors. Tucker looked toward the beach. Through the foliage, blinking red-and-green lights headed toward the shoreline.

"Too much to hope it's a rescue party?" Jane said wryly.

Kane slipped through the brush and joined them, panting lightly, his eyes bright in the darkness. Tucker patted the dog's side, welcoming him back. Kane didn't wag his tail, still on full alert. Under his palm, Tucker felt the tremble of tension in the dog's flank muscles. After Kane's near suffocation in the collapsed tunnel, Tucker feared he might be pushing the dog too far, too quickly.

"Follow," he whispered to Kane, but it was less an order than a plea.

Even Kane heard this change in tone and gave him a small whisk of his tail, as if to say he was okay.

That's a good boy.

With Jane under one arm, he set off deeper into the forest, driven by the growing thump of helicopter rotors. Ducking and weaving through the undergrowth, he headed inland until he had covered a hundred yards.

"Let's stop here," he said, now all but carrying Jane.

He lowered her down and dropped to a knee beside her. Half of her face was covered in blood, seeping from her head wound. His heart thudded in his chest. Kane pressed his body against Tucker's thigh—both reassuring him and looking for the same in return.

Tucker stroked the dog's head while listening with an ear cocked.

By now, the sound of the rotors had faded. Though unable to see the helicopter, he knew such aircraft well enough to tell from the sound of the engines that it must be hovering over the beach. He twisted in that direction. As he did so, the helicopter's spotlight flared through breaks in the foliage. The onboard crew must be inspecting the runabout's wreckage for bodies or signs of survivors. It wouldn't take them long to discover the set of footprints and paw prints leaving the surf.

As if cued by this thought, the spotlight slid sideways, toward where he and the others had entered the jungle.

The engine began spooling down as the helicopter prepared to land. They'd be offloading a search team in moments. He had no doubt Lyon would be with that party. Back at the hotel, the former soldier had struck Tucker as a hands-on type of guy.

He stared over at Jane. She had seen enough combat herself to recognize the same. "We have to keep moving," she said.

He nodded.

But to where?

Tucker got Jane back on her feet. He tried to recall the geography of Patos Island. The tallest and most thickly forested sections were to the northeast, so Tucker headed that way.

As he set off, the helicopter's engine whined down, and a voice shouted from the direction of the beach, echoing through the trees. There was no mistaking the harsh French accent.

"*. . . three teams . . . that way . . . head north . . .*"

Even if those teams were only two men each, that meant a minimum of six combatants. With those bad odds, they needed an advantage—and there was only one way to achieve that.

Dread iced Tucker's gut. He stopped and leaned Jane against a tree. As she rested there, he crouched before Kane and looked into those trusting eyes. It took all of Tucker's effort to lift his arm and point west, away from their path.

A string of orders flowed from his lips. "Hide and seek. Make noise. Elude and cover. Shadow attack bravo."

While these commands were simple enough by themselves, when they were strung together as an action plan, only a handful of dogs were smart enough to understand what was being asked of them. He was ordering Kane to play cat and mouse with the enemy, like the shepherd had done outside the cabins at Redstone. Only now, Tucker was also asking his partner to purposefully make noise and lure Lyon's men away from Tucker and Jane's trail, to risk his life for their sakes.

Tucker leaned down, pressed his face against Kane's snout, and kissed it. With guilt eating a hole in his heart, he whispered, "Go."

Kane follows the acrid note of burning oil that cuts through the forest, carried by the night breeze off the ocean. Other scents fill out his world in this strange new place: the rot of leaf under his paws as he runs, the decay of mold on the fallen trunk he vaults over, the bitter spoor under a nest in a tree.

All is cast in salt by the sea.

Even his own coat is brackish from his short swim.

But he stays focused.

*As he nears the beach, a more familiar odor is carried on the stiffer gusts off the sea: sweat rising from skin, smoke on breath, unwashed clothes ripe with bodily stains. Obeying the first of his orders—*HIDE AND SEEK*—he circles that swell of scents. He notes his targets' positions, listening to the cracking of twigs, the crush of undergrowth, the rip of cloth on thorn. Once satisfied, he shifts in the direction his partner had ordered, away from where he takes the woman.*

Only then does he reveal himself, following his next instruction.

MAKE NOISE.

Kane draws his chest full—and howls into the dark forest. As his challenge echoes through the trees, shouts rise behind him. Branches now break, boots smash through brush, even the pant of breath reaches his taut ears. The enemy closes upon him, but he is already gone, gliding farther into the forest, away from his partner.

He barks again, to make sure the others keep on his trail.

ELUDE AND COVER.

Scents and sounds paint the world around him as vividly as anything his eyes reveal. He senses the enemy being dragged in his wake.

He howls again as he runs, this time not to draw the others with him, but to call to his partner, to let him know he lives, but also to share one certain truth.

I'm a good boy.

"Is he going to be okay?" Jane asked, leaning heavily on Tucker, her boots half dragging beneath her.

Tucker kept a firm grip around her waist. His own breath had grown ragged by now, partly from the exertion, but also from the anxiety as he listened to Kane's barks and yips.

"Of course he'll be okay," he answered, but his words of reassurance were more for his own benefit than for Jane's.

Occasional shouts echoed through the forest as Lyon's hunters pursued the shepherd's trail. The task he had given Kane was a daunting one, a challenge that would tax even Kane's substantial experience. While over the years his partner had proven adept at this game of cat and mouse, this night there were too many cats in the field, all intent on killing them.

Still, Tucker trudged on, intending to use every second that Kane bought them to get Jane somewhere safe. He continued northeast, while Kane drew Lyon's men to the west. The jungle thickened around him, and the grade steepened as they neared a low hill of broken cliffs that rose on this end of the island.

As he plodded along with Jane, Tucker kept one ear on Kane's progress and the other listening intently for any sign of pursuit on their trail. Lyon was not one to be easily fooled. After a time, the soldier would come to realize—if he didn't already—that a skilled dog like Kane would not give away his position so readily.

Knowing that, Tucker did his best to mask their trail, carefully placing one foot after another. Kane barked sporadically, sounding farther and farther away, changing pitch and direction, drawing his pursuers first one way, then another. Tucker desperately wanted to look at his phone's screen and check on his partner, but it was all he could do to stay upright on his burning legs.

"There," Jane gasped in his ear.

He pulled his attention forward, to where Jane pointed.

"Is that a cave?" she asked.

Through a break in the canopy, moonlight shone down on a section of cliff to his right. At the base was a jumble of moss-encrusted boulders, but in the shadow of that nest was a darker patch in the rock face.

"Maybe," he said, and marched them closer.

Lowering Jane to sit, he took out his penlight, blinked it once, and inspected the opening. The space was less a cave than an alcove, barely enough to hold one person.

Jane noted the same. "I can fit in there."

"Janie . . ."

Her eyes glowed back at him. "Cover the entrance, then go find Kane. He can't do this alone. I'll be fine."

As if to prove this, she wriggled into the narrow space and pulled in her knees. "See? Snug as a bug."

The blast of a rifle in the distance was far more convincing than her assurances. He searched over his shoulder as more gunfire erupted.

Kane . . .

Kane's ears ring with the chatter of gunfire, stripping him of one of his senses. His world is smaller now, edged by panic.

He ducks his head low as he runs, pivoting off one hind leg, then the other.

A moment ago, he had failed to note a squat shape lying in ambush under a tangle of deadfall. The moldering mound of fallen trees and branches, redolent with rot and fungus, had masked the hunter's odor—until it was too late. Once close enough, Kane had caught the barest whiff of a familiar scent, one he recognized from days ago.

From back in the swamps, in the building of rust and concrete dust.

It was the same hunter as before.

With this brief warning, Kane had dodged at the last moment. Still, the round had glanced across the flank of his thick vest, bruising his ribs.

He ignores the pain and keeps running.

Gunfire chases him deeper into the forest.

Only after it dies down does Kane slow. He circles back around. His hearing slowly returns, filling in the blank spaces of his world. But he leans on a keener sense. He has latched on to the scent of the hidden hunter—and once captured, it is his.

He follows it around to come quietly upon the deadfall from behind.

While he could have continued to flee—which he wanted the other to believe he had—Kane's last order burned brightly behind his eyes.

Shadow attack bravo.

He reaches the hunter's hiding spot in time to hear the man crawl free. The crackle of a radio marks his position. The man's voice hardens with command as he stands. Kane skulks forward enough to see him point toward where his partner and the woman had retreated.

Kane does not understand the man's words, but the threat is plain in his voice. Fury burns brightly in Kane's chest. As the man turns away, he reads the anger in the other's scowl, a ferocity that matches his own.

Kane knows the hunter now suspects the true intent of the game here.

Before the man can head off in that direction, Kane lunges out of the shadows behind the man. He moves silently, not even offering a growl of challenge. Instead, he snaps at the tender flesh below the other's knee. Fangs sink deep. A toss of his head rips flesh and throws the man down.

But this is no ordinary prey.

The man makes no sound of surprise or complaint. A knife flashes, whisking past the tip of Kane's ears. Kane rolls away from that threat, bunches his hind legs, and bolts back into the forest.

He runs again as a spatter of rounds rip leaves and shatters branches overhead.

He keeps going, knowing the hunter, wounded and angry, would send others after him. Maybe not all, but enough to help his partner.

Crouched at the entrance to the small cave, Tucker listened as the fresh spate of gunfire died away. Jane must have read his concern.

"Go," she said, shifting deeper into the tiny space. "That's an order, soldier."

Tucker nodded, knowing she was right. In her state, Jane could not travel much farther. This spot was likely the best place for her to hole up, while he and Kane kept attention away from her.

He began gathering palm fronds to hide the cave entrance. "Try not to fall asleep," he warned her as he began covering the opening, fearful that her concussion could worsen.

"Fall asleep?" she offered him a weak smile. "Not a chance in hell."

Good.

As he leaned down to place the last frond, Jane abruptly reached up, cupped his cheek, and drew him closer. "One last order, soldier." She kissed him on the lips, lingering for a moment, then settled back, her eyes aglow. "Come back."

"Abandon you on this desolate rock? Not a chance in hell."

Another spatter of gunfire erupted behind him.

Jane waved him away. "Get moving. Your partner needs you."

Tucker obeyed. He freed his SIG Sauer from its shoulder holster and started making his way back down the forested slope. He moved swiftly at first, aiming west, toward where Kane had been engaging the enemy. His heart pounded in his throat. After that last round of gunfire, Kane had gone silent. With each step, Tucker's dread grew.

Had Kane been shot?

He had to stamp down that fear and keep moving, which soon became harder. As Tucker neared the western reaches of the island, he entered the search grid of his pursuers. It was now his turn to play hide-and-seek. To continue, he stuck to the deepest shadows and placed each boot down with great care. Through the forest, the sounds of the hunters grew all around him: the squelch of radios, murmured voices, the faint crunch of footfalls.

"This way," a voice whispered on his right, sounding only yards away.

Tucker dropped flat, rolled under the low branches of a thorny bush, and lay perfectly still.

The boots of a soldier in combat gear passed within a foot of his nose.

Another followed behind him.

Tucker held his breath.

The first man leaned his cheek to a shoulder radio. "Sector Delta clear."

As the pair moved on, Tucker slowly let out the trapped air in his lungs. He gained his feet and set off, angling away from the soldiers' trail. Two more times, he had to quickly hide, but eventually the sounds of Lyon's search parties fell behind him, growing fainter.

Still, there was no further sign of Kane: no barking, no growls of attack.

Where are you, buddy?

Tucker forged on for another ten minutes, moving at a glacial pace when all he wanted to do was rush to his partner's side. After hearing no sign of Lyon's men for several minutes, Tucker risked breaking radio silence. He tapped the small microphone taped to his throat and subvocalized a single quiet word.

"KANE."

The shepherd had been trained only to respond if doing so

wouldn't endanger his position. Tucker pushed the radio earpiece more firmly in place, but he still heard only silence.

"KANE," he tried again.

Then a faint growl tickled his ear.

Tucker closed his eyes, relieved but still fearful. For Kane to have responded, the dog must be hiding somewhere safe at the moment. Tucker intended to make sure he remained that way.

"STAY IN COVER."

Tucker pulled up the map on his satellite phone and pinpointed the pulsing green dot that marked the GPS transmitter built into Kane's vest. He started moving in that direction. His gaze alternated between his screen and the terrain before him. As he drew closer, his pace grew faster, anxious to reach Kane's side.

Almost there, buddy.

Distracted, he stepped around the bole of a palm and found a soldier blocking his path. The man seemed equally surprised to see Tucker pop out of the shadows. Unlucky for Tucker, the man's assault rifle was casually pointed in his direction. The muzzle of the rifle flicked toward Tucker's chest. As the soldier fired, Tucker twisted sideways. A trio of rounds spat past his rib cage. Tucker lifted his pistol—but before he could fire, the man suddenly came tumbling forward with a gasp of surprise, sprawling facedown.

Kane bowled over the body and clamped his powerful jaws on the man's forearm. The assault rifle clattered to the side. But the soldier rolled, hooked a leg around Kane's body, and threw the dog down hard.

Tucker charged forward with his pistol raised, but he refrained from firing, fearful of hitting Kane as the two wrestled. The soldier's free arm rose. Moonlight glinted off a knife blade. It seemed to hover there—then plunged into the dog's body.

Kane yelped, but he kept his grip on the man's arm.

Tucker's heart filled his throat. As the man's hand arced upward again, Tucker dove headfirst. He caught the soldier's wrist between his palms, yanked the captured arm straight up, then shifted his hips and levered the man's arm across his own belly. With a muffled pop, the elbow gave way.

The man let out an agonized scream.

Tucker wrenched the dagger from his grasp and stabbed the blade into the hollow of the man's throat. The soldier's scream turned into a strangled cry. Tucker twisted the blade, blood gushing over his fingers. The man's body flailed for a breath, then went still.

Tucker rolled off the limp form and signaled Kane to his side. They had no time for a warm greeting or to check Kane's injuries. Lyon and his men had surely heard the commotion. Tucker headed out with Kane, moving farther west, away from Jane.

As he fled, the forest grew thinner around them. Ahead, he heard the pound of surf on rock. He was running out of island.

Behind him, panicked shouts rose.

"Here! I need some help!"

"Gleason's down!"

"Leave him. Spread out!"

The last command was frosted with a French accent.

Lyon . . .

Tucker ran faster. He weighed the odds of cutting back north to where the jungles were thicker, but Kane had started limping. The shepherd slowed rapidly, panting hard in pain. No way Kane could move swiftly enough to stay ahead of the closing net behind them, and Tucker would never abandon his partner.

Tucker kept them going straight. In less than a minute, they reached a cliff. Standing at the edge, he stared down at the dark water crashing against the rocks below. He could only imagine the currents, riptides, and undertows beneath those churning waters. To his right, he spotted a tiny area of flat water—no larger than a kiddie pool—sheltered in a U-shaped pocket of an outcropping.

It'll have to do.

He looked down at his friend. "Ready, pal?"

Kane wagged his tail.

Good enough.

Tucker holstered his pistol, reached down, and hauled the shepherd into his arms. Kane winced. Fresh blood squeezed out of the dog's fur and warmed Tucker's palm. The dagger had cut deep—but *how* deep would have to wait.

"Sorry, buddy," he whispered in Kane's ear. "Here we go!"

He tightened his arms and jumped.

28

With Kane wrapped tightly against his chest, Tucker plunged beneath the surface of the roiling surf. He didn't know how deep this pool was, so he kept his legs slightly bent against the coming impact. Still, the collision with the seabed drove him to his knees, then forward onto his face. The air shot from his lungs. Pain flashed behind his eyes.

Pinned under Tucker's torso, Kane got slammed flat into the sand and began squirming. Tucker rolled and shoved the dog upward, then followed. They broke the surface together.

At Tucker's side, Kane paddled hard, his mouth agape, his eyes wild with fear. Surf crashed against the nearby rocks, heaving up in great plumes of saltwater.

Tucker grabbed the dog's collar and pulled him close. "Easy, buddy, easy . . . it's okay, you're okay."

Kane relaxed in his grip. The shepherd's head lolled back, and a hot tongue licked Tucker's cheek and chin.

Love you, too, big guy.

Then from above, a shout rose over the pound of the waves. *"Got tracks over here! Headin' toward the cliff!"*

Tucker kicked madly toward the rocks, fearful of being spotted. Once close enough, he boosted Kane onto the outcropping that framed the pool and crawled up after him. He searched for a hiding place, but there was no convenient sea cave in sight. Their best bet was a slight overhang, a lip of rock that stuck out less than a foot from the cliff's face. With his boots sliding on the slick surface, he led Kane to the spot and hugged the wall under the overhang.

Kane followed suit, pressing against the rock at Tucker's feet.

As they hid, rocks and dirt cascaded past their hiding spot from above.

"*Watch your feet!*" someone shouted from above. "*Edge is crumbling away!*"

"*See anything?*"

A pair of flashlight beams speared down from the top of the cliff and panned over the rocks, skimming just past Tucker's chest. He sucked in a breath, trying to narrow his silhouette. He could only watch as the beam skittered at his toes.

"*Nothing. Sonofabitch. Better let Lyon know. Hopefully the bastard and his dog drowned.*"

"*Let's make sure. You search right and I'll go left. We'll meet back here.*"

The beams split to either side and scanned the surrounding cliffs and surf.

Tucker shivered as he waited. His hands started to shake—but not from the cold.

Here he was hunted and hiding again. He flashed to Afghanistan, where that was his life, day in and day out, separated by bouts of numbing boredom, which only heightened the moments of tension and stress. Such highs and lows rewired your brain. Perhaps irrevocably. While Tucker's PTSD was better, it was far from cured. He still had no control over the stomach-churning ebb and flow of his anxiety.

Tucker squeezed his eyes shut and balled his fists.

Don't try to control it, he reminded himself. *Manage it . . . cope with it.*

Instead, he counted his blessings, most of which were bundled up in fur at his feet. He also pictured Jane's face, remembering her kiss, her lips. The warmth of that memory—overlaid with those happier times with her and with Kane in the past—helped calm the trembling in his body.

"*Anything?*" a voice asked above as the beams converged back on this section of the cliff.

"Guy's gone."

"Lyon's not going to be happy without a body."

"He'll have to be. We're running down to the zero hour."

A radio crackled above. After a few seconds, one of the men said, *"Roger that, on our way."* The man then informed his partner. *"What did I tell you? Boss wants us back at the helo. It's go time."*

"What about our targets?"

"If that bastard and his dog are still around here somewhere, they're going to wish we had shot them quickly."

A harsh laugh followed. *"Let's get the hell off this rock before it blows."*

Footsteps pounded away.

Tucker waited several painstaking minutes. In the distance, he heard the faint whir of the helicopter's engines spooling up. On that cue, he got Kane moving along the battered shoreline to where a section of the cliff had broken into a flow of steep rubble. He hauled Kane over his shoulders in a fireman's carry and scaled the slope, with one hand holding the dog steady.

I got you, buddy.

Once at the top, Tucker continued to carry Kane. The thump of helicopter blades grew louder as the aircraft lifted off the nearby beach. Tucker hurried and reached the cover of the canopy, where he finally put Kane down. A quick inspection revealed a three-inch laceration in the dog's left shoulder. Tucker stanched the bleeding and wrapped the wound with a roll of gauze from the first-aid kit tucked in one of Kane's waterproof vest pockets. Still, the dog could no longer put weight on the limb.

He led the shepherd back to the edge of the beach, and from the tree line, caught sight of the helicopter's lights sweeping across the Bocas del Dragón Strait toward Trinidad. Sensing time was running short, he ordered Kane to stay hidden in the beachside brush and then ran headlong into the jungle. He clicked his penlight on to help guide him back to Jane, not worrying if Lyon had left any men on the island. Especially as the last words of the soldiers had lit a fire under Tucker.

Let's get the hell off this rock before it blows.

Tucker intended to heed that sage advice.

10:34 P.M.

By the time Tucker retraced his steps to Jane, his legs burned and his breath came in gasps. Before he could reach her cave, she kicked away the layer of fronds and flew out of the alcove and into his arms.

"Thank God. I saw the helicopter lift off. I didn't know . . ." She hugged him even tighter, then pulled back. She searched the jungle around them, her eyes going wide. "Wh—Where's Kane?"

"Safe, but hurt. I left him at the beach." He grabbed her arm and searched her face. "How are you doing?"

"Still feel a bit hungover, but better."

"Good. Because we need to haul ass back to the beach."

He got her moving, trying to support her, but she shook off his arm and moved on her own. She was definitely better. Relief helped shed the exhaustion from Tucker's own limbs. He explained the danger as they rushed toward the beach.

As the threat sank in, Jane's gaze swept the jungle all around. "You think they're going to bomb this place?"

"Sounded that way." Tucker pictured the cluster bombs raining down upon the derelict town in New Mexico. "We don't want to be on this island when that happens."

They reached Kane, who greeted them with a wagging tail. As they stumbled out onto the beach, the dog was already beginning to bear weight on his injured leg.

"Oh my God," Jane gasped out.

Beyond the dark waters of the strait, orange flames rose from Port of Spain. Near the city center, a small mushroom cloud erupted and lit up the night sky. A few seconds later, the rumble of the explosions washed over to them, sounding like distant fireworks.

Jane's voice grew hushed with horror. "We're too late. It's already started."

Zero hour, Tucker thought, remembering the conversation he had overheard. As he stared, fireballs rolled into the night sky above the city skyline. He pictured Warhawks and Shrikes ripping through clouds of smoke.

"Those poor people." Jane turned to him. "And what about Frank and Nora?"

Tucker already had his sat phone in hand and dialed the Hyatt, but all he got was a prerecorded emergency message. He shook his head, answering Jane's silent question.

He swung away, casting aside his fears for his friends. "We can't do anything to help them from here. Hopefully Rex gave them enough warning to get somewhere safe." He headed toward the ruins of their runabout, its bulk shattered in a trail of debris across the sand. "Help me salvage anything that could float. Life jackets, sections of wooden decking, empty fuel cans. We have to fashion some sort of raft and get the hell off this rock."

Tucker grabbed a curved section of the broken bow and began dragging it toward the water. They could never swim to safety through the hard currents that wrapped around the island. To survive, they needed some means of staying afloat. The Venezuelan coastline was only four or five miles to the west of the island. They had a slim chance of making it there if they hurried.

Jane climbed and sifted through the debris. She pulled out the remains of an orange life vest and tossed it toward him.

"Lyon must have lured us to this godforsaken place," Tucker realized aloud. "I should have seen this coming. Tracking that bastard here had been too easy. Somebody like him doesn't make those kinds of mistakes." He pictured the Shrike that had come up from behind their boat and attacked. It had flown from the direction of Trinidad, not this tiny island. "Patos was never their base of operations."

Jane inspected a red fuel can, but a round had perforated it. She threw it angrily into the jungle. "He clearly wanted us out of the way and trapped us here."

Where he could kill us at his leisure.

Tucker attempted to get the broken section of bow to float, but it sank to the sandy bottom of the cove. Exhausted and frustrated, he glanced toward the burning city and listened to the distant thunder of the bombardment.

"We're running out of time," he said, sensing it with a soldier's intuition.

Jane stared at him.

"I think the only reason this speck of an island hasn't already been bombed," Tucker explained, "is that Lyon didn't want to show his hand early. If he had blown this place up first, he could have inadvertently alerted Trinidad's military."

"But now that the attack is under way—"

"We're free game."

Knowing this, they redoubled their efforts, but it was to no avail. Kane rose to his haunches. His nose pointed to the night sky, and a growl of warning flowed from his throat.

Between bursts of explosion, a new noise intruded, the familiar buzz of a drone's engines echoing over the water. The noise grew and trebled. Tucker cursed, knowing what that meant. Lyon was not taking any chances. The bastard had sent a cadre of drones their way.

Tucker scowled at the sunken section of broken bow.

We're not getting off this island anytime soon.

"Back into the jungle," he ordered, waving toward cover.

They barely made it under the canopy when the first drone glided low over the water of the cove. The Warhawk reached the beach and arced higher, skimming across the treetops, rustling the leaves with its passage.

In its wake, another pair followed.

A moment later, a shattering boom rocked the island. A fiery burst lit the forest to the west. Tucker stepped out of cover long enough to study the damage. A spiral of flame shot high into the air, roiling through a black cloud. This was no cluster bomb like before. A gust of wind brought a burning, chemical smell, not unlike gasoline, but this wasn't anything you'd want in the tank of your car.

"What is it?" Jane called to him.

He dashed back to her as a second and third explosion erupted from the heart of the island.

"The drones are dropping napalm. Lyon must be planning on burning this island down to the bedrock."

With us on it.

11:04 P.M. EDT
Smith Island, Maryland

Pruitt Kellerman stalked along the banks of television monitors mounted across the wall of his office. The screens displayed broadcasts from the various channels that Horizon Media Corp owned. Talking heads spoke animatedly, though Pruitt had the volume muted. He would occasionally read the updates from Trinidad scrolling along the bottom edges. Or if some new live feed from Port of Spain popped up on one of the screens, he would use his remote to raise the volume.

But his best source of information sat at his desk. His daughter crouched over her personal laptop, an iPad Pro, and his own desktop, manipulating all three devices with the skill of a master pianist. Laura was the one person who he ever allowed to sit on his leather chair, which was only fitting.

Someday all of this will be hers.

He hoped it was a legacy that she would one day make legitimate.

New footage drew his attention to one of the televisions. A church was engulfed in flames. Its Gothic steeple lay broken and charred. Fires glowed through the rosette of a stained-glass window, casting its beauty in a hellish light.

Clenching his jaw in fury, he turned up the volume. He had instructed the technicians overseeing the attack to spare the city's historic buildings.

The anchor on the screen wore an equally angry expression. *". . . latest from Port of Spain. We have footage of the Cathedral of the Holy Trinity. One of the city's oldest landmarks, dating back to 1818. Chaos and panic still grips the capital city. Martial law has been declared. The military is still struggling to combat this terrorist attack, one believed at this time to be orchestrated by a revolutionary group, the Trinidadian People's Party. As soon as—"*

He muted the sound again. At least that much of the campaign was sticking to the game plan. The bombing was meant to cause chaos, while beneath the fire and smoke, the true war was being waged. The drone fleet's suite of electronic warfare tools had already hacked into the island's communication infrastructure, allowing the programming's psy-ops—psychological operations—to disseminate misinformation through all of the commandeered channels.

The programming spread rumors and innuendos, while simultaneously sowing false reports throughout the media. As he well knew, if someone read or heard it in the news, it was believed. And even better, when finessed just right, that misinformation multiplied from one source to another, spreading like digital wildfire, laying waste to the truth and leaving only the fabricated story in its wake.

He turned to his daughter for confirmation. As Horizon's director of communications, she was monitoring all the social media coming out of the area, keeping her finger on a pulse far more current than any broadcast news channel. Over the past hours, he had to tread carefully to keep Laura in the dark about his role in all of this. But her presence here also offered an opportunity.

If Laura could not discern the real story behind the fabrication, then no other media outlet would likely be able to do any better.

"What are you hearing about this revolutionary party?" he asked.

She shook her head. "Everyone seems to think it's this TPP group behind the attacks and bombings. The Twitter feed from the region is rife with speculation about whether the party leaders knew about this attack or if it's a splinter group that's to blame."

"What about *how* these terrorists could have orchestrated such a coordinated attack?"

"That's what has everyone panicked." Laura brushed a few auburn curls from her face as she glanced up. She looked exhausted but determined. "Some reports are saying that armored vehicles were seen firing rocket-propelled grenades at various targets. Others saw helicopters dropping bombs from the air."

Pruitt nodded. He knew very well *where* those stories had come from: out of thin air. They were the first stage of the psy-ops package. Soon fabricated images—fuzzy videos, handheld camera footage, and grainy photos—would be obtained by the media from anonymous sources, all to further support the story that Pruitt wanted told, of a terrorist attack orchestrated by a party aligned against the current Trinidadian administration.

But would it work?

That was the purpose of this trial run, a proof of concept for the next generation of warfare. The cost to pull this off was surprisingly minimal. The entire operation only involved a small drone fleet: three Warhawks for the heavy lifting, a pair of Shrikes to add to the chaos, and a handful of the tiny Wasps to hack into the city's digital infrastructure.

With the stealth technology and the cover of night, no word of strange craft in the sky had made it into the mainstream media. He suspected some people might have reported such sightings, but as part of the psy-ops protocol, any mention would be quashed, replaced with more false stories and fabricated videos.

"Oh my God . . ." Laura gasped out.

He turned his attention back on his daughter. "What?"

"A high school was just bombed. Rescue services are trying to get inside."

He checked the wall clock. "It's nearing midnight out there. Surely there were no children on the premises."

Laura stared at him. Her face had gone pale, which made her freckles stand out all the more. "According to a series of Facebook posts, the school was having an early Halloween party. When the attack began, they kept the children indoors for their protection."

Pruitt winced—not so much at the potential loss of life, but at how to spin this to his advantage. He wanted to make some calls, but instead he crossed to Laura's side and pulled her close.

She didn't resist, settling her cheek against his chest. "Why . . . ?" she mumbled. "Who could be so cruel?"

He just pulled her tighter, trying to protect her from the harshness of life, as he always had. He prayed she would find a way to balance her sense of justice with the realities of the world. It was what he wanted to give to her, to her children: the power and wealth to make a better world.

Even if I must bloody my own hands to accomplish it.

That was one part of the Kellerman legacy he didn't want to bequeath to her. Over the course of U.S. history, many captains of industry—Rockefeller, J. P. Morgan, Andrew Carnegie—were ruthless in ambition, drive, and practices, but later in life became philanthropists for the betterment of mankind. He intended to follow that example.

Let me be ruthless, so she can be kind.

"Why don't you take a break," he said. "I can man the fort for now."

She pulled back and stared up at him. "Dad, I can—"

"I know you *can*. But humor your old man."

She smiled, though tears still glistened in her eyes. "Okay, just for twenty minutes. I'll grab us both some coffee. It'll be a long night."

That was definitely true.

"Go on then," he said, helping her out of his chair.

She hugged him before leaving. "I love you, Dad."

"Me too, honey."

He stayed rooted until she left and still stared at the door for several breaths, waiting for his guilt to ebb and girding himself for what must be done next. He found his center again in one firm determination.

She must never know my hand in all of this.

To that end, he slipped out his private phone and dialed Rafael Lyon's number. As the connection was made, he demanded an update, settling at the end on the one threat that continued to plague these operations.

"What about our friends who arrived in Port of Spain?" he asked.

Lyon sighed. "I see now why Webster had such difficulty dealing with that man—and his dog. Little fucker nearly took a chunk out of my leg."

"I'll take more than your leg if that group isn't dealt with."

"Not a problem, sir. They're trapped on a deserted island with no way off. I've dispatched all three Warhawks from Trinidad to burn that place to a blackened cinder. And if they should try to swim away, I have a Shrike patrolling the waters."

Pruitt smiled, recognizing why he had placed such trust in the French soldier. "So you're telling me they're toast."

Lyon chuckled. "Extra burnt."

29

Panicked and panting, Tucker sped low across the beach.

Bitter smoke cloaked the skies overhead, while dozens of fires churned across the island, joining into a hellish conflagration that glowed through the dark trees. As he ran back to Jane and Kane, fiery ash rained down across the beach and floated atop the water of the cove.

"Anything?" Jane asked, her voice muffled by a wet cloth tied across her nose and mouth. Kane lay next to her with a damp handkerchief draped over his muzzle.

He shook his head. "No sea caves on that side either." He had searched both ends of the beach for somewhere to hole up, somewhere to weather this firestorm. "We'll have to swim out and let the current draw us farther along the cliffs. Try to find a deep enough cave to protect us."

That is, if the currents don't simply drag us all to a watery grave.

Jane's eyes seemed to hold the same fear. They were all too weak to fight the riptides and unpredictable currents that made up the Bocas del Dragón Strait. There was a reason these waters had been named the Dragon's Mouth. Many had been swallowed up by that dark beast.

Still, Jane nodded, knowing they had no other choice, not if she ever wanted to see her son again.

Behind them, napalm bombs continued to explode in great gouts of smoke and flame. Tucker's ears rang with the blasts. Occasionally the ghostly passage of a Warhawk stirred the pall over the beach as one of the drones banked out to sea and back again. It was only a matter of time before a Warhawk unloaded its weapon's bay upon this strip of sand or the wildfires swept down from the burning jungle.

"Let's go," Tucker said.

He patted Kane on his flank and got the dog up. At least Kane was back to gingerly bearing weight on his wounded leg—but how long would the dog's strength last battling the tides and currents of the Caribbean Sea?

Jane looked worse, still clearly compromised by the blow to the head.

With no better options, he led the pair across the sand and into the ash-strewn waters. Another explosion erupted behind them, close enough to feel the blast wave of overheated air push them forward. The reek of burned gasoline rolled over them, setting Jane to coughing harshly.

"Keep going!" Tucker urged, waving an arm. "We need to get clear of the cove!"

Kane paddled next to him, his nose held high, riding the swells. After wading waist deep in the water, Tucker leaned forward to dive into the waves, when a new noise intruded, cutting through the ringing in his ears.

He paused and glanced to Jane. She had also stopped, clearly hearing the same. It was the whine of an engine, echoing over the water. It took Tucker a breath to pinpoint the direction. From around the cliffs to the left, a silver powerboat sped across the mouth of the cove, cutting them off. It banked into a sharp turn, coming full around as the pilot must have spotted them.

The boat rocked in the swells as the engine cut to a rumbling idle.

Tucker momentarily held out hope that it was a rescue party, someone who had come to the besieged island looking for survivors.

He stared as the lone occupant rose from behind the wheel.

Tucker instantly recognized his adversary.

It was Karl Webster.

The man lifted the black tube of a rocket launcher to his shoulder and pointed it toward them. Tucker had no time to free his Sig Sauer from its shoulder holster under his wet clothes. He glanced to the smoky inferno behind him, then back to Webster.

Out of the frying pan and into the fire.

Webster pulled the trigger.

Tucker ducked at the noise of the blast. Webster's form was obscured by the weapon's smoky exhaust. The rocket-propelled grenade shot past overhead, sailing high, trailing a ribbon of smoke.

Tucker twisted around to see the round hit its target above the beach. The blast of fire revealed a wedge-shaped threat hidden in the smoke. It was a Warhawk. The drone shattered above the tree line at the beach's edge and rained debris across the sand and into the water.

Webster yelled, "Get your asses over here!"

Jane was already moving, half wading, half paddling. Tucker followed, pushing Kane ahead of him. He didn't have a clue what was happening, only that there was a way off this fiery rock.

Webster met them with the boat, then leaned over the gunwale to grab Jane's arm. He hauled her inside, then bent over the rail, grabbed Kane's vest with two hands, and pulled the dog to safety. Tucker leaped high enough to catch a grip and climbed aboard on his own.

With everyone in, Webster gunned the engine, yanked the wheel, and sent the boat careening around and away from the island. Once clear of the cove, he turned to the group, his eyes settling on one of them.

"Janie, are you okay?" Webster asked.

Jane looked to Tucker, then back to Tangent's security head. She nodded. "Better now, Karl."

"What the fuck?" Tucker gasped out. He seldom used that phrase, but this situation certainly deserved it.

Jane touched his arm. "I can explain later."

Tucker fought his wet clothes and freed his SIG Sauer. He pointed it at Webster. "Screw *later*. What the hell is going on?"

"What does it look like?" Webster yelled back, ignoring the threat. "I'm pulling your asses out of the fire."

"But . . . but *why*?"

Jane forced his pistol down. "It was Karl who helped me survive the purge at Project 623."

Tucker struggled to understand. He gaped at Jane as conflicting emotions flooded through him: betrayal, relief, bewilderment, anger, and feelings the English language had no words to describe.

Webster used his moment of confused silence and asked, "Nora . . . I know she made it out of Redstone. What about her team-mates? Stan, Takashi, and Diane?"

At the mention of those names, Tucker's swirl of emotions finally settled on one.

Fury.

"What the hell do you care?" he spat out, lifting his weapon again.

Webster nodded at his rebuke. "I did what I could," he muttered, his words all but drowned out by the boat's engine. He glanced to Jane. "I didn't have any choice, Janie. You gotta know that. Back in Silver Spring, just before Project 623 was shut down, that bastard Lyon showed me pictures of my ex-wife and my daughter, Amanda. He was blunt. I either kept silent or I would end up in a shallow grave alongside them."

Tucker read the pain in the man's eyes as he glanced guiltily away.

"I didn't kill any of the others," Webster said. "You gotta know that, too. But by going along, I figured I could save you. You were smart and had connections. It wasn't that hard to make Lyon believe you escaped on your own. Plus, Janie, you know how I felt about you."

Jane sank into one of the seats. "Karl . . ."

"I know you didn't feel the same, but it didn't make what I felt any less real."

Tucker stared at the back of the man's head. He remembered Nora describing how the intimate, close quarters of such research groups often made for strange bedfellows.

"When I was transferred to oversee The Odisha Group at Red-stone," Webster continued, "I was already in too deep. I convinced myself into believing I could do something to protect this new group with my position."

"What about Sandy Conlon?" Jane asked.

"Again, that was Lyon and his men cleaning house after Sandy's success in creating the AI core for the drones. They no longer had a use for her or her team. But I knew Sandy was doing something else, something in private. The girl was clever at covering her bases. I tried to have her back, too . . . though she never knew it."

"And what about us?" Tucker asked.

Webster looked back at Tucker, then to Kane. "At first I had no clue who you were. I thought maybe you were working for Lyon or some unknown third party. Eventually I learned that Jane had sent you sniffing around Redstone." He waved to Jane. "When I picked you both up on a surveillance camera at White Sands, I kept quiet and tried to see if I could find you before all hell broke loose. But doing so put me on Lyon's radar."

Tucker remembered his conversation with the French soldier. Lyon had eventually learned about his group's trespass onto the military base. Apparently it was one too many mistakes for Lyon to swallow or accept.

"I had to run. I got Amanda and Helen whisked away to safety, then I checked in with a couple guys still loyal to me at Tangent. From them, I learned what Lyon was planning for you all, so I came down here. Still, I barely made it. Lyon had pushed up the timetable for operations here by a day. When I saw the island blow up, I figured you were all dead, but I had to check."

Tucker stared toward the fires glowing through the smoke that clouded Port of Spain's skyline. "What the hell is the plan for Trinidad?"

Karl shook his head. "I'm not entirely sure. But Trinidad is a real-world test for something much larger scheduled for three days from now. In fact, the secondary goal of this mission was to distract world attention, to get all eyes looking here, while the real attack occurred elsewhere."

"Where?" Jane asked.

"I don't know . . . I truly don't."

Tucker had a more important question. "Who's behind all of this? Who does Lyon work for?"

Webster turned toward him with a frown. "You don't know?"

"How could we?"

"Lyon works for Pruitt Keller—"

Webster's chest exploded outward, spattering Tucker with gore and blood. The deadly round struck the empty seat next to Jane. As the man fell from behind the wheel, Tucker caught sight of the shimmering passage of a drone against the stars.

It was a Shrike, likely the same one that had ambushed the runabout.

The drone banked around for another attack run on its target.

"Get down!" Tucker hollered.

He dashed forward and rolled Webster's body to the side, freeing the length of the rocket launcher from under his dead weight. Upon entering the boat, Tucker had noted an open box of RPG rounds on the floor next to the pilot's seat. He grabbed a grenade, shoved it into the barrel of the launcher, and rolled onto his backside. He lifted the weapon to his shoulder and centered the sight upon that blurry patch of stars.

He waited until the drone dipped toward the boat.

Now, time for a little payback.

He fixed his aim and fired. The blast was deafening and enveloped him in a cloud of smoke. Still, through the pall, a flash of flame lit the sky, revealing the shattered form of the Shrike. The grenade had struck one of the drone's fixed wings, sending the war machine spiraling into the sea.

As a plume of water shot high, Tucker gained the pilot's seat and grabbed the wheel. "Hold on!"

He shoved the throttle forward and raced across the flat waters, not knowing if there were any other Shrikes in the air or if the remaining two Warhawks bombarding Patos Island would be given new instructions and dispatched their way.

In the rearview mirror, Tucker saw the island was cloaked in smoke, fires smoldering at its heart. A fresh spiral of flames shot high into the night sky, marking the continuing destruction of the island.

Tucker turned his attention forward, flying the powerboat toward the fiery skyline of Port of Spain.

Though he was relieved to have survived, a worry plagued him.

What had happened to Frank and Nora?

11:58 P.M.

Tucker eased back the throttle and let their boat coast to a stop a hundred yards from the commercial docks of Port of Spain. The acrid stench of fire was thick in the air. A cacophony of emergency sirens, car alarms, and loudspeaker-enhanced voices echoed across the water.

Several shore-side warehouses still burned, but the docks themselves were mostly intact. Unfortunately the same could not be said of the Hyatt.

The main hotel tower was a column of flame, wrapped in smoke.

"Nora and Frank . . ." Jane moaned.

"They could have gotten out," Tucker reminded her. "Rex had their backs."

But even he had trouble putting much conviction in his voice.

As he aimed the boat toward the nearest dock, he noted that the main coastal highway was choked with evacuees, the road packed with unmoving or abandoned vehicles. Military trucks raced along the shoulders, some heading toward the city, others away. The central business district looked the worst hit, transformed into a fiery wasteland of blasted skyscrapers.

"Why would they do this?" Jane asked as Tucker reached the docks and tied them off. "Why?"

Tucker remembered their earlier suppositions that this all had something to do with controlling a new oil field. But if Webster was right, that was only an ancillary benefit. The true objective of the attack was a test run for something even worse.

Tucker helped Jane and Kane out of the boat. They had covered Webster's body with a tarp. Though Tucker was still angry with the man, the guy had saved all their lives. When the time was right, they would get his body back home to his loved ones.

Just like with Sandy's remains.

Tucker stared across the devastated city, trying to fathom the number of deaths, of other loved ones who would mourn this night for what was stolen from them. A deep-seated fury settled into his bones.

"If Nora and Frank survived," Jane asked, "how do we even begin to find them?"

"There must be some sort of emergency command center, a place for the injured or homeless to find shelter. If Frank is thinking straight, that's where he'll take Nora."

"What about trying your phone again?"

He had attempted multiple times while en route, both calling the hotel and trying to raise someone in the States. "Still nothing. I think they're jamming outgoing transmissions, keeping the islands locked down. We're going to have to hoof it."

He set off with Jane on one side and Kane on the other. They were lucky to still be alive, and he could only hope that same good fortune extended to Nora and Frank.

In short order, an emergency crew directed them to Queen's Park Savannah, where a makeshift refugee camp was being set up. Normally the park's two hundred acres were recreation space, complete with cricket fields, rugby pitches, and a botanical garden. Now thousands of people filled the fields, milling around or huddling together on the grass or on benches.

At the park's center, a score of white canvas tents had been erected; most appeared to be dedicated to first aid, but a few were serving food and distributing bottled water. Emergency workers in orange vinyl vests moved through the crowd with clipboards, collecting personal data or reports of damage to various neighborhoods.

Jane looked forlorn. Even finding their friends amid this chaos was a daunting task. Kane suddenly sat down, as if he also realized the futility of this search, or maybe he was simply exhausted. The shepherd stared up quizzically at him.

"What's wrong, big guy?" he asked.

Kane cocked his head and pawed at his ear with his hind leg, letting out a whine of complaint. Tucker knelt next to him. Up to now, he hadn't bothered to strip off Kane's tactical gear. With all the emergency personnel around, the shepherd looked like any of a number of search-and-rescue dogs working the aftermath of the attack.

"What's bothering him?" Jane asked.

"I think it's his earpiece."

Tucker pushed away the dog's scratching limb and removed the wireless receiver. He inspected Kane's ear for any damage, but all seemed fine. As he palmed the earpiece, he felt a slight vibration in the unit. He lifted it to the side of his head and heard music playing from it.

"What is it?" Jane asked.

"It's the Beatles."

She scrunched her nose. "What?"

"It's their song 'Help!' "

Tucker slipped his own transceiver into his ear and secured his mike. He heard the melody more clearly now. Someone was broadcasting on the same radio frequency. Maybe it was pure happenstance, but he tapped his mike. "Hello?"

Static followed, then a familiar voice answered. *"Tucker, is that you?"* Frank asked.

Relief flooded through him. "Where are you? Is Nora okay?"

"We're both fine, but we have quite the story to tell you. We're over at Queen's Park, at a picnic table behind the emergency tents."

"We'll be right there."

Jane looked expectantly at him.

"They're alive. They're fine. C'mon."

He hurried toward the row of emergency tents, and after a bit of hunting spotted Frank waving at them. Nora was seated at the bench before a plate with a half-eaten sandwich on it.

Tucker gave Frank a bear hug, while Jane greeted Nora as warmly. Kane danced around them all, his tail swishing happily. When they finally broke apart, Tucker kept a hand on Frank's shoulder.

"How did you pull off that bit of magic with the radio?"

Frank gazed toward the sky. "With a little help from a friend. After we realized there was no way you could reach us by normal means, I set Rex to locally broadcasting the best of the Beatles, figuring you or Kane might pick it up."

"Smart," Jane said.

Tucker frowned. "But how did you know our radio frequency?" He had never shared that information with Frank, nor with anyone.

Frank shrugged. "With a little help from *another* friend."

Nora pointed behind Tucker. He turned to see a familiar figure strolling toward them with two plates loaded with food.

"Now there's my big stud," the woman said upon joining them— but she was talking to Kane.

It was Ruth Harper.

The tall woman bent down and placed a plate before the shepherd, then straightened, brushing back a fall of blond hair, revealing tanned features and a set of amazingly high cheekbones. She wore jeans and a green blouse, along with a pair of thick-rimmed rectangular eyeglasses perched on her nose, which added a certain studious sexiness to her looks.

"You and Jane will have to share the other sandwiches," Ruth said, setting the remaining plate on the table.

"How . . . what're you doing here?" Tucker asked, finally understanding how Frank had obtained the radio frequency. Nothing escaped the grasp of Ruth Harper.

She shrugged. "You declined any Sigma operatives for this mission, so I thought I'd use up some vacation time for a short trip to a Caribbean island, to work on my tan."

"Does your boss know you're down here?"

She coyly raised an eyebrow at this foolish question. *Of course, he did.* Like Ruth, nothing escaped the attention of her boss, Sigma's director, Painter Crowe. Instead, she glanced across the breadth of the fiery ruins of Port of Spain.

"Unfortunately, I got here a tad late. You certainly love to leave a path of destruction in your wake, Captain Wayne." She turned toward him. "I certainly hope it was worth it."

Tucker sighed.

Only time will tell.

30

Half a day later, Tucker stood on a balcony overlooking the coastal town of San Fernando, some thirty miles south of Port of Spain. In the distance, a black pall still marred the blue skies to the north, looking like a storm brewing on the horizon.

Which was certainly true.

After making it out of the city, they had settled here to nurse their wounds and sleep. All morning, they had been monitoring reports, taking measure of the aftermath of the attack. Most of the fires had been extinguished, but even this far south, the trade winds carried the smell of smoke, burning tires, and charred petroleum.

Exhausted from his efforts the previous day, Kane was curled up on a chaise longue on the balcony, fast asleep. Last night, Tucker had clipped the fur around his laceration and had slathered the wound with antibiotics before applying a fresh bandage.

"What's the current death toll?" Jane asked from inside the hotel suite. She stood behind Frank and Nora as the pair worked on their laptops, gathering updates from local news sources. A television droned in the background.

"Most counts are estimating eight or nine hundred," Nora reported. "But search-and-rescue units are still scouring the worst-hit areas."

Tucker closed his eyes. Despite the irrationality of it, his mind was stuck in an *if-only* loop, second-guessing all that had happened. While Lyon's trap at Patos Island hadn't killed him, it had gotten him out of the way. Still, he wasn't sure he could've done anything if he had been in the city.

Frank had told him the story of the night's attack, how Rex had alerted them of the incoming aerial assault shortly after Ruth Harper arrived. The trio had fled the hotel before it was bombed, hitting the fire alarm on their way out, likely saving many other lives.

"All the media is blaming the Trinidadian People's Party," Nora said, "but that's all smoke and mirrors."

Tucker turned from the balcony and joined the others inside. "But how?" he asked.

"A combination of electronic warfare and psychological operations," Frank answered. "Rex tapped into and collected reams of data from the drone fleet. The stories were preprepared and spread into every news source and social media outlet. Even now, I'm having a hard time separating fact from fiction, and I was at ground zero."

"Further clouding the matter," Nora said, "I think the TPP was tricked into being patsies in all of this. There are reports of a handful of armed attacks on police stations and government buildings. The raiders who were killed were wearing TPP uniforms, but the bodies number less than twenty."

Tucker shook his head. "Which gives the government enough flesh-and-blood evidence to blame the rest of the destruction on these revolutionaries."

Jane spoke and turned up the volume on the television. "Looks like President D'Abreo is making a statement."

Tucker and the others gathered around the set.

The president had donned a military uniform for this speech. *". . . for this reason, and in mutual agreement with Prime Minister Magaray, the minister of national security, and the chief of the defense staff, I am declaring a national state of emergency. Martial law will remain in effect until the perpetrators of this cowardly and bloody attack are brought to justice. Upon my order, all members of the Trinidadian People's Party are being rounded up for questioning or arrest. But let me assure the people of Trinidad—and all the peoples of the world—we will survive this attack and be all the stronger for it."*

Jane muted the sound. "What do you think?"

Tucker contemplated the news, then described his take on it.

"Let's see. A radical faction uses violence and bloodshed to try to oust the current government within days of the election. Its beloved president and prime minister have come to the rescue, promising to quash the militants and provide aid and comfort to thousands."

Jane crossed her arms. "In other words, an election that was likely to be lost is now assured of victory."

He nodded. "This attack wasn't a coup. It was an *anti*coup, intended to bolster the current administration."

"And President D'Abreo will owe a debt to his mysterious bene-factor," Nora added. "Not only will someone profit to the tune of hundreds of millions of dollars in rebuilding costs and infrastruc-ture repairs, there's no question to *whom* D'Abreo will grant control of the new Salybia Bay oil fields."

"Pruitt Kellerman," Ruth said behind them all. She had just stepped in from one of the bedrooms where she had been on the telephone all morning.

Tucker had already told her what Webster had revealed before he died.

Pruitt Keller—

It hadn't taken a genius to flesh out the rest of that name. Any American who had even a passing knowledge of the country's media industry knew Pruitt Kellerman. Horizon Media Corp was the sin-gle largest owner of newspapers, television and radio stations, social media sites, and, according to some people, even state and federal politicians. In addition, Pruitt Kellerman had been extending his reach into Europe and Asia.

Not that there weren't detractors.

Kellerman was currently fighting a firestorm of allegations that he had used Horizon Media's position to tap phones and intercept e-mails—not only of business competitors and personal enemies but of beltway legislators in charge of regulating the telecom industry.

"What's the word from Washington?" Jane asked.

Ruth sighed. "The attack here seemed to have caught everyone off guard, including the entire U.S. intelligence community. Every-one is scrambling to catch up."

Tucker remembered Webster mentioning that one of the objec-tives of this operation was to distract attention, to turn all eyes toward Trinidad.

Mission accomplished.

"We have to stop him," Nora said. "Expose him."

"That'll be hard, especially as all we have are the dying words of a traitor," Ruth said. "While Tangent Aerospace is owned by Horizon Media, the corporation is only one shell of a game involving hundreds of companies and subsidiaries, insulating the man at the top from culpability, leaving him plenty of room for deniability. In fact, Sigma has had its eye on Kellerman for years, but nothing ever sticks."

"As my mother would say," Frank said, thickening his Alabama twang, "he's slicker than pig snot on a doorknob."

Ruth offered a small smile. "That he is. We know he's a majority stockholder in Tangent, but Tangent has no fingerprints here in Trinidad." She nodded to Nora. "But thanks to your and Rex's help in pinpointing where the drone fleet was launched from in Trinidad, we have another name. Switchplate Engineering. The company— another subsidiary of Horizon—leased the patch of airstrip and land that was used as the base of operations here. It's now a bombed-out hole in the jungle."

"To further cover up any evidence," Tucker said.

"Yet, it's one more piece to the puzzle," Ruth added. "Though plainly not enough to go after Kellerman directly. We'll need more pieces of this corporate puzzle before pursuing him."

Nora spoke up from her laptop. "If nothing else, I may have uncovered a *noncorporate* piece." She stared over at Jane and Tucker. "Thanks to Sandy."

"What do you mean?"

"Remember the date of the last entry in Alan Turing's journal, the one that detailed his algorithms that Sandy was shown?"

"What about it?"

"It was dated April 24, 1940. Just two days before a mysterious fire nearly destroyed Bletchley Park, a fire some believed might have covered up a secret attack on the place."

Tucker squinted at Nora. "You and Sandy thought Turing's journal might have been stolen at that time. Maybe even made it back to the U.S."

Nora typed rapidly. "I did some digging into Pruitt Kellerman's past, to see if I could turn up anything of interest. His father, Traf-ford Kellerman, killed himself and Pruitt's mother in a drunk driving accident when Pruitt was four years old. He went to live with his grandparents, Bryson and Gail, in 1969. His grandfather died when Pruitt was twenty-one. His grandmother passed a few years later. Pruitt was their sole heir."

Frank leaned over her shoulder as she worked. "What of it?"

Nora leaned back. "Look here. I hacked into old military records and found this."

Tucker joined Frank. On the screen was a faded copy of a U.S. Army form:

WD AGO 55
Honorable Discharge from the Army of the United States.
Name: Kellerman, Bryson Gale
Date of Active Duty: 29 September 1927
Date of Separation: 8 August 1940
DOB: 11 November 1906

Nora scrolled down the form, which listed myriad details pertinent to Pruitt's grandfather's discharge. "Bryson Kellerman retired from service at the age of thirty-three, just a couple of months after that mysterious fire at Bletchley Park."

"You think he somehow obtained Turing's journal?"

"Maybe. Look at what else I found." She pulled up a heavily redacted version of Bryson Kellerman's service record. "He was a colonel with army intelligence, though in what capacity is blotted out. But prior to his discharge, Kellerman had served in almost every theater of the war, including a last assignment in Britain."

"What are you thinking?" Ruth asked.

"I think he somehow obtained Turing's journal, maybe stole it even. Either way, he likely thought it was important enough to keep secret. Maybe he hoped to use Turing's work to make a profit. You have to remember that postwar America was an industrial powerhouse, the leader of scientific innovation, a legacy left in the wake of the birth of the atomic bomb. Everyone was looking for the next big innovation. During the war, Bryson must have had the foresight to recognize the potential locked in Turing's papers and spirited them away for himself."

"So what did Bryson end up doing after the war?" Tucker asked.

Nora shrugged. "He sold insurance." Upon Tucker's frown, she continued. "Though Bryson likely had an inkling of the importance of what he had stolen, no one in the world at the time could turn Turing's algorithms into real-world applications. But I could easily see a proud grandfather sharing the trophies of his war years with his grandson and showing him those stolen pages."

Tucker rubbed his chin. "Pruitt must have remembered those papers and waited for the world to catch up with Turing's genius, then sought a way to put them to use."

"But what is Kellerman's ultimate goal?" Jane asked.

"Power," Tucker answered. "If you look at the trajectory of Horizon Media, it's less about accumulating wealth and more about gathering power, of controlling events."

Jane nodded. "We're at the cusp of a new way of waging war, of abandoning the atomic age of Pruitt's grandfather and entering the era of the digital battlefield. These are wars being funded by corporations and fought by private defense contractors, where profit margins are as important as winning."

Tucker sighed. "And Kellerman is determined to be the master of this new world."

Frank looked sick. "If Trinidad was some sort of proof-of-concept trial, that is one scary world. From the data that Rex was able to pull before we hightailed it out of the Hyatt, Nora and I estimate this attack was carried out with only a handful of drones."

"But what's he planning next?" Jane asked.

Ruth checked her watch. "I have a video conference scheduled with Director Crowe in a few minutes. He has Sigma digging into that very question. Hopefully he'll have something for us."

Tucker stared toward the open balcony door, to the pall of smoke sitting on the horizon to the north.

He had better hurry.

1:18 P.M.

Tucker found himself back on the balcony after a brief lunch. Kane had returned to his chaise longue, luxuriating in the warm sunshine. Jane joined them, stepping to the rail beside Tucker. She slipped an arm around his waist, but he stiffened.

She felt it and removed her arm. "Tuck . . ."

They hadn't had a real chance to discuss the matter concerning Webster. "You should have told me," he muttered.

"I tried—"

"Not hard enough."

"I know that now. But Karl helped keep me alive, protected my son. He risked his own daughter to do so." She gripped the rail with both hands, her knuckles going white. "Karl and I spent a lot of time working together, perhaps too much time, enough for Karl to grow fond of me, even of Nate. But our relationship didn't pass beyond that of mutual colleagues."

Perhaps from your perspective . . .

Jane shook her head. "At the very least, I owed Karl my silence. I thought the less you knew about that arrangement the safer it would be for Nathan, even for Karl's family."

"But at what cost?" He pictured Takashi's head exploding from a sniper round, saw Sandy's bloated face floating out of the dark trunk of her car. "If I had known beforehand . . ."

Jane turned to him, her eyes hardening. "What would you have done differently? I had no further communication with Karl after I left. I had no idea what was happening at Redstone. I knew only that Sandy was at risk and the pattern of deaths following the purge of Project 623 seemed to be happening again. I had no way of knowing how deeply Karl was still involved."

Angry, Tucker refused to accept her explanation. "Yet you sent me and Kane in blind."

Jane was silent for a while, then sighed. "Maybe it was stupid and shortsighted to do that, but Nathan is my entire life. I'm not going to apologize for doing everything in my power to protect him." She gave a small shake of her head. "I could have stayed in hiding and done nothing, but I risked reaching out to you. At the time, it was the best compromise I could come up with."

Tucker saw her hands tremble on the rail, knowing she was seeing the blood on them from her decision. He recognized that familiar tremor, having experienced it all too often himself. He remembered the term one of his counselors had used to refine his diagnosis of PTSD: *moral injury*. It occurred when someone's understanding of right and wrong was deeply violated. Jane clearly struggled with that now.

He wanted to reach an arm around her, pull her close, but instead he turned away and headed inside. He tapped his thigh to get Kane to follow, leaving Jane alone with her demons. He had no choice.

I have too many demons of my own.

2:02 P.M.

Tucker stared at the laptop screen, which showed a dark-haired man seated behind a desk with a wall-mounted monitor over his shoulder. The screen ran with silent footage from the attack on Port of Spain. The man tucked a single snowy lock, a stark contrast to his black hair, behind one ear, as if securing a white feather. Blue eyes shone from a tanned face, seeming to stare straight at Tucker.

The director of Sigma, Painter Crowe, straightened in his chair. "Kellerman's financial network has proven to be a tough nut to crack. Even for Sigma. Though we've made some progress, we could use your help."

Ruth Harper had called them all into the room for this video powwow with Director Crowe. Tucker rankled at being summoned in this manner. While he personally liked Painter Crowe, he wasn't fond of the system to which the man belonged—namely the government. Plus, Tucker girded himself against any possibility that this operation might be stripped from him.

As he had told Ruth a few moments ago, *if the director tries to jerk the rug out from under me, he's in for a fight.* And Tucker meant it. Too much blood had been spilled for him to willingly walk away now.

"We face several obstacles," Painter continued. "The foremost being Pruitt Kellerman himself. He's a titan, and not only in the business world. His influence and power are far reaching, even within our own government. Kellerman's not someone to be taken lightly. We're going to need as much proof as possible to go after him directly."

"Not to mention stopping what he's planning next," Tucker added.

Painter's gaze flicked to Ruth, who was seated at the bedroom desk. Tucker read both the director's expression and Ruth's body language.

"You know something," he accused them.

Painter nodded. "It's something you could've figured out given enough time and resources. But you gave us all the pieces to put it together."

"Like what?" Jane asked.

Ruth answered. "Like that list of Soviet equipment you saw destroyed at White Sands."

Tucker pictured the armored Russian tank. Earlier he had told Ruth how he believed the hardware at White Sands had been specifically chosen, a way of testing the drone's capabilities against military targets.

"All that old Soviet equipment," Painter explained, "is still in use in a handful of Eastern Bloc countries. We think Kellerman's next attack is aimed at one of those nations."

"But which one?" Tucker asked.

"We have a suspicion," Painter said. "It was only a matter of pinning down which country Kellerman might have the most interest in . . . a country with the most financial ties to his vast conglomerate."

"And let me guess," Tucker said. "Considering Trinidad was a test run, the second target is likely another country under political tension, a powder keg waiting to be exploited."

"Exactly," Painter acknowledged. "We pursued that very angle and discovered another company in which Kellerman holds a major stockholder position, namely Skaxis Mining."

Tucker shook his head. "Never heard of them."

"The company oversees the mining of rare-earth minerals. Scarce elements like scandium used in aerospace framework, lanthanum for hydrogen storage, gadolinium for nuclear reactor shielding. And on and on."

"In other words, everything you'd need as a supply line for drone development."

Painter nodded. "It's also a multibillion-dollar industry and growing."

"Where's Skaxis based out of?" Jane asked.

Painter smiled grimly. "A former Soviet Bloc country."

"Serbia," Ruth explained.

Frank let out a low whistle. "Talk about political tension."

Tucker agreed. Following the breakup of Yugoslavia into a scatter of independent countries, the area had been a hotbed of insurrection, wars, assassinations, skirmishes, even ethnic cleansing going back decades. And while that corner of Europe had quieted of late, it remained an uneasy peace.

"If Kellerman ignites that powder keg," Tucker said, "all hell could break loose across Europe."

Painter stood up and leaned on his desk. "And we have twenty-four hours to stop it."

"That's impossible," Frank muttered.

Nora spoke up from the back of the group. "I know how we can do it."

Everyone turned to her.

She faced the scrutiny without flinching. "Sandy gave us the answer. But it'll take all of us to pull this off."

FIFTH

STORMING
THE CASTLE

31

Twelve hours later and half a world away from Trinidad, Tucker bounced along in a new rental SUV. The temperature at this early hour in the southern mountains of Serbia was below freezing as a cold front moved over the Balkan region. The roads were icy and a steady sleet fell from low clouds that had settled over the green peaks of the Dinaric Alps.

"Not exactly the balmy Caribbean, is it?" Frank said from the backseat.

No, it's not.

Tucker was driving a polar-white ŠKODA Yeti, a vehicle manufactured by a Czech company and commonly seen in the mountainous regions of Serbia. Ruth Harper had arranged the particular transportation to blend in with the locals, not that their group exactly fit in.

Cleared medically, Jane sat in the front passenger seat, bundled in a thick down coat, while Frank and Nora shared the backseat with Kane between them. The final member of their party—Rex—lay under a tarp in the rear compartment.

The group had landed outside the small town of Kraljevo in southern Serbia, flying overnight aboard yet another private jet, a Bombardier Global Express, which made the leap from Trinidad to Serbia in a single intercontinental bound. Ruth had chosen this remote mountain town and its small regional airport for two reasons.

First, to avoid making the same mistake twice. After blowing two of Tangent's drones out of the skies, they had to assume Lyon might suspect Tucker and company had survived the assault on Patos Island, and the French soldier might have placed the main airport in Belgrade under watch. An hour ago, they had landed at Kraljevo's small airport under EU call signs and bearing Greek passports, courtesy of the good folks at Sigma. Still, as a precaution, the group had exited the plane in heavy jackets, their hoods pulled up, with both Rex and Kane in closed crates.

Jane studied a folded map in her lap and brought up the other reason for this choice of location. "The Skaxis Mining complex lies only sixty miles farther into the mountains. To reach it, you'll want to take a road marked E-761, which heads toward Serbia's border with Montenegro."

He nodded.

Last night, Painter had reported an increase in commercial cargo helicopters landing at the sprawling mining complex, along with the arrival of a caravan of trucks. They were all gambling that whatever Kellerman had in store for the region had its base of operations at Skaxis Mining.

In the backseat, Kane let out a jaw-cracking yawn.

I feel you, buddy.

With time ticking down, Tucker's group had caught what little sleep they could aboard the jet, though Frank and Nora had spent most of the flight bent with their heads together over a laptop. Even now the two mumbled behind him, speaking in what had to be a foreign language about coding and algorithms.

Much of what was to come depended on those two, especially Nora. She was the one most familiar with Sandy's work, while Frank offered a sounding board for the young woman. Tucker and Kane were nothing more than glorified bodyguards to get Nora where she needed to be.

Jane rubbed a gloved palm over the window next to her to wipe away some of the steamy moisture. He had wanted to leave Jane behind—both to keep her safe and because a part of him was still angry with her. They had barely spoken a word on the flight here. Even Kane felt the tension, slinking back and forth across the cabin between them as if trying to draw the pack together by sheer will.

In the end, Tucker conceded that he could use Jane's help. Despite everything, he trusted her more than anyone else, even the Sigma operatives who Ruth had suggested accompany them. Jane had blood in the game, both her own and those of her friends. He also read the haunted look in her eyes whenever she thought no one was staring. He recognized that expression, having seen it often enough in the mirror when his own anxiety and despair flared. Over the years, he had dealt with the core of that pain by trying to right the wrongs around him, to perhaps one day find his center again.

He could not deny Jane the chance to do the same.

She needed to see this through.

In the end, with the timeline this narrow, Ruth had agreed—after a brief argument—to allow Tucker's group to head into enemy territory as an advanced surgical strike team. She had flown back to DC to arrange for a backup to follow Tucker's group into the field. She was also coordinating with Painter to deal with Pruitt Kellerman.

So for now the group was on its own.

Tucker glanced to Nora in the rearview mirror. He could see the weight on her shoulders, from the shadows under her eyes to the slump in her back. But there remained a steady determination in her face, to exact revenge for the woman she loved by wielding the sword Sandy had left for her.

Even now Nora clutched Sandy's thumb drive in her fist.

Sandy had perfected Turing's algorithms and stored her results on that bit of electronics, allowing Nora and Frank to outfit Rex with those improved algorithms. Doing so had already helped them stay one foot ahead in all of this—but to take down everything from here would require accessing the last remaining file on the thumb drive, Sandy's masterwork in reverse engineering.

Tucker pictured the file he had seen a few days back—and its name.

Lobotomy.

The file held the key to dismantling anything that bore a copy of Sandy's original work, especially the AI cores of the drones. The code was capable of stripping the brains out of the warcraft, turning them into scrap metal. The team had considered using Rex as a delivery system, but the tiny drone's capabilities were too limited. Rex could at best commandeer *one* drone, like he had done back at White Sands. To take out an entire fleet would require delivering Sandy's code into the master control unit of the operation, where it could be broadcast far and wide. In order to accomplish that feat, they would first need to reach Kellerman's local command center.

With that objective in mind, Tucker headed higher into the mountains, all too aware of the region's history. He had heard stories from senior Rangers who had served both covertly and openly during the Kosovo War, stories of mass graves, of entire villages razed, of women raped and mutilated, of concentration camps that rivaled those of Nazi Germany. And though that war had ended almost two decades ago, the tensions in the region remained.

How could Kellerman even think of throwing a lighted match into this powder keg?

5:02 A.M. EDT
Smith Island, Maryland

"Are you getting cold feet again, Mr. President?"

Pruitt stifled a yawn as he took this early morning video call from the Serbian president, Marco Davidovic. The sun had yet to rise on the East Coast, but Pruitt had already been awake for the past hour. Too much was at stake for anything to go wrong today.

Davidovic leaned closer to the screen, revealing a nervous sheen to his pale skin, which highlighted the dark circles under his eyes. From the fireplace in the background, it appeared the president was calling from his private office at his palace in Belgrade.

"Not at all," Davidovic said haltingly. "I just wanted to make sure all was in order. I will play my part as scripted, but I am putting much at risk."

"As I am," Pruitt countered, keeping his voice even, suppressing his irritation. He didn't need the Serbian president second-guessing him, especially at this late stage. He just needed the bastard to sit in his palace and continue to swill that sickeningly sweet plum brandy of his.

Was that too much to ask?

"We're fully on schedule at the border," Pruitt assured the president. "At sundown, operations will commence—and by dawn, you'll have your revenge upon Montenegro, while gaining the enduring love of your people."

And I will possess the mineral rights to hundreds of square miles of land rich in rare-earth elements.

"You have nothing to worry about, Marco," Pruitt said in a firm, confident voice.

Davidovic nodded and leaned back. "Good. Then there will be no need to speak of this again . . . at least not for a while."

We shouldn't even be speaking now.

Still, Pruitt kept a smile fixed to his face until the call ended, then he scowled and reached for his phone. He dialed Rafael Lyon.

"Give me an update," he demanded as the secure connection was made.

"All is in order on the ground," Lyon reported. "We're running a final systems' check on the fleet. But so far everything is green-lit to go."

As Lyon filled in more details and answered several more questions, the man's voice grew irritated, a mirror to Pruitt's own frustration a moment ago. Like Pruitt, the soldier didn't appreciate being second-guessed.

"And what about the other matter?" Pruitt asked.

"It's not a concern," Lyon said, his irritation turning to anger. "After Trinidad, we've had no further sightings of the others. I have eyes and ears throughout the airport in Belgrade, even Sarajevo. Nothing."

Lyon seemed to think these assurances would put Pruitt at ease. *Far from it.*

Pruitt began to pace his office. Over the years, he had learned that the *unknown* was far more dangerous than the *known*.

"Sir, they're likely all dead," Lyon said. "And in a few hours it won't make a difference."

Pruitt wasn't satisfied with this answer.

First, Davidovic gets cold feet . . . now this lingering threat hanging over our heads.

He saw only one way to deal with both situations at once.

"We're moving up the timetable," Pruitt decided. "It's no longer set for sundown."

Lyon was silent for a breath, but he took the change of plans in stride, ever the good soldier. "Then when?"

Pruitt calculated the time change in his head. In Serbia, it was just past ten o'clock in the morning. "Noon . . . make it noon your time."

"Understood."

As the call ended, Pruitt clutched the phone, feeling more relaxed and confident.

No one can stop this now . . .

10:18 A.M. CET
Brodarevo, Serbia

Tucker trundled their SUV over a bridge. It had taken them more than two hours to cross the sixty miles of winding mountain roads, challenging the Czech vehicle's four-wheel-drive capabilities in the ice and rain. But at least the clouds had begun to clear, showing streaks of blue through the dark gray overcast.

"Where are we?" Frank asked as they cleared the bridge.

"According to the map, that was the River Lim," Jane noted, "which would make that the village of Brodarevo ahead."

She pointed to a road marker, as if proving her case, but the sign was inscribed in indecipherable Serbian Cyrillic and could mean anything.

Let's hope Jane's navigation is correct.

As a precaution, they had disabled the SUV's GPS, so it couldn't be tracked. But now he wondered if that was the wisest choice. On the way here, they had driven through countless towns and villages, all of which seemed to be made up of a hodgepodge of consonants. It would be easy to get lost with one wrong turn.

Still, the route up into the mountains had been strangely idyllic, with stacked stone bridges fording bubbling creeks and sod-roofed farmhouses with split-rail fences. They had also passed pieces of Serbia's history, like a Byzantine monastery tucked away in a lush valley and a medieval mosque perched atop a ridgeline, its slender minarets silhouetted against the stormy horizon.

Even the quaint village of Brodarevo, like many of the other alpine hamlets, was composed of a mishmash of picturesque houses with terra-cotta roofs and whitewashed facades. The inhabitants paid them no heed as they drove past, save for the occasional wave or smile.

"Skaxis Mining should be another four miles to the northwest,"

Jane reported, "in the mountains above a place called Kamena Gora, which hugs the Serbian border."

As they left the town, she directed them along a winding road, which offered glimpses of boulder-choked ravines and moss-covered cliffs. After a couple of miles, the road changed from blacktop to gravel. Over the next ridge, the trail snaked down into a valley bisected by a narrow gorge roiling with white water.

"Are you sure this is the right way?" Nora asked.

Jane remained worrisomely silent, poring over the map and occasionally glancing up. As they rose again out of the gorge, Tucker spotted a scatter of red-tiled roofs in the distance, with stone chimneys trickling smoke. The village ahead was mostly obscured by forest, with the homes climbing the mountainside in a series of tiers.

"Could that be Kamena Gora?" he asked.

"I think so." She pointed to the valley on the opposite side. "If I'm right, somewhere over there should be Serbia's border with Montenegro."

"And where's Skaxis Mining?" he asked.

She swung her arm back over the village to the mountain on this side. "In that direction." She took out a set of binoculars and searched. "I can almost make out the scar of a quarry up there. Skaxis Mining covers over fifty square miles of those mountains."

Tucker slowed, pulled the SUV off the road, and turned to Frank. "How about we send Rex up for a quick look around?"

Frank nodded, and in short order had the drone set up in a clearing out of direct view of the road. They gathered around Frank's shoulders as he set Rex's propellers to spinning and did a short test of the drone's systems.

Kane spent this time sniffing at some trees and making sure each was properly marked. He was moving well again on his leg. His knife wound had been sutured before leaving Trinidad, but Tucker wagered it was the past forty-eight hours of rest that had done Kane the most good.

"All set," Frank said.

"Keep Rex low," Tucker warned. "Don't want him spotted in broad daylight."

"Got it. I've activated all of his electronic defenses to help hide him, and I'm keeping his sensor array in passive mode. Like you said, he's only going for a look, right?"

Tucker patted Frank's shoulder. A moment later, the drone sailed off the grass with a humming buzz and into the cold air. Upon reaching the level of the treetops, it sped away. Tucker watched on the screen as Rex skimmed the trees, whisking back and forth. Again most of the flying seemed to be self-guided with little input from Frank at the controls.

"Picking up anything on the EM?" Nora asked.

Frank brought up another screen. Tucker remembered it from before. It was a frequency map. "Hmm . . ." Frank mumbled to himself and adjusted a few dials, while getting some guidance from Nora.

Then suddenly there was a blue spike wavering on the map.

"M-band," Nora said, lowering her voice.

Frank turned to Tucker. "There's another Wasp in the air."

"Probably a patrol," Nora said.

"Careful," Jane whispered.

As Rex skirted the enemy and forged higher into the mountains, more spikes popped up, shimmering and overlapping on the screen in the same band.

"Make that more than one Wasp," Frank commented.

"Get Rex back here before he's spotted," Tucker ordered. "For now we have what we need."

Jane turned to him.

Tucker was suddenly sorry he doubted her navigation skills.

"This confirms we're at the right place," he said. "Now we just need to find a way inside—and stay alive in the process."

32

Once back on the road, Tucker set about canvassing the area around the Skaxis Mining complex. They traveled rural paths, farm tracts, and muddy roads, circling the location from a distance, sending Rex aloft in short hops to try to triangulate the source of the transmissions between the Wasps in the air and the communication center on the ground.

They were trying to pinpoint the operation's C3 hub: command, communication, and control. The only hope of stopping Kellerman and Lyon was to discover where that central hub might be located. Jane had an aerial map of the mining facility as part of the package prepared by Ruth beforehand. But pinpointing *where* the C3 structure might be hidden among the fifty square miles of quarries, pits, and mining buildings was proving to be a daunting challenge.

"How 'bout up there," Frank said, and pointed to another road that seemed to head in the general direction of the mining complex, flanking its western side.

Tucker slowed, but a wooden black-and-white-striped barricade blocked access in that direction. Bolted to its front was a placard emblazoned with red Cyrillic lettering and the Serbian coat of arms: a gold crown atop a double-headed eagle.

Jane used a program on her iPad to translate the warning. *"Access restricted by order of the Ministry of Agriculture and Forestry. Trespassers will be arrested and prosecuted."*

Tucker remembered a similar warning posted by the EPA outside the flooded quarry where Sandy's body lay drowned.

Jane waved them on. "We should keep going. That looks legitimate."

Angry, Tucker braked to a stop. "Let's see what's up there."

Before anyone could protest, he hopped out with a reluctant Frank, and together they wrestled the barricade aside, enough for Jane to squeeze the Yeti through. The SUV's polar-white exterior was now covered in mud and grime from the windows on down.

Tucker secured the barricade again, regained the wheel, and started up the forestry road. The way quickly grew steep, setting the vehicle's four wheels to spinning to keep them moving uphill. The road became a set of serpentine switchbacks climbing the flank of a mountain. Unfortunately the path was slowly taking them the wrong way, in the opposite direction from Skaxis Mining.

"This is a waste of time," Jane said as the Yeti fishtailed around a corner. "We should turn back."

"Just a little farther," Tucker insisted. "If we can get near the summit, we might be able to get a view over to the neighboring complex."

"Rex can do that a lot easier," Nora suggested, clutching the handgrip by her window in back.

"But he also could be spotted from the air."

After another agonizing ten minutes, they reached the top of the crest. Tucker kept the vehicle among the densely packed fir trees and climbed out. The panoramic view from the ridgeline revealed the true breadth of the challenge ahead.

Skaxis Mining was a vast scar across the verdant countryside. Entire mountaintops had been carved away, with valleys filled with tailings and debris from the digging. Toxic green pools dotted the broken landscape, amid lumbering equipment and clusters of concrete buildings belching black smoke from tall chimneys.

"I've seen this sort of destruction back in the Appalachians," Frank said. "It's called MTR, mountaintop removal mining."

"And right now it looks like business as usual." Tucker watched a helicopter lift off, hauling aloft a metal bin full of debris and whisking it toward a dumpsite.

"But we know there are Wasps patrolling the area," Nora reminded him. "So this must be the right place."

He nodded toward the activity below. "With the mine operational like this, Lyon and company must be keeping their activities secret from the workers."

"But where are they hiding?" Jane asked.

Frank shrugged. "A few more trips by Rex, and we should be able to pinpoint that command center."

Jane still looked unconvinced. "That's a lot of land to cover."

Tucker searched past the mining complex and down to the red-tiled roofs of the village of Kamena Gora. From this height, he could spot other hamlets in the distance. They were tucked into neighboring valleys that spread out like five fingers of a hand. The palm stretched south in a series of lower hills and patchy forests, with the wrist marking the boundary with Serbia's neighbor Montenegro.

Tucker studied that border.

What is Kellerman planning? And why here?

He knew of the historical tensions between these two countries and suspected it was the key to all of this and what was to come. Back in Trinidad, Kellerman had exploited the internal political tension of that island republic. He must be planning on taking advantage of similar conflicts here in the Balkans.

But how did he intend to play this out?

Tucker turned to Frank and pointed south. "Does Rex have enough juice to do a sweep of the Montenegro border?"

"If we got closer. Maybe launched him from outside that town." Frank waved down to Kamena Gora. "I might even be able to hit two birds with one stone."

Tucker looked at him.

Frank explained. "If I fly Rex south from that village, I bet I can get the final reading I need to pinpoint the location of the C3 hub for this operation."

"I'm not taking that bet. I know what you can do with Rex."

Frank scowled. "And here I thought I could get a free beer out of you."

"You find where everything is being controlled from up here, and I'll buy you a case of beer."

Frank grinned. "Done."

11:40 A.M.

Back in the SUV, Tucker cleared them out of the forest-service lands and down to the neighboring valley floor. As they reached the outskirts of Kamena Gora, rustic cabins began to line the road, skirted by goat pens and pigsties. Well-kept picket fences, painted a stark white, ran in rambling lines across green meadows.

"Feels like I'm back home in the mountains around Huntsville," Frank muttered.

Nora chuckled. "Sandy would've liked it here, too."

As they entered the village proper, one difference became evident. The inhabitants showed none of the insular paranoia of the Appalachian mountain folk. Old men waved at them; small children laughed and chased after the car. Tucker pulled into the village's central square and parked beside a raised fountain topped by a lichen-splotched statue of a soldier in midcharge, his bayonet extended toward his unseen enemy.

"Why are we stopping?" Jane asked.

"I'm going to check if anyone speaks English. See if there's anything I can learn." He turned to Jane. "You take the others to the southern edge of town and get Rex in the air, then come back for me."

Tucker twisted toward Kane in the backseat. "You stay with them, too, buddy."

It was risky enough showing his face so close to Skaxis, but with Kane in tow, he would stand out. People might talk about an American stranger and his dog. So he left the others with the Yeti, pulled up the hood of his coat, and tugged the edge of a scarf over his chin. Before exiting, he also donned a pair of sunglasses, not that they were needed on this overcast day.

As the SUV headed away, he strode over to a middle-aged woman wearing a blue kerchief on her head. She cradled a thick loaf of bread the size of a small child and noted his approach. She smiled, bowing her head slightly when he joined her.

"Is there somewhere to get something to eat?" He pantomimed putting food in his mouth. From past experience, he knew the best place for gossip was usually the local watering hole or diner.

"I speak Engleski," the woman said, her smile widening at his poor attempt to communicate via sign language. "Come. I show you. Good food."

She headed across the square toward a white-brick building with a sign in Cyrillic hanging from it.

"You American?" she asked.

"Canadian," he corrected, doing his best to further mask his presence.

Everyone loves Canadians.

"I am Bozena." She placed a palm on her chest and looked at him.

Figuring Lyon probably still didn't know his true name, he gave it up to this woman. "Tucker."

"Tucker," she repeated, as if testing his name, then nodded, apparently finding it acceptable.

"You come good time. Lunch today is *Jagnjeća čorba.* Lamb soup. Very good on cold day."

"Sounds wonderful."

Her smile widened as she led him through the door. Heat from a stone fireplace washed the chill from his bones almost immediately. The dining space consisted of two long plank tables and benches before the roaring fire and a tiny bar with shelves of dusty bottles behind it. A set of stairs led up to what were likely rooms for rent.

Apparently he had stumbled into the Serbian equivalent of a bed-and-breakfast.

Bozena spoke to the proprietor, a bent-backed old man holding a large pot and ladle, and pointed to Tucker. The only other patrons were two rough-looking young men in work clothes with beige caps next to their elbows on the tabletop. Their thick, callused hands were clean but bore ages of dirt and oil under their nail beds.

Miners, he imagined.

Tucker shed his coat and scarf, keeping half an eye on his two lunch companions, but after giving him a brief, dismissive glance, they returned to their bowls of soup.

Bozena stepped over and made an introduction. "This is Josif. He will take good care of you."

"Thank you," Tucker said as the woman headed out.

"You eat?" Josif asked. He lifted his ladle, which clearly doubled as the menu.

"I eat." Tucker nodded and sat at the other table.

The old man returned with a big bowl and filled it with generous scoops from his pot.

Tucker leaned slightly aside and asked him, "Miners, yes?" He cocked his head toward the other diners. "Must be good for business with Skaxis nearby."

The old man may not have understood, but he clearly recognized the name of the mine. "Skaxis." He made a spitting motion toward the corner. The two men ignored him, huddled over their bowls, plainly too hungry and exhausted to care.

"Skaxis want us to go away," Josif explained, waving his hand. "Want everything under us. But we say *ne*." He stamped a foot as emphasis. "But they buy everything, even my sons."

He turned and scowled at the two miners—apparently Josif's sons—saying something to them in Serbian that caused the pair to hunch further over their bowls, plainly accustomed to this tongue-lashing.

Tucker began to get an inkling about what Kellerman might want out of a conflict in this area.

More land to expand his operations and exploit the wealth under-foot.

Before Tucker could inquire further, the mud-stained form of the Yeti braked hard outside the square. Frank hopped out, quickly tucking the CUCS unit under his coat and casting around with a panicked look.

Not good.

"Excuse me," Tucker said and stepped outside and waved Frank over.

Frank hurried inside and joined him at the table. "You better see this."

He placed the CUCS device on the table and cradled it from view in the crook of his arm. "Rex has spotted something. Sitting almost on top of the border, about two miles south of here."

Frank brought up an aerial view of a copse of trees, maybe a quarter mile long and fifty yards wide. From a distance, nothing seemed out of the ordinary, but upon closer inspection, there was something *wrong* with the treetops.

"Camouflage netting," Frank explained. "I risked having Rex do a radar sweep."

The image changed, showing angular shapes beneath the treetops, spread in neat lines. Large vehicles were parked under there, including several that sprouted long barrel-shaped noses. Though the view was fuzzy, Tucker knew what he was seeing. He pictured the Soviet hardware outside the derelict town at White Sands: infantry fighting vehicles and T-55 medium tanks. Beyond those neat rows were other shadowy images. He could guess what those were, too.

D-30 artillery pieces . . . same as at White Sands.

Tucker's heart began pounding in his throat.

All the hidden vehicles and armament were facing north toward Serbia.

"How much you wanna bet those tanks are covered in Montenegrin army emblems?" Frank asked.

Tucker didn't want to take that bet any more than the one earlier. "They must be planning a false-flag invasion. Like the Gleiwitz incident."

"What?" Frank asked, his voice edgy.

"At the start of World War II, Nazi commandos donned the uniforms of Polish soldiers and attacked the German town of Gleiwitz. Hitler used that fabricated aggression to justify his invasion of Poland."

"You think the same's about to happen here?"

"Maybe."

He pictured the little hamlets strewn across this side of the valley. If Kellerman razed these villages, made it look like an act of aggression by Montenegrin forces, it would give the Serbian government the excuse it needed to invade.

Tucker peered out the window toward Montenegro, certainty growing inside him. Kellerman didn't just want the land under this town. The bastard had far greater ambitions.

"The question is, *when* does it all begin?" Tucker mumbled.

The answer came with a distant boom. A puff of smoke rose from the tree line miles to the south—then a breath later, a hillside exploded two hundred yards south of the village. Chunks of shattered trees and earth erupted in a geyser. A shudder rippled through the earth.

Tucker jumped to his feet.

It's started . . .

33

Tucker burst out the door of the restaurant and onto the street. Another boom shook the ground. A moment later, an artillery shell screamed past overhead and hit the mountain slope above the village. Trees shattered and boulders rained down, crashing through the red-tiled roofs of the upper village.

From a tiny school across the square, a stream of children and a teacher came rushing out amid panicked shouts and crying.

The Yeti's engine growled from where it was parked and leaped into reverse, then jackknifed toward him, driven by Jane.

Frank pushed up behind Tucker, along with Josif and his two sons, who chattered angrily in Serbian.

"What do we do?" Frank shouted.

Jane skidded the vehicle alongside him. Nora popped the door open as Jane yelled, "Get inside!"

Kane barked, as if urging the same, his ears pressed back on his skull as another shell exploded to the west, striking a building and sending smoke and debris sailing high into the air.

Frank stepped around to obey, but Tucker stared across the square, now milling with older men, women, and more children. Most of the town's able-bodied men must have been sucked up into the neighboring mines.

Tucker grabbed Frank's shoulder. "We . . . we can't just leave these people to be slaughtered."

Frank's eyes were wide with panic, but he winced and nodded. "What can we do?"

Tucker pictured the destruction of the desert town at White Sands—and how they had survived. He turned to Josif and pointed to his toes. "Do you have cellars, caves, anything underground?"

The old man must have seen his fair share of hard times, and rather than being panicked, he looked angry and determined. "*Da*. Many root cellars. Also caves." He waved toward the west side of the village.

Tucker stared the man hard in the eyes. "Show me those caves. Get your boys moving everyone into cellars or over to those caves."

Josif nodded and spoke rapidly to his sons.

"Tuck!" Jane called to him.

He stepped to the open door, glancing across the chaos in the square. Most of the children stayed with their teacher, huddling around her, grasping her skirt and sobbing. A scatter of other children fled down nearby paths and streets.

"Jane, I'm going to help get these children to some caves at the west side of the village. Take the Yeti and collect as many other pe—"

Another artillery round whooshed overhead and crashed into a home on the opposite side of the square. Cedar shingles and white bricks exploded outward, zinging across the open space and peppering the fountain. The statue of the soldier teetered sideways and crashed into the fountain's basin. To his right, a boy of ten or eleven flew through the smoke, then crashed across the ground, his body shredded by shrapnel.

Frank started heading that way, but Tucker grabbed his arm.

The boy was already dead.

Josif waved for Tucker to follow. His sons spread out, grabbing younger children and swinging them up into their strong arms, while herding older children ahead of them.

"*Zuri, zuri!*" the pair shouted, urging their charges to move faster.

Tucker turned to Jane. "Circle the town! Stuff as many people in with you as you can and meet us on the west side!"

She looked scared but nodded.

"Kane, to me," he said.

The shepherd leaped to his side.

As the SUV whipped around to make a pass through the village, he and Frank followed Josif and his two sons. Tucker grabbed a young girl hiding behind a bench.

Frank waved his arms, parroting the two brothers. *"Zuri, zuri!"*

Upon Tucker's signal, Kane ran back and forth, barking to get any stunned stragglers to move. Tucker pulled out his satellite phone and tried to raise Ruth, but he could find no signal.

Frank noted his effort. "Bastards must be jamming this region, like back in Trinidad, blocking outgoing satellite, cell, and landline."

"What about Rex?"

Frank checked the CUCS unit. "Still connected. Makes sense. They'd have to keep local transmissions and frequencies open in order to control the drones."

Another thunderous blast echoed from the southwest. A plume of orange rose into the sky past the shoulder of the neighboring mountain.

Frank looked aghast. "They've begun shelling the other villages."

As Tucker continued through the town, he caught glimpses of the southern border. A pall of smoke hung there, marking the location of the artillery guns and tanks.

He could guess the enemy's strategy.

They're softening up these places before the tanks start rolling.

Afterward, there would be survivors, along with footage of bombed-out homes, of Montenegrin tanks grinding along village streets, and of bodies, too many of them children.

"How can they do this?" Frank gasped out.

Tucker didn't care. He had only one purpose glowing behind his eyes.

To stop them before those tanks got here.

Frank dashed down a side street and helped a pregnant woman cradling her stomach who struggled toward them. He rejoined Tucker, with an arm around the woman's waist.

After an interminable slog, they finally neared the village outskirts. Far up ahead, one of the brothers waved to Tucker and pointed down a side street, directing the parade of refugees that way.

Tucker needed no encouragement to keep moving.

Another bomb struck the square behind them all, casting up smoke and fire. The blast wave pushed them forward. The artillery barrage was in full swing now, moving back and forth across the valley, sending up plumes of flame and debris. Smoke filled the air, the stench of it thick in Tucker's nostrils. Shouts and the cries of frightened children echoed throughout the quickly emptying streets. Dozens of people now followed behind Tucker, while others sprinted past.

A honk drew his attention to the right. The Yeti came hurtling down a steep street from one of the upper tiers of the village. The vehicle barely fit down the narrow path. Through the windshield, now obscured by a skitter of cracks, Jane wore a hard, fixed expression. He remembered it from Afghanistan, Jane in battle mode.

Relieved to see her, he let out a breath he hadn't known he'd been holding.

She reached the stream of villagers and rode alongside Tucker. She had the Yeti packed from stem to stern with people sprawled on top of each other. She even had a young boy of two or three balanced on her knee, clutching him with one arm as if he were her own son.

With her window rolled down, she spoke while driving alongside him. "I got as many as I could, but it's hell up there. Did you see the explosions in the distance?"

He nodded. From the worry in her eyes, she clearly knew the implication, too.

Tucker and his group reached the edge of the village and turned north, where one of Josif's sons stood beside a set of double doors that opened into a chunk of hillside. He was cajoling and shoving people through the entrance.

Jane explained, noting his attention, "I learned from a passenger that the caves on this side of town are used as a communal root cellar. They burrow deep into the mountain for a ways. Should offer some protection."

He hoped so.

As they reached the entrance, Jane unloaded the Yeti and passed the young boy in her lap to an old woman who seemed to recognize the lad. Still, Jane stared after the boy as he was carried through the doors, her face a mask of concern, plainly thinking of her own child.

With Frank and Nora's help, Tucker got the remaining refugees below, then climbed down the steps into the cavern cellars.

The doors were closed behind them, sealing them all inside.

12:19 P.M.

At the bottom of the cellar stairs, kerosene lanterns had been lit. The yellow glow flickered off worried faces and huddled bodies. A low babbling and murmuring echoed from deeper inside the labyrinth.

Outside, shells continued to slam into the earth, sending shockwaves under their feet. Dirt trickled from the ceiling. Tucker could feel each *thwump* in his belly.

"We got to do something," Frank mumbled to him.

Tucker took a deep breath to collect himself. But deep in the back of his skull, old anxieties stirred, making it hard to think. He found the others' eyes upon him.

Then Kane was there, leaning against him, sensing he needed the support. Those dark eyes stared up at him, warmly reflecting the lamplight. The shepherd's body trembled slightly against his thigh. Being underground after being almost buried alive had left the dog unnerved, and rightly so.

Still, Kane stuck by him, ever loyal.

Tucker took strength from his companion and turned to Frank. "Is Rex still in the air?"

Frank pulled out the CUCS unit from his pocket. "I left him hovering in silent mode when I spotted all that military equipment. But he's running low on juice."

Frank showed the screen to Nora, who still looked shell-shocked but seemed relieved to have something to distract her. "I'd say Rex has fifty, maybe sixty minutes of charge left."

"Were you guys able to get that final triangulation on the central command hub?"

Frank winced, plainly having forgotten about this detail in the rush of events. "Let me see." He worked for a few breaths with Nora at his side. "I . . . I think we got it."

"You think or you do?"

Nora explained the hesitation. "We never instructed Rex to perform this last reading, but he must've done it on his own."

On his own?

"Sandy's amazing . . ." Nora muttered, smiling softly.

Frank nodded. "I think Rex is *learning*. He performed the task under his own volition, perhaps sensing what was needed from the earlier hops, recording the information in case we wanted it."

"Which we do." Tucker faced Jane. "Do you still have the map of Skaxis?"

She nodded and pulled out the folded topographic map. "What's the coordinate for the C3 hub?"

As the three of them worked together, spreading the map on one of the earthen walls, someone touched his arm. He turned to find Bozena standing with Josif.

The old man gave a stiff but polite bow of his head. "*Hvala vam.*"

"Thank you," Bozena said, both translating and adding her own appreciation of their efforts.

Don't thank us yet.

Bozena, her face a mask of fear, clearly recognized the ongoing danger. She cringed as another blast shook the ground. No one was safe yet—especially if those tanks started rolling.

Tucker faced Bozena and Josif. "We need your help." He glanced to the old man's two sons. "Someone who knows Skaxis Mining well."

Josif scowled at that name again. "*Zašto?*"

"Why?" Bozena asked, her expression confused.

Tucker didn't have time to explain and feared something would be lost in the translation anyway. "With enough help, I might be able to stop this."

Plainly suspicious, Josif turned and spoke with Bozena, who seemed to offer some reassurance to the old man, waving a hand at Tucker's group, then at the people huddled in the caves.

Finally, Josif sighed and waved one of his boys over. "My son Pravi. He know mines."

Tucker drew Pravi over to the map. "Show him where Rex seems to think the C3 hub is located."

Frank pointed to a spot on the map on the far side of the complex, in what appeared to be a remote corner, away from the attention of the main mining facility.

Tucker faced Pravi. "Do you know where that is?"

The tall young man leaned closer, swiping some blond hair from his eyes, then straightened. "*Manstir, da.*" He bobbed his head but questioned them. "*Zašto?*"

"Can you get us there?"

Pravi frowned. "Place be high and"—he made an angle with one hand—"*strm.*"

Steep, Tucker guessed, which he could also tell from the map's topography. He began to despair, knowing they didn't have much time.

Pravi offered a thin hope, grinning slyly. "But maybe I know way."

34

Tucker careened the ŠKODA Yeti up the mountain road. Pravi sat in the passenger seat, acting as their navigator, while Jane and Nora shared the back with Kane. The shepherd was again fully outfitted in his gear.

The final member of their party whispered in Tucker's earpiece on a channel Rex had encrypted and kept masked from eavesdroppers. *"Tucker, the tanks are beginning to roll across the border . . . headed our way."*

He had left Frank with the villagers at the cavern cellars. Tucker hated to leave the man behind, but Frank had insisted. He was determined to use the last of Rex's battery life to keep an eye on the border and use the drone's electronic warfare suite to protect the people as best he could. To do that, he needed to remain in the village.

"They'll be on us in the next twenty minutes," Frank warned, adding pressure to the already strained timetable.

Even without Frank's call, Tucker could have guessed the tanks would begin to roll. The artillery barrage had fallen silent for the past several minutes. Apparently the rain of shells had softened the cluster of hamlets sufficiently enough. Now would come the true terror.

Tucker touched his throat mike. "We're almost to the perimeter of Skaxis Mining. Do your best to hold the fort."

Pravi was taking them up a rutted tract. It was an overgrown old cart road dating from medieval times, a path only the locals knew about. It was so narrow and heavily forested that the SUV's side mirrors brushed through low pine branches. Several of the men from Kamena Gora used this shortcut to come and go from the mines. It ended at an abandoned section of the complex, where the ground had been emptied of its rare-earth minerals, leaving behind a deep scar.

The C3 hub lay almost directly across from that spot, a good seven miles away.

Pravi had offered a solution for quickly traversing that distance.

Frank radioed again. "*Tucker! I just sent Rex for a high pass over those tanks. Something ain't right here.*"

"What?" he asked while struggling to keep the SUV on the muddy tract.

"*Rex is picking up electromagnetic signatures from the tanks, identical to Tangent's drones. Same across every frequency.*"

"What're you getting at?"

"I think the tanks are drones, too. I think they're unmanned."

Is that possible?

Tucker called back to Nora and explained the situation.

She leaned forward. "He could be right. Odisha was only one of a scatter of labs around the country. There were rumors that other places were working on ground versions of our aerial fleet."

Tucker realized that such unmanned vehicles might work to Kellerman's advantage. Back at White Sands, all that had remained after the Warhawks' bombardment of the Soviet hardware was smoldering slag. With no bodies inside, Kellerman could further mask his involvement.

But this thought gave Tucker another idea.

"Frank," he radioed back, "do you think you could use Rex to hack into one of those tanks and commandeer it to the defense of the village, like you were able to pull off with the Warhawk in New Mexico?"

Tucker pictured that winged drone crashing into the desert bunker.

"*Maybe,*" Frank said. "*But Rex is flying on fumes, so to speak. If he can manage it, it won't last long.*"

Still, it could buy them a few extra minutes.

"Give it your best," Tucker encouraged him.

Pravi pointed to a clearing at the side of the road, where the trail ended at a moonscape of jumbled boulders and pyramidal mounds of gravel and dirt. A single battered open-bed truck was parked in the clearing, likely another of the miners' vehicles.

Tucker parked his muddy SUV next to it.

"We go," Pravi said, and climbed out his side.

Tucker bailed with the others. The young man led them through the remaining edge of the forest, then along a winding path across the rubble. Tucker felt exposed out in the open, but they had no choice. Before leaving, Josif had gathered heavy coats and jackets from the locals, to better hide them from any casual scrutiny. Still, Tucker hoped all eyes were on the battle in the valley and not on this remote corner of the complex.

That certainly seemed to be the case at the moment. Several groups of men stood atop the surrounding slag heaps and rock piles, watching the destruction below. Tucker could only imagine what they were thinking. How many of them had family among the villages? How many had abandoned the mines to go to the defense of their loved ones? He could almost feel the anger flowing down the slopes from those standing in furious vigil.

With that much pent-up hostility, it would not take much to stoke that fire into an all-out attack on Montenegro.

Leading them steadily onward, Pravi eventually took them to where two cargo helicopters rested on concrete pads. Pravi had them hold with a raised palm. He hurried over to a neighboring shed next to a pair of large red fuel tanks.

Jane sidled next to Tucker, her arms crossed over her chest. Both of them had holstered pistols—the same SIG Sauers from Trinidad—under their coats. Flying in under EU call signs and passports, they hadn't needed to pass through customs, so ferrying the weapons in hadn't been a problem. She stared now toward the shed, clearly wary, likely wondering if she would have to use her weapon in another moment.

Pravi appeared again and waved them forward. He headed to one of the helicopters with a pair of fellow workers in tow. Tucker didn't know what Pravi had told the men to gain their cooperation, but if they were locals, it might not have taken much.

Pravi spoke to one man, who then climbed behind the controls of the helicopter. The other worker dragged a thick cable and secured it to the undercarriage of the aircraft. The other end snaked to a large metal ore bin.

Pravi rushed them in that direction. *"Zuri!"* he urged them.

Pravi had suggested using one of the company's choppers to reach the coordinates in the mountainous corner on the complex's far side, but Tucker had come up with this last detail of the plan. He had remembered watching one of the cargo helicopters hauling debris. He hoped such a means could also be used to deliver a secret payload of passengers to the destination atop the distant ridge.

It was risky—but they had no better option.

As the helicopter began warming its engine, Tucker helped Nora inside the tall-walled bin, then he and Jane got Kane up and over the lip. Tucker tossed his pack inside, and he and Jane scrambled up and over to join the others.

Pravi threw in a folded tarp and said something in Serbian that Tucker could guess meant *keep out of sight.* Tucker shook out the tarp and got everyone under it. Before ducking away, he watched Pravi climb into the helicopter.

Moments later, the helicopter's rotors began churning faster and the engine whined into a growl. Rotor wash whipped across the mouth of the bin, requiring all of them to hold fast to the tarp before it was ripped away.

Then the helicopter rose from its pad, the metal cable slithering over the concrete.

"Hang on," Tucker warned.

The bin jerked sideways, tilting scarily and scraping a couple of feet to the left—then it lifted skyward.

Here we go.

12:49 P.M.

As they flew, Tucker leaned his palm against his ear to hear Frank's report. But his friend's voice was cutting in and out as they passed beyond the radio's range.

"The tanks . . . two headed to each village. ETA . . . be here four or five minutes."

"Any luck commandeering one?" Tucker yelled.

"Still . . . working . . . Rex . . . not as familiar with these ground drones as his fellow winged brothers."

"Keep at it."

Frank tried to respond, but the transmission became too garbled.

Tucker finally gave up. For now, it was up to Frank to protect the village. He turned to Nora. "Are you ready with Sandy's code?"

She patted her jacket pocket. "I'd better be."

Kane crouched next to Jane. She absently rubbed the shepherd's head, her gaze gone again into that thousand-yard stare. He shifted next to her and took her hand. She flinched, but he gripped harder.

She finally looked at him, her eyes focusing back. "I'm okay."

No, you're not.

All too often, he had heard that refrain—*I'm okay*—from his fellow soldiers. It was what one said, what was expected of you. The stigma of asking for help, especially among those in Special Forces, was deeply ingrained.

Suck it up was as much a motto as *semper fi.*

He pulled her closer. "I'm sorry, Jane. I shouldn't have been so hard on you earlier. I know you're harder on yourself than anyone."

Especially when it comes to protecting Nathan.

She swallowed and nodded. There were no tears, but he suspected they would come with time. "I'll be all right."

That he could believe.

Happy to have made these meager amends with her, Tucker scooted up and peeked out from under the tarp. Cold winds stung his eyes, but he squinted against the burn. Ahead the carved landscape of the mines ended at a tumble of sheer cliffs, topped by green forests. This corner of the complex looked untouched by the strip-mining.

Why?

Tucker pulled out a set of binoculars.

He scanned the area, trying to discern where across those escarpments the C3 hub might be hidden. Then he noted a shadow halfway up one cliff face, four stories above the ground.

A structure perched there, its facade protruding from the rock's sheer surface. At the top were two towers, separated by a rampart of waist-high crenellated battlements, several sections of which had crumbled away, giving them the appearance of a row of chipped teeth. Below the ramparts stretched a set of tall narrow windows, peaked at their tops. And under them stood massive oak doors, criss-crossed with iron braces.

Tucker remembered Pravi saying something in Serbian when this spot was pointed to on the map.

Manastir, da . . .

He now understood: *manastir* meant *monastery*. While driving from the airport, Tucker had spotted other such churches, dating back centuries, nestled and hidden in valleys.

No wonder this section of the mine had been spared.

Besides the monastery's historical value, the religious piety of the locals likely kept this old church preserved—not that it hadn't been repurposed at the moment.

Tucker spotted cables running along the switchback of narrow steps that led up to those iron-framed doors. At the foot of the cliff, camouflage netting obscured a barricaded compound, where there were generators humming and trucks parked. Swinging his gaze back to the top, he noted rows of parabolic dishes positioned along the ramparts, all aimed toward the south.

This definitely must be the operation's C3 hub.

But how are we going to storm that castle?

The original plan had been for the helicopter to swing low over the highland forests, pretending to be workers fleeing the battle at the border. Once near enough, the helicopter would dip low—hovering briefly enough for Tucker's group to offload into the dense forest—then it would continue north again.

Once safely on the ground, Tucker had hoped to sneak overland to the compound and reach the servers that controlled this operation, where Nora would hack Sandy's lobotomy code into the transmission systems.

Tucker suddenly had no faith in these plans—especially when he spotted something wing out of a ravine to the left and sweep into the sky.

A Shrike.

Lyon's group must be using the nearby valleys and rifts to hide their fleet, readying for phase two of these plans, which was surely to finish the destruction and destroy the invading tanks and vehicles.

But that was not this drone's objective. It banked around and fired at the helicopter. Tucker craned up and watched rounds rip through the bulk of the aircraft. Smoke burst forth from its engine. The helicopter bobbled, whipping the bin wildly beneath it.

Tucker got tossed to the floor.

The Shrike streaked past, its work done.

The helicopter tipped and plummeted toward the ground.

7:50 A.M. EDT
Smith Island, Maryland

Locked securely in his office, Pruitt Kellerman stood once again before his bank of wall monitors. A few screens showed news channels beginning to receive word of the skirmish along the Serbian border. Reports remained preliminary, full of speculation due to the remoteness of the mountainous region. But even at this early stage, he had false information being threaded through various media outlets, using an advanced encryption algorithm based on Alan Turing's old papers.

All due to the foresight of my grandfather.

The remaining monitors ran with secure feeds from the operation center at Skaxis Mining. One screen showed the smoky image of a village on fire. Another revealed a bombed-out armory near the Montenegrin city of Bijelo Polje, courtesy of a late-morning airstrike by a Warhawk, which left nothing but a cratered ruin in its wake. More faked reports had already been seeded, which would show fabricated grainy footage of a caravan of Montenegrin tanks and military vehicles leaving that armory two days prior, headed for the Serbian border. Kellerman had needed some explanation for the source of military hardware that would be found demolished at the border.

"Sir!" a voice shouted from the largest wall monitor.

Pruitt stepped closer to this live feed from the Serbian command center.

Rafael Lyon's face filled the screen as he leaned close to the camera. Still, past his shoulders, various drone control stations bustled with technicians as the next stage of the operation was about to commence.

"We've just received word that six leaders of the Serbian parliament were successfully assassinated in Belgrade. The news outlets are going nuts."

Pruitt frowned. "But didn't we target *eight* politicians? Wasn't that the plan?"

"With the timetable moved up, we lost the opportunity on two."

Pruitt nodded. Weeks ago, he and Marco Davidovic had handpicked a mix of Christian and Muslim moderates, whose deaths would be blamed on the Balkan Islamic Front. And in another day, that same terrorist group would be shown to have ties to Montenegro's National Security Agency, all to further implicate Serbia's neighbor while inciting the radicals in Davidovic's party.

Just one more nail in the coffin.

Pruitt doubted the CIA or the old KGB could have done any better.

"We have everything locked down here," Lyon continued. "Communications are jammed, and I've got the drones patrolling the skies and roads. No one's leaving the area."

"Keep it that way."

"Yes, sir. And we're right on schedule. On your word, we can commence with stage two."

"Very good. Proceed."

Despite the hiccups, everything was running like clockwork. Pruitt stepped back, clasping his hands behind his back, all too aware of the blood on them.

But what's a little spilled milk in the long run?

35

"Brace yourselves!" Tucker hollered as the smoking helicopter plummeted toward the dense highland forest. The bin swung and bobbled. Residual gravel rattled across the metal floor, pelting the trapped group.

Tucker jammed his legs against one metal wall and his shoulders against the other. He had a hold of Kane's vest collar and another fist wrapped in the hood of Nora's coat. At his feet on the other side, Jane pinned herself in the corner, with an arm wrapped around his leg.

He caught Jane's eye, glad he had started to make peace with her a moment ago, wishing he could hold her, kiss her one last time. But he knew her thoughts were elsewhere. Fear and loss shone from her every pore.

Then the bottom of the container scraped across treetops.

Tucker turned every muscle fiber to iron to hold the group in place. The bin dropped lower, ripping through branches and bouncing off trunks. With the steel tub acting as an anchor, the helicopter's momentum slowed, and its bulk got thrown nose-first toward the forest. The bin continued to tear through the trees, dragged by the falling chopper.

Then the container's cable broke with a teeth-jarring twang.

The helicopter flipped and crashed with a splintering of wood and a crumple of metal. The bin followed. It dropped heavily through the tree branches, struck the ground, rolled once, and finally came to rest on its side.

Tucker crawled out, dizzy and dazed. Jane and Nora followed

on hands and knees. They all looked shocked to be alive, except for Kane, who hopped free and shook it all off as if it had been nothing.

Tucker rolled to a hip and stared back at the path of destruction through the branches and trees. The thick forest had saved them, bleeding away the energy of the crash, turning the impact from bone shattering to body bruising. But they were not out of danger.

He stood with a groan, retrieved his pack, and stared toward the smoking ruins of the helicopter. *Pravi and the pilot . . . ?* He took a step in that direction when the chopper's engine exploded, throwing him back and rolling a fireball into the sky.

Tucker turned to find Nora clutching a fist at her throat, her eyes terrified. Jane looked lost. He gathered everyone together and dropped to a knee before Kane. He pointed south into the forest, away from the wreckage.

"CLOSE SCOUT," he ordered. "GO."

Kane took off, swiftly gliding away.

Tucker stood and got the two women moving after the shepherd. "We can't stay here in case a patrol is sent to check on the Shrike's handiwork."

As they hurried, he tugged out his satellite phone and pulled up Kane's video feed. He kept an eye on the dog, while watching where he stepped. Though many handlers had difficulty with this, considering it like tapping your head and rubbing your stomach at the same time, Tucker had no problem. He felt one with Kane, sharing the shepherd's eyes while using his own.

Jane kept to Tucker's heels. "What . . . what's the plan?"

"I'm pretty sure we crashed a half mile or so north of the C3 hub, in the plateau above the monastery."

"What monastery?" Nora asked.

He forgot that neither woman had spied the fortified encampment like he had. He explained what he saw. "If we can reach the cliffs above that old church," he finished, "we might be able to rappel down to the roof."

"That's if we truly crashed where you hoped we did," Jane warned, staring at the thick forest. "All I see are trees and more trees."

Tucker, though, had another set of eyes. On the screen, he watched Kane slip through undergrowth, wet branches sliding past the camera lens. He kept watch on that screen and almost missed it.

"STOP," Tucker ordered—speaking to both Kane and the two women.

Kane froze and lay down.

Something's not right.

A few yards ahead of the shepherd, the tree trunks stood out more starkly. At first Tucker had thought it was a trick of lighting. Then he realized those trees were too straight and were stripped of their dark bark.

Posts . . .

He turned to Jane. "Someone erected a cluster of wooden stanchions in the next section of forest."

"What for?"

"Let's see." Tucker radioed Kane. "SLOW ADVANCE."

The shepherd crept forward one paw at a time. Again Tucker felt that blurring of senses as he continued to give orders to his partner.

"PAN UP . . . TURN LEFT . . ."

Slowly Tucker understood what Kane had stumbled upon, what the shepherd was showing him.

"There's camouflage netting strung about twenty feet off the ground, supported by wooden posts and pine trees." He glanced to Jane and Nora. "I saw the same at the foot of the cliffs."

"Then you were right," Jane admitted. "We must be almost right on top of them."

Tucker grinned. "Only one way to find out."

He set off again, keeping Kane still on point. Eventually Tucker and the women crept under that netting. They found evidence of a staging ground under there: open crates, pry bars, and a scatter of sagging tents. The place appeared to be abandoned.

"This must be where they airlifted in supplies to help set up their command center at the church," Jane whispered.

Kane reached the far side of the camouflaged area and stopped at the edge of a drop-off, staying hidden in some low bushes. Tucker and the others joined him. He had the women hold back, while he crawled on his belly next to Kane. He rubbed the dog's flank.

"Good boy."

He peered beyond the edge. Two stories down, the crenellated battlements of the rampart stretched between the two towers of the church. The facade of the monastery was flush against the cliffs, suggesting the main bulk of the church was likely built into the mountainside, carved out centuries ago with painstaking effort and devotion.

The same could not be said for the new caretakers.

Rows of parabolic antennas had been bolted to the old stone. Wrist-thick cables twisted and snaked across the rampart and vanished down a hole crudely drilled through its surface. A diesel generator chugged loudly in one corner.

Tucker studied the dishes, all of which pointed toward the border. He hoped the attention of those inside was focused in the same direction.

He scooted back and rejoined Jane and Nora. He described what he saw while opening his backpack. Knowing the team had been headed into the Dinaric Alps, he had packed ropes and climbing gear.

"I'll head down first with Kane, then you and Nora follow."

He got nods all around.

Tucker quickly tied one end of the rope to a tree trunk, then back-stepped to the cliff, laying down the line. At the edge, he slipped into a rappelling harness and hooked Kane's vest to carabineers at Tucker's backside. Slung behind him, Kane would hang there while Tucker rappelled below. After double-checking everything, he leaned his butt over the edge and descended in short hops. Kane dangled behind him, remaining calm, an old hand at rope work.

Moments later, their six legs landed atop the rampart.

Tucker crouched, freed Kane, and pulled out his SIG Sauer. He covered the two women as they made their descent, but so far no alarm had been raised.

Then a distant boom made them all crouch even lower. Tucker crab walked between two of the antenna dishes and stared beyond the parapets toward the distant valley. A column of fresh smoke rose from where Kamena Gora lay hidden in the lower forests.

Jane followed him, staring past his shoulder. "The tanks . . ."

More booms echoed, accompanied by flashes from massive guns, raising new flags of smoke. Then to either side of the monastery, a familiar hum arose. Wedge-shaped Warhawks and smaller Shrikes shot out of the neighboring valleys. They swept wide, climbing high, then dove toward the cluster of hamlets.

"It's the beginning of the end," Jane whispered.

1:14 P.M.

As the bombardment commenced, Tucker crouched by one of the parabolic dishes, examining the thick cable that ran to it. It ended at a padlocked juncture box. He tested the cable. It was warm and vibrated with power.

Probably fry my ass if I tried yanking it loose, but it might be worth it.

"Don't," Nora warned, pulling him back. "I know what you're contemplating. You think if you take out these dishes, you can stop any orders from being transmitted to those drones."

Tucker twisted to her. "What's wrong with that plan?"

"Tangent's drones aren't just remote-control cars and airplanes. They have brains, the AI cores designed by Sandy. And while they may not be as highly tuned as our new and improved Rex, they still have rudimentary intelligence. The attack orders have already been transmitted. If you knock out these dishes, those orders will still stand. The drones will continue, perhaps improvising and revising on their own, but surely proceeding with their bombing run."

Tucker remembered how Rex had operated under his own volition to gain the final triangulation to this command center.

Jane offered another reason to leave the dishes alone. "We'll also need these antennas intact if we hope to transmit the lobotomy codes out to those drones."

Tucker realized the women were right.

"But first I need to get down to the servers," Nora reminded him.

He glanced over to where Kane sniffed at a door into one of the towers. The dog's body was taut, tail straight, ears low. He knew Kane's behavior enough to know the shepherd had found a scent trail, one he recognized.

There could only be *one* person who Kane would remember by smell.

Rafael Lyon.

Ever thorough, that bastard would surely have spent some time up here, inspecting every final detail. A deep-seated anger burned inside Tucker. He could still hear the blast of the mortar shell that had struck the village square earlier. He pictured the boy's body, shredded by shrapnel, crumpling like a broken doll onto the cobbles.

Lyon and his boss were already responsible for the deaths of hundreds of innocent people, and more would die this day.

It had to stop.

"C'mon," Tucker said, heading toward Kane. "Let's find those servers."

The tower door was steel, clearly new, but it was unlocked. Either Lyon trusted no one had access to this back entrance, or maybe technicians simply needed to come and go to adjust the dishes.

Tucker didn't care.

He edged the door open and discovered a set of worn stone steps spiraling down the center of the tower. A string of bare bulbs lit the way, but they were spaced far enough apart to leave shadowy gaps between. Tucker signaled Kane by lowering a palm before his nose, then pointing a finger toward the steps.

STAY LOW, TAKE POINT.

Kane stuck close to the wall, slinking along his belly, slipping from one shadow to another. Tucker followed with the others, leading with his SIG Sauer. He kept his phone in his other hand, using Kane's eyes to see a turn or two ahead of them.

As they descended, Nora's breathing rasped behind him.

Jane's boots lightly scuffed the stone steps at the rear of the group.

Kane passed a landing. To one side stood an ancient door of rotted wood held together by straps of iron. It hung crooked on broken hinges, revealing peeks into a dark passage festooned with cobwebs, the walls splotched with lichen and mold.

No one had walked that hall in centuries.

"KEEP GOING," Tucker radioed his partner.

Kane continued down the stairs, around and around, until he reached the next landing.

"HOLD," Tucker instructed, stopping the women several steps up from the landing below.

While Tucker saw no one through Kane's camera, he heard voices echoing up the spiral stair, but it was difficult to tell the source. Another passage split off from the steps, identical to the one above, but here there was no door blocking the threshold, only broken hinges from where someone must have ripped the original away.

Jane whispered in his ear, leaning at his shoulder. "Look at those cables on the floor."

He had noted them, too. A bundle of black snakes stretched across the landing, both extending into the passageway and continuing down the spiral of the stairs.

"Look like power and insulated data lines," Nora offered.

"But which way do we go?" Tucker asked.

"Down the stairs," Nora said without hesitation. "They'd need to keep the servers as cool and insulated as possible."

With no better plan, Tucker crept around the curve of steps and joined Kane. The voices had grown louder, clearly rising from the passageway to the left. Kane sniffed in that direction, his hackles raised, again clearly picking up a scent trail.

Lyon.

One more reason not to go that way.

Tucker reached Kane and sent the shepherd moving down the steps again, following the cables. This time, the spiral ran around three turns and ended at another steel door. The cables ran through a hole cored through the neighboring wall.

Kane reached the door first, sniffing along the sill—then backed a step and lowered to a crouch with his neck stiff, his nose pointed toward the door. Kane was silently signaling his partner.

Someone's inside there.

Tucker spotted no cameras, so he had Jane and Nora remain on the stairs and crossed to the door. He pressed his ear and could vaguely hear someone whistling inside. Considering all that was happening, the casual, nonchalant noise pissed him off more than any blistering curse.

He gently tested the door latch with a finger.

Locked.

Screw it.

Tucker straightened and boldly rapped his knuckles on the steel.

This time Tucker got a curse, followed by a muffled inquiry. "What?"

Tucker growled his response, matching the other's irritation. "Lyon needs you up top. I'm supposed to cover you."

"What for?"

Tucker heard the worry and fear in this question; plainly their boss ruled with an iron fist. Tucker took advantage of this.

"Who the fuck knows?" he said. "Just get your ass moving if you know what's good for you."

Another curse followed, and the lock unlatched.

Tucker retreated a step. As the door opened, he grabbed the edge and yanked. The man inside, his grip still on the knob, got pulled off balance. As his body fell forward, Tucker punched the guard in the hollow of this throat. With a strangled cry, the man buckled forward. Tucker sidestepped him, palmed the back of the man's head, and slammed his forehead into the steel jamb.

Bone crunched, and his victim collapsed limply to the floor.

Stepping over the body, Tucker scanned the next space with his SIG Sauer leveled. It wasn't a room as much as an arched tunnel carved into the bare rock that delved deeper into the mountainside, extending beyond the reach of the pool of light cast by a pair of halogen pole lamps. He could make out a couple of broken copper-banded wooden barrels in the darkness.

Must be the old wine cellar for the monastery.

But the naturally insulated space had been repurposed.

Along both sides of the tunnel were banks of six-foot-tall server bays, blinking with lights and entangled by cabling. A small steel workstation sat to one side with a keyboard and monitor.

Tucker did a quick sweep, then rasped softly, "Clear."

He returned to the door, grabbed the downed man's ankles, and dragged his body into the room. Jane and Nora followed him inside. Tucker signaled Kane to keep watch on the stairs.

Nora looked at the sprawled figure on the floor. "Is he d—?"

"Yep." Tucker crouched down and frisked the man, freeing a compact assault rifle and pulling it over his own shoulder. The weight felt good as he stood.

Jane turned to Nora after studying the servers. "Is this what you were looking for?"

"I think so." She strode over to the workstation and began typing at the keyboard as if she had worked here for ages, which considering her prior employment was partly true. She glanced to them and pulled out a familiar thumb drive. "This is the right place, but I'm going to need time to hack Sandy's new code into these systems and broadcast them."

"How much time?" Tucker asked, picturing the attack on the valley.

Nora looked worried and doubtful. "I'm not sure. Sandy was brilliant. I don't know if I can—"

Jane put a hand on her shoulder. "Sandy left this drive for *you*. She knew you could handle it. If you don't trust yourself, trust her."

Nora took a deep breath, nodded, and set to work.

Jane joined Tucker. "We need to know what's going on up there. Not to mention a backup plan if . . ." She glanced to Nora.

If Nora can't pull this off.

Tucker understood. "I'll take Kane and scout the other passageway, see if I can spy on the nerve center and get a bead on what's going on. If nothing else, I can create a distraction if necessary."

Jane followed him to the door.

He stopped at the threshold, fished in a pocket, and passed Jane one of his spare radio earpieces to keep in contact with her. "You lock up behind me and guard Nora."

"I will, but you be careful."

He sighed. "If I did that, I certainly wouldn't be in this mess."

He turned away, but she grabbed his collar, pulled his head close, and kissed him hard. She then looked at him, struggling to put into words what glowed from her eyes.

"I know," he whispered, and stepped away, pulling the door closed behind him.

He rushed the steps, gathered Kane to his side, and headed up.

As he climbed, he pictured the smug face of Rafael Lyon.

It's him or us now.

36

With Kane at his side, Tucker retraced his steps to the landing. He listened to the voices echoing from the passageway. Kane's hackles rose again, picking up a scent that clearly stoked a deep-seated fury in the dog.

He silently signaled Kane to proceed.

CLOSE GUARD.

The shepherd eased ahead, sticking to the ancient stone wall.

Tucker followed with the confiscated assault rifle at his shoulder.

As the voices grew stronger, so did the light. He also heard distant booms and the occasional loud cheer closer at hand. Clearly everyone's attention remained on this final stage of the attack.

The hall ended in another ten yards, dumping into a cavernous space just past a carved wooden archway. Tucker joined Kane and crouched by a pillar at the base of the arch. Beyond the threshold, stone columns and giant oak crossbeams graced the expanse.

It was the monastery's main church.

The archway opened upon the back of the nave on its second level, likely a former choir loft. The balcony spread across the breadth of the back of the church and extended along the walls to the right and left. Directly ahead was the wall of the church that faced out from the cliff face. Arched windows showed the sky, while below were the ten-foot-tall doors he had spotted earlier. One section had been pushed ajar, letting in daylight, along with the sharper sounds of the valley explosions.

A handful of men stood at that opening, watching the carnage to the south.

But the real action occupied the church floor. The main nave had been converted into a makeshift C3 suite. Down the middle of the room stretched a long trestle table laden with food staples and bottled water. To either side were U-shaped stations of computer consoles, topped by large rectangular monitors. Pairs of technicians stood or sat at those stations, calling out reports and updates.

From his vantage, Tucker spotted screens that showed aerial views of the smoky battlefield, coming from live feeds from the drones in the air. He also spotted what appeared to be black-and-white thermal imaging and a 3-D topographic map done in vivid colors.

A loud order barked to his left, out of view under the balcony on that side. "What's wrong with that tank? Why's it stopped?"

Tucker sneered upon hearing that accent, even Kane tensed.

Rafael Lyon.

Directly ahead of Tucker, a narrow spiral stair led down from the balcony to the floor of the nave. Wanting to get a better lay of the land, he sent Kane to the stretch of loft that ran along the church's left side, while he ducked low and ran to the right. He kept away from the balcony's balustrade and circled wide to reach the loft on that side.

As he made the turn, a shadow shifted along the rail ahead, half hidden behind one of the stone columns. An armed guard. The man had his back to Tucker, his attention on the activity below. Tucker crept up behind him, then burst forward at the last step. Wrapping his left forearm across the guard's windpipe in a strangling choke, he drew the man down and back behind the thick column. With the guard on the floor, he clamped down on his victim's carotid artery. He waited until the man went limp, then draped his body to the floor.

Hidden behind the column, Tucker quickly stripped the guard of spare magazines for his rifle and pocketed them. He also checked on Kane's status with his phone. He had Kane pan right and left, but there appeared to be no man stationed on that side.

Must be the only patrol up here.

Tucker crab walked around the column to the edge of the balcony. He stayed crouched and was able to spy between the stone spindles of the balustrade.

Lyon shouted again. "Why is it just sitting there?"

The French soldier stalked back and forth behind one of the techs seated at a station. Tucker had a full view of the work space. The tech tapped and swiped at a touchscreen, while typing on a keyboard with his other hand.

"I don't understand. It's not responding."

On the monitors above the tech's head, a glowing map showed what appeared to be the town of Kamena Gora. Many areas were blackened out. Another screen showed an aerial view of the fields to the south. A tank rolled across the meadow, crushing through the pigsty of an outlying home. Sows ran through the grass. Other infantry fighting vehicles rocked across the meadow in the tank's wake, guns blazing from atop the armored cabins, firing toward the town. All the while, a second tank sat idle in the field, as if silently watching the ongoing destruction.

"Get that bastard moving," Lyon ordered.

"I can't. It's dead."

But as they all watched, the turret of the parked tank turned. Smoke and flame burst from the gun muzzle as it fired. The shell struck the lead tank from only thirty yards away, blasting it up onto one set of treads, enveloping it with smoke. When it crashed back to the earth, half its turret was gone.

As if not satisfied with the one kill, the tank's gun swung toward one of the infantry vehicles and fired again. The round missed, but the turret kept turning, readying for another shot.

While Lyon and the tech were baffled by the tank's behavior, Tucker was not.

Good going, Frank.

Frank must have finally been able to remotely commandeer one of the tanks, to bring it to Kamena Gora's defense.

Lyon turned to another station, pointing to the man seated there. "Send in a Warhawk. Bomb that bastard."

The tech worked quickly, but even his body language screamed his frustration. "I can't get a targeting lock, sir. Not from any of the birds. It's as if all our systems are blind to that tank."

"But I can see it right there!" Lyon complained.

Tucker grinned. Rex must be electronically masking the tank, similar to how the CUCS unit had protected Kane and Tucker back in the Alabama swamp.

The tank fired again. The shell struck the armored infantry unit broadside and sent it rolling across the meadow, a gaping hole through its flank. But Frank wasn't done. Treads churned grass and the forty-ton beast began to pursue other vehicles, gaining speed.

C'mon, big guy . . .

"Wait!" the tech in front of Lyon called out. "I think . . . I think I'm regaining control again."

On the screen, the tank slowed, its barrel swinging erratically—then steadied.

"Got it!" the tech announced triumphantly. "Green lights across the board!"

From the neighboring station came equally good news. "And I've got a targeting lock on it finally."

Tucker silently cursed. Apparently Frank's defense was short-lived. Rex must have finally run out of juice.

"Do you want me to still destroy the tank?" one tech asked.

Lyon squinted at the glowing 3-D map. "No. Leave it where it is." He tapped a spot on the screen, almost shaking with fury. "Send these coordinates to that tank and have it unload its remaining arsenal here. According to our premission briefing, most of the remaining townspeople are probably holed up in some caves on the western edge of the village. Blast the fuck out of this spot. If anyone survives the shelling, they'll still be buried alive."

"Yes, sir." The tech started tapping in the coordinates.

Lyon strode across the length of the nave. "We end this now! Bring all guns to bear on those villages. Begin dropping the incendiaries and cluster bombs from the Warhawks. One last firestorm, men, then we clean up and get the hell out of this godforsaken place."

He got muted cheers and a few *hoo-rahs.*

Tucker sank back behind the column and touched his throat mike. "Jane," he whispered.

A long moment of silence stretched, then he got a static-frosted response. *"How're things up there?"*

"Bad . . . and about to get worse. You?"

"Nora's still working. Needs maybe another five or six minutes."

Tucker winced. They didn't have that much time. "I'll see what I can do at my end."

Knowing he had to stop the shelling of the caves, Tucker rolled back to the balustrade and eased up enough to balance the barrel of his rifle on the stone rail. He centered his sights on the technician at the control terminal for the tanks.

The man turned toward Lyon. "I'm ready—"

Tucker let out a breath and squeezed the trigger. The technician's head snapped to the side in a halo of red mist. His body crumpled over the terminal. It was a cold-blooded kill but a necessary one.

As shouts arose, Tucker ran along the rail, firing below, snapping off shots at random targets. He tried to take out Lyon first, but the soldier was too skilled to panic. Upon the first crack of Tucker's rifle, he had dived for cover behind one of the stations.

Tucker touched his throat. "Kane," he radioed. "MAKE NOISE. STAY IN COVER."

From across the nave, the shepherd howled. The ululating cry echoed off the oak rafters and stone walls, seemingly coming from everywhere at once. The unnerving acoustics even set Tucker's teeth on edge.

Tucker dropped back into the shadows as men fired blindly up at the balcony. From the corner of his eye, he watched several technicians and armed guards hightailing it out the open church doors.

Lyon, perhaps sensing he was losing control, shot one of the deserters in the back and shouted brightly. "Hold fast! All stations . . . transmit final orders! Now!"

Crap . . .

Tucker rounded the back corner to the balcony, aiming for the stretch of the loft along the rear of the church, but the way was blocked by a pair of men running up the spiral stairs from below, both in full combat gear.

Tucker crouched at the corner and fired at the first man's legs as he appeared, blasting out a kneecap. The guard tumbled with a cry, tripping up the second man—but these were seasoned soldiers.

Though falling, the second man dove and rolled over his partner into the passageway across from the stairs—where Tucker had hidden moments earlier and spied upon the church. The first soldier, clearly in agony, had the wherewithal to roll to one shoulder and fire at Tucker's position, driving him back. His partner then lunged out, grabbed his free arm, and hauled him into the hallway.

Both men opened fire in Tucker's direction, laying down a deafening barrage. Rounds pelted the stone, ricocheting everywhere. Tucker felt a hammer blow in his hip that spun him sideways. He toppled backward onto his butt, rolled on his side, and emptied his rifle in their direction.

Once out of ammo, he struggled to free a fresh magazine from his pocket.

As if sensing this opportunity, the uninjured guard barreled out of hiding, firing toward Tucker's position behind a column. Rounds chipped at the stone as the man circled for a clean shot.

Not gonna make it . . .

Then two sharper pops cut through the barrage of automatic fire.

The wounded man who was still in the hallway fell face-forward onto the balcony. His partner turned, only to take a bullet through the throat, blowing out his cervical spine. He crashed to the ground.

Jane appeared and dropped to a knee under the hallway arch, a smoking pistol in her hand.

He wanted to both hug and curse her—but now was not the time for either action.

He tapped his throat. "Kane, RETURN."

They needed to retreat to safer quarters.

The order shines behind Kane's eyes, glowing with the urgency in his partner's voice, but he remains in hiding. A scent carries to him from the deeper shadows, wafting through a door that opened, drafting up from a hidden stairwell.

He knows this particular scent of sweat, salt, and smoke, remembers it from the deadfall in the forest. It marks the hunter who had ambushed him.

The man tries to do the same again now, intending to come upon him and his partner from behind. But Kane waits, crouched by a trunk of this stone forest.

Kane will be the hunter this time.

He watches the man slink out of the doorway, hugging a wall, angling away. Kane watches his prey draw up a long tube to his shoulder and balance it there.

Not a gun.

Something worse.

Knowing this, Kane can no longer wait for his prey to come to him.

He bunches his legs and bursts out of hiding, barreling toward his target.

He hits the man as an explosion blasts overhead.

Tucker ducked as fire flashed from the shadows to his left, accompanied by a deep-throated explosion. Something screamed past the balustrade and flew across the church, trailing a spiral of smoke. The rocket-propelled grenade struck a far column and detonated, shattering the old stone with a thunderous crack.

Tucker ignored the damage, hearing a savage growling from the shadows closer at hand.

Kane . . .

Waving Jane forward, Tucker passed her his rifle and had her take a position at the top of the spiral stairs. "Fire at anything."

A brief glance below suggested it was already too late.

Technicians were abandoning their stations, running for the open door, encouraged by a pair of guards waving them out. The final instructions must have been transmitted to the fleet, ordering the complete annihilation of the valley's hamlets.

Tucker had a more immediate concern.

Gunfire erupted from the shadows, a muzzle flashing in the darkness. It was enough to reveal a pair wrestling near the loft's back wall. He hobbled in that direction, his hip on fire, a trail of heat running down his leg.

Hang on, Kane.

Blood flows over his tongue.

Kane ducks a flash of knife and snaps at a wrist. He catches cloth and flesh, but not enough to sink his fangs into. He gets tossed aside. He rolls as a pistol fires at him. Two rounds strike the stone before his paws; a third hits his chest. The impact cracks ribs and knocks the breath from him, but his vest holds. He launches through the air with every fiber in his hind legs.

Not to escape—but to attack again.

His body slams into his prey. The other crashes into the wall and goes down. But still an arm rises as Kane rebounds off. Fire flashes in the dark. Kane's shoulder explodes with agony, collapsing his leg on that side.

He struggles to get up.

The man is faster, looming over him, pistol pointed down.

He fires.

Still yards away, Tucker unloaded his SIG Sauer toward the shadowy figure of Lyon—at the same time, the other squeezed the trigger of his pistol. Seeing his partner in danger, Tucker shot wildly. A bullet managed to graze Lyon's forearm, throwing off the bastard's aim. The round sparked harmlessly off the stone near Kane's nose.

Tucker kept firing, closing the distance, driving the man away from Kane and toward the balustrade.

As Lyon retreated, he swung his weapon and shot twice at Tucker, his aim just as wild. Then his pistol's slide popped, its magazine empty.

Tucker stood over Kane and centered his aim. "It's over."

Lyon sneered and threw himself over the railing. Tucker got off a round, but Lyon was no longer there. Tucker rushed forward. He leaned over the balustrade in time to see Lyon crash atop one of the tall workstations and roll off it. Before Tucker could bring his pistol to bear, the soldier dove under the thick trestle table in the center of the room, using the cover to crawl toward the open door.

Men loyal to Lyon fired at Tucker from that doorway, forcing him back.

"There's nothing you can do," Lyon called up to him. "What's now in motion can't be stopped!"

A new voice interrupted. "I wouldn't be so sure of that, asshole!"

Tucker turned to see Nora crouched with Jane by the balcony stairs.

"Take a look!" Jane added.

From his hiding place by the balustrade, Tucker peered through the upper arcade of arched windows. In the distance, small dark specks fell from the sky, tumbling down and crashing into the valley. On the monitors, he witnessed the same: Warhawks and Shrikes raining from above and crashing leadenly to the ground, like so many poisoned birds brought low.

And they had been *poisoned*.

Nora yelled down to Lyon. "Sandy says *go fuck yourself.*"

Lyon rolled out of hiding and hopped toward the open door on a broken ankle. His men covered him from the doorway.

"Like I said," Tucker hollered, "it's over."

"For you."

Tucker didn't like the sound of that and peered over the balustrade

Lyon had paused at the door, standing in plain sight. He lifted something boxy and black in his hand and pressed a button on it. Blasts rose from below, igniting charges set at the bases of the columns. Other booms sounded from above. The forest of pillars began to topple, taking sections of the roof with it. Stones and chunks of wooden rafters rained down.

Tucker remembered how Kellerman had destroyed the command center in Trinidad, bombing it to ruin to hide any evidence of its presence. They were planning on doing the same here.

Lyon laughed. "Lock 'em all in here!"

Tucker fired toward the doorway. He struck a man trying to haul the heavy door closed. It was a clean head shot. The other guard took flight.

But not Lyon.

The soldier gained an assault rifle and returned fire—but not at Tucker this time. The bastard was smarter than that. He aimed for Tucker's weak spot. He strafed toward the top of the spiral stair at the back of the church.

A gasp and cry rose from over there.

Nora yelled to him. "Tucker . . . help!"

Jane . . .

Lyon laughed again, stepped back, and reached to close the door himself. But through the smoke and roil of dust, another hunter closed upon its prey.

. . . .

Kane races low under the tables, avoiding the crash and thunder all around him. He ignores the pain in his ribs, the agony in his left leg. The scent of his prey fills his skull, leaving little else but rage.

He has followed the scent trail of his target by backtracking it through the side door and down the secret stairs to this lower level.

He speeds now under tables and across the last of the distance, toward daylight, toward his target. The man realizes the danger too late, one hand on the door, the other holding his gun high.

Kane hits him low, bounding forth with both hind legs, a snarl fixed to his lip. He strikes his prey in the stomach, bending him over, knocking him back. Then the man tumbles farther backward, his arms flailing, his weapon flying . . . and falls over the cliff's edge.

Unable to stop, still in the air, Kane follows.

37

No!

Tucker watched Kane barrel into Lyon. Seventy pounds of rage and bloodlust bowled into the soldier, knocking him away from the door and over the cliff outside. Kane's momentum carried the dog past the same edge, where he plunged away.

Tucker flung himself around.

It was a four-story drop to the rocks below.

He sprinted to the spiral stairs, to where Nora cradled Jane on the floor. Nora had a wad of cloth pressed to Jane's shoulder. Jane's face was a mask of agony—but perhaps not solely from the bullet wound.

"Go!" Jane gasped. "Find Kane!"

Nora helped her stand, scooting an arm under Jane's arms. "I got her."

Jane pushed Tucker toward the stairs with her good arm. "We'll be right behind you."

As more of the monastery crashed around them, Tucker led the way down to the nave and across the floor. He skirted around toppled sections of column. Rock dust choked the air. A massive beam cracked overhead and plunged down, striking the trestle table and smashing through it, sending bottles of water and boxes of rations flying high.

Tucker reached the front door to find the threshold deserted. Lyon's men had fled the destruction, leaving their dead behind. He stepped out of the church to the cliff's edge and searched below—but a thunderous boom shook the ground as an upper level of the monastery collapsed upon itself. Tucker came close to losing his own footing, but Nora grabbed him with her free arm and pulled him back.

A parabolic dish tumbled past his nose.

"It's all coming down!" Jane yelled, still under Nora's other arm. "Keep going!"

Recognizing the danger, Tucker took to the narrow steps that led down the cliff face. Despite their steepness and treacherous footing, Tucker bounded along, crossing from one switchback to the other, skipping stairs in his haste. He ignored the pain in his left hip with each jarring leap. Once on the ground, he stared up to orient himself to the monastery doors and rushed to the spot below them.

It didn't take long to find Lyon. The soldier lay faceup, his back broken over a boulder, blood flowing from his mouth. Tucker ignored the body and searched for his friend. He spun a full circle.

Nothing.

He cupped his mouth and bellowed, "Kane!"

Ever obedient, a mewling cry answered him. He followed the whimper, but he still could not find the source.

"Kane!"

A muffled bark drew his attention up and to the left. A form struggled within the camouflage netting that was spread over the treetops.

Kane . . .

Tucker hurried toward his partner, noting the hole in the netting where Lyon had punched through before meeting his end. Tucker dropped his pistol and snatched his knife from its sheath. He gripped the handle between his teeth and scaled the fir tree to reach Kane.

"I gotcha, buddy."

Tucker reached his fingers through the tangle of netting and rubbed Kane's neck to calm and reassure him. Then he grabbed his blade and carefully sliced the netting under the shepherd. Kane slid out of the opening like a newborn calf. Tucker caught the dog's weight atop a shoulder and steadied Kane there.

"Hold still," he whispered.

Both supporting and balancing his partner on his shoulder, Tucker climbed down. Once his boots touched ground, Tucker cradled Kane around and got the shepherd back on his feet—or at least, three of them. Kane held up his left front limb. Blood dripped from his paw.

Tucker dropped to a knee to examine the injury, only to get a warm lap of a tongue on his face. Kane panted and gave a weak wag of his tail.

"Yeah, I'm glad to see you, too."

But the reunion would have to wait. More debris rained down from above, crashing around the base of the cliff, ripping through the netting.

"Tucker!" Nora called as she reached the bottom of the steps.

Jane hung in her arms, clearly weakening.

Tucker noted a handful of trucks and SUVs still parked in the makeshift garrison at the foot of the escarpment. They were going to need a vehicle. He stepped over to Lyon's body and patted down the man's pockets, figuring Lyon would have his own truck, not trusting anyone else to do the driving.

Tucker found a set of keys in the man's jacket and yanked them free. As he did so, a groan rose from Lyon. The soldier's eyes fluttered, and he coughed blood from his lips. Tucker stepped back, but the man was no longer a threat, his spine shattered, his limbs paralyzed. Still, eyes rolled toward Tucker—then Kane.

"Little fucker," Lyon moaned. ". . . more like a cat . . . got nine lives."

Tucker kept a protective hand on the dog. "But he needs to learn to land on his feet. Maybe you should've, too."

Nora and Jane hobbled closer to them. Tucker pressed the key fob, setting one of the trucks to chirping. He tossed the keys to Nora and took Jane from her.

"Get that truck over here. We need to find out what happened to Frank."

Nora nodded and sprinted off.

A cough drew Tucker's attention back to Lyon. Bloodshot eyes centered on him. "You think . . . won. Kellerman . . . you've got nothing on him."

Tucker was ready to laugh at this assessment, but Jane sighed.

"Bastard may be right," she said. "When Nora lobotomized the drones, the code erased everything. With Webster gone, there's no one else who can directly implicate Kellerman's personal involvement. And layered in corporate shells, he's well insulated from liability."

A weak laugh flowed from Lyon's throat, along with more blood. His head lolled back, and his chest gave one final heave—then his body slackened. His eyes stared up at the sky, but they clearly saw nothing.

With a growl from the truck's engine, Nora backed over to them.

Tucker helped Jane onto the bench seat in front. Then he hauled Kane up into his arms and hopped into the back bed. He slapped the rear window, and Nora took off across the mine's grounds.

Behind him, Tucker watched the monastery crumble and crack, slowly falling to ruin at the base of the cliff.

Kane dropped his head heavily into Tucker's lap and let out a world-weary sigh.

"Don't ya know it, buddy."

Tucker shook his head, picturing Pruitt Kellerman.

We won the battle, but lost the war.

38

The ringmaster of this circus sat front and center before the closed-door Senate hearing. From the half-filled gallery at the back of the judicial chamber, Tucker watched Pruitt Kellerman lean toward one of his lawyers, smiling, offering a chuckle of reassurance to his bevy of legal counsel.

Tucker clenched a fist on his knee.

This was the third such hearing in three weeks, after what the news media had come to label "The Siege at Kamena Gora." With the array of military hardware found strewn across those fields and forests—both aerial drones and their land-based counterparts—investigations continued, involving the military, intelligence services, and civilian police agencies across Europe and the United States. Conspiracies abounded, and villains were propped up daily, only to be cleared later.

Only one person seemed to deflect any blame.

Kellerman continued to deny any personal involvement, cladding himself with mountains of legal defenses and layers of corporate protection. But the CEO of Horizon Media had an even stronger tool to attack his accusers: a very loud and broad pulpit. Horizon Media Corp and its hundreds of affiliates continued to sculpt the story. For every allegation or claim, Kellerman had talking heads that would shout loudly from those many pulpits, drowning out discourse, declaring this all a witch hunt or worse—an attack on the foundations of America.

Tucker shook his head. Jane had been right.

The bastard's good.

Jane hadn't even bothered to attend this hearing, spending the crisp fall morning with her son, Nathan. She was out of the hospital after having a bullet removed from her shoulder and wanted every possible moment with her boy.

Tucker couldn't blame her. He shifted in his own hard seat. After catching a ricocheted round in his hip, he was still in pain if he sat for long—or maybe it was simply he hated being idle, being stuck in one place. After weeks in DC dealing with the aftermath of all this, a certain wanderlust had begun to set in. He longed to finish his trip with Kane to Yellowstone. Winter would be the ideal time to visit the snowy, frozen wilderness, offering the perfect place to clear his head. But that would have to wait. Not only was Kane still recovering from his injuries—a broken rib and a bullet wound of his own—but Tucker had some unfinished business here.

Nora sat next to him, her arms folded over her chest. Fury shone in her eyes as Pruitt laughed at a joke by one of his lawyers. Tucker didn't know if Pruitt recognized Nora in the gallery as one of the survivors of Redstone, but she remained here for her friends, for Stan, for Takashi, and for many others. Diane was the only other person to walk away from that purge, and she did so now on only one leg. The wound she had sustained from the escape, a deep laceration to her leg, had developed an infection that required amputation. She was still in rehabilitation.

"How're you holding up?" Tucker asked her.

She lowered her chin and glowered. "Give me a minute alone with that asshole."

You and me both, sister.

After another fifteen minutes of jostling and points of order, Senator Fred Mason of Utah, the chairman of the Senate Judiciary Committee, banged his gavel. A hush fell over the space.

Kellerman sat stiffly at a polished wooden table before the committee's six highest-ranking members for this closed-door session. The CEO of Horizon Media was flanked by the same number of lawyers, ready to face and contest any new allegations.

No one knew why this hearing had been called so suddenly and under such clandestine circumstances. A lone television camera sat unmanned and idle. Wall-mounted monitors to either side of the chamber were dark. Those in attendance had been granted special clearance. The hearing was beyond merely *closed-door*. It was hermetically sealed and locked up tight.

"I call this hearing to order," Mason announced. "And for all our benefits, I'll get straight to the point, Mr. Kellerman. A witness has recently emerged who will testify and provide evidence of your personal involvement in treasonous and criminal activities, covering events not only in Serbia but also here in the United States and in the Republic of Trinidad and Tobago."

Kellerman's chief counsel leaned and whispered in his ear, but the CEO gave an annoyed wave of his hand. "What witness, Senator? What activities?"

Mason shifted forward, looking over the rims of his eyeglasses. "Mr. Kellerman, before the committee calls this witness, is there any statement you'd like to make? This is your last opportunity."

The chief counsel began to lean toward Kellerman, only to be held off. Kellerman's next words were meant for his lawyer, but his microphone picked them up. "They're bluffing. There's no witness. This is all a show."

Tucker smiled.

It was a safe gamble—and came very close to being the truth.

Mason signaled a uniformed guard stationed at a set of double doors to the left of the senators' raised dais. The doors were opened, and the witness entered.

Frank stepped into the chamber, smartly outfitted in his army dress uniform. He limped on a leg with a shoe splint strapped to his foot. After Tucker and company had vacated Skaxis Mining and rode wildly down to Kamena Gora, they had discovered that Frank's efforts at stalling and taking out the one tank had saved a majority of the hamlet's villagers. His only injury was a twisted ankle—and not from the fighting or barrage, but from slipping on a patch of ice the next day as the Sigma team, which Ruth had sent into Serbia, evacuated Tucker's group from the region.

"Master Sergeant Frank Ballenger," Mason introduced, then waved the man to a seat. "Thank you for your help and cooperation."

With a pinched brow, Kellerman studied Frank, plainly wondering who this newcomer was. While Kellerman likely knew Tucker was working with Jane and had support from Nora, Frank was apparently still an unknown commodity to the CEO.

Tucker savored the flicker of worry in Kellerman's eyes.

Here is one bastard who does not like surprises.

And Kellerman was about to get a huge one—because Frank was *not* the witness.

Frank withdrew a familiar CUCS unit from inside his jacket. He hunched over it and manipulated its controls. A moment later, a low humming buzz reached the hushed chamber. A small drone flew slowly through the still open doors, circled around the senators' dais, and came to a hover in the middle of the chamber.

"Say hello to Rex," Mason said.

Suddenly every cell phone in the room began ringing, even those in silent mode. Tucker's satellite phone was no exception. He removed it and saw someone—or something—had commandeered it. Upon the screen, video footage showed tanks firing upon a mountainside hamlet. Across the room, the dark monitors flickered to life, showing other images: a child's body on the street, the guttered and smoking ruins of a home, the sweep of a Warhawk through the air.

Kellerman was on his feet.

To one side, the robotic television camera charged with power, lifting its dark lens, while green lights flashed.

Good boy, Rex.

"He's getting better at this," Tucker whispered.

Nora grinned. "And he's only getting started."

In the aftermath of events at the border, Rex had been recovered from a field by Frank and the Sigma team. The drone had broken a propeller or two after finally losing power and tumbling like a fallen leaf out of the sky. And lucky it had. With no juice, Rex had never received the code that Nora had broadcasted out from the C3 hub. He was never lobotomized, never mind-wiped like the other drones.

Once the industrial little drone had powered back up, Frank and Nora had discovered it had been busier than anyone suspected, performing operations once again that had been part of its subroutine in the past. Rex was built and designed as a data miner. While flying in Serbia, he had done just that, tapping into the transmissions feed sent out by the command station and sucking data out of the C3 hub.

On a screen to the left of the chamber, the face of a ghost

appeared, flickering, then speaking. Rafael Lyon leaned closer to the video camera for this chat. *"We've just received word that six leaders of the Serbian parliament were successfully assassinated in Belgrade. The news outlets are going nuts."*

Across the chamber, another monitor glowed to life, showing Kellerman standing in his office, his shirtsleeves rolled up. He faced the camera and frowned. *"But didn't we target eight politicians? Wasn't that the plan?"*

Lyon answered from across the chamber, *"With the timetable moved up, we lost the opportunity on two."*

The exchange went back and forth as the two plotted the time-table and destruction of a handful of Serbian hamlets.

Senator Mason lifted a hand. "That's enough. Thank you, Master Sergeant Ballenger."

The screens went dark, leaving the room in stunned silence, but the television camera lights remained green, broadcasting what had just been revealed far and wide.

"We have much more," Mason said.

And they did. Two nights ago, Frank and Nora had sent Rex on a little hunting expedition across the Chesapeake Bay to Horizon's headquarters on Smith Island. Rex had performed like a charm, drawing out more incriminating evidence.

"What do you have to say for yourself?" Mason asked as the tele-vision camera pointed at Kellerman.

From the man's expression, Tucker imagined the CEO of Hori-zon Media wanted to ask for a new set of adult diapers.

But before Kellerman could respond, the monitors bloomed to life again, showing the face of another ghost. Sandy smiled from all the monitors—and likely on television screens around the nation. It was the last fleeting glimpse of her from the footage on her thumb drive.

Bravo, Sandy . . . bravo.

Nora clutched Tucker's hand, choking with emotion. "We . . . we never told Rex to show that."

Tucker looked over to the woman, to the tears welling and roll-ing across her cheeks.

Rex *was* learning.

Tucker pulled Nora close. "Alan Turing would have been proud," he whispered. "Of both of you."

5:14 P.M. EST
Smith Island, Maryland

Pruitt Kellerman stood before the expanse of glass overlooking the bay. A haze hung over the water, casting the distant skyline of Washington into a ghostly mirage. As the sun set, he could almost feel the city fading from his reach.

Elsewhere, both here and across the bay, lawyers were in full emergency mode, dealing with the repercussions, the allegations, and the charges that were still being filed. He'd had his passport stripped from him, and the entire island was under watch in case he tried to escape.

But there's no escaping this.

Not just the island, but any of it.

He was savvy enough to know he had lost. All that was left was the fallout.

His office door opened behind him. He was momentarily surprised, as he had locked it. Only one person had a passkey that would allow them access.

He turned to face his daughter.

Laura took two steps into the office, tried a third, but came to a stop, as if the air in here were too polluted for her to wade through. He circled past his desk and closed the distance.

"Laura . . ."

She turned half away, plainly ashamed to look at him. He was wrong. She swung back around and slapped him full across the face. He didn't try to block her.

She stumbled back a step. "How could you?" she seethed. "So many children . . ."

He didn't try to deny anything. She was his daughter. She knew the truth as readily as he did.

She turned away, this time for real. "I'll never speak to you again."

She stormed off, slamming the door after her.

Pruitt stood there for a long time, feeling the sting of her palm on his cheek. He wasn't angry, hurt, or disappointed. In fact, he was relieved.

Good girl.

If nothing else, he had raised her right.

Let that be my legacy.

But he knew this was one prayer that would not be answered. To either side of the door, silent monitors showed his face. Words scrolled along the bottom of a screen, declaring in bold letters: THE BUTCHER OF KAMENA GORA.

And this was feed from one of Horizon's own stations.

It was definitely over.

He headed across his office to a wall safe and unlocked it by placing his palm on a reader. Bolts slid free, and he opened the thick door. He pulled out a worn folder and ran a thumb over the faded stencil inscribed into it.

THE ARES PROJECT

The file was empty now, the papers inside shredded and burned three weeks ago as he covered his tracks. He shook the empty folder.

Here is all that's left of my grandfather's legacy.

He threw the file aside. But the safe held one last memento from Bryson Kellerman, the agent known as the *Geist*.

"The Ghost . . ." Pruitt whispered, a sad smile forming.

Like Pruitt, his grandfather was a master of shadow and smoke, of illusion and fabrication, but he had also been a cunning spy, one with secret ambitions and lofty goals—and someone willing to bloody his hand to accomplish them.

Pruitt reached into the safe and removed the small German Mauser, a pistol dating from World War II. He ran his hands over the butt of the gun, imagining his grandfather's palm upon it. He knew the story of this pistol, of the final time it had been fired inside a lonely barn in the British countryside.

Pruitt crossed to the window. He always kept the weapon oiled and maintained, as a quiet testament to his grandfather—though now he wondered. Maybe he had performed this ritual for a more practical reason, knowing he might need it one day.

As a final bit of legacy.

To prove that justice could never truly be thwarted.

Pruitt stepped to the window, lifted the gun to his temple, and pulled the trigger.

39

Beatrice Conlon gave Tucker a huge bear hug, practically squeezing the air from his lungs as they stood on the woman's porch. He had just dropped Sandy's mother back at her place after the funeral in Poplar Grove.

"Thank you for what you did," she said, letting him go but still gripping both shoulders. "For my girl . . . for everyone."

He nodded, feeling his cheeks warm, uncomfortable with the attention. "The service was beautiful," he mumbled.

He had returned to these mountains to attend Sandy's long-delayed funeral, though in the end, it was more like a party, which Sandy would have appreciated.

Nora called from inside. "Where are the lemons, Bea?"

Sandy's mother leaned back and hollered, "In a paper sack by the fridge, hon!" She then patted Tucker's shoulder. "Why don't you all get on out of here? Nora's spending the night. Gonna teach her how to make raccoon stew."

Tucker must have winced.

She cackled. "Just pullin' your leg, city boy. We're having pizza and beer with some gals that are coming over tonight."

"All right then, you have fun."

Bea still gripped his arm. Tucker felt the tremble in her fingers. The woman put on a happy face, but the pain was still there. He was glad Nora was staying here.

Bea stared over at his SUV. Jane waited in the front seat, with Kane half in her lap. Nathan was still back in Washington, being baby-sat by friends. Jane had opted not to bring her little boy to this funeral in the middle of the Appalachian Mountains.

"You got a good gal there," Bea said. "You remember that. Don't take it for granted."

"Don't worry. She won't let me."

Bea smiled, a touch more genuinely now. "Then you should listen to her."

"Yes, ma'am."

Bea hugged him a final time. "You take care of yourself . . . and that big, strappin' dog of yours."

"I will."

She kissed him on the cheek and sent him on his way. As he high-stepped through the weeds to the truck, he heard the screen door clap shut behind him and Bea's voice call to Nora. "Not the powdered sugar, for crying out loud! Didn't your momma ever show you how to make proper lemonade?"

Tucker grinned and climbed behind the wheel.

"How's Bea holding up?"

"I think it's Nora who's in trouble."

"What do you—?"

"Never mind. It's not important." He reversed the SUV off the Conlon property and headed back to Huntsville.

Kane hopped into the backseat and stuck his head out the open passenger window, soaking in the last of the afternoon. His tail patted the leather.

"That's one happy dog," Jane said.

He reached over and took her hand. "Make that two dogs."

They continued along the back roads in silence, meandering their way slowly toward their motel in Huntsville. They had no schedule, only a dinner with Frank set for this evening. Frank had headed straight back after the funeral, needing to finalize some details over at Redstone. He and Nora were continuing to work with Rex, but the pair had taken steps to encrypt the drone's code, a fail-safe against anyone trying to circumvent their authority over the drone.

Nora had taken one extra precaution. She had released Sandy's lobotomy file to the world at large, as an open-source code. If anyone tried to repeat what the late Pruitt Kellerman had attempted, the world would have the means to stop it.

At least for now.

Tucker knew that genie was out of the bottle. For better or worse, the battlefield was changing from one of flesh and blood to one of codes and robots. He wondered how long it would be until he and Kane were obsolete.

Maybe that'll be a good thing.

Still, he stared over at Jane, unsure about everything.

When Tucker pulled up to their motel, he found someone seated outside his door. Her legs were crossed, and she kicked a booted foot up and down.

"What is it about women just turning up on my doorstep?" Tucker asked.

Jane patted him on the knee. "Worked pretty damn well for me."

Tucker parked the car, and they all unloaded.

Ruth Harper stood up and met them. "There you all are. I expected you back an hour ago."

"Took the long way home." Tucker unlocked the door and waved Kane and Jane inside. He blocked the way with his body. "What is it, Ruth?"

"I just came to give you an update. Laura Kellerman is proving a woman of her word. As new CEO, she's been divesting Horizon's assets and promised to help rebuild both Port of Spain and the villages along the Serbian border. She's also reaching out to the families involved in Project 623 and Odisha, offering restitution."

"Money's not going to bring back the dead."

"Of course not, but she's doing her best. All evidence, even from Rex, seems to suggest she is blameless in all of this. Don't paint her with the same brush as her father."

Tucker leaned against the doorjamb, suddenly exhausted. "What about the other players who are to blame? In Serbia? In Trinidad?"

"Marco Davidovic is already in prison, being held on war-crime charges. Everyone's still hunting for President D'Abreo of Trinidad. He vanished shortly after the news broke—he's either on the run or dead already. It's still chaos down there."

"Which keeps the world turning," Tucker said.

"And why Sigma could use your help." Her eyes twinkled with mischief.

"Ruth . . ."

"I know, honey. Just putting it out there." She passed him a shiny black card. "Here's the real reason I came all the way down here."

He flipped the card back and forth. It was blank, but if he tilted it just right, he could make out a holographic silver Σ, the symbol for Sigma.

"What is it?"

"The key to the kingdom."

Tucker suspected what he held. Back in DC, he had briefly been allowed access to Sigma's command center, located in a warren of old bunkers beneath the Smithsonian Castle on the National Mall. This must be one of the command center's encrypted access cards.

"As a thank-you," Ruth explained and began to turn away—then stopped and shrugged. "Or maybe consider it a standing invitation."

Tucker weighed whether or not to throw the card back at her feet, but instead he sighed and shoved it into his pocket.

What the hell . . .

Ruth smiled, turned on a heel, and left, but not before mumbling a single word. "Progress."

Tucker shook his head and closed the door. He found Jane play-wrestling with Kane on one of the beds. The shepherd bounded about like a puppy, pretending to snap at her hands. Jane laughed and giggled like the girl he remembered from long ago, when he was a different man, one less scarred.

Again he felt that gulf between now and then, yawning wide, stirring his gut with vertigo.

Across the room, Jane finally collapsed on her side atop the bed, staring over at him, smiling a silent invitation, reminding him this was now, not then.

He took one step, then another, closing that gap.

Could it be that simple?

Jane's smile grew as he approached. "Hey, handsome."

Tucker matched her grin—knowing this time she wasn't talking about Kane.

AUTHOR'S NOTE TO READERS: TRUTH OR FICTION

This novel addressed the blurring line between truth and stories fabricated by the media, so I thought I had better come clean here in these last pages and try to separate fact from fiction . . . at least for this story.

Military War Dogs and Their Handlers

Tucker and Kane first appeared in the Sigma Force novel *Bloodline*, but I knew they had a story much richer still to tell. In real life, I first encountered this unique heroic pairing of soldier and war dog while on a USO tour to Iraq and Kuwait. Seeing these pairs' capabilities and recognizing their unique bonds, I wanted to try to capture and honor those relationships.

To accomplish that, I spoke to veterinarians in the U.S. Veterinary Corps, interviewed handlers, met with dogs, and saw how these duos grew together to become a single fighting unit. Some may read this account of Tucker and Kane and wonder how much is truly possible. Can a dog and his handler truly do so much? I vetted the first book in this series with handlers, who told me that not only are such actions plausible, if anything these dogs could do so much more. I tried to capture that in this book, showing how those military war dogs could not only understand diverse commands but were capable of following a string of orders.

If you'd like to know more about war dogs and their handlers, I highly recommend two books by the author Maria Goodavage: *Soldier Dogs: The Untold Story of America's Canine Heroes* and *Top Dog: The Story of Marine Hero Lucca.*

Post-Traumatic Stress Disorder

Another topic raised in this novel is a new understanding of one aspect of PTSD. It goes by the name of *moral injury* and is explored in this book through the character of Tucker. It relates to a shattering of moral and ethical expectations, and according to the U.S. Department of Veteran Affairs, it can manifest as shame, guilt, anxiety, and anger, along with behavioral changes, such as alienation, withdrawal, and self-harming (including suicide). We see shades of this in Tucker in this book, and as with most veterans, there is no quick fix. For those afflicted, it's an ongoing process to find their center again.

Alan Turing and His Oracle

Sadly, the history of the mathematical genius Alan Turing depicted here is mostly accurate. During World War II, he broke the Nazis' Enigma code, which was integral to the Allies winning the war, but he was later convicted of gross indecency for being homosexual and had his security clearance revoked. Given the choice of prison or chemical castration, he chose the latter and eventually killed himself.

Turing is also considered to be the father of the modern computer, from the crude electromechanical machines he used to break the German code to his theoretical "oracle," the first artificially intelligent computer. He did indeed at one point suggest to his bosses at the U.K. National Physical Laboratory that they should throw radioactive radium into one of his computing devices to see if the randomness of atomic decay could trigger the "unpredictability" that he believed (as do others today) may be the key to creating his "oracle."

Most historians believe Turing didn't go beyond *theorizing* the creation of an artificially intelligent computer, but there are others who wonder, which became the basis for this novel.

Drones, Drones, and More Drones

One only has to read the newspaper to understand and appreciate how prevalent the use of drones has become in modern warfare. There is currently an arms race under way to develop new and improved robotic warriors. This raises a fundamental question: will the use of drones save lives or will the ease of their use—killing from afar—make us more likely to go to war? Will we begin to shoot first and ask questions later? For a full exploration of these moral questions, along with a peek at what is coming next in drone development, please check out the frightening book *Wired For War: The Robotics Revolution and Conflict in the 21st Century*, by P. W. Singer.

This all brings us to the next topic concerning *who* will control these drones.

When Corporations Go to War

As with the advancements in drone warfare, the battlefield is changing in a unique and disturbing way. We are seeing the lines blurring between military forces and those armies employed by corporations—not just private defense contractors, but also full fighting forces—which raises the concern about profitability, accountability, and who truly *is* in charge. To save money and balance budgets, governments, including our own, are handing over military powers once overseen by command structures to corporate boardrooms. To read about this threat in more depth, I recommend *Corporate Warriors: The Rise of the Privatized Military Industry*, by P. W. Singer.

This brings us to the final glimpse at what's to come, an example of which is found in the pages of this story.

The Age of Information Wars

This novel explores a new battlefield that is already being waged by ISIS in the Middle East, by Russia in Ukraine, and by China on U.S. shores. It is a digital battleground with real-world consequences.

This story casts a light on three critical components of this *information* theater of war: electronic warfare, cyber attacks, and the most insidious of all, psychological operations. To learn about where war is headed next, read this article by Professor David Stupples (which can be found on various websites, including Gizmodo.com): "The Next Big War Will Be Digital—and We're Not Ready for It."

So that's where I'll end this book—but not the story of Tucker and his stalwart companion, Kane. Their adventures are just beginning.